Praise for Spring Castle

Michiko Ishimure is one of the greatest writers of modern Japanese literature. In *Spring Castle*, she tells the political, social and historical story of the Shimabara Rebellion while also depicting in vivid detail the daily lives of farmers and fishermen, so that their lives are not overshadowed by their deaths.

—Hiromi Itō, *author*

An eloquent translation of Ishimure's most powerful novel, *Spring Castle* takes readers on a fascinating journey back to the 17th century, skillfully weaving together narratives that uncannily resonate with many of the challenges facing us today.

—Karen L. Thornber

Harry Tuchman Levin Professor in Literature and Professor of East Asian Languages and Civilizations, Harvard University; President, Phi Beta Kappa Alpha Iota of Massachusetts

Bruce Allen has recreated in English Ishimure Michiko's magnum opus *Spring Castle*, capturing the colloquial intimacy and moral intensity of Ishimure's historical fiction.

—Scott Slovic

University Distinguished Professor, University of Idaho

Bruce Allen's animated translation of the local details and multiple dialects of peasants who are finally driven to engage in a desperate rebellion of David and Goliath proportions is a must-read for anyone interested in historical fiction.

—Christine L. Marran

Professor, Department of Asian and Middle Eastern Studies, College of Liberal Arts, University of Minnesota

In recent decades, much has been written by historians about Japan's so-called "Christian century" (c.1550-1650) and the subsequent two centuries that ended with the emergence from hiding of a group of Christians who had kept the faith alive over some ten generations. Ishimure Michiko offers fresh insights into one of the most significant milestones in this history: the Christians' last stand at the Shimabara Rebellion, which saw the round-up and execution of some 37,000 sympathizers to the cause.

—Mark Williams
Formerly, Professor of Japanese Studies, University of Leeds, UK; Currently, Vice President, International Christian University, Tokyo, Japan

In *Spring Castle*, nature moves, and therefore, people move—not vice versa. Approximately 100 species of local plants are referred to in the novel, in order to eloquently tell of the historical environment in which the Christian martyrs lived and died. Ishimure Michiko believed that those plants were the clocks that told time and seasonal changes, as well as witnesses to human history.

—Ken'ichi Noda
Professor Emeritus, Rikkyo University, Tokyo, Japan

Spring Castle is a magnificent historical novel extolling the virtues and exposing the vices of human beings. Ishimure Michiko masterfully interweaves psychological dimensions of individual people with the historical context they are in.

Bruce Allen's masterful translation—fluid and engaging—reads as if *Spring Castle* were written in English. He succeeds in presenting the historical novel as a classic of contemporary relevance.

—Sajed Kamal, *EdD, poet, artist, literary translator, renewable energy and sustainable development educator*

—Rosemary Kamal, *EdD, educator and environmentalist*

Spring Castle

SPRING CASTLE

MICHIKO ISHIMURE

TRANSLATED BY BRUCE ALLEN

TUTTLE Publishing

Tokyo | Rutland, Vermont | Singapore

Contents

INTRODUCTION

Bruce Allen

The fifteenth of April, 1638, marked the defeat of an estimated 37,000 Japanese peasant farmers, fishers and former samurai who had risen up in the Shimabara Rebellion. On that last day, inside the stone walls of the abandoned Hara Castle—the "Spring Castle" of this novel—the shogun's forces slaughtered in battle or beheaded every remaining man, woman and child who had taken part in the uprising. It is reported that 10,000 of the rebels' heads were set on stakes around the perimeter of the castle as a grim warning to others. The rebels had occupied the abandoned castle in their desperate last stand against oppressive local feudal lords and central government forces.[1]

This number of 37,000 people, most of them killed in battle or beheaded on that one day, must stand as a particularly grisly figure in the world's history of warfare. But the complex history behind this figure and event has for the most part remained shrouded in a narrow victor's reporting of events. This accounting has almost completely erased the stories of the lives of the tens of thousands of mostly Christian Japanese peasants and a small number of others who joined in the rebellion.

The Shimabara Rebellion, also known as the Shimabara-Amakusa Rebellion, stemmed from tensions that had been steadily mounting during the 1630s on the Shimabara Peninsula and nearby Amakusa Islands of Kyushu, many days journey from the seat of government in Edo (present-day Tokyo). Hara Castle, located on a headland of the Shimabara coast, had been abandoned in 1614 when its former Christian lord from the Arima clan was

1. John Dougill, *In Search of Japan's Hidden Christians: A Story of Suppression, Secrecy and Survival.* (Tuttle, 2012) 116.

exiled by the central government following its recent proscription of Christianity. When a new lord from the Matsukura clan was appointed, he began construction of a new castle, after dismantling and removing most of the usable building materials from Hara Castle, leaving the site with just its massive stone walls and moats. The rebels seized the abandoned Hara Castle and hastily refitted it as a fortress from which they could wage their improbable quest, led by a charismatic fifteen- or sixteen-year-old boy named Masuda Shirō, hoping to gain freedom and establish a Christian domain within Japan. Their valiant but increasingly desperate occupation of Hara Castle lasted from December 17, 1637 to April 15, 1638. On the final day, the approximately 37,000 rebels inside the castle, including women and children, fought government forces that numbered over 125,000 trained soldiers, backed up by greatly superior stores of guns, munitions, food, horses and other supplies and augmented by naval support, cannons and munitions supplied by the Dutch East India Company.

Spring Castle is Ishimure Michiko's[2] fictional telling, based on extensive historical research, of the erased history of the lives, places and stories of those who organized, took part in and were defeated in the Shimabara Rebellion.

Ishimure Michiko (1927-2018)

The roots of Ishimure's interest in, and compassion for, the people of the Shimabara Rebellion lay in the deep ties of her family with local history. She was born on Lower Amakusa Island and raised in the nearby small city of Minamata, just across a bay of the inland Shiranui Sea. In an interview she gave in a documentary about her life, Ishimure discussed her commitment and hopes in writing *Spring Castle*:

> Only the number of the peasants who died in the uprising has been recorded. But certainly, they all had names, and so I gave them names. There were parents, brothers, sisters and

---

2. Here, and throughout the translation, I have written all Japanese names, including the author's, in the Japanese order, with family name first.

> grandparents. But the names of those people—not even one of them remains. And their dead bodies were thrown away like the tossing out of tattered rags. I think of myself as a descendent of those who survived, so I thought I needed to give them names ... In the novel, I created scenes that showed how those peasants must have brought happiness to the people around them.
>
> There is no proof that this has helped to give those souls peace. I don't know what kind of people my ancestors actually were, but I am connected to this land, and so I couldn't help but think of a requiem for their souls. This was an island where people were sent in exile. Those people would not even tell the islanders their real names. Amakusa was an island of prisoners. And so, some of my ancestors, too, probably were thieves and murderers ... None of these exiles and rebels were allowed burial in proper graves that showed their names ... In the world's history of punishment this massacre stands out as an unparalleled instance of brutal retribution.[3]

Ishimure's gradual work on the novel extended over a period of some fifty years. In the 1960s, her experiences as a writer and activist in exposing the Minamata Disease incident—the world's first recognized case of industrial environmental pollution, caused by the discharge of methyl mercury into Minamata Bay by the Chisso Corporation—brought her to consider more deeply the events that had taken place some four centuries earlier in Amakusa and Shimabara. In the Preface to *Spring Castle,* she further explains her initial calling to this history and to writing the novel:

> My first thoughts of writing this book came to me back at the time when I was protesting at the Tokyo headquarters of the Chisso Corporation, together with ... the Minamata disease victims who had been denied government certification. That was on December 6, 1971. The negotiations with

3. *Toward the Paradise of Flowers*, directed by Kin Taii, trans. Bruce Allen (Fujiwara Shoten, 2013) DVD.

> Chisso were a difficult struggle, and several days later we were forced out by the police. After that, we set up tents in front of their head office and continued to negotiate. On a bitterly cold night, we were sleeping by the street, together with student supporters, with the falling leaves of the plane trees swirling about and sticking to our cheeks … At the time of our protest, I deeply imagined and sympathized with the situation of the unnamed people who had suffered long ago inside Hara Castle.

Building on this initial inspiration, Ishimure spent decades doing meticulous research and journalistic reporting on the historical background of the Rebellion. In this research she not only engaged in a scholarly reporting of dates, documents and facts, but immersed herself deeply in conveying the spirit of the people and places in which this history was enacted.

In Japan, Ishimure is regarded as one of the country's most important modern writers. She was the author of over 50 volumes, written in a wide range of genres, including novels, short stories, poetry, Noh drama, children's stories, essays and memoirs. Most of these works, including *Spring Castle,* were written in her characteristic, pioneering style which combines the use of reportage, nonfiction and fiction, narrated in the rich local dialects of its characters. Her best-known work, *Kugai jōdo: waga Minamata-byō* (1969), often translated as *Paradise in the Sea of Sorrow: Our Minamata Disease*, went through over 30 printings in Japan and has been translated into English and other languages. This work, along with two other books and a Noh play that also focused on the Minamata Disease incident, led to her being referred to as the "mother of the Japanese environmental movement" and the "Rachel Carson of Japan." While the majority of Ishimure's earlier literary work focused on life in modern Japanese society, *Spring Castle* is her one work that was set in the distant past. *Spring Castle* has gained critical acclaim in Japan as a masterpiece of modern literature and as the magnum opus of her writings.

Ishimure was the recipient of numerous international and Japanese literary awards, including the Ramon Magsaysay Award from the Philippines (1973) and the Asahi Prize for literature in Japan (2001). Her collected works have been published in an 18-volume critical edition by Fujiwara Shoten Press. *Spring Castle* was first published in a serialized edition from 1998 to 1999 in several local Kyushu newspapers under the title *Haru no shiro* (*Spring Castle*). It was then published in a book edition in 1999 by Chikuma Shobo Press but, owing to issues that temporarily prevented the use of the title *Haru no shiro*, it appeared under the title *Anima no tori*, meaning "spirit birds." In 2017 it was republished as part of the Fujiwara critical edition of her collected works, with its title restored to her preferred choice, *Haru no shiro*.

Ishimure devoted her life work to telling the stories of people and places whose lives and histories were being threatened and erased in the face of society's striving for material development and progress. Her writing provides a requiem for the victims of this process, along with a call for recognition, responsibility, reconciliation and renewal.

The Shimabara Rebellion

The Shimabara Rebellion, the focal event of *Spring Castle*, emerged from the background of Japan's Warring States period, partly coinciding with its initial century of contact with Europeans and Christianity. During the Warring States period, usually dated from 1467 to 1573, local feudal lords fought for dominance in establishing a unified national government. However, after 1573, regional conflicts lingered on, especially in the southern Kyushu area, until the final victory of the combined forces of the third Tokugawa Shogun, Iemitsu, at the Shimabara Rebellion in 1638.

Japan's century of contact with Europeans opened in 1534, when a ship carrying Portuguese traders was blown off course onto the island of Tanegashima, about 23 nautical miles off the southern coast of Kyushu. This period lasted until 1640, when, in the aftermath of the Shimabara Rebellion, the Tokugawa shoguns strictly enforced their policy of maritime prohibition that marked the beginning of the Edo period of international isolation.

The Rebellion emerged from a complex amalgam of local, national and international stresses. At the local level, peasants in the

Shimabara Peninsula had become angered by the exorbitant taxes levied on them by their callous, demanding and sometimes brutal lords. During the 1630s, the taxation demands of the Matsukura lords had grown increasingly excessive, in spite of the farmers having suffered through years of droughts, alternating at times with excessive rains, resulting in severe crop failures and starvation. Although it had become nearly impossible for the peasants to pay their taxes—demanded in grain payments—the lords meted out draconian punishments, including torture and the taking of women and children as hostages. Similar conditions were suffered by the neighboring peasants in the Amakusa Islands under their Terasawa clan lords. The people in the Shimabara and Amakusa regions had remained in close contact, being physically separated only by the narrow Straits of Hayasaki, which mark the starting and ending points of *Spring Castle.*

These local tensions, in turn, were connected to unstable national conditions related to the recent civil wars, and then on up to the international level, where Japan was rapidly becoming involved in dealings with Europeans. Furthermore, and critical to the events of this story, these tensions involved the fragile presence of the newly-introduced religion of Christianity. Over a period of several generations, Christianity had emerged as the predominant religion in the Shimabara Peninsula and Amakusa Islands. In other parts of Japan, an initial flame of attraction to European culture, trade, technology and religion had waxed, and then waned. By late 1637, when the Rebellion broke out, the central government's attitude toward Christianity had changed from initial interest to suspicion, and then to active suppression, as Christianity came to be judged an instrument of European designs for colonizing Japan. This suppression was enforced by increasingly severe edicts, backed up by the use of torture and execution of both foreign priests and members of the native population.

The first recorded Western "visitors" to Japan were the Portuguese crewmembers of the ship that was stranded on Tanegashima. These sailors were regarded with great suspicion by the Japanese, but from this chance initial contact, seeds of interest in Europeans sprouted quickly. Important among these interests was the possibility of establishing lucrative international trading relations.

Furthermore, the locals were fascinated by some of the Europeans' curious implements. On Tanegashima, Japanese got their first look at guns and ammunition. Within months after the sailors' arrival, local artisans and metalsmiths had copied, manufactured and even improved upon the design of the European matchlock rifles. Japan quickly established gun manufacturing as an important domestic and export industry. It has been estimated that, at the height of this century of European contact, Japan had changed from being a country with no guns to the one with the best and highest proportion of guns per capita in the world.[4] Remarkably, shortly after the government gained its victory in the Shimabara Rebellion, it collected and destroyed almost all of the guns in the country and prohibited their use for some 250 years, until the Meiji era.

Soon after the arrival of the Portuguese sailors, a succession of Jesuit, Dominican and Franciscan missionaries came to Japan, starting with the Jesuit Francisco Xavier in 1549. With considerable success, these missionaries attracted receptive and talented converts. Their new religion, with its strange, heretical notion of only one God—a deity they called "Deus" and regarded as supreme, even above the emperor—was judged with suspicion by many leaders, but it proved comforting to many others, both among the peasantry and the nobility. There may have been as many as 300,000 Japanese Christians at the peak of Christianity's spread in the country in the 1590s (out of a total population of about 17 million).[5]

The speed of this spread and the extent to which Christian teachings were comprehended and absorbed was impressive. During this "Christian century," missionaries set up a number of *collegia* and *seminaria* in Amakusa and Shimabara, where they taught Western languages, culture and religion. Many of their students were said to have excelled in Spanish, Portuguese, Latin and other subjects, some even surpassing the abilities of the priests' former European students.

In 1587, missionaries also brought to Japan the first printing press, which was used at their school in Amakusa. In *Spring Castle*,

---

4. Dougill, p. 8.

5. Jonathan Clements, *Christ's Samurai: The True Story of the Shimabara Rebellion.* (Robinson, 2016) 201.

evidence of this event appears when a young Japanese Christian scholar recites to an audience from a printed version of the classic *Tale of the Heike*, one that would have been printed in the Romanized phonetic alphabet on the press in Amakusa. The advent of the printing press signaled the introduction of a tool, a technology and a medium that perhaps resounded in Japan with even greater implications than that of the gun, as it ushered in the era of printed texts, the practice of private reading among the samurai, merchant classes and even the general public, and other changes that would one day link the country with the modern world of electronic media, IT and AI. The implications of this transition from an oral-based society to a modern media-based one was an underlying concern in all of Ishimure's writing.

But although a few members of the Japanese nobility were attracted to Christianity, by the end of the 16th century, most top national leaders had become wary of the growing Christian presence. Far from being unaware of international developments, they had taken critical note of increasing reports about neighboring countries being colonized by European countries. Toyotomi Hideyoshi, the imperial regent and de facto head of the government, became convinced that the missionaries represented the vanguard forces of European countries intent on colonizing Japan. Hideyoshi, followed by the Tokugawa shoguns Ieyasu, Hidetada and Iemitsu, issued a series of increasingly harsh edicts against the religious practices of the priests, and subsequently against all of their native Christian converts. A series of executions—considered martyrdoms by the Christians—followed. It has been estimated that about two thousand Japanese believers and foreign missionaries were killed in the enforcement of the edicts against Christianity.[6]

After the rebels' defeat in the Shimabara Rebellion, Christians and Christianity disappeared almost entirely from Japan. Many in the government believed that the Catholic missionaries in particular, and the trading and cultural practices that accompanied them, had been largely responsible for the Rebellion and for endangering

6. Yvette Tan, "The Japanese Christians forced to trample on Christ," *BBC News*, Nov. 24, 2019.

the country with Western colonialism. The shoguns forced any remaining believers to choose either apostasy or execution. Nonetheless, a few Christians—no one knows for certain how many—maintained their faith in secret for over two centuries, spanning some ten generations, until Christianity was again legally permitted by the Meiji government in 1873. In 1865, a small group of these faith-keepers, known as *kakure* (hidden) Christians, emerged from secrecy and announced their existence in public to a priest who had been permitted to preach to the recently-gathered foreign congregation in Nagasaki—much to the astonishment of the priest, the church in Europe and the Japanese public. At present, Christians comprise about 1.1 percent of the Japanese population.[7]

While *Spring Castle* brings to light stories of the religious persecution and bloody warfare that took place in the Shimabara Rebellion, it also highlights the deep ties that existed between many Christians and Buddhists, and it suggests possibilities for reconciliation and alternatives to intolerance. A central character in the novel, a peasant woman named Oume, embodies such possibilities. Oume, born into a devout Buddhist family—one which we learn had experienced persecution from the Christian priests—becomes the beloved, lifelong assistant of the Christian Hasuda family. In her simple, powerful words, she teaches the fundamental meaning of religion to those around her for whom complicated doctrines and petty animosities had threatened to obscure the universal roots of religion. It is Oume, the untutored Buddhist peasant, who most effectively demonstrates to others the practical application of the biblical—indeed the universal—Golden Rule of doing unto others as we would have them do unto us.

Moreover, amidst its scenes of suffering and tragedy, a major emphasis of *Spring Castle* is devoted to depicting the pleasures and beauties of the daily lives of the people of Shimabara and Amakusa, including their foods, stories, environment and celebrations. Some one hundred different plants are mentioned in the text, many

7. Japan Agency for Cultural Affairs, *Shukyo nenkan Reiwa 3 nenban* (Annual report on religion, 2021), December 2021, https://www.bunka.go.jp/tokei_hakusho_shuppan/hakusho_nenjihokokusho/shukyo_nenkan/pdf/r03nenkan.pdf

accompanied by specific information regarding their use in food preparation and health care. Because of this prevailing attention to the joys of simple daily life and the beauties of nature, the overall tone of *Spring Castle* remains surprisingly bright.

All of the characters in the novel who belong to the noble and samurai classes were based on historical figures. Masuda Shirō, the Rebellion's young leader, was born to a well-documented Christian samurai family from Amakusa. He was regarded as a charismatic figure and legend has it that he could perform magic and supernatural feats. But as for the story's peasants and commoners, about whom all records had been erased and discussion largely tabooed, Ishimure had to create their names, lives and histories completely from her imagination. It was to tell their stories and honor their lives that she wrote *Spring Castle*.

Narrative and oral imagination

From the first time I met Ishimure Michiko at a reading she gave of her work in 1995, I was deeply impressed—and initially somewhat puzzled—by the unusual but exquisite range of sounds, rhythms, and narrative time-space she brings to her work. Readers of *Spring Castle* may also initially encounter a certain "strangeness" in Ishimure's style of narration and storytelling. In this novel, as in her other writings, she remains a lover, preserver and innovator of the traditions of oral storytelling, language and imagination. Her writing inhabits the space that exists between and unites the worlds of traditional oral and modern written language. She writes with a distinctive, orally-based, non-linear sense of time-space that relates history as a spiraling, recursive, emotional process linking past, present and future, rather than as a merely rationally-ordered, linear progression moving inexorably from past to future. As Ishimure scholar Ken'ichi Noda has aptly said, "*Spring Castle* has no clock time. The time passing in the story is shown simply by nature, mainly by plants growing and withering and the changes of the seasons."[8] History, in Ishimure's world, is recounted as the collective stories of people who are in and of nature.

8. Personal discussion, June 5, 2023.

In creating this world in *Spring Castle*, Ishimure employs three basic narrative forms. The first is a sinuous kind of third-person, authorial narrative. It may begin in a more standard form of modern Japanese, but often it takes surprising turns. Abruptly, it may change into eerie, dream-like language that evokes the spirit of Noh drama, stream-of-conscious associations, meditations and spiritual conjectures. The second narrative form derives from the spoken conversations of the stories' characters, narrated in their distinctive, often rough local dialects. This includes Ishimure's imaginative re-creations of the 400-year-old dialects of Japanese peasants, fishers and samurai, as well as those of the Spanish and Portuguese missionaries who would have used a strange mixture of their own native languages, ecclesiastical rhetoric and Latin, along with their labored attempts to speak Japanese. The third is Ishimure's distinctive "internal monologue" narrative form, through which she relates characters' intimate thoughts and dreams about matters that even they would not be able to put into words. Some scholars have given this range of imaginative dialects in Ishimure's writing the special term "Michiko-ben" (Michiko dialect). This rich mixture of narrative elements comprises Ishimure's distinctive, pioneering hybrid style that unites the older oral tradition with contemporary literary narrative forms.

Translation considerations

Among the most difficult challenges for me as a translator of Ishimure's literature has been that of conveying her use of dialects and the "sound spaces" she creates. While it may not be possible to fully translate the richly varied dialects of the peasants, fishers and missionaries of 400 years ago that Ishimure employs in *Spring Castle*, I have worked closely from my sense of the novel's essential world of sounds and rhythms. In Ishimure's attention to this world of sounds, the voices of winds, waves, plants, animals and all of nature are given equal standing to those of humans. In translating this oral-aural world, I have kept in mind the advice that the poet Robert Frost used to give students about reading: "Be an ear reader," he urged. In this spirit, I have tried to work as an "ear translator," guided by Ishimure's profound attention to the world of sounds and their oral transmission.

Ishimure's choice of the novel's title, *Haru no shiro* (lit. "castle of spring") itself involves a subtle but important sound-play with words that resonates with the spirit of the novel. The castle's historical name was Hara Castle (*hara jō*), but in the novel, Ishimure works into this name the additional, suggestive name of Haru Castle (*haru no shiro*). In Japanese, *hara* means "field," while *haru* means "spring"; *jō* and *shiro* are two readings of the character meaning "castle." Using these two words in close association, she transforms the historical "Field Castle" into the "Spring Castle" of the Christian rebels. Being so close in sound—especially when pronounced in the local Kyushu dialect—the similar aural, visual and metaphorical overtones of these words *hara* and *haru* help to represent the faith that the people who joined the Rebellion held for achieving a spring-like rebirth.

Because the use of Japanese honorific suffixes and prefixes is such an essential linguistic element of the novel, I have preserved them in translation. For readers unfamiliar with these honorifics, a brief explanation may be in order. Japanese honorifics supply important information regarding characters' position, status, gender and age. They may also suggest such nuances as the ironic use of humor, teasing and mock seriousness. The most common honorary suffix used in *Spring Castle* is "-san," which is usually attached after family names, but sometimes after given names as well. The suffix "-yan" is a local variant, expressing closer intimacy. The suffix "-sama" is a more formal, respectful version of "-san." The suffix "-dono," and its abbreviated form "-don," are used to express respect for persons of higher class. The respectful prefix "O-" is added to adult women's names. Young girls are not given "O-" prefixes, but in some situations, they may be addressed using the suffixes "-san" or "-yan." The honorific term "danna-sama" is sometimes used to denote the master of a household.

In writing Japanese personal names, I have preserved the Japanese order, with family names written first, followed by given names. In a few instances, where it might be difficult for readers to keep track of characters whose names are referred to with multiple variations, I have added their family or given names to those written in the original.

I have written all dates following the Japanese text, which uses the old Japanese lunar calendar, rather than the modern Gregorian solar calendar. Thus, the dates in this book are about 45 days behind what they would be in the modern calendar. For example, "the first day of the first month" corresponds to February 14 in the modern calendar.

Likewise, I have followed the Japanese text in writing people's ages according to the traditional system. Ages start from one year at birth and thus appear one year older than in the modern system of counting ages; a boy who is "fourteen years old" in this text would be thirteen by the modern system.

Toward the Future

Spring Castle deals with a vast range of historical issues and events. In particular, it provides insights into Japan's early experiences in dealing with Western people, religion, economy, technology and culture. It sheds light on a wide range of the challenges faced in the process of internationalization, touching on such persistent issues as human trafficking, slavery and prejudice, and on the difficulties of accepting and integrating people of differing religions, races and customs. It also provides critical insight into Japan's ecological conditions at the time, notably its severe cycles of droughts and excessive rainfalls, and it warns of the problems that can follow when governments ignore or exacerbate such environmental-social conditions. The novel's accounting of the historical events of the Rebellion, expressed from the rebels' and Christians' perspective, provides fresh insight into the late stages of Japan's period of civil uprisings and its formation of a unified nation. The novel also encourages a deeper questioning of Westerners' plans for the colonization of Japan, in connection with their hopes for opening lucrative foreign trading relations, practicing religious conversion and exerting economic and political power. Furthermore, it invites new considerations about the effects of introducing Western technologies, notably firearms and the printing press. Along with raising such concerns, it also highlights the joys that common people have found in the beauty of nature and community life, and the ways they have kept hope alive, even in the midst of the tragedies of war and social collapse.

In an interview Ishimure gave near the end of her life, in which she discussed such challenges in relation to her thoughts about writing, beauty and hope, she reflected:

> Our hoping for what we cannot accomplish through human power, our hoping for what is not even possible to be hoped for; this is the essence of our aspiration for beauty. And it is this sense that I have hoped to put into literature … My hope is that, at the very end, we may die with aspiration.[9]

9. Taii, *Toward the Paradise of Flowers.*

ACKNOWLEDGMENTS

Although translation can be a rather solitary process, my experience in translating *Spring Castle* has been a remarkably shared, cooperative one. The wide scope of this novel, involving difficult questions about matters such as historical background, narrative voice and dialects, has necessitated my asking for and receiving assistance from many people.

Ishimure Michiko generously encouraged me and assisted me in working with others who have given me further support and understanding about her work. Thanks to my conversations with Ishimure-san, I gained a deeper appreciation of the oral-based narrative imagination of her writing. To my sadness, I was unable to complete this translation before her passing, but she kindly encouraged me to take as much time as I needed to bring it to life. For this I am deeply grateful.

My wife, Mitsue, has been my fundamental assistant, mentor and supporter through the years we have spent in seeing this translation to fruition. Her continuing enthusiasm, encouragement, and advice have been essential to this work.

A wide network of other friends, readers and helpers has also been essential. Among them are Yuko Aihara, Yuri Yokota, Ken Noda, Karen Thornber, Christine Marran, Jonathan Mack, Scott Slovic, Sajed and Rosie Kamal, Mark Williams and Mark Selden. My initial introduction to Ishimure Michiko and her writing came from the activities and members of the Associations for the Study of Literature and Environment in Japan and the US. Seisen University in Tokyo has supported my translation work for many years. Fujiwara Yoshio and the Fujiwara Shoten publishing company, primary supporters of Ishimure Michiko's writing in Japan, have given me important encouragement for this translation. Winnie

Bird, my ever-enthusiastic and perceptive editor at Tuttle Publishing, has helped me wrestle with interpreting difficult sections of the text and improving the English expression. It has been a joy to work with all these people. To all of them, and to many others too numerous to mention here, I express my deep gratitude.

This translation is dedicated to my wife, Mitsue, and to the memory of Ishimure Michiko.

PREFACE

Ishimure Michiko

This work was originally published in serialized form from 1998 to 1999 in seven local newspapers (from April of 1998 to March of 1999 it was published in the *Kumamoto nichinichi shinbun* newspaper). In the serialized edition, it appeared under the title *Haru no shiro* (*Spring Castle*), but owing to unavoidable circumstances, the title was changed to *Anima no tori* (Spirit birds) when first published in book form.

My first thoughts of writing this book came to me back when I was protesting at the Tokyo headquarters of the Chisso Corporation with the late Kawamoto Teruo and other Minamata disease victims who had been denied government certification. That was on December 6, 1971. The negotiations with Chisso Corporation were a difficult struggle and several days later we were forced out by the police. After that, we set up tents in front of their head office and continued to negotiate. One bitterly cold night we were sleeping by the street, together with student supporters, with the falling leaves of plane trees swirling about and sticking to our cheeks. As it turned out, the next book I finished writing was *Ten no uo* (Fish of heaven), but during the protest I deeply imagined and sympathized with the unnamed people who had suffered long ago inside Hara Castle.

From that time on, it remained my fervent wish to tell the story of the Shimabara Rebellion, and in 1991, with encouragement from the *Kumamoto nichinichi shimbun*, I started publishing a series of travel sketches titled *Kusa no michi* (Grass road). With that start, my long-held wish began to gradually take shape. It was fortunate that I started writing this novel in serial form for a newspaper, for without that pressure to continue, being the lazy person that I am, I likely never would have finished. I wish to express my deep appreciation to the many people who have supported and encouraged me.

LIST OF MAIN CHARACTERS

Masuda Family

Home in Ebe Village, near Uto in the Hosokawa clan domain on the Kyushu mainland. Some of the men are living in Miyazu Village on nearby Ōyano Island. Christians who were formerly samurai under the Christian Lord Konishi Yukinaga, but lost samurai status following the prohibition of Christianity and exile of their lord:

Shirō	15- or 16-year-old charismatic prodigy who is chosen as leader of the Rebellion. Also called Masuda Shirō Tokisada
Jinbei	Shirō's father, a main organizer of the Rebellion and ex-samurai of Lord Konishi
Oine	Shirō's mother (pronounced O-inay)
Man	Granddaughter of Jinbei and Oine
Kohei	Grandson of Jinbei and Oine

Extended family relatives; Christians, living on Ōyano Island:

Watanabe Denbei	Former headman of Ōyano Island, now headman of Amura Village
Watanabe Kozaemon	Denbei's older son, current headman of Ōyano Island
Watanabe Satarō	Kozaemon's younger brother

Okayo's Family (no family name given)

Home in Uchino Village on Lower Amakusa Island. Farmers, Buddhists, but with some Christian members through marriage:

Okayo	Daughter of Seibei and Onobu, marries Daisuke of Hasuda family
Seibei	Okayo's father, village leader of Uchino

Onobu	Okayo's mother, from Christian family; dies before the story begins
Ofuji	Okayo's grandmother, from Christian family
Sasuke	Okayo's older brother (pronounced Saskay)
Nana	Okayo's younger sister
Oshizu	Sasuke's wife

Hasuda Family

Home in Kuchinotsu, on Shimabara Peninsula. Christians, village headman family, big farming household, non-samurai background, leaders of Rebellion:

Nisuke	Headman of Kuchinotsu (pronounced Niskay)
Omiyo	Wife of Nisuke
Daisuke	Son of Nisuke and Omiyo, marries Okayo (pronounced Daiskay)
Ayame	Daughter of Okayo and Daisuke (pronounced Ayamay)
Oume	Chief household assistant, midwife, lifetime assistant of Omiyo (pronounced O-oomay)
Suzu	Young girl adopted by Hasuda family, becomes caretaker of Ayame
Matsukichi	Older household manager
Kumagorō	Young household worker, adopted by Hasudas after father was martyred

Ninagawa Family

Home in Kuchinotsu, Shimabara Peninsula. Christians, former samurai, leading family in Kuchinotsu, organizers of the Rebellion:

Ukon	Young Christian scholar and teacher, close friend of Shirō, Rebellion leader
Sakyō	Ukon's father
Mizuna	Ukon's sister
Takematsu	Household worker, fisher, heavy drinker, becomes a cook at Spring Castle

Other Important Characters

Yazō	Leader of fishers' group, provides sea transport of supplies and communications for Rebellion, cousin of Daisuke's mother Omiyo
Onami ("Okattsama")	Nagasaki businesswoman, former prostitute, Christian, guides Shirō in his studies
Umeo Shichibei	Headman of Kōtsuura on Upper Amakusa Island. His house is used as temporary rebel headquarters during early stage of the Rebellion.
Okiku	Umeo Shichibei's wife
Osato	Umeo Shichibei's mother
Tsunekichi	"Town crier" messenger of Kōtsuura and Upper Amakusa Island, fisher, confidant of Osato
Sankichi	Son of Christian martyr, builds woodshed shrine in Kita Arima Village
Yamada Yomosaku	Artist
Yozaemon	Leading farmer of Kuchinotsu area, often donates grain to poor families
Otaki	Wife of Yozaemon
Chōichi	Son of Yozaemon
Okimi	Wife of Chōichi
Henmi Juan	Elder Christian scholar, former Arima clan samurai, Rebellion organizer (pronounced Jew-an)
Kazusa Hyōgo	Former Arima clan samurai, Rebellion organizer
Chijiiwa Bannai	Former Arima clan samurai, Rebellion organizer
Matsushima Sadonokami	Headman of Kita Arima Village in Shimabara, former Arima samurai

Sainen	Ikkō sect Buddhist monk who joins Christians in the Rebellion
Matsukura clan	Shigenobu, Shigemasa and Katsuie: Successive lords of the Shimabara region, appointed after the prohibition of Christianity and exile of Christian Arima lords in 1614
Tada Kurōbei	Magistrate of Matsukura clan
Matsuda Gonzaemon	Magistrate of Matsukura clan (after Tada Kurōbei)
Okamoto Shinbei	Chief Matsukura counsellor, leads fight against rebels at Shimabara Castle
Suzuki Saburō Kurō Shigenari	(often, just "Shigenari") Shogun's engineering and munitions advisor, appointed governor of Amakusa after the Rebellion

References

In Japanese:
Original text of *Spring Castle* by Ishimure Michiko (published under separate titles, but with same text):

—*Haru no shiro* (*Spring Castle*). Fujiwara Shoten, 2017.

—*Anima no tori* (Spirit birds). Chikuma Shobo, 1999.

In English:
Allen, Bruce, and Yuki Masami, ed. *Ishimure Michiko's Writing in Ecocritical Perspective: Between Sea and Sky*. Lexington Books, 2016.

Clements, Jonathan. *Christ's Samurai: The True Story of the Shimabara Rebellion*. Robinson, 2016.

Dougill, John. *In Search of Japan's Hidden Christians: A Story of Suppression, Secrecy and Survival.* Tuttle, 2012.

Ellison, George. *Deus Destroyed: The Image of Christianity in Early Modern Japan*. Harvard University Press, 1988.

Ishimure, Michiko. *Lake of Heaven* (*Tenko*). Trans. Bruce Allen. Lexington Books, 2008.

Whelan, Christal, trans. *The Beginnings of Heaven and Earth: The Sacred Book of Japan's Hidden Christians*. University of Hawai'i Press, 1996.

Spring Castle Area Circa 1637

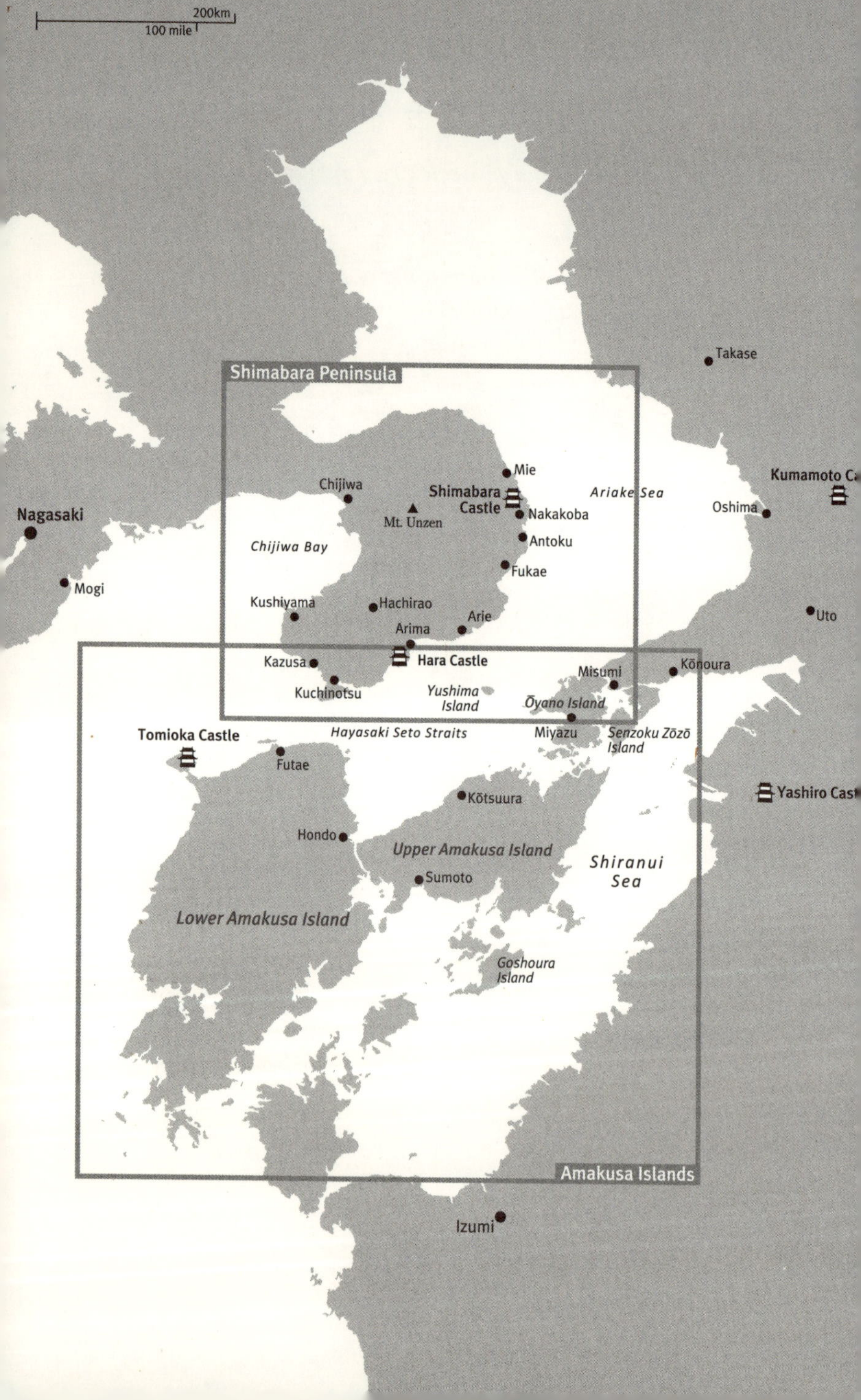

200km
100 mile

Shimabara Peninsula
Takase
Mie
Chijiwa
Shimabara Castle
Ariake Sea
Kumamoto C
Nagasaki
Mt. Unzen
Nakakoba
Oshima
Chijiwa Bay
Antoku
Mogi
Fukae
Kushiyama
Hachirao
Arie
Uto
Arima
Kazusa
Hara Castle
Misumi
Kōnoura
Kuchinotsu
Yushima Island
Ōyano Island
Tomioka Castle
Hayasaki Seto Straits
Miyazu
Senzoku Zōzō Island
Futae
Yashiro Cas
Kōtsuura
Hondo
Upper Amakusa Island
Shiranui Sea
Sumoto
Lower Amakusa Island
Goshoura Island
Amakusa Islands
Izumi

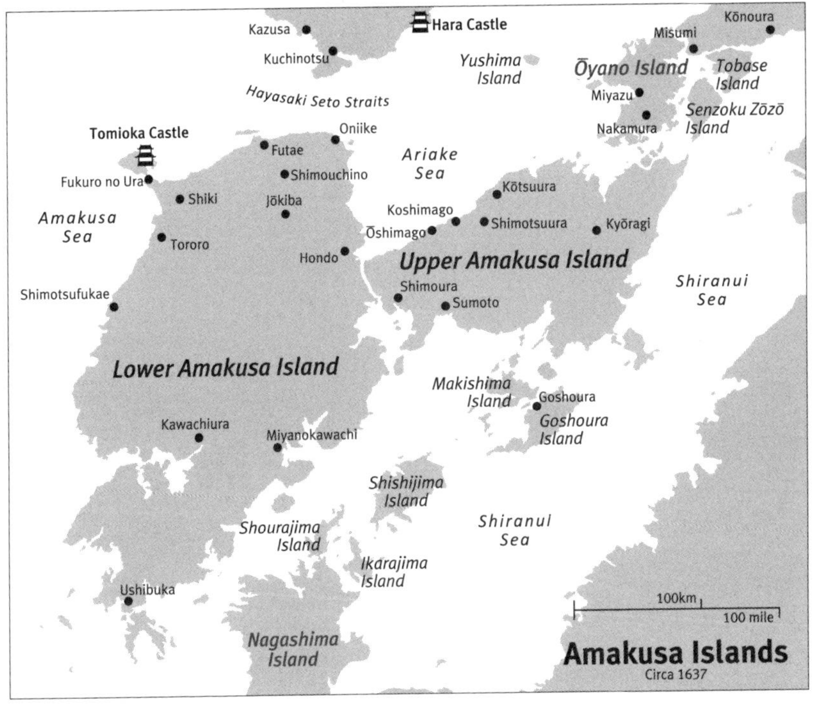
Kazusa
Hara Castle
Kōnoura
Misumi
Kuchinotsu
Yushima Island
Ōyano Island
Tobase Island
Hayasaki Seto Straits
Miyazu
Nakamura
Senzoku Zōzō Island
Tomioka Castle
Oniike
Futae
Ariake Sea
Shimouchino
Fukuro no Ura
Kōtsuura
Shiki
Jōkiba
Amakusa Sea
Koshimago
Shimotsuura
Kyōragi
Ōshimago
Tororo
Hondo
Upper Amakusa Island
Shiranui Sea
Shimoura
Shimotsufukae
Sumoto
Lower Amakusa Island
Makishima Island
Goshoura
Goshoura Island
Kawachiura
Miyanokawachi
Shishijima Island
Shiranul Sea
Shourajima Island
Ikarajima Island
Ushibuka
100km
100 mile
Nagashima Island
Amakusa Islands
Circa 1637

Shimabara Peninsula
Circa 1637
100km
50 mile
Taira
Iko
Yue
Higashi Koga
Moriyama
Ōno
Noi
Aizu
Mie
Chijiwa
Shimabara Castle
Ariake Sea
Mt. Unzen
Nakakoba
Antoku
Chijiwa Bay
Fukae
Obama
Futsu
Hachirao
Dōsaki
Kushiyama
Hinoe Castle
Arie
Sugawa
Kita Arima
Minami Arima
Hara Castle
Kazusa
Ōe
Kuchinotsu
Yushima Island
Misumi
Ōyano Island
Miyazu

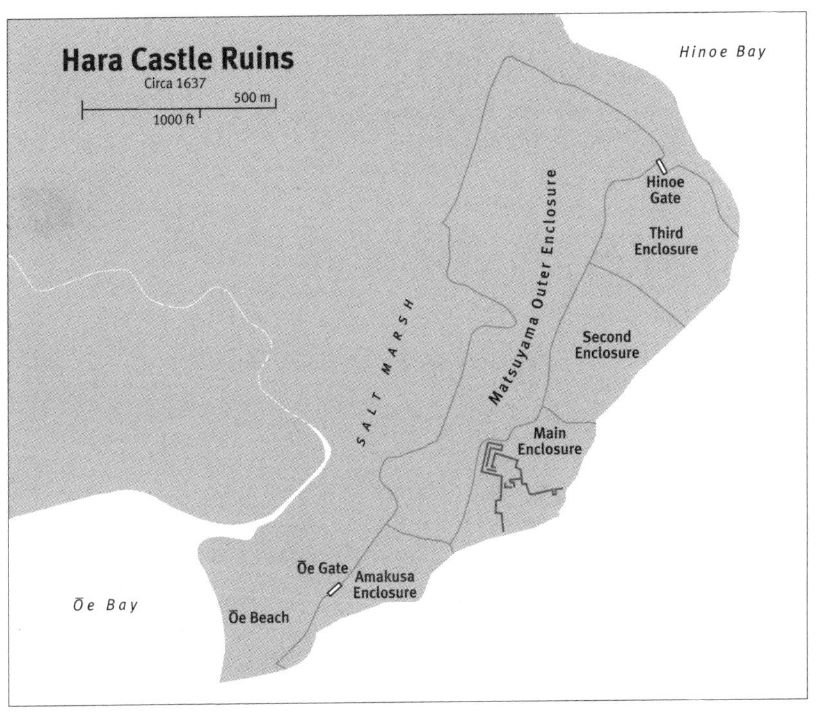
Hara Castle Ruins
Circa 1637
500 m
1000 ft
Hinoe Bay
Hinoe Gate
Third Enclosure
Matsuyama Outer Enclosure
Second Enclosure
SALT MARSH
Main Enclosure
Ōe Gate
Amakusa Enclosure
Ōe Bay
Ōe Beach

CHAPTER ONE

The Straits of Hayasaki Seto

The boat that would carry Okayo to her wedding was set to make the crossing on a day with favorable currents.

The man who would accompany her came to give her a message:

"When we get to the beach at Futae, the boatman Shichigorō, who you know well, will be waiting. You'll be in good hands."

He assured Okayo that everything was ready at Nisuke's house in Kuchinotsu, and that as soon as the boat arrived there, she and her family would be guided to the wedding ceremony. The bride's party included Okayo, her father Seibei, her grandmother Ofuji, her elder brother and his wife, her younger sister Nana, and her uncle and aunt.

If it hadn't been for the introduction from this man Yazō—the *benzashi*, leader of the net fishers—her marriage might never have taken place.

There had been plenty of other proposals, but Seibei had rejected them all without so much as a word to Okayo. "We couldn't, we haven't taught her the things a wife should know," he would say, although she was twenty-one[1] already. Or, "She's my mother's favorite and she's been with us all her life. If we married her off now, I reckon Grandma would keel right over." And on it went. All the rejected suitors could do was smile. *Grandma, eh? Seems you're the one likely to keel over, Seibei.* Okayo was the image of her late mother Onobu, whom Seibei had loved dearly, and the villagers knew he

1. This is her age according to the traditional system, in which babies are considered one year old at birth. By the modern system, she would be twenty.

wouldn't let her go easily. And so, when they heard that the latest marriage proposal had been accepted, everyone was surprised.

"So Yazō from Kuchinotsu brought the bridegroom over in the flesh, did he? He's a stubborn one, that Yazō. Once his mind's made up, he's not budging."

Every year the *benzashi* visited all the villages to buy the fermented astringent juice of persimmons to dye fishing nets, and people everywhere knew him by his hearty laugh.

When Yazō visited Seibei's house, the first thing he had done was to take from his inside breast pocket a lovely ball, finely decorated with colored threads, and place it in Nana's hand. With a big smile he told them:

"My cousin married into a family of farmers in Kuchinotsu, and she likes to make this sort of thing. When she heard you had a little girl in the house, she asked me to bring this for her. She stays up nights making them, says it tickles her fancy to give them out as presents.

"The household in Kuchinotsu she married into is no small one—they need five or six people to help at harvest time, that's how many fields they have. She doesn't work much in the fields, though, since she's so busy helping her husband. He has a lot to do as head of the household. They asked me to find a nice young woman for their son. He's the heir, just turned twenty-three this year. I've been looking for a good woman, and I admire Okayo-sama's character. That's why I'm here. I'll tell you one thing, and not just as a matchmaker—my cousin's a more generous woman than most. Her helpers all say she's easier to work for than the usual mistress."

Okayo's grandmother Ofuji nodded as she listened to Yazō talk. *A mother-in-law like that could teach Okayo needlework and weaving. Okayo is my precious grandchild, but we can't keep her forever.* She made up her mind to place the possibility of Okayo's wedding in Yazō's hands.

"May I ask one thing?" she said, a little hesitantly.

"Why, anything at all," Yazo replied calmly, as if he had been expecting the question.

"The family's religion ... ?"

It had been worrying her.

"Everyone in their family has been Christian from birth—same as everyone in their village."

"I see," Ofuji answered, lowering her head. "Actually, Okayo's mother's family was born into that religion, but our temple and our prayers are different."

"Well, that doesn't matter, as long as she's a good, kind person. Christians don't lead different lives from other people. The family belongs to a benevolence group. They take care of the sick and poor, and orphans too. So, really, it's just about the same as what people try to do in this village."

"A benevolence group?" Ofuji blinked for a moment and then, looking down, continued in a low voice, "Well, thank you so much for your help. Seibei will give you his reply soon."

After Okayo's marriage was decided, word got around that she was marrying into the family of the headman of Kuchinotsu. "Such a delicate girl, think she'll last?" some villagers wondered, half from envy.

Yazō assured her family again and again that they needn't fuss over the preparations. "They just want to meet your daughter as soon as they can. Bring yourselves, nothing else."

To each other, Seibei and Ofuji said, "Farmers or not, they're a family of high standing, and she's marrying the heir. If we don't pull together what we can, she'll come off like an orphan." Then the aunts had discussed things, coming and going endlessly, and finally, everything was ready.

On her wedding day, in remembrance of her mother, Okayo wore Onobu's kimono. Onobu's father had been the *benzashi* of Shiki and had done business with the *goshuinsen* trading ships authorized by the shogunate. On Onobu's wedding day he had presented his cherished daughter with a kimono made of cotton crepe, brought from Nagasaki. It was such an elegant gown. Its white was the hue of moonflowers. After wearing it just one time at her wedding, Onobu had placed it in a closet and never put it on again. Twenty days after giving birth to Nana, Onobu had called Okayo to her bedside and, just before she died, asked Okayo to take care of her baby sister. "When the time comes for you to marry, I hope you'll wear this kimono," she had added.

Before Okayo left home, her grandmother Ofuji had taken up the hem a bit at the bottom and asked Okayo to put it on.

"Oh," Ofuji sighed, "the blue in the embroidery of the crane and the flowers is like dragon balls. It will be just perfect for the celebration." "Dragon balls" were the round blue berries Okayo and Nana used for beads when they played *ohajiki*.

"She left this as a keepsake, just before she died. I was planning to teach you to weave, but everything's been so rushed. I wish we had more time. You'll be a wonderful daughter-in-law. I'm sure your mother-in law will like you and teach you well."

It was so pleasing to see Okayo straightening the collar of her kimono and nodding, her cheeks full and charming. She looked just like her mother when she had come as a bride. Ofuji understood why Seibei hadn't wanted Okayo to leave, and it filled her with sadness.

Noticing her younger sister staring in wonder, Okayo said to her, "Nana, when you get married, I'll give you this kimono—all right?" Her lighthearted voice, too, was just like her mother's.

A group of elderly neighbors had gathered to see Okayo off. "What a beautiful day for a wedding," one said, looking up at the sky. "The winds over the Hayasaki Straits should be calm."

Okayo turned and took in the scene around her house. Red and white deutzias were starting to bloom beside the mossy stone bridge out front. Her aunt arranged the carefully-combed hair around Okayo's shoulders and tied it with gold and silver ceremonial paper strings. The tresses that fell from her temples over her rounded cheeks looked fresh and her lips were colored with a trace of red lipstick. Okayo glanced at the green apricots and turned toward her grandmother.

"Grandma, soon the apricots will be ripe."

"Yes, the apricots—let's put them up in salt," Ofuji answered, but then grew sad. *When will she come back to eat them?* As a girl, Okayo had liked to stand under the tree when the fruit ripened and pester her—*apricots, apricots!*

"They're good salted, but nothing beats the tart fresh ones," Okayo said, looking down and smiling.

"Be sure and send her some of those apricots when she's pregnant—right, Grandma?"one of the women seeing off the wedding party called.

The wind swept over the soft grasses along the riverbank on the fine late spring morning. From the grain fields and squash patches, villagers watched the party walk along the road by the river. They bowed to them, removing the kerchiefs from their heads.

"Look—the Ofusa family are bowing," Ofuji said, pointing as she glanced back.

"And Sister—" Nana cried out. "Look! In the field over there, too, people are bowing!"

Nana was the first to return their bows, and in response, the couple in the field stood up straight and laughed. Her father and uncle, both dressed in formal kimonos, walked in front and Okayo and their grandmother followed behind. Nana walked between them, sometimes lagging behind or skipping ahead.

"I'm so grateful, seeing everyone celebrating the wedding like this," Grandma exclaimed, her voice choking with joy.

Each time she bowed in return, Okayo shed tears. She felt the soft grass beneath her sandals. The familiar landscape around the riverbank settled deeply into her heart. They walked more slowly than usual because Grandma was using a cane.

"Look at that nice mugwort! It's ready to pick," Okayo's sister-in-law called out as a patch of the plants swayed in the wind. Before, when Okayo had come to pick the first mugwort of the season, the river wind had still been cold and her marriage had not yet been arranged. Now she reflected on all she had been doing while the plants grew.

"We sure have been busy," Ofuji said with a sigh as she gazed over the field. She was an inch or two shorter than Okayo.

"All of this happened so quickly, we've been late in starting the grain crops," she added.

"Everyone else's fields look a lot greener than ours," the sister-in-law continued in a voice that carried well.

Okayo's aunt, who was walking at the very end of the line, called back loud enough for Ofuji to hear: "Grandmother, after the wedding let's work the fields together, and soon we'll turn them green. We'll help, and we'll bring some horse manure from our place, too."

"Well, thanks. I just wish we had more rain. We haven't had much of late."

Just then, without knowing why, everyone stopped and looked up at the sky. The fields on the low hills across the river were spread out in a patchwork and the new grain stood about six inches high.

"Sister," Nana asked, "when are you going to make mugwort cakes for me?" The five-year-old peered up at Okayo's face, playing with the sleeve of her kimono. Nana was so happy to see her sister wearing the silk wedding kimono, and she loved to touch it. Usually, Okayo wore a kimono of simple indigo cotton. Okayo found it difficult to reply. *Will I still be able to make mugwort cakes after I'm married?* she wondered.

"Why yes, mugwort cakes," her grandmother put in, taking over for Okayo. "Your sister is marrying into another family, so you and I and Oshizu will pick the mugwort." Oshizu was Okayo's sister-in-law.

When Okayo heard her grandmother say this, tears welled up in her eyes.

Although her brother and his wife lived nearby and many people would come to help with the farming, Okayo had been worrying about what would happen to her father, sister and grandmother, who was over sixty now. *Will their lives be harder after I leave home?*

"I'll be back next year at Girls' Festival ..." Okayo managed to reply, but her words caught in her throat as she coughed and choked back tears.

Okayo made a point of mentioning next year's Girl's Festival because she remembered that Nana had made Yazō promise that her sister would return for the event.

On the night the marriage was decided, Nana had gazed intently through the flickering candlelight at the face of the guest who recently had been visiting the house so often. Being a child, and thinking the discussion was over as soon as the visitor had changed from sitting formally to sitting cross-legged, Nana had asked her father, "Papa, will Sister be able to come back and make mugwort cakes for me?" The guest had smiled warmly. "Well, you certainly understand what's going on. What a smart girl! Yes, yes, she'll be back. So—you like mugwort cakes, do you?"

Nana had nodded solemnly and replied, "I heard our mother liked them."

Everyone had laughed a little and then grown pensive. *Just how far is it from here in Uchino to Kuchinotsu?*

"She's getting married, but the house is just on the other side of the straits," Yazō went on. "Riding the currents, she can go and come back on the anniversary of your mama's death."

"Will you bring my sister back on your boat?" Nana had asked. Her child's eyes had been fixed on the eyes of the guest, this ruggedly-built man in his prime. Charmed by her tone, Yazō had nodded immediately.

"Sure, I'll bring your sister back on my boat across those rough Hayasaki Straits. So I hope you'll come, Okayo-sama. And Nana, don't you worry."

As she clung to Okayo's waist, perhaps Nana, too, was recalling Yazō's words. She looked up at her sister as if stamping her feet.

"When will it be next year?"

"Well, next year will be …"

When Okayo paused, not knowing how to reply, Ofuji took over again:

"This is the year of the boar, so next year will be the year of the mouse. That's next year."

"So, how many nights will I have to sleep until we get to the year of the mouse?"

"Well, you'll have to sleep a whole lot of nights—and then, still some more."

"A lot of nights?" Nana repeated. She was walking just behind Okayo, stroking the sash of her kimono.

"I want you to come back sooner—please!"

"Well, yes, I hope I can come back soon. Right, Grandma?"

"Yes, I hope so too, but those Hayasaki Straits are rough."

Surprised, Nana asked, "The Hayasaki Straits are rough?"

"They sure are. The tide comes in at night and it rises and falls, and it makes whooshing and swirling sounds."

"Whooshing and swirling? What's it doing?"

"It's making whirlpools."

"Oh—I know whirlpools. I've seen the *okera* bugs whirling

around in the fields when we get the big rains."

"Yes, but the tide is much wilder and fiercer than what you see with the *okera* bugs. It's Ryūjin-sama—the Sea Dragon god."

Seeing Nana gazing up at her wide-eyed, Ofuji softened her voice. "Sometimes that fierce old Sea Dragon comes up from the bottom of the sea, along with other sea creatures, and he plays along the shores."

"And, and then the young octopuses swirl around and come in from the Hayasaki Straits, and then they go up onto the land and pick wild plums," Nana cried.

"That's right! The other day at the Girls' Festival you were playing with the young octopuses and sea cucumbers at the shore, weren't you?" Ofuji replied. Nana shrieked with glee.

She was no doubt recalling what she had heard from the grownups about octopuses—that the parents and children came in with the tide and floated their way up the river mouths and then climbed the wild plum trees along the shore and pulled off the small branches that bore ripe red fruit and decorated their heads with them and then swam back to the sea.

Whatever the topic of conversation, Nana was just happy to be walking along with her whole family, all dressed up for the wedding.

"My goodness! While Nana's been talking about octopuses, the tide has already come in so much. Soon we'll be at Futae Beach."

Ofuji pointed across the river to where it widened considerably. Okayo watched intently as the tide rose and mingled with the river, flowing in among the reeds. The Uchino River wasn't particularly big, but it nurtured life for the little villages hidden in the heart of the mountains. On occasion, in hard rains, it would rise and flood, but as long as the rains weren't too heavy, it gently watered all the fields. At the spring tides, the fry of striped mullets, sea bass and gobies came up to play among the reeds in the ditches of the fields. Crabs came all the way to the upper reaches of the Edagawa River and people plopped them into the cooking pots in their hearths and savored them in their soup.

Okayo thought back on the days when her mother Onobu was still alive and they had waited together for the beginning of spring. She, her grandmother and her mother would go down to the beaches, passing over the riverbanks, to gather mugwort and silverleaf. From spring to early summer this had been their greatest pleasure—not only for her family, but for all the women in the village. Until summer arrived, the outskirts of the mountains, the thickets and the beaches were filled with the cheerful voices of women. It was such a peaceful time. Okayo loved those places. Since her childhood, she had enjoyed learning how her grandmother and mother worked, and she had learned how to soak the roots of bracken ferns and kudzu, after getting the men to dig them up, and how to crush the soaked roots and collect their starch.

"You'll have to remember all of this, since you never know when we might have another famine," her grandmother had told her.

Since they had been able to harvest some wheat the year before, Okayo and her sister-in-law had ground it and added some mugwort they had boiled and dried for making cakes for the memorial of her mother's death. Ofuji had told her they could also make delicious cakes from kudzu starch, and Okayo had wanted to try it. But before she could, the wedding date had been decided. Now she thought about how she would like to make those cakes with Nana when she returned for the memorial.

Ofuji continued walking along just ahead of Okayo, her chin buried in the collar of her kimono and her head bobbing along in rhythm. As she followed right behind, Okayo thought again about how her grandmother had been the one to bring her up.

As Ofuji walked along, her chest swelled with emotions. *Even though Okayo could be taking her place in front of me, she's chosen to walk behind me, worrying about my steps. How often I walked this grassy path with her on my back. Will I ever walk it with her again before I die?*

"I'm worried that after I get married you won't have enough rice," Okayo said suddenly. Ofuji turned around and looked at her in surprise.

"What's this? You've been worrying about such things? I hadn't expected to hear you talking about our rice supply. So far, thank goodness, our rice bin has never gone empty. Well, sometimes we've only found some beans and chestnuts in it, but there's always been at least something left."

"So there has," Okayo said, laughing softly as she gently touched

Ofuji's back, the way she always had. "I'm not sure why, but I've been thinking about it these days. I never paid enough attention to it before, but recently I've started to hear about the rice and grain situation in other families."

"Well, your brother's here with us—you remember? And your father Seibei—he's still in good shape, too. The workers who help us sure will be surprised to hear you're worrying about us having enough rice."

"I guess I've just been a child. I'd never thought much about these things."

"You can't stay a child now that you're marrying into a big family. But it would be a shame for your new family if we saddled you with worries about your parents' house," Ofuji said, remembering how Okayo had been going off to the mountains behind their house recently to gather acorns.

In the flurry of marriage preparations, Ofuji had asked Okayo, "Did you polish the mirror as a keepsake of your mother?" and "Have you changed the neckband of your work kimono?" and other such questions, but Okayo had only nodded absent-mindedly and then gone off to gather acorns in the mountains behind the house.

"You aren't going to take those acorns with you when you get married, are you?" Ofuji had teased. *Since she was three or four she's been going off by herself to play in the hills behind our house and gather acorns and chinquapins. I love those roasted acorns as much as the children do. The ones just about the size of soybeans, with that rich aroma and sweetness when you crunch them in your mouth. Maybe now that she's decided to marry, she's been trying to reassure herself that her ties with the mountains she grew up with will continue.*

"Last year," Okayo added, "with all the dry weather, we couldn't take in much grain or chestnuts, and Father often said our dinner pot was looking more humble than usual."

Ofuji was touched to hear Okayo talking of such things, as if excusing herself for going off to gather nuts in the midst of the marriage preparations.

"You know your father; he's always gotten his way, ever since he was a child. No matter how many times I tell him not to complain about what we have in the dinner pot, he never learns, even at his age. Isn't that right, Nana?"

Hearing the word "father," Seibei turned around. Okayo shrugged and shook the sleeves of her moonflower-hued kimono in front of her face. Her father cut in, "I heard you talking about me. And, you know, I used to follow you ladies to the beach at the spring tides in March. I wonder how many times I've walked this path."

"And thanks to you, Father, we always got lots of hijiki and other kinds of seaweed," Okayo answered in a soft, kind voice. "It would leach salt into the straw bags and really smell. Remember, Grandma?"

"And, Okayo, we still have some dried daikon from last year in a big pot," her sister-in-law Oshizu added, joining the conversation. "And we picked silverleaf and bracken ferns and boiled and dried them. We'll wait till you come back, and then we'll make *nishime* with stewed vegetables and chicken. Why don't you bring some of your new family with you? We planted extra soybeans for making miso, and extra *sasage* beans for the Obon festival. And this year the ume trees are really doing well. It looks like we may be able to put up enough pickled plums for two years, don't you think, Grandma?"

"Oh, come on Oshizu—you're exaggerating again. There's probably enough for about one year. We ought to talk about such things modestly."

Even the people in back who couldn't really hear what Ofuji was saying started chuckling when they heard the ripple of laughter from the front.

Rows of small red crabs were marching down to the river, crossing the roadway that the people were walking along.

"Looks like there's lots more crabs this year. You think you can walk through them all, Mother?" Seibei asked, watching her feet.

"Oh, the crabs? Well, since you're walking in front, they're not bothering me a bit," Ofuji replied. As she spoke, she remembered something and smiled.

"Speaking of crabs, remember how they used to bite Okayo and make her cry? Just like a little kitten."

"That's right. One day when I was off in the woods cutting oak trees, I heard her sobbing and wailing, so I dashed back home. How old was she then?"

"You're no better yourself, Seibei—that time when a crab pinched your finger, you ran around with it hanging down by its claw and you howled like a wild puppy who'd just had its tail cut off."

"You did that, Papa?" Nana squealed in delight, "Do you cry, too, Papa, when you get pinched by a crab?"

"Well, that was a long, long time ago—back when I was really small. Much smaller than you, Nana."

As the breeze swept down along the river and softly touched the grasses on the banks, it wafted the lighthearted conversation out toward the seashore. Seeing the budding deutzias on the riverbanks and hillsides swelling and swaying gently in the wind, the women sighed in admiration and suggested they pick some for the family memorial altar.

Taking in the pungent sea smell, the group realized they were nearing a fishing village. The smell was completely different from that of the mountain villages. Whenever Okayo smelled the sea, she felt as if she herself was almost becoming a fish, and it always filled her with energy. She wondered about the smells in Kuchinotsu. *What will it be like there?*

As the roadway widened, small hamlets appeared here and there along the way. Seibei, in the lead, raised his hand, turned and signaled that they should stop and draw water from the Igawa well. The branches of its familiar hackberry trees stretched all the way down to the beach.

Whenever people from the mountain villages traveled to the shore, they drew water from the Igawa. Everyone in the party now fashioned their own small cups out of the round leaves of the silverleaf plants that grew among the rocks. Respectfully, Seibei offered a prayer and then scooped up some water with the wooden ladle that was kept there and poured it into each of the leaf cups. With reverence, they all drank the water from the little cups that looked like children's playthings.

"Mm—such sweet water. You won't find water anywhere that tastes better than this."

In this area, the word "igawa" meant a wellspring. White strips of Shinto ceremonial paper had been hung around it. The water had a bluish color, indicating its depth. People said that the water in this well was "female water." This kind of spring was found at a number of places along the shore. There was "male water," too. It was less cloudy, but harder. The female water was softer and sweeter. Okayo, too, could taste the difference.

While the others were washing their hands and resting, Ofuji pointed at the rock beside her and asked Seibei and Okayo to sit.

"When you become a member of the new family, you may get baptized," Ofuji remarked, looking at Okayo intently. Okayo was surprised by her grandmother's serious look—a look she had never seen before. She nodded quickly, even before hearing the rest of what Ofuji had to say.

"We brought this," Ofuji went on, taking a *furoshiki* bundle from Seibei and starting to unfold it on her lap. "Last night, Seibei and I were talking and we thought it would be a good idea if you took some of this water to your new family as a present."

Nodding, Seibei added, "You may already know this, but this water is so special that the tuna fishers from Kuchinotsu and the whalers from Ōyano all come here for it—for its sacred protective powers. This will make a very nice present."

"Now listen to me," Ofuji continued. "In the religion of your new family, water is highly revered. When a baby is born, they do a ceremony using water to purify its soul and keep it from evil. Before your mother Onobu died, the people from her family came and gave her some water to send her to Heaven—*Paraizo*, they called it. You were there too, Okayo, weren't you? I'll never forget the beauty of your mother's face at that time. There are no words for it."

Ofuji's voice suddenly grew plaintive, and she paused. Then she continued:

"Now I can imagine how much Onobu wanted to purify you with water when you were born. But she wasn't able to talk about it then because she had married into a family with a different religion. For a long time, I've felt sorry for her. And now, since it's been decided that you'll marry into a Christian family, this is what I've been thinking about. Seibei and I talked about it last night."

"So, Okayo, that's what's going to happen."

Seibei looked into his daughter's eyes with concern and explained, "The family you're marrying into will probably talk to you about this purification with water. And if they do, you can use this water. So we brought this as our present."

Ofuji opened the *furoshiki* and uncovered a white sake bottle. Painted in blue brushwork on its surface was a peony. Seibei drew some well water and filled the container silently. After Ofuji had retied the cloth, she looked up.

"Seibei, what was Onobu's other name—the name from her religion?"

"Magdalena."

"Magdalena, that's an easy name to say. So Okayo, if they're going to give you a name in their religion, you should ask them to call you Magdalena—your mother's name."

As the family stepped onto the boat, the boatman greeted them warmly.

"Since you're Daisuke-sama's precious bride, I'm going to take special care in getting you there." Okayo gazed at the sky above Uchino, which now seemed so far away.

The boatman tightened the cloth wrapped about his head and looked up at the dazzling sky. A few white sea birds were soaring slowly alongside the boat. Okayo stared for the first time into the powerful currents of the Hayasaki Seto Straits, with their dark waters torn by tidal currents that knocked each other and swirled about.

"My mother's name was Magdalena," she murmured.

As they approached the beach at Kuchinotsu, they could see a group of children pointing toward the boat, jostling each other and romping about on the rocks among the protruding roots of banyan trees. It seemed that each of the children was holding some kind of flower. Shichigorō, the boatman, rowed slowly and called out to the children, glancing at Okayo:

"Say there—it looks like everyone's here. What? Is something happening today?"

Now the children's giggling voices could be heard clearly. It was apparent that the children and Shichigorō knew each other well. A lively voice replied:

"We came to welcome the bride."

"So *that's* why you all look so cleaned up today—and without any runny noses."

Quickly, some of the children wiped their noses with their sleeves, but they all gazed at Okayo in a daze and ran along, following the boat.

"And whose bride is it you're welcoming?"

"She's the bride of Nisuke's eldest son."

"And where's the bride?"

The children shouted gleefully and threw some light pink bindweed flowers up into the air. The flowers fell onto the sea around the boat and floated on the waves. Some had been tied loosely into wreaths, but they came undone and scattered about here and there on the waves.

"Look, it's the bride!" a boy about nine or ten years old cried out, pointing at Okayo. Standing close behind him, sticking together like dumplings, a group of boys was rubbing their hands and shuffling their feet. Among them was one dressed in worn-out, much-patched clothing. His testicles showed below the hem of his short, quilted kimono, just like the boys in Futae. It was such an unexpected welcome.

"Well now—how gracious of you to come and welcome the bride. And who was it that asked you to come here today?" Shichigorō asked.

"Nisuke's mother. And she said she'd give us rice cakes if we came and welcomed the bride."

"We're going to get some rice cakes and then we'll go back home," the children piped up gaily.

"I see—so you came here to get some rice cakes, did you?" Shichigorō teased. Everyone on the boat laughed.

Nana, who had been frightened by the big whirlpools and had been clinging to her father, seemed relieved to see children her age. Her brother lifted her onto his back and then lowered her again to the ground. Her gaze met that of a girl holding a flower wreath. Both girls seemed bashful and hesitated to greet each other.

When Yazō and the bridegroom Daisuke appeared from beneath the shade of the big banyan tree on the beach, the children ran to them.

"Say—don't you have a special job today?" Yazō asked, encouraging the children.

At that, the children all called out a name: "Suzu!"

Lifting her head, the girl who was holding the small wreath of white flowers took a step toward Okayo, knelt on one knee and crossed herself, blushing.

"We welcome you and we thank you for coming. This is for your celebration. *Amen.*"

On her small feet were straw sandals that looked as if they had been made that very morning. Her knees showed beneath her short kimono. The kimono had patches around the shoulders and knees that were of particular interest to Ofuji. To her, the stitching on those patches was especially beautiful. She had seen that same stitching before. When Yazō had first introduced Daisuke, who was to become Okayo's husband, he had worn work clothes with patches. Ofuji had been fascinated by their stitching. That, too, must have been the work of Okayo's future mother-in-law.

Ofuji was even more surprised when she heard the word *amen*—and so soon. Since Yazō had told her that the bridegroom's family were Christians, she had been prepared to hear the word at some point. But she hadn't expected to hear it spoken by a child, and just as soon as she got off the boat. After this girl named Suzu recited a short prayer, all the children crossed themselves in unison with their small hands. Suzu held out her hands and gestured to Okayo to put the wreath on her head. Okayo bent her head forward, half sitting. Ofuji was about to cross herself. For in fact, Ofuji, too, was from a Christian family.

"Thank you so much," Seibei said in a muffled voice, and Ofuji looked up. She felt a sense of peace in finding her own palms joined together, yet she also felt a bit strange and uneasy. With flushed cheeks, Okayo, too, placed her palms together and lowered her head.

"All right my little ones, let's go now," said Yazō. "You can take the flower wreaths back to show Nisuke's mother you've done your job—and that will make her happy." The children placed the wreaths on their heads and completed their roles as ushers with dance-like steps.

The channel that led into the harbor at Kuchinotsu was deeper than the one in Futae and it appeared that boats would be well protected from storms once they passed through it. In this town there were many more boats and houses, and its surrounding fields looked much larger too. As she walked along, Okayo was amazed to think that for many years this vast land had been a bay of Christians.

She had hardly spoken with Daisuke. He was three years older than she. The calm look in his large eyes made her feel at peace.

The children called him "elder brother Daisuke" and followed him about, clinging to him. This assured Okayo that he had the trust of the villagers. When he first visited Okayo's house, he had played ball with Nana while Yazō and her grandmother discussed the most important issue, that of the marriage. When the talk was almost settled, Okayo had served tea to Daisuke, who was sitting at ease. With smiling eyes, he said, "My only merit is my strength. If you marry me, I'll put you in a mulberry basket and carry you on my back to show you around our town." For a moment, everyone had looked at him blankly, but soon they had burst into laughter.

"That girl Suzu, she looks really smart. Is she Daisuke's sister?" Ofuji asked Yazō, who was walking beside her.

"Actually, she's not. She's an orphan, but she's really become a member of the family."

"An orphan?"

Ofuji felt her heart pierced as she gazed at Suzu's retreating figure. Kicking up the hem of her knee-length kimono, Suzu stretched out her tanned legs as she walked along holding the hand of a young child.

"Suzu's mother died when she was young, and her father was lost at sea, fishing for tuna."

"When was that?"

"The year before last. After the funeral we couldn't just leave her alone in her little house, so Daisuke's mother asked her if she'd like to come live with her. Suzu looked up at her and answered, 'I can fetch water and collect driftwood—I can do anything. Please, please let me stay with you.'"

Daisuke's mother was a cousin of Yazō. Holding the young girl, she had wept. *Suzu is young, but already she's thinking of fetching water and gathering wood. I'll give her a little pail for drawing water, and she can pick up branches. And before she gets married, I'll teach her how to cook and sew. But she's just turned six—she should be playing children's games!*

When she came to live with the family, Suzu had sung a song, alone:

One, two, three, and four,
a little child without a mother.
Four, five, six, and seven,
a little child without a father.
Calling, "Mother!"
Calling, "Father!"
No answer coming back,
just flowers of eggplants,
and flowers of gourds.

The other children in the village had started singing her song. They had felt so sad when they heard the words, *A little child without a mother, a little child without a father.*

"Yes, it sure is a sad one. And since then, has she been living at Daisuke's place?"

"Yes, Suzu's really become attached to the family. People often ask Daisuke if she's his little sister, although he doesn't have one. Well, it's not much trouble for that family, since they usually have so many people at their table anyhow. Suzu's really growing up. She acts like an adult and she carries water, and this year she's turned eight."

"I suppose that's what the benevolence group is for."

"Well, that's part of it; but there's more to it than that. This family has never turned its back on anyone in trouble. Perhaps that's why the role of helping her came to them."

Ofuji had been wondering when, and to whom, she should mention the water they had brought. Thinking it might be good to tell Yazō about it, she called to Seibei, who was walking just in front of her.

"Seibei, about the water ..."

Seibei seemed to be thinking the same thing, and he looked back as he walked alongside Yazō. Bowing his head, he began to speak in a lower tone.

"Actually, there's something we were thinking of talking to you about when we arrive at Daisuke-dono's house, but please allow us to mention it now, since we don't want to sound too serious then. We have a present we'd like to give the family when we get there."

Sensing that some matter of special importance was about to be brought up, Yazō responded in a particularly polite manner.

"And what might that be? I wonder if I'm the appropriate person to hear of it first."

"Well, we thought you'd be the most appropriate, and we'd like to tell you about it."

Seibei showed him the *furoshiki* in his hand.

"This is some water we brought from the Igawa well by the hackberry trees in Futae."

The twinge of tension in Yazō's face didn't escape Ofuji's notice.

"Ah yes, the Igawa in Futae. I get water there too—every time I stop by Futae on my boat. That water brings a great blessing."

"Well, if you already know about it, then I suppose we don't need to say much. Don't you agree, Mother?"

"But I think we should mention it properly. We have to explain it well."

Being spoken to so pointedly—something he had rarely experienced from his mother—Seibei assumed a more reflective attitude and replied, "I've heard that the whalers from Ōyano get water there. And they say *amen,* and after that they bring home a big catch."

"Seibei—you're straying from the point," Ofuji scolded, and then continued. "We're not talking about earthly rewards. We're talking about religion; about the religion of this family. About a group of people who carry out acts of mercy."

Yazō's face grew more serious as he tried to follow the conversation.

"We're sharing some family matters with you now, and it's quite all right if you forget this."

Seibei began to talk about his late wife, Onobu. He explained that she had been born in the town of Shiki and that she had been a Christian. Shiki, like Kuchinotsu, had been a bustling town where the Jesuit Fathers had lived a long time ago, and where all the high-ranking families, including that of the feudal lord, had been Christians.

Seibei had felt sorry about Onobu's marrying into a family of a different religion. She had been a very modest woman. She had chanted her Christian prayers in the mornings and evenings without drawing attention to herself, and had respected the Shinto gods and the Buddha, so he had never asked her to change her religion.

Every time Seibei spoke his wife's name, his voice filled with deep affection.

"Onobu was given her Christian name by Father Valignano, who's no longer in Japan. Although she never met him, she revered him deeply. Her father was a *benzashi*—like you—and Father Valignano rode on his boats quite a few times. Through this connection, my wife received the name Magdalena. That's what I heard.

"When I asked for her hand, my father-in-law made me promise I would remember what the priest had told him: 'I will give this beautiful name to your baby as a memento, upon my leaving Japan.' I've always wondered about the meaning of that name, but both my father-in-law and my wife died before I asked them about it.

"This has left a cloud in my heart, and in my mother's, but now we will be close to a Christian family. This water from the Igawa well makes the very best tea. In our village we use this water as an offering when we pray for rain. My mother and I had a talk about how Okayo is about to marry into this family, and about the possibility of a baptism, so we decided to bring this water as a present. Perhaps I'm rushing things in talking about this now, but I thought things might get too formal if we talked about it while sitting in a room; but here, walking along and talking like this, you can just listen and, if you like, you can just forget it all. Well, all right then—so now I've told you just about everything."

As he listened, Yazō seemed more serious than usual. He replied politely:

"Well, you've just told me something that's more important than anything I could have imagined. Father Valignano had strong connections with the people of Kuchinotsu and with the family you're going to meet. Nisuke and his wife will be very happy to hear this. I'll certainly pass on your story to them. And, come to think of it, tonight a man who was taught in his childhood by that same Father Valignano is going to be present at the wedding."

Surrounded by children's cheerful voices, Nisuke's wife appeared carrying a tray of rice cakes. Seeing that her face was as sweet as a child's, Ofuji felt greatly relieved.

Before the wedding festivities began, Yazō and Nisuke led the family to a room where a silver-haired man with a short sword at his waist was waiting. With great respect, the two men introduced him to everyone.

"This is Henmi Juan-sama. All of us here rely on him greatly. He's a former samurai of Lord Arima. When Lord Arima renounced Christianity and his fief was transferred to Hyūga, his Christian samurai decided to stay here and Henmi-sama became the leader."

Smiling a bit bashfully, the elderly samurai started to speak freely:

"Actually, it was only after I lost my connections with Lord Arima that I began to think seriously about the farmers—and especially about the importance of growing one's own food. It took me a long time, but finally I realized that a country's foundation lies with its farmers."

Okayo looked on in surprise as the samurai continued talking about matters she had never thought about before.

"Your name is Okayo, isn't it? I just heard from Yazō that the priest who gave your mother her Christian name was Father Valignano. It brings me tremendous joy to hear his dear name. I wanted to meet you right away."

The elder looked intently at Daisuke and then at Okayo.

"Daisuke, I'm very happy that you've found a bride like this. I never expected to hear the name of Father Valignano at this wedding. Nisuke, back in his time, your father offered the priest a place to stay, didn't he?"

"Well yes, that's true. So this is quite an amazing turn of fate."

Nisuke and his son looked deeply moved.

"When I was young, I studied at the Arima Seminary that Father Valignano founded. Later, it was moved from Shiki in Amakusa to Kazusa, and then to Hachirao. I got a very well-rounded education there and it helped me become a man. Father Valignano left Japan about thirty years ago, and now he's no longer in this world. It's wonderful to hear he gave the baby that name as a remembrance on leaving Japan."

Watching as Henmi Juan closed his eyes and placed his hands on his knees, Okayo and her family sat up and listened respectfully as Yazō spoke:

"In regard to the water you brought from the Igawa well, the family will receive it sincerely as a farewell gift and use it for Okayo's baptism. And Grandmother, you understand that Okayo will be baptized, don't you?"

Ofuji's neck flushed at this sudden question, but immediately she made up her mind. "I have no objection. Now, at last, I'll be able to fulfill my responsibility to my late daughter-in-law. Will this be all right, Seibei?"

Seibei nodded. *Even if Okayo converts to Christianity, she can keep her ties with the Japanese gods and the Buddha, since they've been in that sacred water from ancient times*, Ofuji reflected.

The cakes that were handed out to the children were not actually made of rice, but of wheat flour, rolled thin and baked. In a low voice, Daisuke's mother Omiyo explained to Ofuji how people had once used mochi rice cakes at the Masses, but later the padres in Kuchinotsu had taught them how to make unleavened wheat wafers.

"Last year the rice harvest was poor, but the wheat harvest wasn't too bad. We kept some of it away from the mice, and I'm glad we could use it today."

As she watched the children devour the cakes, she looked very happy.

"Next time, I'd like to give them mochi—when we have a grandchild. But I wonder how the rice will fare this year. It should be all right if we get enough rain."

Hearing Omiyo's gentle way of speaking, Ofuji felt confident that Okayo would soon feel close to her new mother-in-law. When Ofuji met the elder samurai who had studied at Arima Seminary she had started to think. She had been twelve years old when the regent Toyotomi Hideyoshi advanced to Kyushu to defeat the Shimazu Clan and then suddenly ordered the expulsion of all the missionaries from Japan. Two years later, the Lord of Shiki—one of the "Five Lords of Amakusa" who governed Shiki, Futae, and Oniike—

had fled to Izumi in Satsuma after losing the battle against Konishi Yukinaga, who became the newly appointed lord of the southern part of Higo. Ofuji still remembered the thunder of the war horses as they rushed through the tall grass in the mountains.

A long time before Ofuji was born, Shiki Rinsen, the lord of Shiki Castle, had been baptized by the padres, along with his vassals, in order to help establish trade with foreign countries. It was said that Shiki's ports had bustled with Portuguese ships back then. But the trading had soon dwindled to a halt, and when no Portuguese ships came into the port, the lord had grown increasingly resentful about his unmet expectations and had turned against the Christians. Nevertheless, the baptized people in his domain had held on to their faith. Ofuji was brought up seeing her parent's generation gather in secret to talk about their faith. After Regent Toyotomi issued the Order of Expulsion of Jesuit Missionaries, many of the padres had fled to Amakusa to escape the oppression. While the Christian Lord Konishi Yukinaga governed the area, more people were baptized and a *residencia* for the padres was set up in Shiki. When Ofuji married into a non-Christian family, she had given up her religion, but no one had seemed opposed to the Christians. After Konishi Yukinaga's death at the Battle of Sekigahara, and even after Lord Terasawa of Karatsu Castle took over as the new ruler of Amakusa, the Christians there had continued to live in peace. Only when Ofuji was in her late thirties had the harsh prohibition of Christianity begun. Twenty years had now passed since rumors began to spread about the bloody executions taking place in Shimabara and Amakusa, and since the priests had disappeared from Japan.

The local farmers had continued to hope for peace and security, and had taken care not to get involved in conflicts with government officials. Ofuji, too, had shared those hopes, but now she couldn't help wondering about the place her granddaughter was coming to. *Kuchinotsu is known as a haven for Christians. I've heard there are still many Christian former samurai of Lord Arima who chose to stay here and keep their faith. Today one of them, Henmi-sama, will baptize Okayo. I imagine these former samurai became leaders who helped the people hold onto their faith after the foreign priests left Japan. But I also heard that Lord Arima's successor, Lord Matsukura, was very repressive of Christianity.*

Filled with emotion, Ofuji gazed at Juan, who appeared to be in a contemplative state. It seemed to her that if many samurai like him lived in the area, the Christians might be able to lead peaceful lives.

Standing in a row, the children started singing a hymn:

Benedictus Dominus
Deus Israel

Ofuji remembered this song. Long ago she had heard a group of boys singing it when they came to pick bayberries in the mountains. The women in the village had whispered, "Look—they're such nice brothers who've come from the seminary." Hearing the song now reminded Ofuji of those days. She could hear Henmi Juan speaking quietly close to her ear:

"One time I went from Kuchinotsu to Shiki to welcome the priests. We sailed on seven boats. Those seven boats, with their sails filled, looked like flowers from Heaven. We recited poems and sang songs in Latin. And there was a bamboo organ, too."

Juan's eyes were filled with a light that reflected the sacred early days of the Christians in Shimabara and Amakusa. The wedding night approached, wrapped gently in the old man's sentiments. Okayo was given her mother's Christian name, Magdalena.

In addition to Henmi Juan, three other former samurai were invited to attend the wedding of Daisuke and Okayo. They all had served under Lord Arima Naozumi, who had subsequently been exiled to Hyūga. The three of them were known as "the ones who abandoned their lord." After the wedding party ended, they went to the house of Ninagawa Sakyō, at his invitation. Among other things, they wanted to continue drinking. Sakyō's wife managed to find some home-brewed chestnut sake to serve the men.

The first to speak was Chijiiwa Bannai:

"Well, village weddings certainly bring a breath of fresh air."

"They sure do," Kazusa Hyōgo said. "And Henmi-dono, he played the role of godfather just right for the special mood of the scene. He had those folks who came over on boats from around the bay in tears. That's his way."

Hyōgo's clothing rustled as he adjusted his sitting posture. He looked ready for a good long drinking session.

"No way yokels like us could have carried off a ceremony like that."

"We haven't seen many good times lately. But today, when I heard the children singing those hymns, it really hit me."

"Well, we've had some rough times, all right, but tonight I felt really fine."

Hyōgo was deftly tearing off the legs of some dried octopus and placing them on a plate.

"I, too—I felt relaxed. And I remembered a lot of things. It brought back lots of memories. You remember the wedding of our young lord and his first wife? That's quite a few years back now."

"Ah, you must be talking of his marriage to Lady Okō. That sure was ages ago. Back then Hinoe Castle was still full of life. The retainers' children still practiced and sang the hymns."

"So they did. Back then, no one could have imagined that our young lord would give up our religion."

"And the children sang those hymns in European languages so beautifully. They had the voices of angels. No one could stop talking about them."

"Things were so different when he married Lady Okuni."

"You can say that again. Shogun Ieyasu forced our lord to marry Okuni, and to divorce his first wife to do it."

"Come to think of it, Lady Okuni was the great-granddaughter of Shogun Ieyasu. And they held their wedding way off—up in Sunpu—before they came here. No way they were going to have a Christian wedding. Ah, I was starting to get things mixed up."

"Come on, Hyōgo-dono—that was thirty years ago. We have to think about our future. We're facing a do-or-die situation."

"What? What's going to be do-or-die?"

"Oh, come on now, you must know. I'm talking about what happened last night. I can't stand the way the Matsukura officials have been talking. And who was it that said 'My sword's been crying at night since it can't do its job, and one of these days it's going to jump right out of its scabbard?'"

Hyōgo tapped his head with his fan.

"All right, it was me who said that. But things sure have changed since yesterday. Tonight, I feel like a completely different man."

All three men were about fifty years old.

Henmi Juan teased them as he entered the room:

"Well now—this is quite the feast you have going on here. You sound like a bunch of rowdy teenagers before a coming-of-age ceremony."

"We're just drinking some divine sake to refresh ourselves," Hyōgo replied, and everyone laughed.

"So, you're talking about the old days, are you? Well, all right then. That may have been the only time we saw the flowers of blazing light at Hinoe Castle."

"Flowers ...? Come to think of it Juan-dono, I heard from the fishers over in Amakusa that while they were out at sea they saw lights from a party in the castle reflected on the waves, and they heard voices in the sky, and they all talked about it."

Waiting to speak after Hyōgo, Chijiiwa Bannai continued, "That Lady Okuni—the granddaughter of Shogun Ieyasu's first son Nobuyasu-dono—she sure was a brazen one. When she showed up, she laughed out loud and said the people of Arima were dark-skinned and looked like raccoon dogs."

"How could that young lord ever have pushed aside the blameless Lady Okō and taken such a stuck-up woman for his wife?" Hyōgo demanded.

Trying to placate the offended Hyōgo, Juan explained, "It couldn't be helped. Young Arima Naozumi had served Ieyasu since he was fifteen and Ieyasu was fond of him. When he was ordered to marry Ieyasu's great-granddaughter Lady Okuni, he couldn't refuse. And when his father Lord Arima Harunobu was martyred, it would have been natural for Naozumi, his eldest son, to commit *seppuku*. But since Naozumi was married to Ieyasu's great-granddaughter, the shogun didn't confiscate his estate. Instead, he ordered him to go back and govern it."

"I can sort of understand that, but I don't get why the shogun cared so much about the Arima clan," Hyōgo said, tilting his head.

"Well, think about it a bit more," Bannai insisted. "Shogun Ieyasu didn't especially care about the Arima, but he was worried about the Christians—and the Arima were at their center. Ieyasu knew that since the young lord Naozumi had been allowed to keep his territory, he'd have to get serious about following the orders to get rid of the Christians. It would work better to have Arima eliminate the Christians than to confiscate his lands."

Hyōgo was four years older than Bannai, but they seemed to get along very well. They made a great pair: Bannai hot-tempered and Hyōgo slightly absent-minded.

Ninagawa Sakyō, the master of the house, poured sake with a quiet smile. He was a generous man who knew how to take care of guests, so his house had become the main meeting place for the former retainers.

"The young lord looked so frightened when he had Taketomi Kannuemon-dono and his men put to death," Ninagawa said. "To show his loyalty to Shogun Ieyasu he was forced to execute the main Christian leaders, like Taketomi-dono, Takahashi-dono, and Hayashida-dono. But I don't think he planned to kill off all the Christians."

Bannai agreed energetically. "Of course—there's no way he could've gotten rid of us all. At the time, his face showed how on edge he was. He was being hounded by problems with Lady Okuni on one side and pressed by the Nagasaki officials on the other. He was a weak young lord."

"You're talking now as if you saw it yourself," Hyōgo cut in teasingly.

"I didn't see it, but everybody knows about it."

"Back then, the Nagasaki magistrate was that guy Hasegawa Sahei, wasn't it?" Sakyō said, unwilling to let the conversation wander. "They say he was almost poisoned by Lord Arima Harunobu."

"Right—the bastard almost got what was coming to him, but he escaped."

"It's a shame Lord Harunobu got tricked by someone like Okamoto Daihachi. That was the beginning of the Arimas' downfall."

As Sakyō listened quietly, Hyōgo continued rambling absent-mindedly.

"Did Lord Harunobu really think he could recover the three areas that had been transferred from him to the Nabeshima Clan by bribing Daihachi?"

"Well, yes—I think that's what he wanted. And Daihachi played on his hopes. Lord Harunobu was too hot-headed, and it was easy to see through what he was hoping for."

The short-tempered Bannai broke in with his usual frankness:

"After getting caught up in an interrogation, Daihachi claimed that Harunobu had planned to poison Hasegawa Sahei out of anger over the outrageous orders Sahei had given when he blew up that Portuguese ship in Nagasaki Bay. So Daihachi dragged Harunobu along with him to Hell—the bastard!"

Juan raised his head calmly.

"How old were you when Lord Harunobu was martyred?" he asked Bannai.

"About twenty-five or six."

"Hmm. When you think about Lord Harunobu's life, he had it pretty rough. After succeeding to head of his family at age ten, he got dragged into family troubles and was attacked by Ryūzōji, and he was pretty much prepared to meet his downfall. That was when Father Valignano saved him."

A deep light gleamed from Juan's eyes as he spoke. The other three men sat up straight.

"In the eighth year of Tenshō (1580), when I was seven or eight, our castle was surrounded by Ryūzōji Takanobu's forces, including some of his like-minded relatives. I remember very well that terrible night when Lord Harunobu and a small band of his men who were still inside the castle prepared to die in battle the next day. Later, Father Valignano refused to take sides in fights among the daimyo, but that was one critical moment when he felt he had to lead and he brought gunpowder into the castle. The Arima clan were saved by his help. Lord Harunobu and his retainers were so moved by the great power of the new God, Deus-sama, that they decided to be baptized.

"Four years later, the Arima's enemy Ryūzōji Takanobu was killed by the Satsuma forces at the Battle of Okita Nawate. The Arima's forces took part in that battle. My father was one of them, and he was killed in the fighting. I joined the seminary right after my father's death. Every day, I found something new there. I was amazed by everything I saw and heard. But that was only the beginning of Lord Harunobu's troubles. Hyōgo-dono—how old were you when Regent Hideyoshi attacked Kyushu?"

"I was born in the eleventh year of Tenshō (1583)—so, how old would I have been then, at the time of the Kyushu fighting ...?"

Hyōgo cocked his head.

"That was in Tenshō 15 (1587), the year I was born. So you must have been five," Bannai cut in.

Everyone burst out laughing.

"So much has changed since then, what with the invasion of Korea and the Battle of Sekigahara," Juan went on. "The world has changed so quickly. I suppose Lord Harunobu did his best to maintain governance. You all know the story well. It was in the Battle of Uto that Hyōgo-dono's leg was injured by gunfire."

"That was a miserable duty," Hyōgo replied. "Lord Harunobu felt close to Konishi-dono because he was a fellow Christian, but also because he'd served with him in the Korean campaign and they'd risked their lives together in battle. Even though Lord Harunobu eventually decided to ally himself with the Eastern forces of the Tokugawas, he wouldn't have wanted to join Lord Kiyomasa in attacking Lord Konishi's castle in Uto."

"Right," Sakyō continued quietly. "And that's why Lord Harunobu claimed he was suffering from eye troubles and appointed his son Naozumi as commander, although he was only fifteen, and then Naozumi sent the troops."

"But Hyōgo-dono was the most unlucky of us all—on top of everything, you got your leg shot up," Bannai said kindly to his older friend.

"I was young then. Stupidly, I yelled out from in front of the moat to the people inside the castle, taunting them, and they shot my left leg. I was eighteen years old and it was my first battle."

"Lord Harunobu went through some terrible hardships, and so did we. His martyrdom was the inevitable outcome of the aftermath of all that," Juan commented, gazing at the Chinese trumpet-creeper flowers arranged in a vase in the alcove.

"Lord Naozumi must have asked for permission to change his domain. I'm pretty sure about that. And like we said earlier, we couldn't just give up our religion—even after the executions of Taketomi-dono and the others."

"Right—it was just like Juan-dono said. Perhaps Lady Okuni begged the shogun to let her family change their domain. And Lord Naozumi—he was in tears—he asked us to just pretend to renounce Christianity. But we couldn't, no matter if he cried. He must have reached his limit."

Bannai emptied his cup and gazed up at the ceiling. Hyōgo, having drunk too much, began swaying a bit every time he spoke.

"When I think about it, I feel sorry for him. If his father had lived, I'd have gone with him to Hyūga."

"How can you talk such nonsense? What would you have done then? Don't you remember that we promised each other we'd stay in Arima?"

"How could I forget?"

Sensing that one of the usual cross-fire arguments between Hyōgo and Bannai might break out, Sakyō changed the subject.

"It looks like Juan-dono has some thoughts on the subject. Let's hear what he has to say."

"Well, we don't really need to talk about it tonight … Anyhow, after we saw off Lord Naozumi on his way to Hyūga and we were left on our own without a master, we got used to tending the fields. But I'm afraid things are changing now. We won't be able to live like this much longer—don't you think?"

"You're talking about Matsukura Shigemasa's administration, aren't you? At first, I thought he was fairly capable. Judging from the number of retainers he brought in from Yamato, he looked pretty powerful," Hyōgo said.

"But Hyōgo—that's precisely why Shigemasa looked suspicious to me," Bannai countered. "Everything that guy did was to impress the shogun. He offered him 100,000 *koku* of rice to help build Edo Castle—even though he only had 40,000 himself. He just wanted to bow and scrape to the Tokugawas. He never thought about the people—*never*!"

"Really? I thought he showed some grit. You remember how

he tried to advance to Luzon in the Philippines? And his treatment of the Christians wasn't as ruthless as that of our present lord. I heard he even showed some mercy to the padres in prison," Hyōgo countered.

"Come on—don't be a fool. Shigemasa was the one who started the Unzen persecutions!" Bannai shouted.

"Damn right! We can never forget that."

"But it's no use complaining about the late Shigemasa," Sakyō interrupted, growing irritated. "What Juan's getting at now are the most recent events—the punishments and executions under our current Lord Matsukura Katsuie."

"True enough, terrible things have been going on since Katsuie took over. He's started levying taxes on cotton, tea, charcoal, cigarettes, spades and hoes ... I've never heard of anything so outrageous."

"And taxes on digging the graves to bury the dead, and taxes on each baby who's born. And taxes on the *irori* hearths, and taxes on the *kotatsu* heating tables, and taxes on shelves and doors—basically, taxes on every damn thing."

"And the way his officials act—busting into our houses and talking to us so viciously. I've had more than I can take."

"I can see why Hyōgo said he could kill them."

Set off by Bannai, Hyōgo's cheeks were flushed.

"Even if we've been cut off from our lord, we're still samurai. I'm not carrying my sword around just for show. I don't give a damn about those worthless Matsukura henchmen."

After quietly sipping some homebrewed *doburoku* sake, Juan set his cup down.

"What you're talking about now is something we should wait on," he said calmly. "At the last moment, if we have no other choices left, then, silently, we may use our swords. But for now, it's more important to take care of the things we've been talking about in our *confuraria* meetings. These are times of big changes. No matter what the officials tell us, we never know what will happen next. The important thing for us now is to keep our roots in the fields, along with the farmers, and to protect our families and our faith."

From outside the *fusuma* sliding door, a quiet voice called,

"Good evening. It's Ukon."

Hyōgo and Bannai looked at each other and sat up straight again. Sakyō's son Ukon was nineteen years old and particularly conscientious and polite for his age. Coughing slightly, Bannai replied:

"Well, Ukon-dono—come right in."

"Since this meeting sounds so cheerful, I was wondering if I might step in and offer my greetings."

As Ukon opened the door, Hyōgo and Bannai quickly yielded their places. Ukon seldom smiled and it was hard to guess what he was thinking. He spent most of his free time reading, so Hyōgo and Bannai felt somewhat uncomfortable around him.

Despite his youth, Ukon was deeply thoughtful. The other day, Takematsu—who often turned rowdy when drinking—had started an argument with a friend. Ukon had calmed him down and avoided another fight just by giving him an unexpected smile. The group had been about to expel Takematsu on account of his repeated behavior while drunk, but Ukon had saved him before it reached that point.

"Well, Ukon-dono, it seems when we see you, somehow we all straighten up," Bannai said, a bit awkwardly.

"Right," Hyōgo continued, "I remember the kinds of things we used to do when we were your age."

"Bannai, I remember how you were great at crab-catching—but not so great at reading."

"Reading isn't enough these days," Ukon said seriously. "We have to think about our food supply. Hyōgo-dono, I'd be grateful if you would teach me your secrets for catching crabs."

"Well, that's just like you Ukon-dono," Hyōgo replied, "But no need to wait till tomorrow—I can teach you tonight. I thought you were just studying things that aren't much concern to us, like the *Catecizumo* and *Wakan roeishu*—those old religious texts and Japanese and Chinese verses. But I see I was wrong."

"If you teach Ukon your tricks, soon your treasure beach is going to be empty," Juan added teasingly.

"Well, maybe so, but if it all goes to Ukon, I won't mind."

Ukon cast his eyes down and smiled.

CHAPTER TWO

THE RED SHIP

Okayo soon grew accustomed to life in Daisuke's household. Coming from a mountain village, what she found especially interesting about her new home was how the sea and the land were so inextricably intertwined in their lives. When Suzu called out, "I'm going to get some wood," it made her realize people here could get firewood not only from the hills, but from the seaside as well. Anyone could pick up the driftwood on the beaches. Being led by Suzu to gather it was a joy.

With Okayo, Suzu was like a sensible younger sister looking after her easygoing but slightly eccentric older sister. Their relationship seemed to have been that way forever. Their conversations made others laugh and brought great comfort to Nisuke and his wife, and to all those around them.

The year after her marriage, Okayo traveled with her husband and Suzu back to her hometown in Uchino during the summer Obon Festival. Keeping her promise to Nana, Okayo prepared mugwort mochi, pounding and mixing together sticky millet with the mugwort she had picked, boiled and dried before her marriage. Nana placed the abalone and turban shells that Okayo had brought as gifts on the narrow porch. Nana watched the live shells squirm about, the tip of her nose sweaty with excitement. Suzu acted like a big sister to Nana, who tended to be quiet. After all, although she was young, Suzu had experienced many difficult things and she knew a lot about the world.

The next morning, Seibei invited Daisuke to go with him to the mountains to dig kudzu and bracken fern roots.

"You probably won't find so many treasures up here in the mountains as you do by the sea," Seibei remarked.

Thinking just the opposite, Daisuke was astonished by the huge kudzu roots and kept calling out, "Amazing—these are incredible!" He returned from their foraging with a heavy bundle.

The following morning, after everyone pounded the kudzu roots they had soaked overnight, a beautiful white starchy liquid seeped from their cracks. After draining off the surface water, the liquid *sen* remained. If they had dried it, the *sen* would have become a smooth flour. But, following Ofuji's orders, they had rolled and steamed it to make beautiful, translucent kudzu cakes.

When Okayo, Daisuke and Suzu left Uchino for Kuchinotsu, Ofuji handed Suzu a cloth bag of chinquapin nuts that Okayo had gathered before her marriage.

"Please look after your big sister," she added.

Nana repeated Ofuji's words exactly and with great seriousness, prompting laughter from everyone. As she headed back to Kuchinotsu, Okayo's steps felt a bit lighter.

The mugwort growing thickly along the riverbank was covered with dust. Suzu romped along the grassy paths, running ahead and sometimes glancing back at Okayo and Daisuke.

"Though she's so dependable, she's still a child. I can see how much fun she's been having," Daisuke commented. He adjusted the mulberry basket filled with gifts for people in Kuchinotsu and then turned toward Okayo.

"I'm glad we took her with us," Okayo said, nodding back at Daisuke and realizing that he, too, was happy. She felt pleased that they had made the visit back to her hometown together.

When Suzu sat down in the midst of some foxtails, Daisuke called out, "Let me carry your bag. And watch your step—it's around the time when the *mamushi* snakes come out. They're poisonous, you know."

Immediately, Suzu stood up. Then she pointed to her feet.

"Look—the cranesbill is in bloom. Let's pick some. It's good for stomachaches," she added and sat down again.

"We can pick cranesbill in Kuchinotsu. Better stay on the path here."

"All right, but wait just a minute. These will make nice presents for the old folks in the home."

"Well, if that's what it's for, then all right. So you've been thinking about presents for the old folks? Wonderful. Let me help you."

Tugging at their roots, Daisuke pulled up some of the medicinal herbs with their lovely reddish-purple flowers.

"Look! I've gathered ten times more than you! Now we'll have plenty."

The old folks were cared for by the *jihi gumi*, the benevolence group that carried out charitable activities. These elders had no one else to look after them and Suzu had become very helpful in caring for them.

Suzu lifted the bag that Ofuji had given her and looked up at Okayo and Daisuke. "Can I roast some of these nuts and give them to the old people?" she asked.

"Why of course. They were given to you—you can use them however you like. It will make them happy."

As Okayo gently stroked Suzu's back, she realized that Daisuke was carefully surveying the rice fields in the valleys that stretched down to the sea.

Recently, some of the elders in the little home had eaten strange things they had gathered from the sea, and had suffered stomach ailments. The reason Suzu wanted to give them chinquapins was because they didn't have much else to put in their cooking pot these days.

Food was always scarcest in the season before the harvest, but this year, with all the bad weather they had faced since spring, there was even greater concern about the fall harvest. Okayo had visited her hometown in Uchino during a long spell of dry weather. On the previous day, and also this morning before they left for Kuchinotsu, her brother had gone to village meetings to pray for rain. Now, once again, she surveyed her surroundings.

She sniffed the dry soil and its smell remained deep in her nose. The mugwort and silvergrass looked wilder now, their leaves rough and dry from lack of rain. With each step, dust rose from under her feet.

Daisuke recalled what Ofuji had said about the chinquapins before they left. She had talked about how Okayo had begun to worry about her family's stock of food after her marriage was decided, and had suddenly started gathering more nuts than usual from the mountains. Perhaps this was partly because she had always loved chinquapins, ever since childhood. But Ofuji said that Okayo seemed to have had a premonition about a poor harvest this year.

"I know big farming families like yours are well-prepared, but still ...." was how Ofuji had put it, as she humbly offered the nuts. Accepting them, Daisuke had felt a pang of worry.

Soon after their marriage, Daisuke's mother Omiyo had taken Okayo inside the family's two storehouses. The first one was dry and dimly lit and filled with the smells of straw and various kinds of grain. The second smelled of dried daikon leaves and grass, mixed with the more pungent odors of dried seaweed and octopus, which had made her cough.

"Our helpers work hard, and they're good at finding things from the sea to eat. Everyone likes going to the shore," Omiyo had said.

"I love it too!" Okayo had added cheerfully.

"Normally we'd have more food stored up, but this year's been different," Omiyo went on, smiling calmly. "It seems things are running short much sooner than usual. Besides the supplies for our daily meals, we save some rice, soybeans and black-eyed peas for making rice cakes and dumplings for Lent, Easter, Christmas and the other festivals. Here's the shelf for these provisions. Oume-yan and Matsukichi have come up with ways to keep the mice away, and they do a great job of looking after things. They'll teach you how to take care of the storehouses."

Okayo thought about the storehouses now, with their dwindling stores of food. Watching Daisuke's broad back as he walked along in front of her, she was gripped by an unfamiliar touch of fear.

A few days after returning to Kuchinotsu from the visit to her hometown, Okayo was serving tea to Daisuke and his mother as they sat and talked on a straw mat in the storehouse. Matuskichi and Oume were in the circle too. Matsukichi was just starting to speak.

"Because of the drought, it looks like not only the upland rice, but the millet, too, won't make it. Yesterday I went to the field to see how badly faded the millet was. When I pulled some up, it was completely dried out, all the way from the roots up to the ears. At this rate, we'll be able to burn it to heat the bath and that's about it. Even the tougher grains like millet won't survive if we don't get some rain in the next five days. They'll all dry out and die."

"Dry out and die? You mean the millet—or the people?" Omiyo asked.

"Both."

"Is that right, Oume-yan?"

"I'm afraid so, Omiyo-sama," Oume replied in a subdued voice as she opened the pods of some black-eyed peas in her apron.

"As you've seen, there's not much left on the festival shelf. And our grain stores are running low, too. Omiyo-sama, please listen—if you keep giving out food to the benevolence group, we'll go hungry. Look, these pods have hardly any peas in them—they're mostly just husks."

"But the wheat harvest this year wasn't too bad."

"This year's wheat harvest? But with just this much left, soon it, too, will be gone. I don't know how we're going to get by until autumn," Oume added and then pointed at the ceiling.

"Look, Omiyo-sama, up there—the seed rice is hanging in those sacks. Don't ever touch that rice, no matter if demons or Deus-sama come asking for it."

Holding back a chuckle, Omiyo chided, "Oume-yan, please don't use the word Deus-sama when you're speaking of such bad things."

"But I'm serious. You say Deus-sama is the only god in this world? Well, if he's the only one, then he must be really powerful. It seems you do everything that Deus-sama asks of you. Actually, the other day . . ."

"Yes, yes, Oume, I understand. From now on, any time I take grain from the storehouse, I'll ask you first."

Oume glanced up at her quickly, as if determined not to be deceived. She remembered how Omiyo had given away five liters of wheat and a half a liter of black-eyed peas to a man who introduced himself as a messenger from a secret Christian training monastery in Nagasaki. Oume had regarded the man with suspicion.

Oume was a Buddhist, and people called her one of the Seven Wonders of the Hasuda household, whose family head was a Christian. She had come to the household along with Omiyo when Omiyo married into the family. She had served as Omiyo's nursemaid, and had been with her ever since. When Omiyo's childhood house burned down, Oume had carried her out on her back and even tossed out six sacks of rice as she escaped. It had become a legend. She was already over fifty.

"If everybody knows you're so good and kind, someone may try to trick you. There are cheats and bad ones even among Christians, you know. With me keeping an eye out, we can strike a balance."

"Yes, you're right, you're right. But then—what were we talking about? Oh—about grain and, yes, about millet cakes. How about the millet cakes?"

"I think we have enough left for five grindings."

"That sounds all right. How about sorghum?"

"We still have some, but we have to save it for the horses," Matsukichi answered, hiking his sleeve up to his elbow.

Omiyo nodded. "We can't survive on just our remaining grain and dried vegetables. Let's ask Yazō-don to send a boat to Hizen to buy some grain," she said briskly.

"Well, all right. But not just Yazō-dono; let's make arrangements with some of the other *benzashi*, too."

Okayo felt reassured as she listened to Daisuke speak. Although she was still too young to be placed in charge of the provisions, she worried about the changes she saw happening in the fields, day by day, wherever she looked. It seemed especially worrisome that even the taro, whose green leaves usually swayed back and forth even in dry weather, had begun to droop and wither.

By the time summer came, the colorful seaweed that had thrived in springtime on the rocks along the seashore had disappeared, as if it had been licked away, leaving the waves pale and seemingly without purpose. Okayo tried to tell herself that seaweed grew there only in springtime and that it was normal for it to be gone in summer, but she couldn't help suspecting that it had all been gathered by families who had rushed to the shores, worrying about a poor harvest to come.

Oume spoke up, her expression suddenly serious.

"Things have been looking pretty bad these days. Until just a while ago, when families in need borrowed wheat or millet from each other, if they promised to return it by a certain time, then they did. Even if they didn't have enough for the next day's meals, they'd return something at night and ask to borrow something again the next day. That's the way it's supposed to be, and it's the way we used to do things. But recently, folks don't return things on time, and they don't even say they're sorry. I know they're not being lazy—they simply can't do it. It's hard on those who lend things, but I guess it's a lot harder on those who can't give things back. If only one or two families were suffering, I know I could talk with you and take some rice or wheat to them, but things just seem impossible now.

"How do you pray to Deus-sama in times like this? The borrowers aren't being negligent, but still, it's natural that the lenders sometimes bear a grudge. How does Deus-sama judge them? Both sides might be sinners. And I—who can't do anything for them—I'm a sinner too. I know that Christians make a *conhisan* when they have problems like this. But, Omiyo-sama, I, too, would like to make a *conhisan* to you about this."

Completely taken by surprise, Omiyo sat up straight.

"How could I hear such a difficult *conhisan*? That's something for a priest or a church elder."

"But there aren't any priests left in Japan ... and I can't keep it to myself any longer."

"I feel the same. And my husband is constantly being summoned by the Matsukura officials. As you know, more and more, families can't pay the land taxes because they're so high. The officials have accused my husband of falling behind in making the tax payments, and they've demanded that he pay up—or else. They've threatened him, even. With all that's going on these days, we don't even have time to talk about Deus-sama."

"Is that what it's come to? I imagine things must be hard for Danna-sama, as the master of our house. Back in Lord Arima's time, the clan used to lend us rice. How things have changed."

"The new lord stays up there in Edo and he's been ordering his retainers to hold hostage the wives and children of farmers who don't pay their taxes."

Okayo couldn't forget the dark expression that settled in Omiyo's eyes as she spoke.

A few days later, Nisuke was summoned to the magistrate's office again. In the past month he had been called in time and time again.

"I've sent my men to your place and I've listened to your endless excuses—but I've had enough! Enough excuses! From now on—no mercy," the magistrate Tada Kurōbei snapped, launching into a tirade. As he glanced around at the village leaders, he seemed to focus particular hostility on the strongly-built Nisuke, who was looking at him with narrowed eyes.

"So—Nisuke. You're a stubborn one, aren't you? You haven't delivered the taxes for years. My officers have asked you for them repeatedly, and courteously. And still you haven't delivered any rice. I'll bet this is more than a delay. It looks to me like you're hatching some sort of a plot. You—a Christian! One of the *jihi yaku*—the leaders of the do-gooders. And you've been treated well. But you've been plotting with the ronin—those ex-samurai Christians, the most forbidden people. I heard you hid some old rice and other crops and gave it to them. Admit it—you're plotting a rebellion, aren't you!"

"How can you say such a thing? We're truly grateful for Lord Matsukura's kindness in helping us build our house for the elderly who have no family to care for them, and for the sick and the orphans. All the fishing people in the area know that porridge is served there."

Repelled by his own words, Nisuke halted in mid-sentence. They owed nothing to Matsukura—and not a shred to this official. In the other domains, all the churches and monasteries had been destroyed. But still the Matsukuras had left untouched the *jihi-in*—the "mercy home" that cared for lepers and other sick people. The local people's use of the Buddhist word *jihi* in its name had served to good effect in keeping it safe.

The Buddhists, although of a different faith, hadn't called for the destruction of the home for the sick. It seemed that Lord Matsukura, in trying to expunge the Arima domain's reputation as a hotbed of Christians, had been acting particularly harshly to make an example of them. But keeping the mercy home open had made him look good at governing his domain. He must have done it to preserve his pride and reputation.

The time had come for Nisuke to resist. He hadn't been able to fully pay the taxes because crops had been failing for years, but also because increasingly unreasonable demands had been placed on the people. Unpaid taxes had piled up. Nisuke was keenly aware of the things that poor peasants in his village were putting into their cooking pots. In fact, he thought, the lord ought to be providing them with grain assistance in the amount of their unpaid taxes. Nisuke had mentioned the mercy house because it had come up earlier that day when he had discussed asking for grain assistance with the other village leaders and elders.

"We understand your request, but life has become extremely difficult for farmers. Entire villages—indeed, the entire region—is like a mercy home. We have no choice but to ask you for some grain assistance. As you can see, we've had a severe drought again this year. If you just take a step outside, you will see that all the fields are parched and cracked. The mountains are so dry they're ready to catch fire. The trout and the carp and all the other things the villagers have been relying on to fill their cooking pots—already they've mostly died."

Nisuke continued his appeal:

"The farmers are barely surviving by digging up the roots of bracken ferns and kudzu to eat. Mothers can hardly nurse their babies. We often get together and talk about how we can meet your demands, but the situation is getting worse day by day. Surely you understand all this."

That Nisuke—it seems he's every bit as clever as I'd heard, Tada Kurōbei concluded. The fact was that, as they sat facing each other, Nisuke appeared far more self-possessed and noble than Kurōbei.

"Since I haven't stopped you, you've talked on brazenly. Do you, a single citizen, plan to lodge accusations against our lord? You mentioned grain assistance, didn't you?"

"Yes, I asked that favor of you."

The other village leaders joined Nisuke and bowed their heads in unison.

"We came here to make this appeal. It is far from a criticism of Matsukura-dono's policies. It's just that—"

"Just that what?"

Everyone could see that Kurōbei was wary of what Nisuke

might say next. When this man spoke, his wide-set eyes peered down condescendingly on people. Perhaps it was only a quirk, but when he lifted his chin, his drooping eyes looked drowsy.

Leaning on an armrest, now and then he placed his hand on his balding pate and a slight gleam of light appeared from deep within his eyes. It was hard to tell if he was looking at a person or not. The men could hear him scratching with his fingernails at the cloth covering on his armrest. To Nisuke, it brought to mind the fetid smell of a sea slug crawling along a beach, but he continued his appeal.

"I've heard that Regent Toyotomi Hideyoshi once said to his vassals that a lord can be replaced but not his farmers, so for a lord to demand unreasonable taxes from his farmers is a crime. We have also heard that this principle of protecting the citizens has not changed in the present Tokugawa era, not a bit."

Ah, that Nisuke has a point, the magistrate, realized. *I shouldn't have let him, with his fancy tongue, gain advantage over me. Forty years have passed since Regent Hideyoshi died. Nisuke brought up an old story, but it's true that the governance of all lords is only temporary. No one knows when unwelcome changes of rank or domain may occur. Indeed, the Katō clan in Higo had their fief confiscated not long ago. When vassals lose their jobs, they immediately become homeless. But the farmers are tied to the land.*

"If all the farmers die, Matsukura-dono will lose forty thousand *koku* of rice. If you ignore the extreme poverty we farmers are facing now, it will shake the whole region. For these reasons, we sincerely ask for your kind indulgence."

The nerve of this guy, calling him "Matsukura-dono." He should address him properly as "our Lord Matsukura," Kurōbei thought, but decided to let it pass. He recalled the main point of his summons. *Stop arguing. I just have to get them to pay their back taxes and make plans to collect the annual tax and the miscellaneous taxes.*

Although there are no longer priests here, everyone knows these people are still Christians. I could accuse them on account of their religion. But that—well, I'll overlook it today. These headmen, still holding on to their little plots of land, they may think they won't be affected. But since they're employers and they have to pay the local farmers and their own helpers, soon they're going to find themselves pushed into a corner.

All right then, I'll try one more push. I bet if I push them a little more, I can get a little more.

Kurōbei shut his eyes for a moment and then resumed his harangue:

"I don't know how much land you own, but your way of talking shows that you may be thinking too lightly about your lord. I've heard that Christians are also taught to serve their master, if they have one. In any case, first you'll have to clear up the matter of your unpaid taxes. Then it will be easier for you to get some assistance. If you keep on resisting at every turn, the Matsukura domain's rice production—which, thanks to our efforts, finally rose from forty thousand *koku* to sixty thousand—is going to fall again. Keeping it up is the only way we can clear this area's bad name as a hotbed of Christians.

"You say you've given up Christianity—at least on the surface, that is. Well, I won't go into that now, but if you ever want to get some grain assistance, you'll have to fill the domain's rice storehouses first. Look, if you plant one eggplant seedling, we only ask you to give us back one eggplant. That's not much, is it? And you have to watch out so the insects don't get at the tobacco leaves. And you've got to follow the rules for gathering things from the seaside and such. And if you can't pay your taxes with things from the sea, well, then you'll have to pay them with silver. Since you have connections with people working in the seaside villages, you must have plenty of ways of getting some silver.

"So, all right then, let's just get a few things straight about our lord. Since none of you farmers served under the Arima Lords Harunobu or Naozumi, you probably don't understand the difference now. Lord Naozumi was a retainer and he was lax in looking after things, but Lord Matsukura Shigemasa was a military commander, and Shogun Ieyasu appointed him to take Naozumi's place because of his distinguished service on the battlefield. Shigemasa made clear his dedication to the shogun by offering ten thousand *koku*—that's two and half times more than the required contribution—to help with the construction of Edo Castle. Unfortunately, Ieyasu died before he could achieve his big plans for conquering the Philippines—that base of heathen Christianity. But Shigemasa gained a strong reputation, and people know the Matsukuras are an important clan here in western Japan. When you get down to it, the troubles here have come about because the Arima region of Shimabara has been a rat's nest of priests for some time, and because the lords and the people here have been captives of this heretical religion. And, of course, there was also the Okamoto Daihachi Incident caused by Lord Arima Harunobu. You can't say you don't remember that."

The magistrate continued:

"Christians infested even the ranks of Ieyasu's close advisors in the capital, along with those close to his military governor in Kyoto. All of them were Christians who'd gained power in Arima and run rampant. Shogun Iemitsu realized that the Christians wouldn't hesitate to destroy the government, and he directly ordered our late lord to get rid of them.

"You should realize that your Christian troubles and your unpaid taxes are part and parcel of the same thing. The records of your payments will be the proof of your service. They will prove, too, that you are innocent of keeping up a divided loyalty to Christianity and our lord. Keep that in mind."

The magistrate had summoned these village headmen and leaders and spoken to them directly because he thought things would remain unsettled if left in the hands of lower officials.

Among the leaders present were some Arima clan ronin who had become farmers after the Matsukura clan took over. As they sat facing the Matsukura magistrate, these former samurai brought a pride of their own that stood up to his. At first, Tada Kurōbei had spoken to them domineeringly. But then, perhaps believing he had started to persuade them, his tone quieted.

With arms folded, Chijiiwa Bannai from Kazusa turned his big eyes toward the ceiling. From time to time he looked at the magistrate as if he were observing some strange animal rather than listening to his tirade.

"You need to give up your attachment to your late lord—and fast," Kurōbei said, then suddenly lowered his voice. "It's still not too late. Depending on your service, I can recommend to our lord that he find you some positions, even if you're ex-vassals of Arima. The look in your eyes suggests you don't wish to work with me, but

I'm tired of it. Stop being stubborn. I've received comments and demands from the Nagasaki commissioner, too. I've had enough of your excuses—you understand?"

After having been insulted with these harsh and unforgivable comments about their respected Lord Harunobu, the village leaders from Arie and Kushiyama walked home in silence with their arms crossed over their chests.

"He sure laid it on thick today. Seems he's really up to something now. What do you make of it?"

"Well, he sure was after something."

"I wonder which village he'll go after first. We'll all have to watch out."

The meeting had been attended by Matsushima Sadonokami and Masuda Sōken from Kita Arima, Hayashida Shichizaemon and Matsushima Gennojō from Arie, Chijiiwa Bannai from Kazusa, and Hasuda Nisuke and Nagai Sōhan from Kuchinotsu.

Since the Matsukura clan took over administration of the area, taxes on the harvest had fully doubled. This year, the tax assessment also seemed to include demands for payment on the harvest from land the farmers didn't even own.

"And if you can't come up with it, there'll be no mercy for the households with women. We'll take women as hostages—you hear me?"

These parting words from Kurōbei, spoken almost casually, had weighed the most heavily on Nisuke.

How can we, who have no rice, be expected to fill the coffers of the clan? Perhaps Kurōbei thought he had to justify his demands, but his words today were outrageous. I guess I wasn't my usual self today. I suppose I ended up giving him a piece of my mind, since the other leaders had told me, "Hasuda-dono, when we have to say something, you speak first."

Nisuke recalled his conversation with the other leaders.

Before going to see the magistrate, they had gathered to discuss their plans. Among the former vassals of the old Arima clan were some headmen and leading farmers from the north and south of the old Arima clan region who had been high-ranking samurai and couldn't help speaking like soldiers. Chijiiwa Bannai from Kazusa, for one, was hot-tempered and poor at talking when things got tense. He would reach for the hilt of his sword before he spoke.

Nisuke, in spite of being a farmer, possessed a dignity that suited him to the role of representative. He could speak before the magistrate without causing unnecessary friction. And because he was head of the *jihi gumi* benevolent association, he was particularly suited to petition for grain assistance. The others had hoped he would open the discussion calmly, and then gradually they could add their comments. They had all gone to the meeting intending to see how things stood and later submit a joint petition.

But despite his best intentions, Nisuke had gotten upset right from the start, even though he knew he was only supposed to make the opening remarks. He had also noticed how Bannai changed; at first he had simply observed Kurōbei, but gradually he had grown more riled up and his eyes had turned bloodshot.

Not only Kurōbei, but the other men, seated in a row, couldn't help noticing the seething anger of the Arima lord's former vassals, although they had hardly spoken.

"I'm very sorry. That went so badly. My words seem to have rubbed the magistrate the wrong way."

Nisuke made his apologies as soon as they left. He said he had been worse than useless; he had added to their troubles.

"Don't worry about it. Kurōbei had no intention of granting our requests. This time the tax assessment is far too high. It's way beyond what the lord who governs the domain should allow. We all think his crackdown on unpaid taxes is a ploy to expose us as Christians and force us out. It's something he can report to the shogun to show his allegiance.

"You know, if you'd lived during the *sengoku* wars, you could've been a great strategist, like Takenaka Hanbei. Your exchange with Kurōbei really impressed me."

Nisuke blushed at Bannai's sincere words. "His coming down here from the so-called 'Yamato Gojō' domain up in Nara and talking to us in that affected language—it really went against the grain of things," Nisuke grumbled. "But then I ended up antagonizing him. Somehow, I should have handled it better and gotten him to drop his demands."

Regrets about the bitter outcome burned in Nisuke's chest.

I'll have to tell Yazō the benzashi *what happened today, although we belong to different* confuraria. *Judging by Kurōbei's talk, it looks like they're going to start squeezing us for taxes on things we gather from the seashore, too.*

The last four or five years had passed somewhat peacefully, but ever since the Matsukura clan took over, they had been going after the ex-vassals of the Arima lords and the village headmen and leaders with special ferocity in their persecution of Christians. Although people throughout the region north of Kuchinotsu—from Minami Arima up to Kita Arima and Arie—had publicly renounced their beliefs, in reality, they were all still Christian. If the officials started rashly going after Christians in the general population now, it would expose the domain leaders' misgovernment. It was obvious that the Matsukuras' deeper motive for punishing the Christian leaders stemmed from a desire to paper over doubts about the clan's compliance with the Shogun's exclusionary policy against Christians and to plant fear among the Christians—while at the same time filling their own pockets and grain stores by collecting the land and rice taxes.

After leaving the magistrate's headquarters, Nisuke and the village leaders headed back to their homes. On both sides of the pathways they passed fields with withered white ears of rice. When Nisuke finally took his leave from the others and stood in front of his house, he didn't feel ready to go in, so he squatted by the flowers in his garden.

What, he wondered, was that magistrate seeing?

The magistrate had insulted the former Lords Arima Harunobu and his son Naozumi. But what could one say about the Matsukura lords? Matsukura Shigemasa had more or less tried to be closer to the people of the domain, but the present Lord Matsukura Katsuie was nothing but a fool. His cruelty far exceeded his father's. He had gotten so zealous about carrying out the shogun's repeated orders to punish Christians that he had turned Mount Unzen into a living hell. He had ordered his men to do things like cut off the heads of the living with bamboo saws and pour salt into their wounds to prolong their suffering, acts that ought to be unthinkable for a ruler to do to living human bodies, even if those humans were thought to be villains and criminals.

When Omiyo saw her husband sitting in front of the white spider lilies, she was taken aback. She could sense the invisible flame of anger rising silently from his back and shoulders.

"My dear, my dear—what's happened?"

She even forgot to say, "Welcome home."

Nisuke turned his head slowly. Omiyo could see that the irises of his eyes were blurred. It was clear that the meeting had gone badly.

"Well, the meeting dragged on for a long time."

Nisuke sighed deeply. It seemed as if his breath had taken on a foul color that stained the earth beneath it. She could see that something very serious had happened. While Omiyo remained silent and apprehensive, her husband, his back still toward her, pointed to the white flowers.

"Look, they're blooming. This year too."

Squatting by his side, she could see that his eyes had become more normal.

"Ah—I can see them now. Before, your eyes looked like they had nothing in them."

Now his eyes held the refreshing white color of the spider lilies.

"If they're blooming, the autumn equinox will be here soon."

"Really? If it's coming, I can make rice with red beans."

Thinking of the dying rice, she changed the topic.

"These white spider lilies, they were a gift from that elderly lady over in Kazusa—how many years has it been now?"

Kazusa was the village next to Kuchinotsu.

"That's right, Hyōgo's grandmother gave them to us. It must have been ten or more years ago. And still they bloom, every year."

"Yes, it was those bulbs. And it's unusual that their flowers are white—not red like most."

"Yes, white."

Gazing at the white spider lilies, Nisuke and Omiyo were able to forget the present for a while.

"You asked the old lady if, in a pinch, we could eat the bulbs, since they looked like arrowhead bulbs."

"Yes, I did. I did!"

"When you asked her that she broke out laughing. She said that, if it was really necessary, we could soak out the poison and eat them, but she hoped we'd just let them grow and enjoy their flowers."

"Even now, when I look at them, I can't help thinking of using their bulbs to ease our hunger a bit. But there are so many people in our house—those bulbs wouldn't even fill one pot."

"You're right. She said the flowers of the red spider lilies are nice, but the white ones are especially beautiful, and they will see us off and welcome us into Heaven. If we were to eat them, we might get stomachaches."

"How well you remember!"

"Well, yes—when it comes to flowers. But come now and get up. I'll make you some tea."

Laughing, Omiyo held out her hand. Nisuke stood up, clinging to it; a rare thing for him to do.

It happened the following morning.

The cicadas were shrieking under a strange, reddish morning sky. And then suddenly, they stopped. People stepped outside and stared up at the sky. There was no wind.

The sea seemed to be swelling up. It looked as if the sky were sucking up the heat of the ocean and burning bright red.

Kumagorō, one of the household workers, called out, "Matsu-yan, the cicadas—they've stopped crying."

Kumagorō had just woken up and was splashing water on his face, but he stopped and looked at Matsukichi, the head of the household workers. Matsukichi's face, too, looked red.

"It's not so strange for cicadas to stop crying for a while."

"I know—but they stopped all of a sudden."

"I guess the cicadas must have business of their own."

"Come on, Matsu-yan. Are your eyes getting that weak? That red in the sky, it's really strange. And your face looks red, too. The cicadas must've been frightened."

"Well, speaking of red, Kuma, you're looking pretty red yourself."

"Don't you think it's a strange sign?"

"Well, yeah, it *is* kind of strange. The red sky this morning is different from usual. It's a warning sign of something to come. Somehow, the cicadas must be telling us this."

"But that's just what I've been trying to tell you!"

"Also, before sunrise, a lot of birds were flying off."

"I didn't notice since I was sleeping."

"Suzu jumped out of bed and followed the birds off to look at the sea."

"Why was that?"

"I don't know, but Suzu's like that. She often runs off when something happens."

"Well, yes, she does seem to run off a lot."

While the two men were chatting, Suzu came running back. Her hair, tied up in back, was bobbing up and down, reflecting the red sky.

"Suzu, if you run around so much, you'll go hungry."

Suzu stared at the two men for a moment, her mouth shut tight, and then pointed at the sea.

"From the red sky, a boat appeared—with a red flag."

The two men looked at each other. Had the morning boats arrived already? They suspected that the fishers, who could predict the weather by reading the sea and sky, had judged it a morning when something strange might happen. Perhaps they had headed back early expecting bad weather.

Feeling neglected by the men, Suzu pointed ahead again. Her child's voice piercing old Matsukichi's eardrums, she insisted, "On the boat—there was an incredibly dazzling, handsome person standing on it."

"Well, well, you saw a dazzling person, did you? If the boat had a red flag, it must've been Yazō's. But what about this dazzling, handsome person?"

As if under a spell, Suzu walked along unsteadily with her bucket in hand to draw the morning water.

"Again, there's less water. Less than yesterday." Her voice echoed from the sides of the well.

Matsukichi, followed by Kumagorō, walked over to the well and both men looked into it. Matsukichi seemed very concerned, but said nothing.

Past noon, clouds appeared in the sky and gradually thickened. The entire sky seemed to be moving forward from behind.

"Well, it looks like rain's coming on."

Here and there, villagers stepped outside, looked up at the

sky, and started talking. It was unusual for Nisuke to be at home. While he was pensively watching the movement of the clouds, Yazō stopped in.

"Well, well, it's been a long time. Come on in. What business brings you here today?"

"No business, really. I just got back from Mogi. I've been going about here and there, trying to look after our boats because of this weather. I thought I'd check on your place, too."

"Well, thanks. I've been thinking about you, too. With this sort of weather, you must be worried about your boats."

"So I am. I just told some of the men to pull them up."

"Pull up the boats—onto the ground? All six?"

"Onto the ground. From the looks of the sky, I'd say we're going to have quite a storm."

"That's what I've been thinking, too. Well, you sure must be tired. Come in and take a break."

"Thanks, but I'm just stopping by. I was concerned about the women here, since you've been summoned away so many times and you're rarely at home these days. Seeing you here now, I feel better. But I'm heading home—I have a guest with me."

"Who's the guest?"

"The son of an acquaintance. He sometimes rides on my boats on his way to and from Nagasaki."

"To and from Nagasaki? ... Is he from Amakusa?"

"Yes. His father is Masuda-sama, from over in Uto. He's a former retainer of Lord Konishi."

"A ronin of Konishi-sama?"

Yazō nodded.

"Right. He's the son of one of Konishi's ronin. His father has connections with the wholesale trade of Chinese goods in Nagasaki, and sometimes he takes his sea products there."

So, Konishi's ronin are taking up the China trade these days.

"But his son has devoted himself to his studies and he's not really interested in business. He's a young man with real talent."

"Then I'd like to meet him. Why don't you both come in—be my guests."

"Well, all right then, thanks. We'll be guests for a bit."

From the opening in the hedge fence, a boy had been watching the two men talk. When his gaze met Nisuke's, he greeted him quietly, his eyes shining like waves rippling in the morning light.

For a moment, Nisuke mistook the boy for an apparition of a flower, perhaps because on this day so many more white spider lilies were blooming than on the previous day. The boy stood against the sky with nothing else around him as heavily piled clouds rose and scurried about strangely. It looked as if he were standing in the center of a slowly swirling sky, with the earth all around him. Nisuke thought he had become dizzy from standing up so quickly. Perhaps it was owing to the mental stress he had been feeling lately. He tried to step firmly. Owing to the movements of the clouds, the earth looked as if it had been cast askew. As he bowed slightly in reply, Nisuke found himself wondering, *Who is this young nobleman?*

Unconsciously, this phrase from an old story had welled up in Nisuke's thoughts. Perhaps it was because, the night before, Ninagawa Sakyō's son Ukon had visited and read a section from a text of the *Tale of the Heike* that had been printed on the mission press in Amakusa. In the scene where Kumagai Naozane beheads the young nobleman Taira no Atsumori, who is carrying a flute at his waist, the old people and women had wiped away their tears many times.

As the Taira fighters flee the battlefield following their defeat at Ichinotani, Kumagai spots a young warrior riding off on a horse through the waves toward the waiting boats.

... Kumagai tightly grasped the sleeve of his enemy's armor, trying to tear off his helmet in order to take his head. When he did, he saw a boy, about fifteen or sixteen years of age, whose teeth had been blackened and whose face had been colored with very light makeup. The boy looked to be about the same age as his own son and was handsome ... Kumagai was certain it was a young nobleman of the Heike clan. How could this boy be his samurai enemy? Surely the feelings of this young nobleman's father would have been similar to his feelings for his own son Kojirō. How sad. Whose son was this young nobleman?

"Tell me your name and I'll help you."

Kumagai had pleaded, but the young nobleman would not identify himself. Instead, he replied:

"I am thy worthy enemy. Take my head now—quickly. You shall

learn my name when the identification of my head is done."

Kumagai had kept trying to think of a way to save him, feeling so deeply for this person who was almost the same age as his own son. But when he saw the rush of approaching warriors, such thoughts vanished and he put him to his sword.

After covering the boy's head, Kumagai noticed his flute, held in a brocade pouch at his waist. How sad. That morning at dawn it must have been this boy and his companions who were playing music inside the castle. Although there were tens of thousands of soldiers in Kumagai's army, not one of them carried a flute onto the battlefield.

Later, with this in mind, Kumagai confirmed that the boy had been the youngest son of Tsunenori, a high official in the Public Works Ministry and brother of Taira-no-Kiyomori. His age was sixteen years.

In tears, Kumagai had gone to Kurō Yoshitsune, the chief of the police and the judiciary and had shown him the head and the flute.

Among those who had heard the flute playing at dawn, *there was not a person who did not weep.*

When Ukon read these words, his voice had faltered. He finished by saying simply that Kumagai Jiro Naozane could no longer continue living as a soldier and had become a monk.

Nisuke, the leader of the meeting, also had been unable to hold back tears when he heard this passage.

Although the situation around Kuchinotsu and Arima differed from that at the Battle of Ichinotani, memories of the great number of martyrs from this area remained fresh. The bravery and helplessness of the children who had been executed along with their parents were in no way less than that of Atsumori. The audience must have felt the same emotions.

Now, seeing Yazō's young guest, Nisuke associated him with the young nobleman in the *Tale of the Heike*, and with the future of this area. Deeply struck, Nisuke stood as if rooted in the ground. When Yazō called to him, "Nisuke-dono, what's wrong?" he came back to himself.

"Ah—I was just feeling a bit dizzy. Yesterday I had to listen to so much vile talk from Kurōbei at the magistrate's office, and I wasn't feeling so well this morning."

"Called you in again, did he? About the same business?"

"Yes. The same old business. But this time there's going to be a lot more trouble."

"It's a shame you're always the one who has to shoulder all these troubles. That old lout is just no good."

"Um-hmm."

Nisuke was speaking less than usual. Yazō could see there would be many more hardships to come.

"Well anyhow, come on in. I need to talk to you, too. Please excuse the mess. And, please, have your guest come in too."

Nisuke bowed respectfully to the young man. He had been worrying about the ominous signs; the trees and grass withering from the severe drought, the unusual red sky that morning, and Kurōbei's talk the day before. But now, in the presence of this serene young guest, he felt refreshed.

It's quite something for Yazō to be bringing a guest, and on a day with such strange weather at that.

More sociable than usual, Yazō assured his guest, "This house is like my own place, so come right in." Nisuke was moved and felt a little better.

The boy stepped into the room, sat, and lay his short sword by his side. Adjusting his posture, he placed his hands on the floor.

"I'm Masuda Shirō. I'm glad to meet you."

The boy looked about fourteen or fifteen. His self-possessed voice resonated pleasantly. He was wearing a splash-patterned white kimono decorated with an intricate motif of flying mosquitos over somewhat short *hakama* trousers. The distinctive weave was old-fashioned, likely chosen by his mother. His appearance was strikingly refined, neat and clean.

Yazō put in a few words of introduction.

"He says his father used to be in the service of Lord Konishi Yukinaga."

"Well, that was in the past. These days my father trades in things from the sea and sells them to wholesalers in the Chinese trade."

"Marine products? I see," Nisuke said, quickly assessing the situation. *If Yazō took the trouble to bring this boy here, he's likely a Christian. Maybe we can speak freely.*

"Well, Yazō-dono, Lord Konishi Yukinaga once ruled Amakusa. He was our neighbor and he kept up an especially good relationship with our late Lord Arima Harunobu, since they were both Christian. Do you remember the trouble when Regent Hideyoshi came to Nagoya in Hizen Province, back at the time of the Korean campaigns of 1592 and 1596? That was a hard time for your family."

"It certainly was. My father talked about it any number of times. When Hideyoshi was in Osaka, the churches and seminaries in the western domains were still protected by Lord Harunobu and stayed fairly well hidden, even after the edict for expelling Christians had been issued. But when Hideyoshi got to Nagoya, things had to change. Certainly, he would have taken note of the Christians' presence and our religious practices. So, Lords Konishi, Ōmura and Arima held secret meetings and helped hide the priests. They moved the seminary and theological school to places where they wouldn't be found—Hachirao in the mountains of Arima and the bay area south of Amakusa. That's when the big problems started. We had to move all the padres, and the students too. My father made so many trips escorting them to safety."

"Right. The boatmen took people from here to Shiki in Amakusa, and then on up to Kazusa in Shimabara. As soon as they reached Kuchinotsu, they returned to Kawachiura in Amakusa. My father said that was the real war for him—even more so than the Korean campaigns."

"I've heard that the lords ordered everything to be carried out in secret before Regent Hideyoshi arrived in Kyushu. They moved just about everything, including the church organs and all the ritual goods, and even the printing press."

"I've heard that Lord Konishi was one of Regent Hideyoshi's favorite retainers. Hideyoshi probably wasn't aware of those secret missions."

"Well, they did a great job of it. After that, my father joined the convoy of our Lord Harunobu and entered the government forces as a leader. Having successfully hidden the priests, both lords went off to fight in Korea with an air of innocence."

"But I heard that later everything came to light."

"Well, that happened after Nabeshima Naoshige and Mōri

Yoshinari became the Nagasaki magistrates."

Listening to the two men talk, Shirō appeared deeply engrossed.

"During the two invasions, warships sailed from Kuchinotsu to Korea. Even today, the old samurai who were on those ships complain about the dangerous high waves they faced and the terrible battles they fought."

"And before they could rest, they had to fight again in the Battle of Sekigahara."

"Our Lord Arima chose the side of Tokugawa Ieyasu and his Kanto forces, while Lord Konishi sided with Ishida Mitsunari, and for that choice he ended up getting beheaded at Rokujōgawara. But even though Lord Arima sided with the Tokugawas, he was implicated in the Okamoto Daihachi incident and, in the end, paid the price with his life."

I've heard that after they lost their master, some of Konishi's ronin took up farming in Amakusa, like those in the old Arima territory. And since the coastline around Amakusa and Ōyano juts in and out so much, I suppose the area is rich in marine products that are good for the Chinese trade. Interesting how some of those men of formerly high rank and culture are now making their living by selling things from the sea. And this fine young boy grew up among them. It's good to see Yazō looking after him with such pleasure. I can see the happiness in his eyes.

"My connection with Shirō-sama's family started when I met his grandfather Genbei-dono," Yazō said. "He gave the evening prayers on my boat on our way to Mogi and I was deeply impressed. It made me think I should behave like him. I'm a rough sort and I often forget my prayers. It was good to have the Mass out on the sea. Since then, I've been happy to take his family on my boats. The other day I had Shirō's father on board with me."

"You're a good man."

"I don't really think so," Yazō muttered with embarrassment.

Just then, Suzu came running along the narrow wooden porch in front of the house.

"Soon it's going to rain," she called out and then looked at the three men.

When her eyes met Shirō's, she gaped in surprise. She glanced down at the bunch of wild herbs she was clutching and tilted her head.

"Hello," Shirō greeted her.

"It looks like you've been picking *ashitaba* today. How about saying hello to our guest?" But it seemed Suzu wasn't really listening.

Mumbling, "… red sky and a ship …" she walked unsteadily toward the shed and then slowly turned around. Suddenly, she held up the bunch of herbs and ran off to the barn.

Omiyo came in with tea.

"Well, Yazō-sama, it looks like these clouds have brought you here today. Where've you been all this time?"

"I just got back from Nagasaki and I brought this guest with me."

Having been friends since childhood, Yazō and Omiyo often chatted casually when they met. The boy looked down and smiled, perhaps because he appreciated the friendliness he found among the people in this house. Nisuke noticed the striking quality of his unaffected manners and how he looked so different from ordinary young people. He understood why Yazō wanted to take such good care of him.

Yazō asked Omiyo if she had made preparations for the strong winds they were expecting. She assured him they were mostly done. Perhaps because Yazō was so preoccupied with attending to his young guest, he kept looking up at the sky and chatting about this and that. But in part he also spoke so that Shirō might hear about certain things.

"Back when the churches were still doing well, Nagasaki Port used to be bustling. Whenever the Portuguese ship the *Nau* arrived, the house of the priest who served as bookkeeper would fill with silks, scarlet woolen cloth, gold brocade cloth, tiger and deer skins, and other items like musk, aloeswood, dried apricots, wine and all sorts of things the regular merchants couldn't get. I visited the church after I heard the rumors that it had become a warehouse of treasures.

"Certainly, there were donations from the Christian lords and believers, but without considerable capital funding it would have been impossible to start the businesses that financed the Christian cloisters, churches, and schools, one after another. Heavy expenses were involved in buying land, constructing buildings, and hiring workers. All the heads of the church who came to Japan from far across the seas, including Valignano-sama, first headed for the capital in Kyoto to get permission from the regent and the family of the shogun. They made long trips there, bringing lavish presents. I've heard that all the expenses were covered by the profits from the Portuguese trading ships.

"Around the time of Lord Arima's death, a rumor circulated that after he died the Nagasaki magistrates and the Christian lords had invested heavily in the *Nau,* which regularly sailed back and forth from Macao. It was also said that Konishi Yukinaga, who was the son of the wealthy Sakai merchant Konishi Ryūsa, had kept an eye out for important maritime business."

After recounting this history, Yazō looked over at Shirō.

According to Yazō, Shirō's father had been a local samurai on Ōyano Island under Lord Konishi, after he started to govern the Amakusa region. The taxes had been reasonable and the Amakusa people still fondly remembered the good days of Konishi's administration. Recently, Shirō's father Jinbei had been living in Ebe Village near Uto, on the mainland across the bay from Ōyano. Nisuke supposed that Jinbei still maintained good relations with the people in Nagasaki he had met doing business in the bay area and supplying the military campaigns of Lord Konishi during the Korean wars. Now Yazō had brought along this good person as a guest. Nisuke felt a little better. Suzu had been right about what she said a while ago: a boat had descended from a red sky with a dazzling, handsome young person standing on it.

As if reading Nisuke's mind, Yazō smiled and said, "Suzu's mood seems to have improved."

Yazō looked up at the sky.

"We won't be able to sail for Ōyano in this weather. We'll have to ask Shirō to stay here for a few days," he said to Nisuke.

"Right. And where's he going to stay?"

"He could stay at our house or at yours. But how about having him stay with the Ninagawas? What do you think?"

"Well, of course we'd like to have him stay with us, but I suppose the Ninagawa's place might be good for him."

"Ukon's in their family. He's a great reader of books. A while back he rode with me to Nagasaki. He met Shirō-dono there and they hit it off."

"Well, in that case, nothing could be better."

Among all the Christian samurai families in the area, no one loved reading and studying more than Ukon, even at his young age. People called him the "god of books."

"I wish we had a seminary in Amakusa or Kazusa. Ukon-dono would show everyone that he's as smart as any of those highbrows who come down from Kyoto."

Nisuke couldn't help staring at Yazō as he emphatically expressed his high regard for Ukon.

Because of his duties as village headman, Nisuke often had the chance to meet a wide range of people, from dying beggars and desperately sick people collapsing in the streets to high-ranking officials. But Yazō had been born into a *benzashi* family and had traveled on his father's boats since he was a boy. He had connections not only with the fishers, but also with Chinese traders in Nagasaki. Still, even with his family background, he could never have run his business so successfully without his own talents. Nisuke imagined that Yazō had acquired his keen ability to size people up from his long experience in the shipping trade. He no doubt knew things Nisuke couldn't even imagine.

"One time, I heard some seminary priests on my boat saying that the young men from Kyoto were different, and more learned. Somehow it really riled me when I heard that."

Yazō had mentioned that he never had the chance to get an academic education himself; perhaps their words made him bitter.

"Well, back in those days, famous scholars used to come down here from Kyoto, but Ukon-dono—he'd be second to none of them."

"Those scholars, who were they?" Shirō asked suddenly.

While Nisuke and Yazō were trading glances, Okayo came in with fresh cups of tea. Sensing an important discussion in progress, she placed the tea tray in front of them without speaking. As she looked up, her husband entered. Daisuke nodded to her and sat down in the back.

After a pause, Nisuke said, "I never met them or heard them talk myself, but I remember the names Yōhōken Paulo-dono and Fukansai Fabian-dono." A bit uncertain of his memory, Nisuke sought confirmation from Yazō.

"Well, I'm no expert either, but I've heard that those two men knew a lot, not only about the Buddha and Confucius, but about Spanish and Portuguese studies as well. People said they were equal in learning to Lord Sugawara no Michizane."

"Fabian-dono taught at the seminary, and they say he helped write books like the *Doctrina Chirishitan*."

Hearing this from Nisuke, the boy's cheeks flushed.

"I keep that book with me always, and I'm studying it now."

"Really? That book? Wonderful!" Yazō and Nisuke responded together.

Daisuke, with his rugged features, was observing the young guest intently. Okayo thought her husband looked especially handsome with that serious expression.

"Not really. I've read the words in the book, but I'm not sure I understand them."

"You're just being modest," Yazō replied. "To tell the truth, when I read the book, words like *Trinidade* and *Mysterio*, they're too difficult. My tongue gets all tied up. And *memoria*, and *entenjimento*—that's intellect, right? I just can't get used to words like that yet. It's only in the parts about *Viruzen Santa Maria* that I feel myself getting close to it."

Listening to Yazō pronouncing with such difficulty the strange foreign words from the *Doctrina Chirishitan*, Shirō was amused. He smiled as he looked intently into Yazō's face.

"Even someone like me can chant those lines," Yazō continued.

And then, with a somewhat more serious expression, he began reciting an *oratio* from the *Doctrina Chirishitan*.

"This is from the part about the valley of tears ... 'O blessed, merciful mother and empress, we thank you. We, the descendants of the wandering children of Eve, with this prayer we cry out to you. Moaning and weeping in this valley of tears, with this prayer we beseech you to turn your merciful eyes upon us.'"

With head bowed and eyes closed, Nisuke asked in a low, diffident voice, "When you say this *oratio*, to whom do you address it?"

"To the Virgin Maria," Yazō replied respectfully.

"And where is the valley of tears?"

"I think it's in the darkness, beyond the hope that exists in this world."

"As I understand it, it's a prayer we say to Maria-sama when we're in that darkness."

As this discussion unfolded before her, it seemed to Okayo that Nisuke looked different from usual. Her father-in-law's expression was calm and his eyes were closed. When they had held the meetings of the *jihi-gumi*, Juan-sama had come and read *oratios*. The congregation had knelt and held hands and followed him. But now Nisuke and Yazō were in a situation more urgent than anything they had faced then.

In asking me these questions, this man is questioning himself, taking me as his own reflection, Yazō thought. *For generations his family has served as village headmen, and back when Father Valignano and the other priests used to come here regularly, they gave them lodging. Not only does he endure the reproach of the clan lord who drives such a hard bargain on the taxes, he also bears the responsibility for sustaining the faith of the villagers, who have pretended to renounce their beliefs in the face of the harsh edicts. He is a man of honesty and sincerity. He must be thinking of the people in this village and blaming himself for not practicing his faith well enough to meet their needs.*

But then—I'd almost forgotten—Omiyo asked me to bring back some grain. I could only find a little. I searched around for more, but it's been such a bad year for crops; far worse than expected. Disturbing rumors are spreading all around us. What excuse can I come up with?

Okayo noticed how the eyes of the young guest gleamed mysteriously as he listened to the conversation between Yazō and her father-in-law. She felt as if her chest was somehow being pressed in. She had never seen Yazō look so serious. Usually he was always cracking jokes in his deep voice and making the people around him laugh.

Okayo glanced at Daisuke. He had shut his eyes and was sitting with his arms folded, like his father. This was the first time since their marriage that she had seen her husband's face take on such a ponderous expression. She loved his generous character, and the way the village children followed after him calling him "Brother Hasuda." But now her husband's brows were deeply knit. With his father facing all these troubles, she imagined that Daisuke, too, must be sharing the burden.

It had taken less than six months after marrying into this family for Okayo's morning and evening devotions to change from the *nenbutsu* of the Buddhists to the *oratio* of the Christians, but she still hadn't thought deeply about the meaning of Christianity.

She knew that her mother, who died young, had been a devout Christian and that she had been given the Christian name Magdalena. She regarded this as important. But as for the difference between the Buddha and Deus, it felt daunting for her to ask questions and find answers, since she thought of herself as not knowing much. And what was the difference between Kannon-sama and Maria-sama? The family she had grown up with respected both of them, and it seemed it would be a sin to place one above or below the other.

And so, in this way, Okayo had become a member of her new family without asking her husband much about such things. But now, right in front of her, these men were discussing the most important matters of the Christian faith; things she had been wanting to know about, from the depth of her heart. When her mother was a baby, she had been given the pure name Magdalena, so Okayo felt assured that her mother had passed on peacefully into *Paraizo*, the paradise of Heaven. And yet, despite this reassurance, simply calling out her mother's name in her heart brought her to tears.

Father-in-Law and Daisuke, and even Yazō, look so different from usual. No doubt the suffering in their hearts has been far deeper than anything I've felt.

And look at the guest. What a dignified young person. Owing to him, there have been such deep discussions about the doctrines and other things they've never discussed so seriously before. Everyone, even Daisuke, was leaning forward as they listened.

My own family has a similar custom of taking care of guests, but this family does it so much that our stores of food are running out; so much that Oume and Matsukichi have been grumbling about it. And now that the storerooms are almost empty, the family is offering its sincerity to this guest. Father-in-Law has been summoned time after time to the magistrate's place and unfairly accused. I suppose that's another reason they're talking like this.

Nisuke looked up and uncrossed his arms. "They say the salvation of *anima* comes after we die, but it seems we're not destined to be saved in this life," he said with a deep sigh.

Anima is a spirit, a soul, possessed by all people; that much Okayo knew. When she was young, she had climbed a persimmon tree at someone's house and tried to take some fruit. She remembered how Ofuji had scolded her: "An evil spirit stole your soul!"

"The teaching about salvation in the afterlife—that too, is so hard to understand," Yazō complained.

"Our Lord died on the cross for our sins," Nisuke answered. "I think that now is the time for us to practice His words, *Do unto others as you would have them do unto you* ... but I don't know how to do that."

Nisuke wanted to take advantage of Yazō's presence to try to explain to his son and daughter-in-law the difficulties he was facing. When he stopped by, Yazō had said he was just waiting for his boats. Yet the fact that he had brought along this somehow unworldly young person seemed to imply that he had planned all along to introduce him.

"Yesterday, when I heard Magistrate Tada Kurōbei talking, it made me think about sinners and criminals. If I, as one person, do something wrong, I can make a confession and ask Maria-sama to take away my sins; but I can't do that for all of Kuchinotsu. And tomorrow—where are we going to find food to eat? When we think of the suffering of our Lord, we should be able to bear our own troubles and be prepared for salvation in the afterlife; but I wonder what our sins are. Is it enough that I, as head of the village, rely on Maria-sama and pray for our salvation in the next world? And even if Maria-sama shines in every corner of my soul and I confess all of my sins, what about the people in this village; can I leave their future unattended? When I think like this, my mind gets all tangled up. The other day, before I knew it, Kurōbei started to look to me like a sea slug. I came to hate him ... But even the thought of beating him to death disgusts me."

Daisuke was shocked to hear his father using words like "beating him to death." Normally, in daily life, he never used such language. It made him realize how violent the whirlpool of emotions swirling in his father's heart must be.

"It's not only the one village of Kuchinotsu. How can I handle the suffering that I see everywhere? Do you think we village leaders can just look on with our arms folded?"

"Well," Yazō responded, "about that—I'm sorry I couldn't get enough to pay off the back taxes; but somehow, as Omiyo asked me to do, I found a little grain, and I've put it in the shed near the boat landing. It's only a small amount; only enough to make a little porridge for the people in the village for four or five days. Daisuke-dono, when night comes, let's get some men together and split ourselves into groups to get it, under cover of darkness. A boat from Yushima just came in carrying some grain from Hizen. It's good the storm hasn't hit yet."

The young guest seemed to be following the adults' discussion very attentively. Okayo rose quietly and slipped out of the room. Watching her, Daisuke imagined she was going to tell Omiyo the news about the boat carrying grain.

Bowing and placing his hands on the floor, Nisuke said, "I'm sorry to always be asking difficult favors of you. You're always the one I call on in times of trouble. But I'm truly grateful. Even if it's just enough grain for a few days, it will certainly make people happier."

Following his father's example, Daisuke bowed with deep respect.

"Whatever I can do, allow me to do it—even a small thing like this." Yazō waved his hand slightly and folded his arms.

"But after this drought ends, hard times are coming. Judging by what I've heard from sailors all around the country, it's not just happening here; crops are failing all over the place. In Satsuma and Higo, and off in Setouchi and Kyoto, too."

As Nisuke raised his head, a sharp pain scurried across his skull.

"You say crop failures are spreading throughout the country? Well, since last year we've been suffering from bad weather and we'd thought it would change this year, but the drought hasn't ended. We tried to save the crops by covering them with cut grass and straw, but it was no use. Everyone's been pitching in whatever they can, but all we can do now is hope for rain—and we can't rely on getting more grain from Hizen."

"Well, somehow, somewhere, I'll get what I can."

The group fell into a gloomy silence.

"This drought's been affecting land and sea alike. The water in the sea around Yushima's changed so much the bream are staying down in the deeper reaches. I'm not so concerned about the afterlife, but I wish we could get some help for all the people who are starving. If Deus-sama and Maria-sama could just get rid of the insects and send some rain for our parched fields, I wouldn't mind being sent down to *Inferuno*."

"Seems you're just as out of sorts as I am. Back when Nakaura Julian-sama was martyred—when he was hung by his feet in that pit at Nishizaka in Nagasaki—before that happened, I took him across the Straits of Hayasaki on my boat."

"Did you have a chance to talk with him?"

"Well, I wanted to have Julian-sama hear my confession. Perhaps I had a premonition that if I missed the chance, I'd never get another one. According to the teachings, the troubles we suffer in this life will bring us salvation in the life to come. But how can a man like me who never manages to follow any of the rules ever make it to *Paraizo*? Still, in spite of everything, I don't want to go to *Inferuno*. So, I confided my worries.

"And then that man—with his calm eyes and sunburned skin like mine—he said to me with a smile, 'It's the same for me.' And when I looked up, I saw Julian-sama looking out over the waves and saying, 'For example, if you think of a doctor treating a patient, he treats the root of the illness and then he teaches you how to lead a healthy life so you don't get sick again. That's the work of a doctor, right? But, as for me, I haven't reached the level of a doctor. When I go around and meet believers, I try to figure out how to take care of my own soul. You feel at peace when you realize there's no one in the world without sin—if they look into the depths of their soul. The hand of our Savior the Lord reaches out to us as sinners. But in my heart, I try to remember and follow the words of Chirisuto-sama, who told us, "Take nothing for the journey—no staff, no baggage, no money, no extra shirt." In other words; I should live like a beggar. That's pretty difficult.'

"Julian-sama said that with a smile. To this day, I still can't forget it. That was in the spring of the year he was arrested. Before he was hung in the pit, he said to the crowd, 'I am Nakaura Julian who has been to Rome . . .' We who are here now, we've never seen Rome. But it wasn't just Rome that Julian-sama saw; all the things that had happened around here, too—on land and sea alike—they all remained in his eyes. But all of that disappeared when he was killed. It's too much to bear."

"Yazō-sama, your eyes—they're like Julian-sama's—they've witnessed so many things that the rest of us don't know about," Shirō said in a low voice.

"Well, I haven't seen much, but I still wonder what was reflected in the depths of Nakaura Julian-sama's eyes. What did he have stored away in them? He was still young, but he'd already crossed the oceans and met with the pope in Rome, and with ranks of kings and noblemen, and served as the representative of the Japanese Christians. And they say his refined behavior was praised by all he met in those foreign countries. When he returned home, he met with Hideyoshi at Jurakudai and was highly regarded. But I've always wondered; what was it that lay in the depths of his eyes?"

"And," Nisuke added, "when he was hung in the pit; I wonder how the world looked to him then."

Okayo was in shock. On this day she had heard her father-in-law speak of terrifying things. Yazō continued, without responding to Nisuke but as if peering into his heart:

"We offer up our present suffering as a dedication to the peace that will come in the next life. We're taught to lead our lives thinking about where our souls will go. But even after I saw Nakaura-sama and heard him speak, still I felt it was difficult to obey the teachings, and I wondered how someone like me could ever make it to *Paraizo*."

"It's the same for me. But I wonder; which of the rules is hardest for you to follow?"

"There are so many, it's hard to say."

At this point, the boy joined the conversation with a serious look.

"Could you tell me what it is that's hard for you to say?"

"Well . . ."

Yazō's face turned red and he glanced up at the ceiling. The young couple looked at each other. Then Yazō continued:

"All right then, I'll confess my sins. First—I sometimes drink so much I get out of control."

Covering her face with her kimono sleeve, Okayo stifled a burst of laughter, since it had always been her job to look after Yazō whenever he drank too much at their house.

"And second—I slander, curse and speak ill of others when I get angry."

At this point, Daisuke looked up at the ceiling and started to chuckle. When Yazō got angry, his fiery tongue was like a flame bursting out from a cooking stove. People could hardly stand to be around him.

"It sounds pretty lively in here," Omiyo called out as she entered the room carrying a tray of snacks. After sitting on the floor and greeting the young guest, she lifted the top from a wooden box, releasing a pleasant fragrance.

"I'm sorry I have nothing much to offer our guest, but we have some chinquapin nuts that Okayo brought back from the mountains in her hometown and I just roasted them. Won't you try some?"

In a small bowl decorated in blue designs were some amber yuzu fruits pickled in miso.

"Well, Shirō-dono, look what we have here," Yazō quipped. "Omiyo is so thrifty, she hardly ever serves yuzu pickles. Please try some and see how they taste."

"But Yazō-dono was just starting his confession. I'm sorry we interrupted him," Nisuke said, opening his eyes and placing some of the special pickles on a small saucer that he set in front of Shirō.

"If this is the sort of confession we're going to have, then it may sound like a choir of angels," Shirō said with such utter seriousness that everyone broke out in laughter. Then they looked again at the young guest. He placed a nut in his hand along with a *yuzu* pickle. After slipping them into his mouth he remarked, "This makes me feel nostalgic. It brings back memories of my mother."

Shirō smiled slightly, and his eyes shone with an indescribable warmth. Seeing his smiling face, Omiyo wished Daisuke had a younger brother like him.

"Next time the sea is calm, please come stay with us."

The entire household echoed this invitation as they saw him off. Shirō looked back toward them. Suzu, who had been following him, was looking up as if she wanted to say something. As Shirō raised one hand, she bent forward impatiently, snapped off a white spider lily flower and held it out in a brash, boyish manner. Taken by surprise, Shirō looked at her. Then, bending slightly toward her, he said, "I'll take this as a remembrance of our meeting today."

Suzu's eyes opened wide, but when Okayo poked her gently in the back, she collapsed in childish embarrassment onto her knees and made the sign of the cross. Between her hands and Shirō's, white flower petals fluttered about, and then a strong wind gusted in, as if it might sweep off their feet all of those who were watching.

All the trees and blossoms were stirring and rustling and dust was swirling along, all the way from the boat dock up to the town, along the fields and the roadways.

"Looks like it's getting close. Let's get going," Yazō said, already walking away.

Amid the banging of hastily shut doors, rapidly darkening clouds filled the sky as the two men disappeared.

Tying back her sleeves as she started to prepare dinner, Okayo gazed toward the moving clouds. She thought of the village of Futae no Ura, far across the Hayasaki Straits, and of the foothills beyond in Uchino. What might her grandmother and sister Nana be doing now? How she missed her hometown of Uchino. Shaking her head and pretending to comb her hair, she wiped away tears. *I mustn't forget to ask Daisuke-dono to repair the chimney of the* kamaya *oven. Unless it's fixed before the big winds hit, no one will be able to open their eyes or mouths because of the smoke blowing in.* Then her husband stepped in behind her. Daisuke was tall and broad-shouldered. With the cloth in her hand, Okayo energetically brushed some cobwebs and dust off his shoulders.

"You know, for the first time in quite a while, Father-in-Law was laughing."

"I'd say it was the first time in ages."

"Looks like he's taken quite a liking to that young fellow Yazō brought with him."

"It seemed to me he had a rare sort of dignity."

"Did you notice when Suzu broke off the spider lily flowers and gave them to him?"

"Well, yes, I saw it."

"It looked like a picture from the old seminary."

"You may be right there. It sure was a nice scene."

"I envy the young."

"What?"

Daisuke looked down at Okayo, who wasn't even as tall as his shoulders. Cobwebs were still sticking to his eyebrows, and dipped down along with them.

"You know, you and I—we're still young."

Although Okayo laughed, Daisuke pretended not to notice as he brushed off his eyebrows.

"The sky this morning looked so threatening. I'm glad we could see those two off safely. And, oh—could you take care of that chimney?"

"Ah, right—that job."

Daisuke grabbed a ladder, set it up, and began working. The chimney also served as a skylight, so closing it too much made the room dark, but opening it too much let in too much wind. It was hard to get just the right balance.

During a pause in his skillful pounding of the nails he had been holding in his mouth, he remarked, "Mother, too, seemed a bit relieved—today, at least."

"Yes, she's been worried that Father-in-Law hasn't been eating well lately."

"He's had too many things to take care of, and so much on his mind."

"Even though you've been helping him?"

"I've been trying to, but even if we work together, I still can't come close to doing the work of my father."

"It's a tough situation and I can hardly understand it."

"Well ... if you put together the villages of Kuchinotsu and Kazusa, there's around six hundred households—that's maybe about thirty-nine hundred people. There are four headmen for the two villages and everyone's lives depend on them. What with trying to pay off the land taxes and the back rice payments and all, quite naturally, none of them are looking good these days."

Okayo sighed as her husband continued.

"The other day, when we had a private meeting at Bannai-sama's house, it was my job to write things down …"

"Ah—that night. I remember you said it was a hard job."

"Since so many boats come and go from here these days, it's rather different from the other bay areas and all sorts of problems have cropped up, one after another. Even if all the town leaders put their heads together, they can't come up with answers to all of them."

Watching her normally easygoing husband sighing as he climbed the ladder, Okayo sensed the immense burden her father-in-law must be bearing.

She started to sort through the purslane she had picked along the edge of the porch earlier. Since purslane was a weed, it held up well in droughts. The stems gave off a sticky, pale peach-colored juice when boiled and were delicious dressed with miso. Even without taking the trouble to plant them, patches sprang up all over, growing in flower gardens and vegetable patches alike. They were especially important in the season when other green vegetables stopped growing.

In Okayo's home village, on the fifteenth day of the Obon festival, people offered miso-dressed purslane to the ancestors. Even if the summer crop of daikon growing in parched ground got eaten up by codling moths before it could finish growing, the hardy purslane would survive, and people were grateful to have it for soup. Perhaps it liked the summer sun. Its fleshy, teardrop-shaped leaves resembled those of portulaca spread out densely over the hardened earth, and when you pulled them up, wrapping them around your fingers, their red stems lifted out easily.

Okayo thought of how the purslane and *ashitaba* greens served as a lifeline in years of drought. Her grandmother Ofuji had often said this. At the joints of the purslane leaves were cases of tiny black seeds, like poppy seeds. When you pulled the plants up, the seeds spilled over the ground, and so the next year you'd find them sprouting all over the place.

From atop the ladder, Daisuske's voice came down.

"When I saw that purslane, it reminded me; is your grandmother in Uchino getting along well?"

"I was just thinking about her too."

"If we can get through this storm, the *higan* week of the autumn equinox will be coming up."

"Yes. And the *higan* spider lilies have just come into bloom."

As she said this, Okayo wondered if people in Christian families, too, held services for the dead during *higan*.

"If we get some rain, we can take down some of the seeds we always plant around *higan*."

Daisuke continued talking on about the season for sowing seeds. He stepped down from the ladder, bent over the stove door, and lit a fire. Smoke rose toward the skylight, but soon a gust of wind blew it back down and it filled the kitchen.

"Whew! Well, I guess it can't be helped. Boil the purslane quickly and then put out the fire. That's the best we can do."

Although Daisuke seldom got involved in kitchen matters, this time it seemed he intended to stick around until the purslane was boiled. He noticed that Okayo had paused in sorting the purslane and was gazing off into the distance. When he asked what the matter was, she laughed self-consciously and said, "I wonder if this wind will reach my family in Uchino."

"Of course it will …"

Supposing that Okayo was feeling homesick, Daisuke searched for something that might cheer her up.

"Okayo, next time we go to Uchino, how about taking one of the Amagatsu dolls to Nana? The ones my mother makes."

"Wouldn't that be too much?"

"Not at all. She gives them to all the children. She makes them so she can see the children smile."

"Your mother is so good with her hands. She can do things in no time at all, and without making a fuss about it."

"Well, Oume-yan helps her a lot behind the scenes, so my mother gets some free time."

"Those two are like sisters."

"Oume-yan started taking care of my mother when she was just a baby."

"Well then, I've got two mothers-in-law, don't I?"

"Um … as you know, Oume-yan doesn't put up with any nonsense. I don't know how many times she slapped me when I was a kid for getting into mischief."

"What sort of mischief?"

"Well, once she found me when I'd caught a snake and was swinging it around."

"That sounds pretty scary."

"Getting slapped by her hand really hurts. It's like being hit with a log."

"I'm sure it hurts. Luckily, I haven't been slapped yet."

"Don't worry. There's no reason it'll happen to you."

"She can be really scary when she needs to be."

"It seems strange when I think back on it, but that was the one time my mother really got shaken up and apologized to Oume-yan."

"What? What did she say?"

"Well, she begged Oume-yan to forgive me for the sake of Deus-sama—and for her own sake as well."

Okayo thought about this for a moment and then burst out laughing, putting her hand over her mouth. The arm beneath her kimono sleeve showed her good health.

"That must've been quite some sight."

Okayo couldn't stop laughing.

"It's true that, for Mother-in-Law, Deus-sama is the only God. But it seems funny now. I wonder why."

"And can you guess what Oume-yan said next?"

Finally catching her breath, Okayo stood up and grabbed the ladder for support as she brushed the dust off her apron.

"Could you pass me the short nails over there?" Daisuke asked, turning toward the skylight. "Oume-yan said, 'You talk about Deus-sama, do you? Well, he must not be a very good god. What's he been teaching this little boy?'"

Passing the nails, Okayo looked puzzled.

"Ah—That's it! That's it! Your expression just now—it looked just like my mother's. She said it wasn't the fault of Deus-sama. Oume-yan replied, 'Well then, I'll have to scold him even harder. In my family, Amida-sama told us never to kill any living being. We were taught that even snakes have former lives and are reborn in the next life. If a snake does something wrong, that's a different matter. But that snake was begging for its life and trying to escape, while this child dragged it along and swung it round! He was so mean! Haven't you ever heard of Buddha's wisdom? Well, if you can't handle this child, I'll have to deal with his bad spirit by myself.' Then, in tears, and with her lips quivering, Oume-yan dragged me off by my collar to that persimmon tree."

"That must've been pretty frightening."

"It sure was. My mother was sobbing and clinging to Oume-yan, begging her to forgive me. And I was apologizing and asking for forgiveness too, in shock at seeing two adults in tears."

"How old were you?"

"Probably not quite nine. I was the head of the kids' gang."

"Ah, that Oume-yan—now I see why Mother-in-Law relies on her so much."

"Thinking of that time, I somehow understand why the old folks around here say that Deus-sama and Amida-sama get along well in the Hasuda family."

"Well ... I guess they're right."

Suddenly she looked up and their eyes met.

"Still ..."

Okayo grabbed the ladder again and it tottered.

"Let go of it, won't you? I'm not getting much work done."

"Sorry. It's just funny to me."

"Well, it's a serious story, but you're right; there's something funny about it."

"Just hearing about those conversations between Mother-in-Law and Oume-yan, I can't help but laugh."

"You've been laughing this whole time—your hands have gone idle."

"Oh, you're right! I was supposed to be making something to put on our plates tonight. But look at yourself—you're dropping your nails."

The water began to boil. Watching his wife as she bent over the oven door, Daisuke placed some more nails in his mouth and took up the hammer again. A strong wind blew in and rain pelted down at a sharp angle from the skylight. The entire house sounded like it was twisting and bending.

CHAPTER THREE

Tree on the Hilltop

Swirling powerfully over the cape off Kuchinotsu Harbor, the first strong gusts of wind swept along with big drops of rain. After so many days of scorching heat, the rain came as a great relief as it fell on people's sweat-drained bodies. Soon after, the wind died down as if by magic, and suddenly, here and there, the sound of hammering rose up. And then, as silence fell, the light of day faded.

Nearby, the sea roared. Okayo, more agitated than usual, gazed at her husband's face with a feeling of helplessness. Daisuke was sitting next to his father, turning the pages of the account ledger. The lamplight was especially weak that evening. As a precaution, on account of the wind, he was reading the small characters by the dim light of a wick floating in a dish of oil.

"Hmm, the tide's out. That's quite a roar from the sea," Daisuke said, sensing Okayo's gaze fixed on him. Matsukichi, who had been weaving straw sandals in the dark, earthen-floored room, stood up, holding his work in his hands.

"Looks like it's going to blow real strong tonight. When the tide comes in, it'll be a high one."

With Matsukichi talking on about the sea, Okayo felt her anxiety ease a bit. Nisuke stopped writing and looked up.

"Well, I'm glad to see it's gotten dark enough. Now's the time. Round up the others, all right?"

Immediately, the men stood up. Gathered there to work in the earthen-floored room while the storm raged, they all had been listening for signs from outside. Daisuke nodded to Matsukichi and they headed out, as if the hushed silence outside were sucking them in.

As she watched their quick movements, Okayo guessed that it had to do with the supply of grain. *They must be trying to get the grain that Yazō unloaded earlier today and stored in the shed by the boat landing. When the tide comes in they won't be able to use the road along the beach. When Nisuke said, "Now's the time," he must have been talking about delivering the grain to the villagers without the officials noticing. If they go now, they'll have time before high tide. And the darkness will help to hide their movements.*

The landing is on the opposite side of the inlet from the lord's rice storehouses. If the guards saw them, they'd confiscate the grain, wouldn't they? The sounds from the sea were growing louder, as if they might swoop down on her. Okayo glanced at her mother-in-law.

Despite the anxiety of the night, Omiyo was starting to sew a finely decorated ball. Calmly, in the dim light, she continued winding red strands of thread around the ball and sewing them in. In the darkened room, with most of the men gone, only the small decorated ball glowed with a faint light.

Oume was slowly crushing some dried mugwort that was spread on a straw mat and sorting out the bits of down that came from its leaves. She was preparing *mogusa* for moxa treatment.

"What with the storm and the drought coming together, we've had quite a spell of it, and today's been so busy. But if we get enough rain and if the rain doesn't bring too much trouble, let's celebrate," Omiyo said to Nisuke, who had been looking quite worried since Daisuke left. Just then, there was a gust of wind so strong it seemed to be sucking out the guts of Heaven.

"Whoa—here it comes!"

Biting off the end of a strand of red thread, Omiyo glanced at her husband. Just as Okayo noticed her mother-in-law smile and thought how much she resembled the Kannon at Igawa in Futae, the lamp blew out. The image of the ball in Omiyo's hand, so like the sacred orb of Kannon-sama, remained imprinted in Okayo's mind. Under the creaking ceiling, the remaining group relit the small wick of the lamp and held an evening Mass.

Although the storm was blowing outside, in Ninagawa Sakyō's house, time passed as if they were deep beneath the waves.

Ever since the Ninagawas' son Ukon had met Shirō in Nagasaki that spring, the two had been close. For a while, Ukon had been worried that the Christian books published in Amakusa, Kazusa and Nagasaki might have been scattered and lost when the government expelled the missionaries. He hoped to find and save any that remained. Henmi Juan had strongly urged him to do this. "While I'm still alive, please collect those books and ask me about anything in them. I want to pass on all the things I learned at the seminary and college," he had told Ukon.

After that, Juan had started visiting the Ninagawa house to discuss academic matters. During the past thirty years or more of oppression, a number of people had been imprisoned simply for possessing Christian writings. Some had burned the books before they were found, and Juan worried that if important books like the *Doctrina Chirishitan* were lost entirely, the carefully-preserved essence of their prayers would also be lost. His worries reflected the pressures that came along with the pleasure he took from scholarly work in his old age.

Fortunately, Yazō had made good use of his extensive connections in Nagasaki to patiently search for any Christian books that had been hidden away. In spring, he had shown up one day when Juan was preparing tea for Ukon and announced with great joy, "I found them—and they're all in one place!" Juan had been so elated that he almost spilled the hot water in the wooden ladle he was holding.

Immediately afterwards, Ukon had gone with Yazō to Nagasaki and met Shirō in the house where he was living temporarily.

First, he had been introduced to the slender woman who was in charge of the house. As Yazō had already explained to Ukon, this woman had been a supporter of the town's Christian charitable center, back when it still existed.

The woman greeted Ukon fondly, as if she already knew a lot about him.

"Well, I'm so glad you've come. I've been hoping there might be someone who could keep these things safe. You've come just in time."

Looking at the two visitors, who seemed surprised to hear such remarks right at the outset, she had continued:

"Yes, listen—just the day before yesterday, the police searched a Chinese ship with no notice whatsoever. There must have been an informant."

"What? A Chinese ship? Did they find anything?"

"They found a Christian book. A Chinese sailor had it, but nobody could read it—or at least that's what they said."

"They couldn't read it because it was written in Chinese?"

"No, it was in some European language. The police could tell it was a prohibited book from the design on the cover. They dragged the sailor off the ship and threw him in jail."

"Hmm. It looks like we'll have to be careful."

"I've been so worried, waiting for you to come. Unless we get these religious writings away from Nagasaki soon and hide them somewhere safe, I'll be too ashamed to face the priests."

"Well, I must say you've protected them very well until now."

"It's such a load off my mind. Are you the one who'll be keeping the books?"

The woman had looked a little over fifty. She gazed at Ukon and sighed deeply.

"I'm so grateful to be allowed to care for such precious books," he replied

"But I'm so grateful to *you*. I've heard a lot about you from Yazō-dono. And now I see that you're just the person I've heard about."

Ukon blushed.

"So—my great thanks. And now, could I ask you to wait here for a moment?"

The woman bowed and went off into the back of the house. Outside, it was already growing dark.

Ukon had heard this was a shop that dealt in Chinese goods. Shelves had been built into both sides of the earthen-floored room that led to the back of the house. They held an old statue of the Buddha, a beautiful brass flower vase, some pieces of ivory and various other items. An indescribable fragrance filled the room. Ukon found himself sniffing the air, wondering if it might be the smell of the musk and aloeswood that Juan had spoken about.

When his eyes had adjusted to the dim light, he realized that the room also contained various kinds of lustrous fabrics with woven designs. He wondered if these might be the kinds of damask silks and figured fabrics from China that his mother had told him about. "Do you find them interesting?" Yazō had asked, rubbing his thigh.

"Very much so. And does she also sell aromatic wood?"

"Yes, she does. Ah, that's right, Ukon-dono—you studied tea ceremony under Juan, so perhaps you have a special interest in this kind of wood?"

"I don't have a particular interest in it, but a while back Juan-sensei said he wished that, sometime, he could burn some aloeswood."

On Christmas Days, Juan had a custom of serving tea to friends who stayed after the ceremony. Although he didn't use incense at most of his tea ceremonies, he seemed to think that Christmas was special and he burned it in the tea room on that occasion. He used to say that Father Valignano had been very knowledgeable about the tea ceremony.

"Some of the Christian daimyo were among the most distinguished followers of the tea master Sen no Rikyū," he explained. "They vied to obtain various kinds of incense to burn. But Valignano-sama used to say that we shouldn't ostentatiously make a lot of smoke when we burn incense, even if it's a good one. Instead, we should burn it sparingly and elegantly."

Together, the two recalled these conversations they had enjoyed with Juan.

Once, Juan had said, "I've never used it myself, but one day I'd like to try burning aloeswood as incense."

Chijiiwa Bannai, who had been at the tea ceremony that day, had jumped in: "Speaking of incense, no one talks about putting it in our helmets to go off to battle anymore."

"In our helmets, going off to battle, eh?"

Juan had fallen silent, a faint light shining from his deeply wrinkled, half-opened eyes.

And so, inside the shop filled with smells so different from those in most houses, Ukon had felt as if Juan's voice were calling to him from that day. When he looked up, he found a boy standing inconspicuously in front of him, holding a lamp with a paper shade.

"Might you be Ukon-sama?"

Immediately, Ukon stood up.

"Okattsama asked me to show you in. Would you please come this way?"

"Okattsama" was Nagasaki dialect for the woman in charge of a large household. Although the sun hadn't yet set, it was already quite dark in the tree-covered courtyard that extended from the dirt-floored entryway. As he turned the lamp around, the boy looked back for a moment.

"Watch out for the roots of the wisteria vines as you walk."

In the lamplight, the wisteria vines looked enormous, like giant snakes. Beyond the trees, a brighter light shone from another room.

Okattsama, who had been waiting for them, untied a purple *furoshiki* and spread it over a sturdy foreign-made desk.

"Well, now I can show you the books. Please look them over."

The boy was about to stand and leave, but she stopped him.

"Could you please bring in the candle stand we use when we read the *oratio*?"

Ukon watched closely as he nodded and left the room.

"He's a bit different, but I've been looking after him," the woman said. Still, Ukon felt uncertain about this young person who acted so unlike most merchants' sons.

Under the light from the candles the boy brought in, Ukon was finally able to take a good look at the treasured books. They included the *Guia do pecador*, the *Hidesu no kyo,* which was the first chapter of the *Symbolum Apostolicum*, the *Apostles' Creed* and *Spiritual Training*.

"Please—pick them up."

After carefully examining the cover of each book, one by one, front and back, Ukon began leafing through their pages. Seated beside him, the boy also looked at the books. Okattsama watched, touched with deep emotion. She glanced at Yazō and they nodded to each other.

On the evening the storm hit, Shirō sensed a certain heaviness at the Ninagawa house where Yazō had brought him to stay, even amidst the gracious reception he received—so gracious that he found it almost painful. Later, he learned that the Ninagawas' second son, who had been his age, had died in an epidemic one year earlier. Perhaps when the Ninagawa family looked at Shirō they saw their own son in him.

When Shirō and Ukon met again this time, they recalled their deep feelings from that evening in Nagasaki. The creaking and groaning that rose up all about the house sounded like the cries of a great trial being visited on them by God.

"When we met before, I wasn't able to ask you about the landlady at the house in Nagasaki. What sort of person is she?"

Ukon wanted to know more about this woman because he had been so moved by her parting words. He remembered how, as he was about to say goodbye on the morning after he received the sacred books, she had spoken to him in a choked voice.

"I've taken care of these books until today, and I've prayed every morning and every night. Twenty years ago—you weren't even born then—I'll never forget it. It was in the year of the tiger, and here in Nagasaki, we risked our lives to hold a sacred procession. We'd heard that the Nagasaki governor had announced he was going to tear down the cathedral—down to its very last stone—and that he was going to force all the Christians—down to the very last believer—to renounce our faith. And so, in groups, we believers got up and swore an oath of allegiance to the faith and asked Deus-sama for mercy and forgiveness of our sins. Then we marched through the city, from church to church.

"Seven groups continued the marches for a number of days, and in the course of the processions some did penance. One man, dressed in purple, carried a cross on his shoulders. The muscles of his shoulders became ripped and torn. He scourged himself with a whip until blood flowed. Children, too, dressed in purple, marched along chanting litanies. It was such a stirring procession. Resigned to fate and carrying a beautiful statue of the infant Yesus-sama on a carriage stand, we marched with our palms pressed together in prayer. Even people of other religions lined up to watch in silence.

"These books were given to me by the padre who stayed at my house during the processions. Soon afterwards, he, too, was crucified … These books hold the memories of that day when litanies rang out in Nagasaki. I present these precious books to you along with the spirit of the people who joined the processions."

Shirō's hesitant voice pulled Ukon back to the present.

"About Okattsama—I don't really know what sort of person she is. Her real name is Onami-sama. She's both very strict and very kind."

"Onami-sama? I've never met a woman like her. I can't forget her. And her house is unusual too."

"It sure is. And there are always lots of women in it."

"Because of her trading business?"

"No. They come to ask for advice. I was told by people who know her that she was once a prostitute."

Ukon looked at him solemnly as he continued.

"Maria Magdalena—she, too, had been a prostitute. She shed her tears on Chirisuto-sama's suffering feet and anointed them with scented oils and wiped them with her long hair."

"I remember that name."

"She was the woman who went to the cemetery after Chirisuto-sama was crucified, and met an angel who foretold his resurrection."

"I can see you know a lot about such things."

"Somehow, I think of Onami-sama as a reincarnation of Maria Magdalena."

"Why is that?"

"Well, other women who look like they might be prostitutes, too, come to see her and she listens to their stories. Afterwards, they seem peaceful. Okattsama sees them off in tears."

From the shadow of the candle's flickering flame, Shirō stared at Ukon through his long lashes, as if projecting a light that shone from the intensity of his thoughts. To Ukon, it seemed strange to hear someone as young as Shirō talk about things like that. *I've never thought about the lives of prostitutes—never even considered that their world might have any connection to mine. But here, this young person has been trying to shine the light of the Savior on their lives. How deep his spirit is.*

Come to think of it, when I left Okattsama's house she whispered to me, "He's been my guardian angel. Please think of him as a brother and help him through the many years."

Since the destruction of the churches, each believer has kept alive an invisible church in their heart. And in her shop she, too, must be doing the work of those invisible Nagasaki churches.

"When I was at her house, Okattsama laughed and said you weren't cut out for business. But it seems to me she does a lot more than tally up figures herself, even if she calls herself a merchant."

Shirō smiled with an almost cherubic expression.

"If we chase after numbers, there's no end to it, and ultimately everything becomes empty."

"Empty? Well, perhaps so."

"But if I say that—then, really, everything becomes meaningless."

Ukon stared at Shirō's mouth, surprised by his words.

"Everything, not just humans, brings about an effect the moment it is born into this world, and, in turn, this effect becomes yet another cause, and so everything is bound together without limit. And I, too, am bound up in this endless chain of cause and effect."

A dense cloud seemed to hover between Shirō's eyebrows, which until then had been moving calmly. He was trying to express things that had never even occurred to Ukon. After a silence during which Shirō seemed to be looking for the right moment to speak, he confided quietly, "To tell the truth, on a Chinese ship, I saw a child with his leg bound in chains."

Ukon silently watched Shirō's face.

"According to Okattsama, that child must have been either sold or kidnapped."

"... Now that you mention it, I've heard that the Portuguese ships trade in slaves, too."

"I wonder where that child was sold from? What kind of parents did he have? His toes were all caked with dirt. One of his ankles—he must have been about ten years old—was shackled in an iron chain."

Ukon thought of his younger brother who had died in the epidemic the year before. Ukon had often washed his ankles when he was an infant. And before laying him in the grave he had held his feet and washed them carefully, even between the toes, and wept. Suddenly, he recalled the story he had heard a number of times from his mother about the martyred family of Hayashida Sukezaemon. An image of their eleven-year-old boy being burned to death along with his parents rose up before his eyes. The flames had touched the boy's clothes and hair at the spot where he was tied to a post, with his parents tied to other posts. Together, they were chanting the name "Santa Maria." And as the rope that bound him burned and fell away, he was calling out for his mother, who was also burning in the flames.

With agonizing breaths, the mother had called out to her child, as if embracing him, and looked up to Heaven. Then she had said:

"Let us go there together."

Ukon wondered if it was right for him to have felt happier for the child who had been called to Heaven in front of all those people than for the child whose shackled leg Shirō had seen. These thoughts weighed so heavily on him that he found it hard to talk about them.

"Just think of how the *capitan* of that ship bought and sold people. And think of the sailors, too. And all of them could read the Scriptures, couldn't they?"

Ukon just nodded.

"Our world is in great chaos now."

"A while ago you said it was empty."

"Yes. You could call it a bottomless void."

"And do you think it's from such a place that our world will be created anew?"

"I suppose that's the way all things are born and pass away."

"But if that's so, then is there no need for Deus-sama?"

"No, that's the very reason for the existence of the One who contemplates the order of the entire world. It seems that we humans are merely spinning round and round, pushed along by all the goings on of the world."

Gravely, the boy listened to the storm howling above him.

"*Inferuno*—what do you think about it?"

"By knowing about the existence of *Inferuno,* people can think about their own sins. When I saw the chain on the leg of that faceless child, I realized deep down that our faults and sins were to blame."

"And at such times, where is Deus-sama?"

"*Beyond* such things."

The sounds of the storm made the two young people feel tense as they stood face to face. A greasy sweat formed on Ukon's brow. The depths of his eyes turned pale and he let out a long breath.

Ukon clenched his fists, trying to calm the shivers running through his entire body, as if he'd been struck from overhead by a bolt of lightning. This was the first time he had ever felt such emotions. With deep affection filling his heart, he found himself gazing wordlessly at Shirō, whose appearance reminded him of his brother. *It seems this boy right here in front of me has been sent to this land tangled in the sufferings of the world to atone for our sadness. But how can I impose such a vision on a boy of barely fifteen?* Shirō was staring at him, his gaze like a flame in water.

Even as the storm raged and howled, Ukon's mother could hear the two young people in the next room talking and occasionally breaking into quiet laughter.

"You know, these days we hardly ever see Ukon looking so happy. What do you suppose they're talking about?" she asked her husband.

"Well, they're young and they have all sorts of things to discuss. But I wonder if they're paying enough attention to this wind and rain. We can't let those precious books get wet."

A strong gust of wind blasted up from beneath the floor, making it feel as if the entire house was being hoisted up. The husband and wife glanced at each other.

Ukon's younger sister Mizuna burst into his room shrieking, "Brother—our house—it's blowing away!" The candle's flame swayed, then suddenly went out. The candle stand was an old one from Portugal that their father secretly took pride in.

"We're not going to be blown away," Ukon said in a cheerful, reassuring voice to Mizuna, who was standing in the dark, looking petrified.

"I'm scared. Let's stay together."

"Mizuna, what's all this fuss about? You should be ashamed," their mother said quietly, coming into the room. Holding a candlestick, she felt her way forward with her toes as the entire house rasped and wheezed.

"Mother, is our house going to be blown away? It's making such awful creaking sounds."

"You're right. It's making sounds."

"I'm scared."

"You're not really scared, are you? How old are you now? Behave yourself."

Mizuna was two years younger than Shirō.

"Brother, let's stay together with Mother."

"Your brother and our guest have important things to talk about.

And also, it will be better if we sit in several places to help hold the house down—right, Ukon?" The candle in her hand cast its flickering light on the smiling faces of Ukon and the guest.

"Here's some oil paper."

After setting down her load, she looked up at the ceiling.

"It looks like the rain hasn't gotten to them yet. Talking is important, but those books—could you ask our guest to help wrap them in this oiled paper so they don't get wet from the rain? And, Mizuna, don't just stand there—would you fix the candles in the stand?"

Ukon woke around daybreak, vaguely sensing some sort of commotion around him. It sounded like fragments of people's voices. He had talked long into the night and worked hard at wrapping the books, and then fallen into a deep sleep. When he woke and looked about, he noticed that pieces of straw had fallen from the ceiling and lay scattered all over the tatami floor, and there was a smell of soot. Soot also spotted the edges of Shirō's futon.

"Last night Ukon talked on so long, you mustn't have gotten much sleep," Ukon's mother said, looking apologetic.

The smell of hot porridge wafted into the room, mixing with the odor of soot, and soon breakfast was underway.

"It sure was a bad storm. The waves are still rough, so the boats won't be going out."

"Please, stay with us as long as you like," Ukon's father Sakyō said. His outer appearance was all conscientious seriousness, but when he spoke his charm showed through.

When Ukon stepped outside and took a look around, he was astonished. The house's thick straw roof was twisted and warped. On top of it lay a large broken bough that had blown over from the neighbor's camphor tree. Limbs and branches had broken off and blown into the front garden that lead to the street. Getting away for other things would have to wait until they did some major cleanup work. While he was surveying the damage, Kumagorō came rushing in, his hair disheveled.

"The people at the old folks' house—they've all been swept away by the waves!"

"What?"

"The entire house was washed away!"

Everyone stood bolt upright.

"Suzu and Okayo-sama are at their wits' ends. They've been going back and forth along the beach. We had a hard time getting them to come back."

"What's happening there now?" Sakyō asked.

"We've formed groups and they're out searching the coastline. But my master says he has something urgent he needs to talk to you about. He said he really should have come here himself; but, as you can imagine, he's completely caught up in the work, so he asked if you could come to him."

Kumagorō's shoulders shook as he looked up at Sakyō from bended knee. After drawing a breath, Sakyō replied:

"I see. Well, I'd like to go right now, but we have a lot to deal with in our group of houses too. Tell him I'll go as soon as I clear up things here a bit."

Sakyō turned to his son.

"All right then, let's get to work. First, we need to look around the neighborhood and find out what's happened. Ukon—I want you to go out and check on things."

"Yes, right away."

"Don't rush—you might overlook something."

"I'll be careful. And Shirō-dono, will you come with me?"

"Yes, I'll go with you."

During this short discussion other people had been rushing in to report on the damage. Soon, Shirō started to understand how the Ninagawa family served as the center of the *confuraria* group. Mizuna worked briskly in cleaning up the soot-covered room. She looked very different from the young girl he had seen the night before. Messengers came in, one after another.

"As far as I can see, not a single house has escaped damage."

"The embankment and the roadway in Ushikubo are all washed out."

"Jisaku's fields are so covered with mud they're unrecognizable."

"And the tide washed up over Yozaemon's land, and the soil in his fields along the river was carried away with the gravel and debris."

"Yozaemon's fields?" Sakyō moaned.

Yozaemon was one of the leading farmers of Kuchinotsu and an important member of Sakyō's *confuraria* as well. His rice fields sat along a small river leading to the ocean, and people knew that his little water wheel always turned faithfully, drawing water into the fields even in times of drought. He'd rigged up various contrivances to ensure that water also reached the neighboring fields, but people couldn't help noticing the especially good color of his own fields. The ears of grain stayed full even when the river dried up, and he could still take in a decent harvest.

He lived simply and frugally, but many times when things got hard in the area, he had opened his grain stores and given freely to others. For that reason, people spoke quietly of "Yozaemon's storehouse of compassion."

Remembering Nisuke's messenger, Sakyō realized just how serious the situation was. His wife, her kimono sleeves tucked back, brought in tea and placed it silently in front of him. Then, in a very small voice, she said, "I have to say, our grain stores are almost empty. Last night, when Yazō-yan came with the guest he brought us about five portions, mixed with some adzuki beans. That's why I was able to make bean porridge this morning for the first time in ages."

Sakyō's face snapped back to attention and he returned his wife's look. She hardly ever mentioned the state of affairs in their kitchen.

I suppose I've taken it for granted that my wife will always take care of things at home whenever something happens. I've been so wrapped up with the land taxes and the unpaid rice levy and all of that, I haven't even asked her about our own household affairs. How has she managed up to now?

"So, you're saying ... our stores are empty?"

"I didn't say they're *empty*. We still have a little millet, and some soybeans. And we have a few of those summer beans from last year, all shrunken and smaller."

"That bad, is it?"

"Well, yes, but with all this rain we've had, perhaps we can plant an autumn crop of vegetables like daikon and some other things."

People continued to come and go as they talked. Sakyō felt uneasy as he realized, once again, that he was not only the leader of a group of Christians and a village, but also the head of his own household. As he watched the people pass along in front of him, he thought of their principles and their faith; matters that connected all of the believers. For them, he would certainly give his life. But even if he did his utmost to memorize and act upon all of the principles of his faith, that seemed of no use in the terrible situation facing them. No; he didn't say it was futile, but the rules and principles alone didn't give him the strength he needed to clear a path through their predicament.

That happy time they had just spent at breakfast—thanks to the grace of God and mixed with the good smells of the adzuki porridge they had enjoyed with their young guest—what had that been? Sakyō raised his head and told himself to stop feeling this way.

Old holly trees had been uprooted and lay upturned on their sides. Though their trunks were hollow, the branches were covered with little green berries. *When winter comes and the berries turn red, birds flock to these trees and pick at them. But I've never heard of humans eating the berries.* Sakyō chided himself for thinking about such stupid things.

He felt reassured to see that Ukon, who was normally so absorbed in his studies that he didn't pay much attention to mundane affairs, was acting different today and had gone out to check on the neighborhood. *The Christian teachings aren't an academic matter. It's at times like this that Ukon has to demonstrate the true, living meaning of the teachings, through his actions. But then, so do I.*

But what should I do, and how? Starvation is about to hit all the villages around here, and I hear that people in other neighborhoods have started whipping themselves in penance, hoping to be saved. I wouldn't do that, but if it's God who does the whipping, then I'll take it. The whip, it seems, comes from both without and within. I'm ready to stand up and walk into the midst of pain.

Sakyō listened attentively to the grave reports of damage, his expression serious. There could be no doubt that the other villages were also in a critical state. He thought it necessary to call an emergency meeting with all the village headmen and leaders who had been summoned the other day to the magistrate's place, so they could quickly make plans and start repairing the damage.

It was after midday, after all the people had been taken care of, when Sakyō was finally able to go to Nisuke's house. One elderly person from the group of houses Sakyō was in charge of had been sent to live in the old folks' house, which was now gone. Soon after Kumagorō left, Sakyō sent some people to Nisuke's house to help search for the missing elderly residents. Word was that huge waves, the likes of which people living along the coast had never seen before, had washed away other houses, too. And more than ten boats were still missing, even though their owners had carefully pulled them up onto land and tied them to banyan trees.

Looking distressed, Nisuke and Daisuke were talking to the people gathered at their house.

"Building that house so near the coast was a mistake. People put their loved ones in my hands, and I failed them."

Nisuke placed his hands on the ground and for a while was unable to lift his head. The decision to build the house in that place had not been his alone. The leaders had decided together.

Everyone in the area, even those who lived near the mountains, grew up loving the seashore and going there often. In their leisure time they watched the boats coming and going and the many people who passed by. When the weather was good, they dug for shellfish and listened to the voices of children playing. The community leaders chose the site because they thought the old people would enjoy these things, and they had carefully checked to be sure the footing wasn't dangerous before constructing the simple building. But now, in spite of everything, the worst had happened. They should have built the house on higher ground.

Without raising his head, Nisuke muttered, "It looks as if we built the house there so it would be washed away …"

"Now don't say that—don't talk that way. It was a natural disaster. It couldn't have been helped. Everybody knows the house was built as well as could be and the old people there were well taken care of," Sakyō said, looking around for Suzu. He'd heard that although she was an orphan taken in by Nisuke's family, she saw it as her responsibility to care for the old people in the house, and in truth she did much more than the adults. She was greatly admired. But now she was nowhere to be seen.

Kumagorō said she was beside herself with grief. Of course she was. She was probably off by herself somewhere, crying.

"We can't undo what's happened," Sakyō added. "So start by taking your hands off the ground. There are lots of urgent things we have to take care of."

Nisuke looked as if he had shrunk. Daisuke was sitting quietly behind him with his mouth firmly shut. His normally easygoing face had turned pale and ghastly.

"Daisuke-dono, how much older are you than my son Ukon?"

"I'm five years older than Ukon-dono. But I'm not much for studying."

"Well, all he does is read books. He doesn't know the first thing about farming or people. Do you think you might teach him something about the insects in the fields and the flowers of the eggplants?"

All around, people laughed, and suddenly the heavy mood lifted. Soon after, Yazō came in with a group of young people.

Those who had been seated half rose. They wanted to thank Yazō for the grain he had brought the night before, and also to express their sympathy for his missing boats. But more than anything, just seeing his face renewed their spirits.

"Well, that sure was some wind we had," they said to one another.

The village headmen and neighborhood leaders met from time to time, but today's group was more varied. Everyone had rushed over without time to fuss about clothing and such, but they were happy simply to see each other after a long absence. And now, with Yazō there, the mood suddenly brightened. By the time Ukon and Shirō got there, the gathering was verging on festive.

When people noticed the unfamiliar young person with Ukon, the boisterous room turned quiet. In the back of the room, Juan puffed smoke from a long-stemmed pipe.

"Sensei, thank you for taking the trouble to join us," Ukon said to him, placing his hands on the floor to bow in greeting.

Taking his pipe from his mouth, Juan replied simply, "It's nothing," then gestured with his jaw toward Nisuke as if to say they should be greeting the others first.

Yazō smiled as he watched the two young men turn respectfully toward Nisuke and Daisuke. It was clear that Ukon and Shirō had renewed their easygoing friendship the night before. He was glad that Shirō had stayed with Ukon's family. Perhaps it was a good thing the day had been so unusual.

After Ukon finished reporting on the places he had checked on, the crowd that had come to help and talk began to leave. Everyone was worried about what was happening at their own place. Before heading home, those who had had elderly family members living at the old people's house took particular care to offer words of consolation to Nisuke. Ukon was deeply moved.

If three days passed without finding any survivors, they would conduct a funeral service on top of a hill overlooking the sea. Until then, they would concentrate on cleaning up. Together, they would make sure there were no more injuries. As Daisuke listened to everyone talking and calling out to each other, he felt deeply grateful. But some casual questions nagged in his thoughts:

"Haven't you seen Suzu?"

"She must be heartbroken."

The words brought tears to Daisuke's eyes and made him feel ashamed. Seeing his father more dejected than he ever had before, he clenched his fists.

I have to get a hold on myself. It would be wrong to ignore the support that Sakyō and Ukon and all the others are giving us by being here. Four people died in one night. Any thoughts of how we might have built the old folks' house on higher ground are just empty hindsight. That house was proof of our unceasing faith and it was built on the tenets of our beliefs.

The okite *commandment tells us to "care for your neighbors as you would for yourself." But the words "as you would for yourself"—what do they mean?*

Daisuke put the question to himself and then looked at his father's back. He noticed that he had let his head droop, as if his neck had caved in.

It seems my father, too, must be taking the okite *to heart. Confession before the Lord—this feeling now, is that what it means? Am I truly a believer?*

Because I was brought up in a Christian family, I've never questioned the foreign practices and rituals my parents taught me. There are some Buddhists in town, but when I hear the old folks reciting their namu amida butsu prayers, they seem like no more than old customs. The padres used to call their beliefs the talk of the devil—though I don't agree. But those so-called "heathens" came running to help us, and they've helped with the searching and the distributing of food.

If I ever felt any superiority towards "heathens," it seems vain and pointless now. And when I think of Suzu's frenzy and despair, I feel ashamed, as if I should just vanish. I feel as if I've been acting for show; as if I were her protector since I'm the son of a village headman. But isn't it Suzu who with her own body has been caring for her neighbors as she would for herself? Me—I've just mouthed the words of the okite *as a matter of form. There's been no real spirit behind my beliefs and my faith.*

When I held Suzu—when she was holding on to that banyan tree, shaking and gazing at the sea—I felt like I'd been struck by a bolt of lightning. With her body shaking, that child—she isn't even ten—she went off searching for the old people she'd been taking care of until just yesterday. She hasn't been able to eat or drink all day.

She stared the adults in the eye, questioningly, and when she realized she couldn't get answers from us, she went and stared at the sea, shaking, not knowing who she could ask about all the things she couldn't hold in her young heart.

I didn't know how to take care of her. I … I couldn't approach her naturally, or quickly. Could it be that this orphan has been sent by our Lord? When I held her, the words of the okite *rang out in my head like reverberations from a cracked bell. I wonder—can we ever truly care for our neighbors as we do for ourselves? These are truly frightening words.*

Those old people who were washed away by the waves, what sort of people were they? I'll have to ask Suzu again. It seems that is my confession.

As Daisuke stared at his father's back, tormented by these questions, he realized that someone was approaching. Turning, he saw Yamada Yomosaku, the artist, sliding across the floor on his knees toward him.

"I'm sorry to ask you about this now with all that's going on, but I wonder if those books and writings you've stored in your house are safe," he asked the Ninagawas, his head thrust forward.

Since most of the crowd had gone home, those who remained heard the conversation clearly.

"Fortunately, they're all right," Ukon said, lowering his head.

Yomosaku sighed in relief.

"Well, I'm glad to hear that. As for my house, ten or so of my precious canvas paintings got soaked by the rain."

"That must be quite a disaster for you," Sakyō said sympathetically, leaning toward him.

Yomosaku nodded gently. He moved the thumb of his right hand against his fingers and mumbled something, as if talking to his fingers.

Yomosaku had studied painting at the art school connected to the Shiki Seminary and had painted the image for the cathedral altar. The believers had called it the "holy figure," and displayed it at every ceremony. During the Arima times he had been supported by the clan, but he had stopped serving them after the apostasy of their lord and the transference of their fief to Hyūga. He showed up occasionally at the gatherings of believers.

Even after the Matsukura clan took over administration of the domain, Yomosaku had continued to do well. People in power valued his talent and commissioned him to paint screens and other things, so he was able to make a living. He had a different temperament from both the samurai and the farmers, and was seen as an unusual person and given special consideration.

With arms folded, Juan asked, "So, will you be able to get some new canvas to make up for it?"

"Well, there might be a way," Yomosaku answered absently. Juan and Sakyō worried that Yazō would have to take care of this. They had heard that Yomosaku's canvases were made of a specially woven silk. For the farmers and fishers who couldn't read, the "holy figure" must have held a particular significance, different from what it meant to the samurai. For the sake of the *confuraria*, it was essential that Yomosaku should continue painting.

As Daisuke listened to them talk, he felt his eyes opening again and realized that even among the believers, there were some unusual people. He felt that this realization gave him a wider perspective. As the remaining visitors watched Yomosaku leave and began to stand up, a young voice said, "Thank you for welcoming me here yesterday when I visited for the first time."

Shirō was placing his hands on the floor, greeting Nisuke.

As if his muffled voice was calling them back, they all stopped to watch the exchange.

"I heard about what happened at the old folks' house. Everyone says you took good care of the people there for a long time. This moves me deeply. It will stay with me throughout my life."

The visitors thought that they, too, had shared words of sympathy; and yet, somehow, there was a difference. Shirō's voice had a quality that moved their hearts. At first, Nisuke seemed lost in thought.

"Well, I ..." he began, but finding himself unable to continue, simply bowed. Even then, he looked as if he were having trouble controlling his emotions.

"I'm sorry to bother you when you're so busy, but I'd like to ask Daisuke-dono a favor," Shirō said.

"All right."

"I'd like to see that young girl Suzu I met yesterday."

Daisuke nodded as if he had expected this. "Could you wait just a minute?" he said, then stood and went out.

Wanting to see what came of the conversation between the two, Juan sat down again slowly. Following his lead, the others, too, sat down, with puzzled expressions.

Soon, Suzu came in, with Okayo holding her shoulder. She seemed surprised to find everyone looking at her. Trying to step backwards, she stumbled and then sat down unsteadily. She looked timid, completely different from the evening before when she gave Shirō the white spider lily.

No one spoke. At the back of the room, Yazō was clearing his throat. A few moments later, Shirō sat down and crossed his legs.

"So, we're meeting again," Shirō said gently.

Suzu, looking surprised, said nothing.

"Everyone told me you did good work at the old people's house."

Suzu looked up at Shirō with expressionless eyes, then looked down again. It seemed she hadn't understood him.

"You've been searching all over for the old men and women. You must be very tired," Shirō said as he glanced at her, his head tilted. "They must have cared a lot for you."

He held her wrist and rubbed the back of her hand. The young girl looked up in surprise. A tiny ray of light, as thin as the eye of a needle, glimmered from her eyes. They glittered as if a dark storm were gathering behind them.

"You worked so hard at picking cranesbill and *ashitaba*."

Suzu shook her head.

"You know, Maria-sama appreciates your work. Here—this is a small present from her for you. Cheer up Suzu, won't you?"

Their conversation seemed to be taking place somewhere else, not in a room filled with people. It was like the tender, pleasant scene of a brother encouraging his younger sister as they stood on a grassy plain with a gentle breeze blowing, or on a boat in the sun.

From beneath his collar, Shirō removed the rosary hanging from his neck and placed it around the neck of the young girl. Its small blue beads glittered in the light.

Looking puzzled, Suzu accepted it and glanced at the men. Then, nervously, she touched the rosary and, after looking at Nisuke, tilted her head to the side. Nisuke held her shoulders and turned her toward Shirō.

"Suzu, he said it's a present for you. Maria-sama appreciates your hard work—it's from her," he said haltingly, his voice choked with emotion.

Suzu turned to her adoptive father and held out her hands, as if asking him for help. Deeply moved, Nisuke embraced her a bit uncomfortably, and started to quietly cry.

A group of people had gathered behind them, watching in silence. The man of nearly fifty years and the young girl embraced each other, both in tears. *Ah*, everyone thought, *this should give Nisuke some solace.*

Nisuke's workers had come to see off the visitors and by chance had witnessed this scene. *Since yesterday morning, strange things have been going on*, Kumagorō thought. *There was that strange red sky at dawn. And Suzu said a dazzlingly handsome man came down from a ship that was flying a red banner. And then, in the midst of the big storm, we brought back that grain. The little house was still standing then.*

Running to the door of the old folks' house, Kumagorō had knocked and called out, "Hey everyone—we brought some barley. Tomorrow you can make a nice porridge. Open the door. Open up!"

"Barley?" the old woman Onatsu had called back. "Ah yes, barley. Well, thank you. I'd like to open the door, but the wind tonight is so strange, we asked to have it boarded up. We can't open it because it's nailed shut from the outside."

Matsukichi and Kumagorō had pried the door open. The room was small and unlit.

"Oh, my goodness—barley!"

Several of the elderly residents had crawled toward the two men and placed their warm hands on them.

"Thank you so much. Coming all this way to bring us grain, and on a night like this."

And then the two men had boarded up the house securely again, as they had been asked to do.

"Early tomorrow morning we'll come back and open the door."

With those words, they had returned home.

The woman's words—*Thank you so much. Coming all this way to bring us grain*—lingered in Kumagorō's ears. And now, moved by Suzu and Nisuke's sobbing, he too began to cry.

Silently, on bended knees, Shirō made the sign of the cross over Suzu and Nisuke. Then, in a barely audible voice, he began reciting:

"We ask, in the name of the Sacrificed One who opens the gates of Heaven, grant us your strength, such that we may receive your assistance. We pray for eternal life in Heaven. *Amen.*"

As if suddenly noticing what was happening, Juan brought his hands together and continued the prayer. One after another, the other men bowed their heads and began to pray. Then the women came in from the kitchen and joined them. With this, the house was unexpectedly turned into a place of worship.

Okayo was behind Daisuke. Although everyone was exhausted and bleary from the past night, Okayo had the strange impression that a pure light was streaming from their bodies, and from her own, as well. Deep in her heart, Okayo felt they were all praying for the dead, and for Suzu and Nisuke, and for themselves as well.

Later, each of them thought back to what had happened. In the past, Juan would have taken the role of the priest. But they had the strong impression that on this night, the voice of the boy had been leading them, and the venerable samurai had humbly followed him in prayer. Not only had those present felt nothing strange about this, they had all joined in rapture.

With everyone asking who this young person was and where he had come from, the Hasuda family and the Ninagawa family felt happy. Even Juan, who wasn't easily excited, smiled and joined eagerly in the discussion:

"We've found a great brother. Now, with such a good young person, and with hard work, we'll be able to pass on the Western learning to future generations. Perhaps we won't be able to build a *seminario* or a *collegio* like the old ones did, but we can call together the people who were connected to those places and start a *confuraria* where young people can study. I too, just once more, want to have a dream. I, too, hope to realize a dream once again."

Juan spoke with high spirits and undaunted enthusiasm.

Yazō's boat was found washed onto the shore near the outlet to the sea, but it was damaged beyond repair. In the fields near the bay there were other washed-up boats, along with all sorts of debris. Tatters of clothing were seen amidst the wreckage. But even after removing the debris, still with hope, no bodies were found. When most of the cleanup work was done, funeral rites for the dead took place on the hill overlooking the sea. Since old Onatsu-sama had been a Buddhist, a Buddhist priest from her family's temple was called in to recite sutras.

This had presented a problem at first, since some villagers said a Buddhist priest shouldn't be there at the funeral, seeing that the padres had called them "devils." They wanted the Buddhist rites done separately.

When this was said, Oume, who normally would never have spoken on such an occasion, had slowly stood up. Wiping her hands on her apron, having just come from the kitchen, she stood for a moment in silence, then turned to face those who had spoken.

"Excuse me, but—"

Her swollen eyelids blinking slowly, she began:

"Are we going to leave old Onatsu-sama alone, even after her death?"

Oume's words brought silence to the entire gathering.

"We all know that Onatsu-sama was a Buddhist. And so am I."

Omiyo glanced anxiously at Nisuke, then looked down again. Oume appeared larger than ever.

"As all of you know, when she was young, Onatsu-sama was sent to Nagasaki and she worked as a prostitute to support her family. When she got older and came back here, she had no family left to look after her. Many times, she used to cry because she didn't have enough money to pay the temple where her ancestors graves were to hold memorial services for her parents. Once she confided to me, 'I've been lucky enough to live in the old folks' home and eat my meals from the same pot as the others, in friendship, but I'm a Buddhist and I wonder if I'll be punished for it.'

"She worried about her future, but she was happy to have been so well cared for by the Christians. Now we're saying we're going to cut our ties with her, just be rid of her? I can't understand that way of thinking."

After this forceful speech, Oume paused, apparently allowing her heated emotions to cool a bit. Slowly she looked up, gazed around at those who were gathered, and continued in a lower voice.

"I, too, have a different religion. But I keep in mind what you call the *okite* about caring for neighbors. 'Care for your neighbors as you would for yourself'—that's what I aim for in my life. In that sense we're all in this together. That is the basic way of all people. It's what my parents taught me, and it's why I'm saying this now. We have to think of all people as just as important as our own selves. As for Onatsu-sama and this talk of holding her funeral in a separate place, I just can't understand it. A group of people with no living relatives were living together, and they died together on the same day ... Is it right for Christians who say *amen* to suggest such a thing? Would you feel good about throwing someone down into *Inferuno*? Has our spirit of mercy been washed away along with the high tide?"

Her body trembling, Oume thrust a big-boned wrist out from the sleeve of her kimono, wiped her tears, and clutched her apron.

Nisuke and Daisuke thought, *She's done it. Oume has done it. Oume, the Buddhist, has taken care of it.*

The murmuring and commotion subsided like the ebbing of the

tide. From then on, the discussion proceeded smoothly, in a deeply emotional atmosphere.

Various people spoke.

"Funerals must be held to comfort the souls of all the dead. Let's hold them beneath the big camphor tree at the top of the hill, facing the sea. Out of consideration for the spirits of Onatsu-sama's ancestors, we'll have a priest from her family's temple come and recite sutras for her. After all, in the old days our own ancestors were connected to that same temple, even if the ties are weak now. After that, we can recite prayers from our own faith."

"Beneath the great camphor tree at the top of the hill—that will truly be a good place. From there we can see the ocean all around. It's the right place for calling out to the souls of the dead. And, yes—that's the tree young children from around here climb up and down, cooling themselves under its shade and eating their lunches, and it's where people watch for boats out at sea and chat together like they have since they were young. The old folks in that house used to sit looking out at the sea and talking, with the young folks running about. Why, when I think back on it now, it was the image of Heaven."

As they talked on, the bitter taste from their earlier discussions wore off. The old folks' talk about creating a heaven in this world seemed to bring a calming effect. It was a wonder how it brought peace to their hearts. Okayo watched Oume-yan nodding along with the conversation, her expression still serious. She wanted to say something to Daisuke, but noticing the strained expression on his face, decided to wait until later.

Around the time when the troubles from the big storm were settling down, Okayo realized that she was pregnant. For some reason, when she first felt the baby move, the image of Oume-yan's solemn face at that meeting came vividly into her mind. At the same time, the image of the great camphor tree on top of the hill, after the funeral when no one was there, hovered about in her thoughts.

Okayo could read hiragana lettering, but she couldn't read kanji characters as her father-in-law and Daisuke could. Oume could understand even fewer of the characters. *What is the history of that great camphor tree? Is it written down somewhere? Do that tree and*

Oume-yan have some special connection? It seems I've known about that big tree and Oume-yan from before I was born. Okayo wondered what Daisuke would say if she were to talk to him of such things.

Okayo talked to the child in her womb about the great tree. In her dreams she saw images of it. With its top branches drawing in rays of sunlight from across the sea, it murmured gently while white clouds scurried above them. Beneath the tree, Oume-yan, with her big eyes squinting in the sunlight as she gazed out over the sea, was cradling a baby in her arms and saying something to it. It was the baby that she, Okayo, had given birth to. When she awoke from her dream, she told Daisuke about it.

"It seems your dream had something to do with deep, divine protection. But what about the baby—did it look like me?"

"Well, I don't really know. It was a baby … so I can't really say."

"That's very vague!"

"What I want to say is, I think Deus-sama and Chirisuto-sama are the most sacred beings in the world, but that big camphor tree is special. I think it might be a god."

"Hmm … well, yes, that tree *is* special."

"I can't help feeling it was that camphor tree, not Deus-sama, that showed me our unborn baby in my dream. Anyhow, I can't say who it looked like, but it was an adorable baby."

"How come you get to have all the good dreams?"

Okayo wanted to say something more about her dream's connections to a deeper world, but their conversation ended there.

A rumor that the magistrate's demands might be eased had spread among the farm workers. Daisuke mentioned to his father that Kumagorō had told him about it.

"No, by no means. We may *want* things to get easier, but it's not going to happen."

With a pained look, Nisuke summoned Matsukichi and Kumagorō.

"We can't start taking it easy just because a rumor's going round. Things are going to get even tougher."

Kumagorō had heard the rumor from his friend Sadaichi. He had rushed in from the rain, saying excitedly, "Those officials, they aren't totally blind. If they just take a look at all the rubble and damage around here, surely they'll understand at a glance, won't they?"

"Right. Once they see the ruins of what used to be fields—why, even fools like us can understand."

"We have the eyes of moles, but those officials, with their good eyes—surely they can see, can't they? What do you say, Kumagorō?"

Sadaichi wasn't the only one hoping this might happen. Matsukichi and Kumagorō had been hearing the same rumor when they traveled around the area repairing roadways and clearing fallen trees. People hoped that for once the officials would hold off on land taxes this year and give them some grain assistance. And hopes led to rumors that the magistrate might actually do such things.

"Well, hope alone won't make things go our way," Matsukichi said matter-of-factly. Oume nodded.

"Maybe we'd have had a chance with our old lord, but when I think about what this one's done so far …"

While she talked, Oume was thinking about teaching Okayo and Suzu how to soak and season some of the *kusagi* leaves she had boiled and dried.

Nisuke often accompanied Daisuke when he visited the Ninagawa family and the people in the neighboring village of Minami Arima. Matsukichi rowed them there in his boat. At those times, Nisuke talked with Daisuke, who was looking more manly recently. Both Omiyo and Okayo found this growing relationship between father and son reassuring, yet they also worried that something serious was about to happen.

From time to time, Daisuke talked to his wife about his thoughts.

"These days, I've been thinking a lot about the teachings of our Lord; about taking care of our neighbors."

"So have I. You've become a lot more important to me than before."

"Don't be silly, talking like that in front of other people."

"What's wrong with it? And it's not only you. With all that's happened, your parents and Oume-yan and everyone else have all become more important to me. They seem more thoughtful, too. Soon, I'm afraid, we may die."

"You're so extreme."

"What I'm saying now isn't extreme. If we don't care for other people, we can't go on living. That's what the word 'important' means, don't you think?"

Impressed by his wife's words, Daisuke gazed at her face. It seemed Okayo had grasped the true meaning of Ninagawa Ukon's lectures on the *Doctrina Chirishitan* without his even realizing it. Or more likely, she'd learned it from the words and actions of Oume-yan the other day.

"Suzu often sits beside Father-in-Law these days, rubbing his back."

"Right."

Daisuke sounded a bit embarrassed.

"Come to think of it, these days I often hear people talking to her."

"Yes, and she's gotten a lot stronger because of it."

"Lately if you ask her about her work, she says she's become Oume-yan's apprentice."

"Aha—so that must be why she's been picking mugwort and *kusagi* a lot lately."

"Yes, although both of those plants are going to seed and starting to dry out."

Doctors came from Shimabara to buy the moxa that Oume made from mugwort. They said hers was so easy to use, that it crumbled beautifully and curled up nicely into balls when they used it. And it didn't leave a lot of burns on the patients when it was used.

"Even though the old folks are gone now, plenty of patients still need it," Oume told Suzu. "If we make moxa, it'll help others."

Oume, of course, also gave out her moxa to those who couldn't see a doctor.

"When I crumble the mugwort to make moxa I recite *namu amida butsu, namu amida butsu*. Then the spirit of Amida-sama burns in each of the moxa preparations and soon the people are well again."

Suzu's eyes opened wide. When Oume saw her face, she smiled with happiness. Then she lowered her voice and continued:

"But Suzu, if you prefer, it will be all right to say *amen*. I wonder what Deus-sama may think about me being your teacher. But surely it won't cause any problems for the people we help."

Already it was harvest time, but the storm had damaged the crops more than expected and they hadn't recovered well. Nevertheless, some spots had escaped the ravages of the winds and water, where they could still gather a little millet, buckwheat, foxtail millet and other grains. People talked with envy about the upland rice growing in a few lucky fields. Although the upland rice ears, with their small grains, had fallen onto the ground, people had been able to harvest and use them. But they realized that, all in all, it was a meager harvest and it wouldn't be enough to carry them through until the next year. They wondered how they would survive on the scarce grain, and a feeling that they were making their last stand spread among them.

A meeting was planned at Yazō's house to tell everyone about the latest orders from the magistrate's office and talk about what to do.

"I'm usually not much use in emergencies since I'm always away from home, but this time I'm here working on my damaged boat, so let me invite everyone to my place. I'll have some of my young workers help people get here and back."

Yazō had a feeling they might ask him to deal with the shortage of food and provisions. To do so, he would need everyone's understanding, and the quickest way to get it would be to hold the meeting at his place. During breaks in the discussions, he could provide a little food to warm everyone's bellies. Such were his plans.

When people heard about Yazō's plan, they thought, *Well, people in the samurai class may have big houses, but everyone feels comfortable about going to Yazō's place—it has a kitchen that's easy for the women to work in, and even if the meeting is depressing, at least we'll feel at ease.*

On the night of the meeting, a surprisingly large group gathered. The smell of boiling water mixed with smoke filled the room. And then, after everyone had hurried in and was starting to relax, Yozaemon made a late appearance, accompanied by his son. His face looked unusually somber. As they acknowledged each other with a glance, Yazō wondered what sort of greeting to give him. He had heard that Yozaemon's fields were ruined, but he hadn't been able to pay him a visit to express his sympathy. Then Ninagawa Sakyō stood up.

"In the midst of the trouble we've been having, it's wonderful that all of you could join us. We're going to have to make all sorts of plans, but first we need to hear from you about the situations in your villages."

One by one, the representatives from the villages, from Kushiyama, Arie, Minami Arima, Kita Arima, Kazusa and others, stood up and reported on what had been happening in their areas. In truth, their reports differed considerably from the actual state of things. Mostly, they reported on what they had heard from their talks with others. But they all agreed that as the days passed, the full extent of the damage was proving more serious than they'd realized.

As the reports continued, the genial mood began to fade and here and there groans slipped out. When the reports were done and Nisuke noticed that the meeting had grown quiet, he stood up and began, in a restrained voice, to recount the demands from the magistrate's office on the day before the typhoon. Perhaps because he was trying so hard to control himself, from time to time his voice sputtered, as if threads had been twisted and cut off, but everyone listened attentively, drawn in by each of his words.

After Nisuke sat down, no one spoke for a while. The silence was broken by the screeching of mating cats, much more noticeable than usual. White-haired Juan stood up, his rosary in his hand.

"Well, it looks like we've finally reached the critical moment when we'll either live or die. We have to gather our courage and make up our minds; otherwise, we won't be able to get things in order. And we have to choose representatives to come up with good plans."

For a while, the meeting separated into groups from each of the villages and they held their own discussions.

No matter what, they needed to inform the magistrate's office about the current situation as clearly as possible. They had to argue that unless the government redressed or delayed the unfair land taxes that had been imposed on them these past few years, and if unreasonable demands continued to be made, the villages could not survive. If the officials would just look at the destroyed houses and the rubble-strewn farmlands, surely even they would realize that the situation was unjust and inhumane. Before they received any strange summons, the people would write petitions and sign a joint statement.

Ukon had been sitting quietly at the back of the meeting, but at this point he was called on to help with the writing, along with Daisuke.

They decided that each village would write its own statement, and then they would present them all to the local government office on the same day. The statements would describe the conditions in the villages and call for two things: reductions and exemptions from this year's land tax, and emergency allotments of grain.

A man with white-flecked hair stood up. It was Isayama Chūbei from Kita Arima.

"After the storm, did anyone from the government offices actually come around to check on our villages?"

"Well …"

Both Sakyō and Nisuke started to speak, but it was Sakyō who continued:

"It's strange that we haven't heard anything from them."

In the group from Arima, there were quite a few samurai. Their presence, sitting silently with arms folded, had created a rather intimidating atmosphere.

"In Arima, two officials working for Kurōbei came to have a look, but I hear that all they did was poke around a bit, jot something down without asking any detailed questions of the people and then leave. As for what they wrote—it beats us all."

Then someone from the Kushiyama group spoke out:

"Some of them came to our place too, and they certainly took out their notebooks from under their robes—and then they put them back again right away."

This was met with snickers.

"What do you suppose they wrote down?"

"We were ready to answer any questions they might ask, but they just left, trying not to look at us."

"Well, yes … it was like they were purposely pretending not to see anything. We'll have to keep our guard up."

"First of all, Kurōbei should have come here himself and surveyed the damage with his own eyes."

Suddenly, a chorus of voices broke out, leaving the two notetakers unable to keep up. Isayama Chūbei signaled with his hand, bringing some order to the commotion.

"It seems the magistrate's office has no intention of looking into our troubles seriously," he said. "I have no objection to writing up a joint statement asking for reductions or cancellation of the taxes and for some grain assistance, but judging from their behavior so far, I can't hold out much hope that they'll respond to our petitions favorably. As for the future, what are we going to do if that's the way things turn out?"

A silence like the depths of a well spread through the room. Chūbei's question had touched on the worry harbored in everyone's hearts. Presently, Juan stood up.

"Isayama-dono, certainly, we need to be resolute, and we also need to be prepared for the worst. And I imagine that everyone has their own ideas. But I think that this is good enough for today. If the magistrate's office rejects our petitions, then we'll deal with it when it happens. In each of our *confuraria* let's make plans, and let's meet again soon."

Sighs were heard all around and it was as if the room had been enveloped in a thick fog.

With the meeting concluded, some of the people from distant villages left for their homes, but others who didn't feel ready to leave stayed on. Because of the day's topic, most of those who had spoken up had been samurai, whereas the smaller-stake farmers and the fishers had mostly remained quiet, but now they felt more at ease and began talking.

Ukon, who had hardly ever taken part in such discussions, listened intently. He was moved by their talk, so filled with premonitions about their grave situation. While Nisuke was waiting for a chance to say some words of comfort to Yozaemon and his son, he heard a familiar voice.

"I'd been worried about getting grain assistance, but now, thanks to everyone, we have some hope—right, Saizō?"

When Nisuke turned, he saw that it was Sadaichi, one of the

farm workers. Saizō was a grumpy fellow, whereas Sadaichi seemed quite easygoing. Sadaichi loved get-togethers, and Nisuke supposed this was why he had come today, but he saw no harm in it.

Since Sadaichi didn't own any land, he had no direct connection with paying land taxes. He was, however, very concerned about the grain assistance, and most likely he had attended the meeting with the pretext of helping Yazō. His comments at meetings were often off the mark and invited scorn, but some of the women enjoyed hearing him. "There goes Sadaichi, spouting off again," they would say.

He hadn't been formally entitled to attend the meeting this evening, so no wild remarks had been heard from him then. But now it seemed he wanted to say something before going home.

"But you know, Sada," Saizō cut in, "we can't take it easy yet. Just a moment ago they said we still don't know if they'll send rice, or rocks—you see what I mean? You should know better."

As usual, after being chided by Saizō, Sadaichi pulled his head down. Saizō was a farmer with his own plot of land, albeit a small one.

Ukon realized that until now he had never really listened to the talk of farmers and fishers like these men. Starting on a new sheet of paper, he rushed to record the comments being exchanged among the four or five men seated there.

"I've been feeling really put out; but getting together like this now, I feel a little better."

"Well, we may *feel* a little better, but in the past we've never been grilled like this about paying the land taxes. Why d'you suppose things have come to this?"

"Don't be a fool—ever since the new lord came in, everything's gone bad."

"All right, I know that already. For one thing, it seems like a shadow's crept over our religious faith."

"Right. Why, I remember how, back in the old days, going to Mass felt so glorious and festive."

"My parents used to take me to the Easter services. We went so many times."

The words "Me too!" sprung up here and there around the room.

"On the days of celebration for Chirisuto-sama, our old lord let us take a rest from working the fields, and we dressed up in holiday clothes and walked together in a procession, and everyone looked so beautiful."

"Now things have gotten so tough, and I miss the old times. We hardly ever hear children singing the hymns these days."

"When you think of it, when we praised Deus-sama in the old days it felt like we were praising Hii-sama—the sun."

"Ahh, that's how I felt too."

"It's not that we've given up our beliefs, but the celebration day services and the teachings of the doctrine and catechism seem to be happening in the shadows."

"And come to think of it, back when we were working the fields in the light of the sun—the light of both Hii-sama and Deus-sama—it sustained our bodies and spirits, and our crops did better, too."

"When we get to talking like this, it seems we're thinking pretty much the same way, after all."

"Seems to me that lately, with all the strange weather and the bad harvests year after year, our feelings have all been under a shadow."

"It's like the growing and withering of the crops is mirroring the feelings of the people tending them."

"My old man worries all the time. He says punishment from Deus-sama is coming."

"You too?" the normally taciturn Saizō said, arms folded. "Well, my mother, too—she says the state of the world now is no laughing matter. She says this has happened because we've been hiding our faith too much. When we cut off the light from Hii-sama and Deus-sama, with our own hands, our crops stopped thriving. The proof is in how well the grains and beans did back when we had a Christian lord. And the festivals for Maria-sama were full of life and joy.

"She keeps telling me that if we could just take in our crops and pay the taxes, then the harassments of the Christians might ease up. But we haven't been able to harvest any grain, and we've been hit with all sorts of disasters. She blames herself and talks about how it would be easier if she weren't here—one less mouth to feed. When old folks start crying, it makes the whole household so grim."

"So that's how it is at your place, too? To tell the truth, my mother heard a bad rumor from her nephew who lives near the castle in Shimabara. He said they'd been hanging Christians by their feet and cutting off their noses and ears, but now it's getting worse. The blacksmiths are making even crueler tools, this time for torture. My mother's been telling me to send our children off to our aunt's place in Chikugo, while there's still a chance. She says she doesn't need to be saved, since she doesn't have much longer to live anyway. She says that if things get too bad, she can be offered up and she's ready to be boiled or burned. She's been crying and saying she has a feeling that the time to leave may be coming soon."

"I doubt it'll come to all that, but I can't help wondering if that's the direction we're heading in," Saizō said. He held his breath for a moment and then let it all out at once.

"It looks to me like there's no other way than going back to the old kind of Christianity," he added.

Nisuke sat down next to Yozaemon and his son.

"I've heard that your fields suffered terribly," Nisuke said. "I'm sorry I couldn't visit you to express my sympathy. Please forgive me."

"Please don't mention it. Your family has also been going through so many troubles. You must be under a terrible strain."

"We're all right. But your fields have always held out, even in times of drought. Losing them now, it's really too much to bear."

The two men sighed together. Several days before Daisuke's marriage, Yozaemon's son had also gotten married, and his bride was also from Amakusa, so the two families had grown even closer than before.

Yozaemon's fields—the fields of Kuchinotsu's leading farmer—had been destroyed on the sea side by the high tides, and on the river side by the surge of gravel, trees, and debris.

"Actually, I have something I need to talk to you about in private."

Yozaemon lowered his voice and slid on his knees closer to Nisuke. His son was behind him. He was slender for a farmer's son, but he had a look of manly toughness.

Nisuke felt that this was not the right place to have a private talk, so he whispered something to Yazō and then led the two men to the back room. Shortly after, Yazō joined them and closed the sliding doors. Yozaemon got right to the point.

"On the night of the storm, you brought that precious grain to our place as an offering to Maria-sama. When I think of your kindness, it brings tears to my eyes. And that's why we've decided to do this."

Yozaemon glanced back at his son.

"Actually, we still have a small store of old grain at our place. Since we've had to put off the tax payments all these years, the number of sacks we owe the magistrate as back payments has increased to over thirty. We can hardly do anything about that, but we've also kept a little in reserve; enough so we wouldn't starve. We still have about eight sacks of the old grain left. My son and I discussed it on the way here, and we decided to offer it to you all—or rather, to Maria-sama—during this time of troubles, before it's eaten by the insects. If these were normal times we'd bring more, but this is all we have this year. We'll be grateful if you'll accept this small offering. You took care of that old man I asked you to look after for so long, and you kindly buried him. I'm sorry that it's old grain, but would you please take this, at least, as a token of his memory?"

Yozaemon stammered as he spoke. Together with his son, he placed his hands on the floor. This was a most unexpected offer. Yazō started to reply, "Well, that's … ," but he couldn't finish his sentence. Nisuke was deeply aware of how Yozaemon had long maintained the spirit of the community in this area as a farmer, even though he wasn't particularly involved in the daily affairs of the *confuraria*.

On the appointed day, all of the petitions from the six villages were delivered to the government office. In hushed anticipation, the people waited for replies.

The village representatives were summoned to the office and told that only the damaged fields would be granted a slight reduction in taxes. As for emergency rice assistance, well, their lord, too, was in difficult straits, so they would not be able to provide assistance any time soon.

At first, to the surprise of the village leaders, Tada Kurōbei had expressed a little sympathy about the storm damage. But then he delivered the heartless official reply, spoken in a most patronizing manner, leaving them dumbfounded. Before they could muster a response, Kurōbei pried open his normally sleepy-looking eyes and glared at them.

"Top officials have made up their minds on this matter, so don't make any further demands. We, too, are trying to make the best of the situation and do what we can under difficult conditions. Because you will be receiving a tax reduction, it's essential that you pay your land taxes. We're all suffering through this together.

"If you fail to pay your taxes this year, we'll add the amount to your other back taxes and you'll have to pay it all back next year. I hope none of you are so foolish as to think that your debts will be cancelled if you keep on delaying.

"Do not underestimate the Matsukuras. I've been dealing with you leniently so far, but it would be a mistake to think I'll continue to do so."

Around the edge of the room where the village representatives were seated, a row of the magistrate's samurai had been posted, their swords thrust into the sashes of their kimonos. Out in the garden just beyond the veranda stood some lower-rank samurai, the naked blades of their spears glistening in the sunlight.

The men remained silent as they filed out the gate. The groups from Arima and Arie headed for their boats to return home.

Ninagawa Sakyō's house was near the Kuchinotsu harbor, so he invited them to stop in for a bit. "I'd feel awful parting like this," he said.

No one objected to the invitation. As soon as they were seated, Chijiiwa Bannai from Kazusa spoke up in a low voice, holding back his anger.

"Well, that's what we heard—so what do you think? Now we'll have to face all the people back home who are waiting to hear how things turned out. This is hardly a good answer for them."

Matsushima Sadonokami, the headman from Kita Arima, spoke up:

"I half expected things would turn out like this ... but the magistrate's office knows the wretched state we're in. Even if they reduced our taxes by half, it still wouldn't be enough."

This man was the leader of the Arima *confuraria*, the group with the largest number of samurai.

"This isn't the decision of one local office," Ezaki Minbu of Kushiyama said. "When Kurōbei announced it, he was speaking for the whole government."

"You're probably right," someone said, and everyone nodded in agreement.

"Lord Matsukura's going to take whatever he can from us, even if we have to live off the roots of grass."

Bannai exploded in anger:

"Just how do they intend to take what we don't even have? And what about those samurai? Did they think we'd be frightened off when they bared their spears with their naked blades shining at us?"

"Well, that angered me too. If they're looking for blood, we can make it fall like rain at the magistrate's house."

Matsushima Sadonokami's words stirred up everyone present.

"But, Chijiiwa-dono, even if it does eventually come to bloodshed, we're not at that point yet. For now, we need to be patient," he concluded, fixing his eyes on each person, one by one, as if trying to read their mood.

"That's a good point for us to keep in mind," Sakyō said. "If we go along with what a person like Kurōbei says, we're sure to fail. It's our duty to find a way for us all to live without shedding blood."

"I'm not saying we should rush into a fight with Matsukura," Bannai responded. "And in any case, how can we think of fighting right now, when we have no prospects of even finding food for tomorrow? But if the bad harvests continue, and if Matsukura keeps pressing us harder for payments until things get really bad, we won't be able to go on like this. What do the two of you think about that?"

At first Sadonokami shut his eyes, but then, slowly and deliberately, he spoke.

"If Matsukura continues to act like this, the time will come when we won't be able to go on living. We from Arima are ready for that. But for now, we're trying to decide whether we should stay quiet and go along with the magistrate's orders, or if we should gather the opinions of the people in our area and then return to the magistrate's office to renegotiate. What about you from Kuchinotsu—what have you decided?"

Sadonokami served as the headman of Kita Arima, where many of the former samurai lived. Although he was an imposing figure, his tough, soldierly face now betrayed signs of worry.

Sakyō responded, "Well, we haven't decided yet. We can't expect people to go along with the present government's demands. But if we petition them again, the response will likely be the same. Each village has to have an honest conversation about it. But let's put aside these discussions for now. How about we relax a bit? I can't give you a feast today, but I have a little millet sake, so let me bring it out."

Sakyō stood up. In the drinking session that followed, it seemed as if the men were drinking down the gravity of their decisions. Hayashida Shichizaemon from Arima drank too much and gave vent to his feelings.

"I feel like quitting as headman, I'm so down about taking all this bad news back to my people. I'd feel better if we were agitating for a rebellion. Dealing with all these negotiations, it's just too nerve-racking."

"Whenever I come here by boat, I can never take my eyes off those grain storehouses in Kuchinotsu," Sadonokami said, breaking the gloomy mood as he smiled like a naughty child.

"Same with me."

"How many sacks do you suppose they hold?" Shichizaemon asked.

Grinning, Bannai replied, "Maybe a thousand or so?"

"You think they post guards there at night?"

"There are some, but they're always dozing off."

Sadonokami flashed a rebellious smile and drained the dregs of his sake.

CHAPTER FOUR

Vocation

In the end, the efforts to petition for a reduction in land taxes were given up. Filing petitions and making pleas had proved of no avail, and people came to no conclusions about proposals such as refusing to make the payments or abandoning their lands and fleeing the villages. The villagers saw no other choice than to defer their payments and hope for better crops in the coming year. Facing the Matsukura administration's utter indifference, a sense of futility quietly settled in.

A coming-of-age ceremony was held for Shirō during the Christmas celebration when he returned to his home in Ebe, in the town of Uto on the Kyushu mainland.

"You're fifteen now. You have to realize that from now on you'll be treated as an adult," his father Jinbei said, seating Shirō in the place of honor.

On the ceremonial table in front of him was a large sea bream that Watanabe Kozaemon, the chief headman of Ōyano Island, had brought with him. People in the neighborhood who had doted on Shirō since his early childhood also came to see him, bringing crabs, octopus, turban shells and other gifts from the seashore. After most of them left, the remaining group included Kozaemon and his younger brother Satarō, who was the brother-in-law of Shirō's elder sister, and Yamazen Uemon, who had been invited from Senzoku Zōzō Island.

"We sent you to Nagasaki to study and to prepare for the business world," Jinbei said to Shirō. "All of this has been for your future. But it seems you're not really cut out for business and, well, that's all right. If you're thinking of supporting yourself as a scholar, however, you should know that as a Christian, you won't be able to get a position in the government service. I can see that you've set your sights high, so I'd like you to tell us what you're hoping to do."

After thinking for a moment, Shirō replied, "I'd like to understand how peoples' minds work—but directly from the people, not from books."

"From the people, and not from books?"

"Yes, but I don't mean I'll throw away the books."

Receiving this unexpected reply, Jinbei felt that perhaps he had asked the question in the wrong way.

"And why do you want to do this?"

"I'd hoped that my academic studies would open my understanding to the whole world, but it seems I've been staring up at the stars without seeing all the things the land down here has given me. As I've come into contact with people around me, I've been feeling ashamed of myself."

"What sort of people?"

"Well, for example ..."

"Who, for example?"

Shirō had wanted to say, "Grandmother," but he hesitated because she was so close to him.

"Yesterday, at sundown, I saw Rokusuke from behind."

"Oh, Rokusuke—you mean the fellow who lives at the edge of town? What was he doing?"

"Well, it was sundown and I was walking along one of the paths by the terraced fields at the outskirts of town, and I heard someone reciting an *oratio*. As I listened, I realized it was Rokusuke."

"Yes, he's a faithful believer," Jinbei said, tilting his head.

"As I listened to his *oratio*, I was so struck by his little field."

Together, Shirō's father and Kozaemon broke into a pleasant laugh.

"He certainly cares about that little field."

"That's what I thought when I saw it."

"Which *oratio* was he reciting?" Kozaemon asked with interest.

"It was part of the familiar one, 'Hail Mary, full of grace.' He was praying on his knees in the fading sunlight. It was the sort of thing you might see anywhere, just an ordinary old man, but for that very reason it struck me even more powerfully."

While Shirō was thinking about how to describe the scene further, his grandmother entered and sat down beside his father. Turning toward her grandson seated in the position of honor, she straightened her back.

"Shirō, I'm so very happy to be present at God's blessing of your coming-of-age today. Here—I want you to take a drink from your grandmother's cup."

When he drank from her sake cup, she grasped his wrist and stroked it reverently, again and again. Then Shirō held her hand, opened its wrinkled palm, and in it placed the cup he had just emptied.

"Grandmother, your hands have worked hard in the fields."

"Not just in the fields—they've changed your diapers too!"

Laughter, filled with deep nostalgia, rose up all around.

"I suppose you must have suffered all sorts of hardships I don't know about."

"Well, it's nice to hear you say that. My work has been my happiness. And I've put these hands together and prayed for you."

"Yes, you've prayed for me."

This time, Shirō stroked her aged palm as he spoke. A long time had passed since they had been able to share a good talk.

"Grandmother, I've just been reading books, and I haven't really looked at the fields. It's really only recently that I started to think seriously about the fields. I've been asking myself, what did I really learn in Nagasaki?"

"Well, it's *because* you studied in Nagasaki—that's why you can really see the fields now."

When she said this, everyone laughed.

"Rokusuke-yan built up the hillside with stone walls to stop the mudslides, and that's how he made his field. It took him decades," she said with deep emotion, nodding her head.

Rokusuke was a peasant who worked for one of the big farmers in the village, but he also had three small fields of his own, scattered here and there. The smallest was only about two *jō*, the size of two tatami mats, and even the biggest was no more than five. After his work as a hired hand was finished, he would walk up to his fields, on some nights with the moon, and on others with the stars. He took great care in looking after them, and when he was done, he never forgot to say a prayer to Maria-sama. Grandmother said that when she looked up at his terraced fields at harvest time, she was so moved to see the golden ears of grain that he had raised with such care, soaking up the light of the setting sun and shining in the evening sky.

"Everyone says it's as if the light of Deus-sama shines down on Rokusuke-yan's fields. They're such lovely fields. They receive a divine blessing."

"And around the rocks in the walls of his fields you can see lots of wild strawberries, with their tendrils drooping down, and just when the grain is ripening, the red strawberries are also ripening. That must be a great pleasure for him," Shirō's mother Oine added eagerly.

Quietly, Shirō joined the conversation. His voice hadn't yet deepened.

"In our religion we respect poverty. When I was on the boat coming home this time, while I was looking up at the mountains of Amakusa I thought about a lot of things. It seemed as if a hand from Heaven had reached out to the poor islands of Amakusa and covered its land with plants and trees. And it seemed that these islands were created as places for living honestly and modestly, according to the wishes of God. Even if our crops are scant and we're often hit by storms, this is a pure garden, granted by God, for the kind-hearted people. That's how it all looked to me.

"And then, when I saw Rokusuke-yan's little field and heard his voice reciting prayers, it seemed to me a clear sign that this place is a gateway leading to Heaven. The grain was just sending up fresh shoots and, Grandmother, it was such a beautiful field."

"Yes—the soil there is soft and workable, and there aren't any stones in it. And with him praying, it's so beautiful."

"The Bible speaks of how *if the grain does not die* . . . I realized for the first time that when a person like him prays there in that field, those become living words."

"It's wonderful to hear this, Shirō. Now we can say you're truly worthy of this coming-of-age celebration."

All around, the men remained silent as they listened to the discussion between Shirō and his grandmother. They realized that

Shirō had become an adult. Or rather, he had grown into a person possessed of a deep understanding of things, deeper even than that of other adults.

"I'm glad you invited me to this wonderful ceremony. It was certainly worth coming. The future is as good as decided—don't you think, Jinbei-sama?" Kozaemon said, his cheeks flushed. Jinbei shut his eyes and nodded deeply.

After the ceremony, Jinbei took Shirō to visit their relatives on Ōyano Island. Jinbei had lived there back when he was a retainer for Lord Konishi, and Kozaemon and many other relatives and in-laws still lived there.

When word got around that Shirō was staying at the home of Kozaemon's brother Satarō, who was Shirō's in-law through his sister's marriage, he received a stream of invitations from distant relatives. Having been regarded as a prodigy since early childhood, Shirō was the pride of his family, including his more distant relatives as well. Now he was back from his studies in Nagasaki and had had his coming-of-age ceremony. Everyone was amazed to see what a promising young man he had become. The men spoke of how he would be the joy of the family in the future, and the women were especially eager to see how he had been changed by life in the big port town of Nagasaki.

Also, the islanders were sociable people. When word got around that Shirō was visiting someone's home, neighbors, too, would gather. Among them were a number of ronin—former samurai of Lord Konishi who were now living in places like Senzoku Island. They had long been close to his father Jinbei and to the Watanabe brothers Kozaemon and Satarō, and they served as spiritual guides when the islanders welcomed Shirō and prayed together.

When they recited the *oratio* in their local dialect, it sounded so different from Ninagawa Ukon's crisp diction when he had recited it in Kuchinotsu. Shirō felt as if he were listening to the chanting of the earliest Christians.

In visiting Ōyano he grasped, for the first time, the seriousness of the fact that crops were failing throughout the entire Amakusa region. During Shirō's coming-of-age ceremony, Yamazen Uemon, an especially close friend of his father who had come over from

Senzoku Island, had spoken of how they had gone to the local office to appeal for rice assistance from the government stores. As he spoke, his drooping eyebrows had lent him a curious expression.

"Things got really heated. Though we were mostly farmers, some whalers from Ōyano were with us, and the mood was pretty rough. Back in the Konishi days, the land taxes weren't so bad, and if the crops got damaged by wind or rain the officials lowered the assessments. So, we all assumed we'd be granted some rice assistance again. Ōyano folks get upset easily, and so do I. Compared to other groups, we had some pretty tough characters, with quick tempers."

It seemed that by telling this story, Uemon was expressing his hopes for Shirō.

While Shirō was staying on Ōyano Island, the new year arrived. It was the fourteenth year of the Kanei era (1637).

One day, Kozaemon announced that he had something he wanted to show Shirō. He pulled out an old document written on heavy paper.

"This is from back in my father's day. It's a copy of the letter that Padre Couros asked my father to write to the pope in Rome. I've been saving it all these years. Would you please take a look at it?"

The letter expressed how the Jesuit priests had devoted themselves faithfully to their missionary work. "During and after the persecution by Ieyasu, they didn't think of their own lives at all," it read. There was mention of some matters testifying to their propagation of the religion, and then a list of village leaders from Kōtsuura and Ōyano Island, including Kozaemon's father, Kozaemon the Elder. The letter was dated twenty years back, in the third year of the Genwa era (1617).

As Kozaemon showed the document to Shirō in the presence of his father Jinbei, Shirō silently tried to imagine Kozaemon's thoughts.

"They presented this document to Padre Couros, the representative of the priests after Padre Marco Ferraro left his church in Kōtsuura. It was written to show that, thanks to the visits and care they had received from the padres, the congregation had been able to maintain the faith, in spite of the severe persecution that was taking place all around the country. Everyone signed their names. A few are still alive today."

Jinbei leaned forward to examine the names on the document.

"I recognize about half of the names here. Your father Denbei-dono became a leader who kept the faith alive here in Ōyano."

Denbei was the name Kozaemon the Elder took after he retired.

"That's true," the younger Kozaemon said. "Twenty years ago, I was just a kid—only seven or eight. My father has passed on the name Kozaemon and the job of chief headman to me, but he doesn't think I'm responsible enough yet and he often asks if I've consulted with you, Jinbei-sama. He really relies on you."

Jinbei was already sixty-three, and the age difference between him and the younger Kozaemon was about the same as that between a father and son.

"No, no—I'm not much use now that I live so far away. But seeing this letter reminds me how long it's been since Father Mamacos left."

"It's already been twenty-five or twenty-six years. Thinking back on it, we've been keeping the spirit and holding on to our faith ever since the padres left. But if the persecution continues, what do you think will happen?"

"Well, about that; just before he was forced to go to Macau, I heard Father Mamacos say that in twenty-six years a truly good person would appear, and that this person would revive the sign of the cross on all the people's heads. Hasn't it been twenty-six years now, just this year?"

"I heard the same thing. Some of the farmers, too, have been saying that a good man will appear and restore the Christian world. And they've been talking about how, last year around the time of the big storms, the sky turned strangely red. They say it was a sign. But if our faith is weak, the good person won't come. I showed you the letter my father wrote for Padre Couros because I have the feeling that, compared with my father's generation, our faith is becoming a formality."

"You're right. Even if I recite *oratios* morning and night, I feel like I'm just going through the motions."

Jinbei turned toward Shirō.

"At your coming-of-age ceremony you spoke of Rokusuke. It's hard for most of us to be as devoted to God in our daily lives as

Rokusuke is, but do you think we all should live the way he does? Tell me your thoughts."

"I think Rokusuke has built an invisible temple in his heart. I was impressed by the way he lives, but I can't become like him."

Shirō's cheeks reddened.

"What do you mean?"

"The important thing is to create on this land a world where people can live according to our true faith. And to create such a place, first we need to pray for it in our hearts."

"You mean we need to build a *Paraizo* on Earth?"

"Heaven isn't a place on this Earth. Being reborn in Heaven is God's plan. We can't speak about it as if it's our plan. What I believe is that there is another world beyond the boundaries of this world."

The two adults stared at each other in silence. Shirō's eyes seemed to shine with a sacred light.

"But to cross over the boundaries of this world, we need all our strength—if we want to pass through the gate to that country."

Shirō paused for a moment. Slowly, he looked up and continued.

"We have to walk the path that Yesus walked. No matter how many times we confess our sins, they will never be completely absolved. Yesus died on the cross to atone for our sins. Going to that other world must be like passing from a burning field into a field of flowers. I can see the fire that's burning the fields and the villages. Unless we make our way through that cosmic fire, we won't be able to reach the land of true faith, will we?"

Wondering what they had just heard, the two adults sank into silence. Then, with some hesitation, Jinbei asked:

"Are you saying you plan to be burned up in that cosmic fire?"

Shirō shut his eyes tightly, and a tear streaked down his cheek.

Jinbei and Kozaemon had often found the word *rebellion* rising in their minds, ever since they saw the state of affairs that led to the plundering of the Terazawa magistrate's offices in Tomioka, and also when they saw the people in Ōyano pushed to their limits by crop failures. They worried about what would happen to people's faith and future if the troubles continued. Shirō's words sank into their hearts as they realized that he had been speaking of a kind of fire from Heaven.

After Jinbei and Shirō returned to their home in Uto, three former samurai who were now living on Ōyano Island came to see Shirō, perhaps because they had heard the rumors about him.

"Excuse us for being so late in coming, but we'd like to offer our congratulations on your son's coming of age."

Despite their overly formal words, their real reasons for coming were to get a look at Shirō and to relieve the depression they were facing in their daily lives. Among them was a man named Yanagi Heibei. He liked to discuss the state of the world, and he got worked up enumerating the causes of the Toyotomi forces' defeat in the Siege of Osaka.

"Okay, but that's long past. It won't help us much now," one of his companions chided.

"Well, with Shirō-dono here, that's about all I can say about it for the moment. From now on we're going to have to rely on the young folks. Our duty is to serve our Lord, Deus-sama. But, to tell the truth, I can't stop hoping I'll find a man I can look up to as a lord in this world, and serve him."

"I know how you feel," Jinbei said calmly. "As far as I know, there is no daimyo in all of Japan who will employ people like us. Just think about it; back when the Katō clan was forced to give up their domain, all the daimyo with ties to Toyotomi had to leave Kyushu. And now it's the Shimazu clan who are currying favor with the *bakufu*. The world is full of ronin like us. As for the old retainers who've been in hiding since the downfall of their Toyotomi-connected lords, we can't really imagine they're tough enough to start stringing their bows and rise up against the Tokugawas, can we?"

"That's just it, Jinbei-dono," Heibei said, raising his reddened face. "I too am just a lowly Christian. At this point I'm not looking to serve a lord who's currying favor with the Tokugawas. Still, I'd like to hear the cry of war horses beneath the banner of the cross just one more time."

Heibei glanced at Jinbei to see how he reacted. Jinbei smiled and said, "That's very bold of you, Yanagi-dono. It seems you're still as tough as the young folks."

Shirō rose quietly. He realized that these men were talking in part just so that he might hear them, so he decided to leave the room. His mind was in other places than the current conversation.

Shirō was not unaware of the poverty the ronin were facing. His family, the Masudas, owned a considerable number of fields, and the men and women who helped them worked hard, so for the time being his family was still not too badly off, but it seemed clear that these ronin were feeling much harder-pressed. Supported by the generous character of the farmers and fishers, they had been able to survive, but something rather twisted, like the hermit crabs along the seashore, showed in their faces.

Oine had sensed a change in her only son's inner life during his latest homecoming. Quietly pulling away the small *ozen* table from which he had hardly eaten anything, she looked at his profile, lost in thought.

Every time he returned from Nagasaki, she wanted to prepare all sorts of food for him, as if he were still a growing child. She would ask him briefly about his studies, but while he was back home, she was more concerned about whether he had missed any foods.

Oine accepted the fact that, sooner or later, sons have to become independent and leave home. Yet she couldn't imagine where her own son would go. All she could do was savor the last of the days God had granted them to be together since his birth. From the beginning, Shirō had been different from other children. Jinbei had sometimes said, "He's our child, but perhaps he was sent here from another world."

Oine had heard that Maria-sama gave up her only son Yesus to atone for the sins of the world. She regarded that as a laudable act, yet she also wanted to shut her ears to it. When she heard people praise her child as being extraordinarily bright, she felt more fearful than happy. When she heard them speak of him as "God's child," she felt like hiding him under the sleeves of her kimono.

Oine couldn't dispel the thought that one day Shirō would fly away from her. Of late she had found it difficult to speak to him. She felt he had started to entertain some rather preposterous ideas. She was afraid that if she asked him things thoughtlessly, she would receive unbearable replies. The best she could do was cook the foods he had liked since childhood and make sure he dressed properly.

Thinking back, he had been well-liked since infancy. The

women and girls in their neighborhood would hold out their arms to pick him up and carry him on their backs. Even now, whenever he came back from Nagasaki, the old women would call out to him with a big grin and say, "Got some tasty *sazae* clams here—won't you try one?" At times like that, Oine couldn't help thinking that all these people had helped to raise him.

The morning of Shirō's departure for Nagasaki arrived. She made him take some dried sea lettuce for Okattsama, despite his protests that she already had everything she needed.

"Maybe so, but our sea lettuce smells different. I'm sure it will make her happy," she insisted, placing the bag in Shirō's hands.

From the deck of the boat bound for Nagasaki, Shirō surveyed once again the landscape along the coastline. He had become familiar with the sea lanes from his regular trips, but this time he saw entirely new meanings in the communities along the coast.

The boat left from Misuminoura, passing between the Yushima and Ōyano Islands before making stops at Kōtsuura on Upper Amakusa Island and at Oshimago. The stops changed depending on where passengers wanted to get on or off and where cargo was to be loaded or unloaded. They left at low tide, when the sailing was swift. The sea breeze felt cold. It wasn't even the middle of the first month of the year yet.

To the right stretched the shore of the Matsukura domain's Shimabara Peninsula, with Mount Unzen rising high in the distance. Shirō could see the houses of what must be Arie and Minami Arima in the foothills.

An elderly passenger said to the captain, "Today the ruins of Hara Castle look real close."

"Aye. You can see 'em good and close today."

The sun broke through the clouds and even the sounds of the oars seemed gentle.

"In cherry blossom time, when you look at the castle remains from Yushima Island you see trees you don't usually notice."

"Aye—those cherry trees. When they're in bloom you can see 'em from way off."

"Even now with the castle buildings gone, the cherry trees keep on blossoming."

After the conversation ended, the sounds of rowing continued. The tide was low and women and children could be seen along the shore. As the boat approached the shore, their faces became visible and their happy, playful voices could be heard. The currents around the Straits of Hayasaki at low tide were known to be very fast, but boats headed for Kuchinotsu passed close to the shore to avoid the rocks. With fresh eyes, Shirō gazed at the people and houses along the shoreline. *Those thatched roofs pelted with sea spray look as if they're withering away. Every single one shows the marks of the recent storm. How different they look from the houses along the streets of Nagasaki. Beneath these roofs, what kinds of lives are people leading?*

The coast was dotted with people bent over the greenish rocks along the shore as they gathered oysters and sea lettuce. Since the houses had looked so forlorn, Shirō felt relieved to see the peaceful scene of people working among the rocks that had begun to take on color. The wind was chilly, but beneath the waves signs of spring were appearing.

Perhaps having heard the oars, a woman looked up. She looked a bit younger than his mother. She wiped the sea spray from an oyster and then brushed away some loose hairs with the back of her hand while she held her knife. She flashed the glimmer of a smile that slipped into his heart. *In Nagasaki I rarely see such a friendly smiling face.* The woman called out:

"Chilly wind, isn't it?"

The sides of the boat and the rocks along the shore were about the same height. The woman's hands and feet had turned red from the cold wind. Shirō returned her smile. Passengers on boats often met the eyes of people on shore, and it was the custom to nod in greeting, just as when people passed on a street in a town. But since he was now the one on the boat, his was the role of being seen off. It left him with a strange sadness.

The woman's voice and smile lingered and the movement of her arms remained imprinted in his mind, mixed with the image of his mother, whom he had just left. He wondered if, at this very moment, back in the shadows of the cliff by the boat dock, his mother and sister might also be gathering oysters, bending over with the same rounded figures as this woman. Although his trip this time would not be a particularly long one, his mother had looked so sad and lonely this morning, as if she thought he was leaving her for the rest of his life. For the very reason that she hadn't expressed her feelings in words, the memory troubled him.

In front of the fields and houses that extended up from the shore, willow shoots and peach blossom buds were swelling. Abundant piles of seaweed covered the rocks around the feet of the children who were standing and crouching to work. Glancing at the camelia bushes bent over the edge of the seashore at low tide, their blossoms bobbing in the water, he noticed some small white-eyed birds flying back and forth. Seeing all this fresh growth, it was hard to imagine the scorching drought of last year.

In the fields planted with early crops, sprouts of grain were already poking up. *Maybe that woman was smiling at the spring that has finally come. And the children's happy voices gliding over the surface of the sea—maybe they, too, were greeting the spring with their entire bodies. Even the woman's reddened hands and feet, blown by the sea winds, seemed caught up in the joys of early spring.*

Buoyed by the waves, a camellia flower floated alongside the boat. Its red color pierced Shirō's eyes. His mother's face seemed to shimmer on the waves, rising and falling in the space around the flower. The image pricked his emotions deeply. Perhaps this was his first premonition that someday he would be cut off from his mother.

Dear Mother who gave me life!

Later, when he returned home again, even in peaceful moments with his mother, the foreboding pain he had felt in his heart at this time always came back to him. He couldn't help gazing at her freckled cheeks.

Ever since Yazō had taken him last autumn to the homes of Hasuda Nisuke and the Ninagawa family in Kuchinotsu, it had seemed that the things he needed to think about had been striking him like arrows of light, stabbing him deep in his breast. He felt as if he had become a target suspended in the air; as if an unseen hand in the darkness was drawing a bow and firing test arrows at him.

I haven't yet become like those trees that stand high on the cliffs, clinging firmly to the rocks, exposed to the elements. Unless I can hold on to the rocks and the earth and root myself to them, I'll be drifting around in my dark, frustrated mind like a kite on an untethered string. But these days I'm drifting less. The arrows have been striking my heart and fixing me to the core of this void.

As he rode along, sitting in the boat surrounded by the creaking of the oars, Shirō was caught up in these thoughts.

This feeling, he realized, had started around the time he learned about Okattsama's past in Nagasaki. She was a friend of his father's cousin. Originally, his family had planned for him to stay at the cousin's house, but after thinking about his background and talents, they had arranged for him to stay with Okattsama instead. That was how their unusual and unexpected connection had been established. Probably Jinbei had suggested that it would be better for him to stay in a Christian home.

The foreigners in Nagasaki said there was no other woman in town they held in such high esteem as a tradesperson. She knew business inside out. She overlooked certain things for the sake of profit, but she always made sure those she did business with benefited, too. People said she was good at gambling, but they also said that she brushed off greedy, aggressive people with a smile, saying simply, "Well then, this will be the end of our relations."

"That smile of Okattsama's is truly fearsome. She just cuts off the relationship, smiling the whole time."

Yang, a Chinese trader who had taught Shirō some magic tricks, had told him this with a shrug of his shoulders.

"You must never use this magic to make money. If you do, Okattsama will cut me off. Tricks—you only perform them at important times. You hear me?"

Despite this warning, Yang nonetheless had urged Shirō to perform some of the tricks when they met his favorite prostitutes. When they went to such places, Shirō dressed himself as a foreigner and didn't speak a word. One time, when a young, short-haired girl touched Shirō on the sleeve of his kimono wondering who the foreigner was, Yang had glared at her and scolded:

"Don't touch him—he's an Acha-sama from India."

In Nagasaki, foreigners who spoke different languages, as well as people who couldn't speak at all, were referred to as "Acha-sama."

The young girls' crimson-painted mouths had fallen open as they stared at the blue silk handkerchief fluttering in Shirō's fingers. They gazed without blinking their eyes.

If I hadn't met Yang, I'd never have seen that child on the Chinese ship, chained at his leg. And Suzu, the orphan at Nisuke's house in Kuchinotsu—her direct gaze became a white flower that floated to me softly. It would be fitting if, someday, the white spider lilies she picked were placed on the ground where I'm buried.

Shirō had performed the magic tricks he had learned from Yang for the young girls, making eggs and doves appear. But what he really wanted to show people, right in front of their eyes, was that child's dirt-covered, chained leg.

It seems the moment I saw it, my sins grew still deeper. My heart can't contain it. All right then, may the hand in the darkness strike my heart.

He had taken hold of the arrow that was piercing his body and was trying to pull it out. Using all of his strength, he had to make that arrow shine, catch it in reverse and hurl it back. Ahead, would there be the devil? Or God? *But no*—he hoped unconsciously—*may that arrow fly back to the land where Suzu, Rokusuke, Mother and Grandmother are living.*

Sea spray struck his cheeks, pulling him back from the depths of his thoughts. Lifting his head, he could see the mountains of the Ōyano and Yushima Islands receding in the distance. As he gazed at the soft, fresh grass of early spring that covered the higher reaches of the islands, his thoughts returned to the present. *When did people start to live here? For how long will they continue to live here? How will the people of the future whom we cannot see feel when they look on these islands? Will they listen to the voices of the islands as we do now?*

As the boat swayed on the waves and Shirō gazed up at the sky, these were his thoughts as a young person who had just finished his coming-of-age ceremony.

When Shirō arrived at Okattsama's shop in the Hakata-machi section of Nagasaki, she was walking toward the wisteria trellis in the courtyard, seeing off some tea ceremony guests. She was a person who never raised her voice, no matter what happened. Now, she quietly placed the water bucket she had been holding at the base of the wisteria vine, then looked him over from head to toe.

"I'm back."

"Well then, welcome back."

As she nodded, Okattsama continued to gaze intently at Shirō's face. Somehow, his eyes looked hollow and his face gaunt. There was a slight bluish shadow beneath his eyes and a wrinkle cut across his lower eyelids. The line on his fresh skin, so thin it could have been etched by the point of a needle, pained her. She imagined he had passed some sleepless nights, thinking too much, as usual.

"Well, it must have been cold out there on the sea. Come inside now."

Her quiet, straightforward greeting brought a rush of nostalgia. The house put him at ease.

"I *thought* you would come back. I've been looking forward to it," Okattsama said.

Secretly, Shirō felt that Okattsama, along with his mother and grandmother, represented the eternal existence of womankind.

First, Okattsama congratulated him on his coming-of-age ceremony.

"Your grandmother must have been so happy and relieved."

As always, her voice was gentle.

"Is your mother getting along well?"

As Okattsama was asking this, Shirō placed the sea lettuce in front of her.

"My goodness—such a wonderful smell! Coming from your place, it really is different. The sea and wind must have been cold when she gathered it."

She raised her hands in gratitude and touched them to her nose.

"By the way, I remember how last autumn you had a rough trip back here because of a terrible storm. This time you could wait for the boat in Kuchinotsu. That's good."

"Yes. And this time I brought a message from Ninagawa-sama, so I came here right away to tell you about it first."

With a touch of hesitation, Okattsama asked, "Were those books I gave you any help?"

"Yes, they brought people a lot of happiness. And since Kuchinotsu was a birthplace of the Christians, receiving the writings was a great honor for the town."

"Well, I'm glad to hear it."

"Since the padres haven't been able to come for such a long time, the Ninagawas and all the other believers who've been living in secret were so pleased. They feel those writings will serve as a guiding light. Already, Ukon-dono is planning to gather the young people from all the *confuraria* and read the books to them."

"So people are making good use of them and it's really worth having them ...?"

Okattsama's voice trembled as her words trailed off. Certainly, the priest who had been crucified after entrusting her with the book would be filled with joy to know what had become of them, and Okattsama had wanted to say this, but her tears were about to overflow and the words wouldn't come.

"Have you become friends with Ukon-dono?"

"Yes. Fortunately, I've been blessed with a great elder brother. From now on he'll be teaching me many things. I feel my world has grown a bit deeper."

"I'm glad to hear it. From the first time I saw Ukon-dono, I knew he'd be like an older brother for you. With him looking after those books—books that will be copied by many hands—a divine light will guide the Christians in Amakusa."

Her eyes glimmering like the lights of a fishing boat far out on the night sea, Okattsama looked closely at Shirō.

"Amakusa is where I was born."

A faint smile, tinged with sadness, rose on her lips. It was the first time she had spoken of her birthplace.

"So ... where in Amakusa were you born?"

"It was a place called Tororo."

Shirō felt a sudden twinge in his chest. He had never been there, but he had seen it from the sea. The village had looked poor, with people living pressed together. Nestled in the sinuous coastline, it had appeared suddenly when his boat passed by. Beneath the towering rocky cliffs of the rough, windswept coast, where white waves crashed forbiddingly, houses and people lay tucked away in what appeared, from a passing glance, to be a remote and desolate hamlet.

How hard it must be for someone to leave such a place. And then, af-

ter leaving, how hard it must be to ever return. The difficult, desolate landscape had burned its image into his memory.

"Even in a town like that, there were Christians, and my parents numbered among them."

Whatever could have led her to become a prostitute in Nagasaki? For a moment, Shirō was stunned. Okattsama blinked and tossed back the frayed strands of her hair, streaked with white. These were matters he couldn't ask her about.

"In that area there are many poor villages. The people have survived on their faith."

Shirō sensed that she was trying to teach him things that he, as a young person, needed to learn.

"When I was a young girl, I thought of throwing myself over the rocky windswept cliffs. I folded my hands, looked out to the distant sea, and prayed to find the *Paraizo* my parents had spoken of."

For a while, Okattsama remained silent. Then words, spoken mainly to herself, began to slip out.

"The boat to *Paraizo* never came. So, instead, I came to the pleasure land of Nagasaki. I was eleven then."

Shirō swallowed hard.

"The prayers of people who live in villages like mine are heartbreaking. Throughout their lives, they rely on Chirisuto-sama and Maria-sama in far-off Heaven. They yearn for them, and they die yearning."

Okattsama bowed her head, apparently sunk deeply in thought. Her words touched him deeply. The Christian writings had no doubt been a mainstay for her spirit. Living hard lives in a little village by the cliffs, barely eking out a living, people had seen a vision of a temple in a foreign country beyond the seas, longed for it, and died. This must have been the spirit that led Okattsama to protect and preserve the Christian writings. Handing them to Ukon must have been the realization of her most cherished wish.

As Shirō stared at the collar of her kimono, she raised her head and asked, "Now that you've had your coming-of-age ceremony, you'll continue your studies with a fresh spirit, won't you?"

"Well, yes ... on my recent trip back I saw with my own eyes the conditions in Kuchinotsu, Uto and Ōyano, with all the droughts and damage they've suffered from wind and rain. And it's the first time I've really thought deeply about the meaning of human life.

"I read a couple of books I borrowed from Ukon-dono, but I realized that my way of learning has changed. True faith comes from the places where people live in the flesh and blood. I, too, need to go to where people actually live. I have a deep attachment to Nagasaki, but this time I've come to say goodbye. I want to take another good look at the places that have been the foundations of our faith, and then I'm going back to Kuchinotsu to help Ukon-dono."

Okattsama was overcome with an ineffable loneliness. She had always known she could not keep Shirō with her forever, yet she was stunned to hear him suddenly announce his departure. Would he ever come back?

This boy was brought to me at the age of twelve and he impressed me from the first time I saw him. It was fate that I met him. I was born to carry not only the sorrows of my own life, but those of my parents, and of my parents' parents. My path has led me to an unknown place, with the sounds of the waves from my far-off hometown as my travelling companions. When I think of it now, this child has been my guide in my later years. Our connection must be thanks to a blessing that transcends this world.

"I understand. It is your decision. Please relax and take your time during your last days here. There are many things that I, too, would like to talk about with you."

Wanting Shirō to enjoy as much time relaxing in Nagasaki as possible, Okattsama prepared a detached room for him. When he wasn't busy outside, he stayed in the room, sunk in thoughts about his past.

The initial agreement had been that he might pursue academic studies along with his apprenticeship to a merchant family. But this arrangement had been set aside by Okattsama a long time ago. She had realized that he wasn't suited for a merchant's life, and so, instead, she had engaged him to work with her as a clerk, assisting in negotiations with foreigners. Sitting in silence, he made quite a nice picture. She kept him at her side when she was assessing art and artefacts. The boy had proven an able critic.

When he was taken onto the Chinese boat and taught magic

tricks by Yang, that, too, had stemmed from Okattsama's interests.

"These magic tricks are different from the affairs of business. They show a refined taste," Yang had said, and Okattsama's eyes had narrowed with delight.

"Is that so? Well, in that case, I'd like you to teach this boy your refined arts."

When people in Okattsama's house worried that Shirō was taking too much interest in books, she just smiled and replied, "That child will be the joy of my later years. It's different from the pleasure I get from trading. It's like I'm caring for a tree in Heaven. I think of him as a kind of divine blessing."

One time, Okattsama had confided to Yazō with a mischievous look:

"When it comes to studying Japanese and Chinese literature, his teachers are astonished by his talent; but as for calculations, well …"

It wasn't that he couldn't use the abacus if he had to; but when he did, he became absent-minded and couldn't concentrate. He would stop and say things like, "Numbers—what meaning do they have?"

That was in the first year, just after he had arrived.

"Even if you subtract a certain number, invisible ones continue on and on. Beyond them, nothingness is always there, hiding. When I think of how everything in the universe comes into being from the infinite mother, the lives in this temporal world seem so insignificant."

And in saying this a tear would drop onto the beads of his abacus.

Shirō had reacted in an unusually strong way when he heard the stories of the processions of Christians that had taken place twenty years earlier. He wanted to know all the details.

"Well, it seems he isn't cut out for a merchant's life. But here in Nagasaki there are people with refined sensibilities, and the foreign influence is still here. He's not much use for calculations, but I'd like to let this child who's come to me from my dreams enjoy himself."

Yazō had seen the look in Okattsama's eyes as she gazed into the distance. From it, he had understood the extraordinary feelings she had for Shirō.

One day Okattsama brought out a thick scroll and showed it to Yazō and Shirō.

"Before he passed away, the leader of my group of believers insisted on giving me this letter. Would you like to see it?"

When they rolled it out and read it, it struck Shirō as similar to the one that Watanabe Kozaemon had shown him. As they read on, they saw that the document had been submitted to the pope by the Rosario Jesus group of Dominican priests in Nagasaki in the eighth year of the Genwa era (1622). It was written by some of the Japanese believers whose spirits had been starting to weaken during the persecutions. It expressed their deep appreciation for the Dominican priests who had made their way to Japan and supported the people and not forsaken them. It noted that, although there were many different orders of Christians in Japan, the number of imprisoned priests from the Dominican order was the largest. That fact was evidence of their exceptional and superior work. The letter also described the amazement of the Japanese believers at these accomplishments, which they praised in most laudatory terms. At the end were the names of the signatories and the villages in which they had lived.

Moving her finger over the names of those believers, Okattsama continued, "By the end of that year, Ishimoto Rōsai-sama was beheaded and Tanaka Paulo-sama was burned at the stake. Both of those men were close friends of mine. I've never forgotten how their lives ended ... The letter we're looking at now is a copy of the one that was sent to the pope in Rome, attesting to the good work of the Dominicans. Since all of the religious orders were devoted to serving Deus-sama, they all wrote and sent this kind of document with joint signatures. But, the fact is, both the padres and we believers as well have risked our lives for our faith."

The letter had been written five years after the one that Kozaemon had shown Shirō. He was impressed by the overflowing of passion he saw in the writings of the believers, recorded in the handwriting of those who had been martyred and were no longer in this world. But at the same time, he was disturbed by the way the Japanese believers had been called on to testify to the achievements of the Jesuits at one time, and to those of the Dominicans, who were opposed to the Jesuits, at another.

In places like Arima and the Himi area of Nagasaki, conflicts had broken out among the Jesuit, Dominican and Franciscan missionaries, and Shirō had heard stories about how this had deeply troubled the local believers. He respected the padres for their missionary work, for undergoing severe persecution, and for embracing martyrdom. But he also wondered about the Japanese believers who had been pressed to testify to people in Rome about the relative successes and fervor of those from different religious orders. *Who possessed the greater virtue—the padres, who believed so steadfastly that they had enlightened the Japanese believers by sacrificing their lives, or the believers, who sheltered the padres and yearned, with all their hearts, to become faithful?*

Like withering, blackened ears in a green field of grain, division and seeds of corrosion are constantly being sown among the religious orders. I know that Chirisuto-sama himself was visited throughout his life by the same kinds of problems.

Shirō decided to climb Mount Inasa, a place he had been wanting to visit for some time. It was not far from Nagasaki, and offered a good view of the harbor from its peak. It wasn't really a difficult climb. As he slowly climbed the slope, he looked back on the town and the sea. Near the start of the trail were some modest shingle-roofed houses, with red quince buds just coming into blossom.

He had heard that the harbor was shaped like the neck of a crane, and when he had climbed about halfway up the mountain he could see this shape clearly. Beyond it was Nobozaki Point, but the mountain now blocked his view of it. With the foreign ships passing along the narrow sea lanes, it called to mind a landscape painting of a great river. The low line of the mountains stretching into the distance lent it a tranquil beauty.

What must those foreigners have thought as they peered out from their ships when they sailed slowly through the narrow sea-lanes and first saw the inner harbor surrounded by mountains? He had heard stories of the great waves in far-off seas, but such things were beyond his imagining. Fishers had told him of how, when they went out to the open seas, each wave appeared huge, like a mountain, and how truly frightening it was when the waves piled on each other, swelling and heaving.

When the padres from foreign places first came to this harbor after passing over those huge waves, did they imagine that they had been led by God to a promised land? As if they had entrusted their lives to a great and gentle river, they must have experienced a time of God's blessing, unable to imagine the trying days to come.

Early spring sun, ringed with a slight halo, shone over the harbor. The surface of the sea stirred with faint sounds and the banks that led the way into the East China Sea stood out softly in the sunlight. What lay beyond remained unseen, lost in the hazy light.

The previous October, when Shirō was back in Uto, some boats had left this harbor. A whaling crew from Ōyano Island had pulled into the harbor and had been watching the scene from the trail that led up Mount Inasa. A rumor had arrived in Uto with flying speed: children born of Nagasaki mothers and Portuguese or Spanish fathers were being expelled and deported to Macau, along with their mothers. Shirō thought about the ones who had left this beautiful harbor, exiled to a land they had never seen.

The people seeing them off had swarmed the banks like clouds, and as the boats left, they cried out in peals of lamentation that sounded like gongs being beaten to bits. The strange, painful shrieks and screams had risen up into the skies above.

One of the whalers who stopped in at Shirō's house had described the scene to him:

"It was too cruel—separating them like that, destroying their hopes for the future. I couldn't see them up close, but I saw them off from Mount Inasa. As I walked back down, I could still see many people gathered along the seaside, stamping their feet, standing up and sitting down, weeping and wailing."

It was likely that some people close to Okattsama were among those who had been sent away. Among Shirō's acquaintances, too, were some children of mixed blood. He had wanted to find out what happened to them, but had hesitated to inquire.

In the yards of the little thatched houses nearby, Shirō could see laundry waving in the breeze. The houses looked so much neater and tidier than those he had seen along the shores of Amakusa.

His eyes turned again toward the town. He had heard from

Ninagawa Sakyō that in the past, for believers who had never seen Rome, Nagasaki had been the center of Christianity. Okattsama had said this too.

"In the old days, the bells at the Church on the Cape used to echo throughout the town. Now that they're gone, we realize their true value."

Some twenty years ago, the Church of Saint Mary of the Mountains at the base of Mount Tateyama, and the Church on the Cape and the Church of the Assumption of the Blessed Virgin were all destroyed and now nothing of them remained.

"Sometimes the believers who came from all over the country to pray at those churches in Nagasaki climbed Mount Inasa. They asked if the place where the pope in Rome lived was like this place."

Back in those days they could still see a number of churches from Mount Inasa, but now it was hard to even locate their remains.

Shirō heard a rustling of footsteps in the fallen leaves, most likely another climber. He sensed they were coming to a stop. Turning around, he saw a young girl holding a hand basket, looking as if she were about to run away.

"Saya ... you're in Nagasaki?" he asked in surprise.

The girl seemed even more surprised.

"Well, my teacher ... yes."

Then she fell silent, with her hand reaching toward some rocks covered by swaying ferns. Her eyes were of a green color that looked as if it had sprung from the depths of the sea. Her skin was uncommonly fair. Her dark black hair was tied up simply in the back and she was wearing pantaloons that could easily have been mistaken for a man's; probably she had worn them for gathering leopard plants and wild parsley. She had put the herbs into her hand basket. When she looked up, her green eyes looked as if they might belong to a being from the spirit world. She bowed.

"Welcome back."

Shirō was unable to reply readily. Until just then, he had been thinking about the waves far below them. He had assumed that this girl was among those who had been sent away on one of the ships. And so, her sudden appearance had seemed like an apparition.

Guessing the reason for Shirō's astonishment from the look on his face, she smiled.

"Last year all the people with Portuguese relations were sent off to Macau. But my father's Dutch, so we escaped the danger."

But then, with an indescribably helpless look, she glanced up at him and her shoulders sagged. During their time apart, her way of speaking had become more grown up.

The previous fall, from the time Shirō arrived at Okattsama's place until his return home, he had been teaching neighborhood children how to write. Saya had been one of his students.

Her Dutch father worked on the ships authorized for foreign trade and was often sent to places like Luzon, Vietnam and Cambodia, so her mother took care of their household while he was away and supported the family by taking in sewing work. Okattsama praised Saya's mother and said she had done a fine job of bringing up her daughter.

Nagasaki had valued the foreign influence and taken good care of the children from mixed marriages, so it seemed that Saya, with her unusual eyes, had grown up in great freedom. She was the oldest of the children Shirō taught, only a year younger than him.

Saya worked well with the younger children. She not only did things like practicing brush writing and preparing the ink, she also led them in cleaning the toilets. Okattsama had noticed how well she behaved.

"I ... I thought you'd already been sent away, but I'm glad I was wrong."

"I've been waiting for you to come back."

Before, Shirō had only seen Saya surrounded by children, acting as a big sister. Meeting her now, face to face amidst the camellias, filled him with emotions that were both unexpectedly painful and sweet.

Shirō had never asked Saya whether her father was Portuguese or Dutch. For him, she was just one of the many mixed-marriage children in Nagasaki, and he had found her looks, with their air of mystery, charming. But now, meeting her in this way for the first time, he felt a pain deep in his chest.

"Saya."

"Yes, my teacher."

"You're only a year younger than me, so would you please stop calling me 'teacher.'"

"But … my teacher."

"Well, I will no longer be … "

Shirō was about to tell her that he had climbed the mountain with the intention of taking a last look at Nagasaki before leaving, but when he saw Saya's eyes, he could no longer say it. What was this feeling? A pain he had never felt before tugged at his heart. He turned and looked toward the sea, then knelt beside her. She was stunned. Facing the sun that was circled by a halo, he began to recite an *oratio*.

"Merciful sweet Maria-sama and blessed Son of the virtuous Maria-sama, whose purity is beyond that of any in this world and who is fairest among all beings, and gentle humble Lord, we beseech thee; remember our pain and poverty. *Amen*."

Saya did not quite understand the situation, but drawn by his low voice echoing with sadness, she, too, knelt in prayer.

Although she knew that her young teacher shared her mother's faith, this was the first time she had heard him recite an *oratio*.

For some reason, whenever her Dutch father was at home, her mother didn't pray. When he was away, her mother recited prayers to Maria-sama morning and night, and taught them to her. In a hushed voice and peering deep into her eyes, her mother had often warned her never to recite the prayers in front of others. If someone were to see or hear them praying, they might be crucified.

When this teacher, whom she secretly loved, knelt in front of her and looked up at the sun, she watched in astonishment. Then, quite beyond anything she could have imagined, from his mouth came words very similar to the ones her mother used in her prayers. Saya glanced around. She worried that he might be crucified if someone were to see or hear him.

Quickly, Saya moved behind Shirō, looked around carefully to make sure no one was near, and then knelt and joined him in prayer.

Since it was too difficult for her to follow Shirō's prayer, in a low voice Saya chanted a simpler one she had often recited with her mother. It was the first time she had prayed outside and it made her tense. She wondered what he was praying for. It sounded so serious.

Saya stood up. Shirō waited while she brushed the moss and dirt from her knees. Then he asked, "For what were you praying?"

The sunlight must have been dazzling, for she placed her fingers over her eyes repeatedly.

"I prayed that you wouldn't be punished for reciting the *oratio*."

Surprised, Shirō laughed and replied, "Well, thank you. From now on I'll be careful. And you, too!"

"All right, I will. And ... may I ask you a question?"

"Ask me anything."

"What kind of *oratio* was it that you were reciting?"

"Well, since I'm such a weak person, I was asking the Lord, and Maria-sama, for their help."

Hearing that even Shirō, her teacher, was lacking in strength troubled Saya. It was only natural to say that her mother and she were sinners before Maria-sama, but now, hearing these words from her teacher who was respected by everyone, she worried that there might be no virtuous people left in the world.

Nevertheless, Saya was attracted by the extraordinarily sorrowful prayer she had just heard. She felt a tremendous sense of sadness. She imagined that he, her teacher, must be bearing an even greater suffering, not only for his own sadness and sins, but for the sufferings of others as well.

"Please sit down over there."

His hand resting on the trunk of a large camphor tree, Shirō pointed to a rock beneath a camellia tree. For a while the two remained in silence. Small birds called from the thicket while sunlight, filtering gently through the trees, played about them.

"It's a surprise to meet you here."

Saya nodded as she fingered the handle of the basket on her lap.

"We can't be sure there'll be another day like this to come."

Today her teacher's voice sounded dejected. Saya thought he must be keeping to himself some very painful things. She wondered how to respond. She shook her head lightly, her hair hanging down loosely. Then, as if knocked free by the slight movement of her hair, a camellia blossom fell from above and landed in front of her. Startled, her face paled.

"I'll ... I'll pray to Maria-sama," she said.

Their eyes met. Shaking her head, she continued.

"I'll pray to her. Please, may I meet …"

For a while, Shirō seemed to search for the words to respond.

"Who is it you hope to meet?" was what he had wanted to ask, but he couldn't say the words.

"In this world, we can't know what will happen, even in the very near future."

Saya felt a deep sorrow. Her green eyes were fixed on Shirō, as if staring at him from the shade of rocks on the bottom of the sea.

"Teacher … will I be able to see you in the world of *anima*?"

Shirō was overcome with emotion. *Saya means a lot to me. And she's so unfortunate. For how long will the* bakufu, *which has already so mercilessly expelled the mixed-blood children of the Portuguese, allow the children of Dutch parents to remain?* For a moment he considered taking Saya back with him to Uto. *What if I were to hide her there? What if I took her to the fields of rapeseed and placed her, with a white veil on her head, under the gate of Heaven in Rokusuke's field?*

Suddenly, Shirō opened his eyes. Released from his dark brooding, he made up his mind to look clearly into the world beyond. He pointed toward the currents in the far-off sea that were shining like a great river.

"Saya, Maria-sama will help you in the world of *anima*."

"Then I'll pray to be on the boat of *anima*."

Saya knelt and prayed, her fingertips colored with the pungent juices of herbs. Flowers were blooming in the wide branches of the old camellia tree, and in the shadow of the tree where she knelt the space was filled with a golden mist of nectar. Her shoulders, covered in a pale gardenia-colored kimono, looked listless.

"In the country of *anima*, you're sure to be one of Maria-sama's followers."

Shirō spoke with his eyes closed.

"Are there many followers of Maria-sama?"

"Yes, there are many."

"And why will I follow Maria-sama?"

"Because of your suffering."

"Suffering … ?"

Saya's face showed deep confusion.

"I don't have any wisdom, so I can't understand such difficult things."

"Wisdom? You're better off without it. It's better not to understand."

"Well …"

Saya couldn't find the words to continue.

"Try to keep on talking."

This was her teacher's usual way of speaking.

"When my mother said the *oratio,* she said she was a sinner. She asked me to say that I'm a child of sin too. What is the sin?"

"It's certain that Maria-sama is watching over you. And Okattsama praises your mother's goodness, doesn't she? Real sin is judged by Deus-sama, so it's best if we remain humble in front of others at all times. That's what I think."

It seemed to Saya that her teacher was different from usual today; he looked much sadder. When he was teaching, he used to close his eyes in thought, and now, too, they were shut.

"A young woman like you shouldn't be out walking alone in the mountains. I'll watch after you, so let's go back early."

On the verge of tears, Saya looked down at her basket. Probably, she had been hoping to fill it.

"It's dangerous up here in the mountains. I'll follow you on the way down, and I'll pick some wild parsley for your basket, so don't worry."

As she turned and looked back, Saya felt that Shirō was like a brother, willing even to pick wild parsley for her. Thinking of how she might ride with this brother on the *anima* boat brightened her spirits.

Here is another person who prays to God for what is not possible to achieve in this world, Shirō reflected. *Perhaps she feels these things more keenly than most children because of her mixed-blood background. At fifteen, some women would already be married. But I have to be careful not to say things that might upset her.* Shirō tried to calm the rush of emotions he felt from having met her alone.

People in Nagasaki are used to seeing children of mixed races and, for the most part, they don't discriminate against them. But Saya, with her Dutch father, will have to manage her own fate. It's said that Maria-

sama became an embodiment of compassion by giving up her beloved son Chirisuto to be crucified upon the Hill of Calvary. Her compassion must have sprung from her deep sorrow. We, her exiled children, cast out from Paradise, are being held in the trembling arms of sorrowful Maria-sama. The sorrows of Saya, this child of mixed blood, will one day become an eternal spring of love, just as it was with Maria-sama.

These were the kinds of things that Shirō had wanted to tell Saya.

Watching the sunlight playing on the sea, he stood up.

From this harbor the sea lanes led boats to Luzon, Cambodia, Jakarta and Goa. They led even to the Hill of Calvary, where Chirisuto-sama died, and on to Rome, where the pope lived. But, more vividly than he could imagine any of the boats that sailed off to other countries, Shirō imagined what Saya had called the boat that would take them to the country of *anima*.

Saya's mother, who always prayed that her sins would be forgiven, had likely taught her daughter about this "boat of *anima*." Or had this phrase sprung suddenly from Saya's mouth? Shirō hadn't known there was a boat of *anima*. It could not be known through ordinary means. Shirō thought his troubles in this world might be lightened if he could ride on that longed-for boat, together with Saya. He followed her as she walked down through the shade of the trees, looking back again and again. She went as far as the entrance to the harbor and then, looking down as if she was having trouble making up her mind, suddenly turned and faced him. With a beautiful smile, she said, "Take care, my teacher." Then she bowed her head politely and walked away.

It seemed to Shirō that he had climbed Mount Inasa so that he could meet Saya. This was the best gift he could have received before leaving Nagasaki. Lately he had felt stifled and weighed down when he thought about difficult matters of doctrine. Saya's words had come as a breath of fresh, sweet air.

Still, what food did I give her soul in return? As Saya passed out of sight he began walking and tried to shake himself free of such doubts. A smile formed on his lips as he thought, *I'd like to ride on that* anima *boat with Saya.*

At the water's edge by the wharf, tiny petals of meadowsweet had drifted down from the houses on the hill and were floating in and out with the tide.

Shirō told Okattsama about his talk with Saya. At first, she seemed to listen with pleasure, but then her face took on a note of concern.

"To tell the truth, I've been worrying about her."

"You mean, because …"

"Yes. Lately, there's been talk that a government edict is going to be issued requiring us to write down all sorts of things, like the number of households and the circumstances of life in our town. Everyone knows that her father is Dutch, but if we have to write it down for the magistrate's office, it could lead to trouble."

"I've heard that the religious sect of the Dutch is different from that of the Spanish and Portuguese; and from ours, too."

"Still, we're all Christians. And now that the government has expelled everyone with Portuguese relatives, they're not likely to overlook the wives and children of the Dutch."

Shirō realized that the fears he had been holding in his heart were quickly becoming reality.

"In two days I'll be leaving. You've taught me things more important than what I could have learned from a thousand books."

"What are you saying? It's thanks to you that I can feel the sun shining on my remaining days. This has been our special fate."

Shirō felt profoundly grateful for the words of this woman whose life experiences had been unfathomably different from his.

"I wanted to prepare something for your coming-of-age celebration, but this was all I could think of."

Okattsama brought out a bundle wrapped in a large *furoshiki*. In it, neatly folded, were a kimono with the image of a bird woven into the silver silk; a crisp, dark blue pair of *hakama* trousers with barely visible silver-violet flowers embroidered on them; and a sleeveless *haori* half-coat made of the same material in a pale greenish tint. A small paulownia wood box was set on top. Wrapped around it was a rosary with ivory beads and an ebony cross. It shone in the light with quiet elegance.

"What is this?"

Shirō sat up and straightened his posture.

"Go ahead," she encouraged him, "pick it up and take a look. It was a gift from the priest who stayed here and then was martyred."

"Such an important thing?"

"Because it's important it's fitting that it should be entrusted to you. It's most suitable for you."

As Okattsama spoke, she pulled the box toward her and lifted its cover. Shiro's eyes were struck by the clear light that shone from within. In the box was a crucifix made of finely wrought gold. Reverently, with both her hands, she raised it up high.

"I've regarded this as a family treasure, but now the time has come to pass it on. If you would kindly accept it, I'm sure its former owner would be pleased. It once belonged to a trading merchant."

Shirō looked as if he was about to speak, but she interrupted him gently.

"This crucifix shines so brightly that it might stand out too much when you wear it. But I imagine you could use it as a relic for rituals when people are gathered for ceremonies."

Okattsama's expression turned deeply serious.

"Your departure will be my departure too."

Surprised, Shirō looked at her again.

"I've traveled many roads, and I can't speak about them adequately in words. Talking with you now, I feel that I too, at last, am standing at the entrance to the country of *anima*. My legs are weak and I need to cast off much baggage from this world before I go."

CHAPTER FIVE

Rapeseed Clouds

Sensing a spiritual bond, Shirō bowed his head as Okattsama placed the ivory rosary over his neck.

He woke to a bright morning with a delicate fragrance in the air and realized that Okattsama had lit incense for his departure. It wafted from the altar in the back of the house. When she asked him to read his favorite passage from the Bible, he opened it without hesitation to the page he had already chosen. She was kneeling, her head covered with a white veil she rarely used. To his surprise, Saya and her mother were there too, kneeling in silence, their heads covered with similar veils.

"Our Lord has told us clearly that he came to bring a fire to the Earth, and that he wished for nothing but this fire. The flame from this altar is a sign, passed on according to the ancient commandments, that this fire will not die. It is a most important sign of this spirit."

Wondering if Saya had understood, he added:

"The light of the *anima* boat, too, comes from this fire."

They ate a late breakfast together and then, just as Shirō was about to say his words of parting, Okattsama brought out something wrapped in a violet *fukusa* cloth and gently held it out to him.

"When you meet Ukon-dono, would you please ask him to give this to Juan-sama? It's aloeswood. It's burned for its fragrance. And here is some for you."

The morning was chilly, with a late frost. Seven or eight students who had studied writing under Shirō joined them and walked together as far as the bead tree. Among them was Saya, her eyes moist with tears.

Shortly after Shirō arrived at the Ninagawa's house in Kuchinotsu, a sack of grain was delivered. Without mentioning anything to him, Okattsama had arranged for it to be loaded onto his boat.

Ninagawa Sakyō's wife looked up at her husband, touched by Okattsama's attentiveness.

"My goodness—she's even thought of things for our house."

Okattsama's thoughtfulness also included the spiritual support she provided to the household through the items she sent with Shirō.

When Shirō brought out the aloeswood for Juan, Ukon responded with deep respect.

"Since this is a gift of such uncommon kindness, I think it would bring greater happiness to our teacher if you, rather than I, were to give it to him," he said, straightening his posture.

At his side, his father Sakyō added, "We all know that Juan-sama has long dreamed of this, but had mostly given up hope. He'll surely be very happy. And as for the young folks' study group, your return will certainly help move it along."

Ukon's mother put some of the grain from Nagasaki into a bag and handed it to Shirō and Ukon as they left to visit Juan.

"Let us share our blessings with our teacher."

People in Okattsama's Nagasaki neighborhood often borrowed and lent miso and grain, and they gave food at weddings and on other occasions just as people did in Shirō's home in Uto. He could see that the same customs were practiced here in Kuchinotsu.

When Shirō presented the aloeswood to Juan, joy and gratitude filled him. Reverently, he held it up and breathed in its fragrance. He asked how long Shirō would be staying and suggested that, before he left, they should hold a tea ceremony.

"By the way, Ukon," Juan said, " . . . about the young people you recommended."

"Yes, I'd like to discuss that."

"Perhaps we're thinking along the same lines."

"But I'd like to hear your thoughts first, as our teacher."

"No need to stand on ceremony—just tell me their names."

"Well, all right. A number of people have expressed a desire to open a school. From Kuchinotsu, there's Migita Banojō-dono and six others. From Minami Arima there's Sasaki Kurabito-dono and five others. And from Kita Arima there's Naito Seiba-dono and seven more. I haven't visited Chijiwa yet, so I don't know the number there, but everyone I just mentioned wants to open the school."

"That's good to hear. If we already have that many young people, we're off to a good start."

"But I'm a bit concerned about a rumor I heard," Ukon added.

"A rumor? What was it?"

"Well, I heard that some of the young people in Kita Arima have been talking about leaving the village. And their parents agree with them, too."

"Hmm, tell me more."

"Well, Kichiji, a farmer in Kita Arima, has been telling his friends that if they go to Nagasaki they can get work on the foreigners' boats and make enough money to eat all they want, and not just barley and wheat—rice, even. He says the foreigners in Nagasaki are inviting young people onto their boats, and the whole economy there is tied up with the foreign ships."

"I've heard some stories like that too, but there's another side to all that slick talk," Juan answered. "Yazō's told me that the foreigners are tough traders. I don't think those stories will be enough to persuade our young people to desert their villages."

"But, as you know, our crops failed last year and the year before. We should have better crops this year, but nothing's certain. The young people are saying they don't want to eat weeds and wild plants from the mountains just to survive. They're saying, 'Why not just go work for a while and come back with some foreign rice? There's plenty of foreign ships in Nagasaki harbor. We may be farmers, but we can row a boat good as anyone.'"

"Perhaps I don't need to tell you this, but the work on those foreign boats can't be pleasant. The fact that people are ready to take a risk like that is all the more reason for us to work together and build that school from the ground up."

Juan unfolded his arms and stared at the two young men.

"This Kichiji—is he a Christian?"

"Well, they say he is. Naito says he shows up at Mass from time to time. They say he's quite a lively fellow."

"I suppose those farmers' sons are a different sort than Nisuke's son. I'd be curious to talk to them some time."

"I'd like to talk to them myself, but I worry my way of thinking and talking is just too different from that of Kichiji and his friends."

"Don't worry about that. I've heard how well you handled the Ninagawa's worker Takematsu the other day when he was about to be thrown out of the group for his heavy drinking."

"I suppose I hit it off well enough with him."

"But it's strange that you, Ukon—who hardly ever touch liquor—can get along so well with a guy like that."

"It must be thanks to Heaven. Since then, we've become good friends."

Juan looked pleased that Ukon had answered his half-joking question so sincerely.

"What sort of things do you talk about with your drinking friend?" Shirō asked with great interest.

"How can I put it? When I talk with Takematsu, it's like a fresh wind is blowing through my narrow mind."

"I see . . . For example?" Juan asked.

"That time when he was acting so rowdy, I asked him why he drank so much, even though he knew that the *confuraria's* rules said he could be thrown out of the group if he kept it up after being warned. In turn, he asked me if I knew anything about the taste of liquor. When I replied that I didn't, he said that I know a lot about the taste of written words and so, even though I'm still young, I do know some things. Then he asked me to explain the taste of writing. He said he'd never opened a book. When I told him that, for me, the taste of writing clears my head and opens up my spirit, he cried out, 'Yes! Yes! That's just what it's like for me with the taste of liquor!

"'My parents were poor,' he said, 'and they were poor because my grandparents were also poor, and plenty of times we didn't have enough to eat, and some nights the snow blew in through the cracks in the doorway and my family—my parents and I, together—we all had to pull the tattered blanket around us and go to sleep hungry. But still, I was thankful to my parents, since they put me between them and—whether it was the smell of my father's sake or from their breathing, I don't know, but they kept me warm between them. At times like that, as we slept in our ragged bedding, my mother used to say that we should be patient while we're alive, for soon Deus-sama would take care of us.'"

Ukon fell silent for a moment and then continued Takematsu's story.

"He told me, 'My parents, they're no longer here, and as the years go by, I miss them. My wife left me, and, as you know, I'm on my own. I can't speak in front of people. Every time I say something, I worry that it will bother people, so I just keep my head down as I walk along . . .

"'But when I have some sake, it's the sweet nectar of Maria-sama, and as long as I'm drinking it, I can feel my parents' thin arms, like when they used to hold me. It warms my spirit and clears my head and I can talk about things. For me, it's the time my spirit's the best and most open.

"'I don't know the first thing about academic matters but, Ukon-sama, when you read books, I suppose you feel like there's nothing and no one between you and Deus-sama. There's just your true self and Him. And when I drink, I can be my true self. Then Maria-sama and my mother become one, and She takes care of me, like her child.

"'Why do you call me a heavy drinker? A person doesn't become a drinker by choice. Drinking lets me be my real self, and it lets me say what I really think. But then I realize that what I think is different from what others think and it starts to get me angry. Even when I'm silent, I'm still thinking. And when I'm feeling free and saying what I really think, it causes people trouble—isn't that so, Ukon-sama?'

"That's what Takematsu told me, and then he laughed."

"Hmm, that sounds interesting," Juan said. "So, how's he getting on now?"

"His small boat was smashed by the big storm last year and it's beyond repair. But he's been diving for fish, and he's proud of his skills."

"And still, he's able to find plenty to drink?"

"They say he sniffs it out."

"Sniffs it out, eh? Well, in any case, he sounds like quite a character."

"He seems like an appealing person," Shirō said, smiling.

The wrinkles around Juan's eyes rippled like waves and he looked up at the ceiling, clearly enjoying himself.

Just then, Sakyō's wife appeared at the sliding door.

"Excuse me, but Hasuda Nisuke-dono's son just arrived and he brought us this gift."

She held out a wicker basket filled with mandarin oranges.

"Ah—Nisuke's son? Ukon, what's his name?"

"Daisuke-dono."

"Ah, right, Daisuke. That's good. Please ask him to come in."

Juan looked to Ukon and Shirō for agreement.

"This is good timing. I was just thinking I'd like to see him," Ukon said enthusiastically.

After exchanging greetings, Daisuke looked cordially at Shirō and Ukon. This was the second time the four had met since the night the old people's house was washed away. A month earlier, Ukon had gone to Daisuke's house but was told that Daisuke had just gone off to Yushima Island, so he had talked at length with Daisuke's father Nisuke before returning home. The purpose of his visit had been to ask the Hasuda family if they would be willing to let their house be used for the proposed school. Juan had thought a location with lots of space would be best, and the Hasuda household seemed ideal. But Juan worried that the Hasudas might have a hard time saying no to him, even if they wanted to, so he had asked Ukon to test the waters first.

Although Ukon had last seen Nisuke less than half a year earlier, it seemed to him that Nisuke had aged considerably. But as they talked, Nisuke had seemed to revive and brighten.

"We've all been worried about the future, but this is a wonderful, encouraging idea. It gives me energy," he had said in a single breath, then sighed in relief. "The people of Shimabara have been losing hope for a long time now. We've fallen on hard times these past few years, what with all the bad harvests and merciless taxes. We've all been feeling like we've reached a dead end. Rich and poor alike, all we can do is stare at each other. I'm the headman of this town, but only in name. I'm like a scarecrow in a withered field with no idea what to do. But what you're saying makes me feel alive again."

Ukon hadn't expected such a reply, and it deepened his respect for Nisuke.

"If we can start a school in Kuchinotsu like the one you're suggesting, it will be a spiritual support for all of us. Those who studied at the *seminario* and the *collegio* will help us. This is truly a cause for rejoicing."

Barely holding back tears, Nisuke had looked up at the ceiling.

"This old place is falling apart, but I've been told that back in my father's time, Almeida-sama stayed here. He died at Kawachiura in Amakusa. My grandmother told me that since Almeida-sama was also a medical doctor, Buddhists as well as Christians would flock to our house when he visited, and she had her hands full in taking care of everyone. That may have been one reason our family became the head of the benevolence group. If we can start a new school here in this house, it will certainly bring great pleasure to my departed parents and grandparents."

Scarcely a month had passed since that day when Nisuke had promised with such pleasure to let them use his house.

Daisuke sat formally with his hands on his knees.

"I'm here tonight to ask about the matter that Ukon-sama brought up when he visited our house. My father is very pleased about the plans, but he's wondering about things like when it will start, and how many people will be coming, and how many bookshelves will be needed and what the plans for the future are."

Juan assured him that they were just about to discuss all of this, and so the four men began their first joint meeting about the details of opening the school. Shirō did not feel out of place with the three from Kuchinotsu, who included him as a founding member.

After they had tentatively settled their plans, Juan stirred the fire with metal tongs as the teakettle puffed out steam.

"This school may not compare with what we had during the good times, but at least we can say we're relighting the lamp of learning," he said. "And I must admit with some mixed emotions that I'm getting old."

"I can certainly appreciate your feelings," Ukon said, sitting up straight. "The other day I visited Nakao Taian in Arie. He's a respected graduate of the Hachirao *seminario*. Since he's somewhat hard of hearing, I showed him a written proposal for the school. When he read it, he stared at me and broke into tears."

"Oh, you mean the one we called Matthias? Later, he went on to the *collegio* in Amakusa and completed the course in Latin. He knew the old stories from China and Japan and the myths and popular tales better than I did."

"That's him. I've heard some stories about him. One time, he and some other students debated in Latin in front of the bishop on whether power is superior to scholarship. The bishop praised their talent and said he felt as if he were listening to Spanish students debating."

"I remember that myself, though for the most part I just listened. We used to debate that sort of thing a lot. Matthias and I were in the same class.

"I wonder where all those people are now, and what they're doing. They came from all over; from Ōmura and Isahaya and Nagasaki, and other places. All that good talent hasn't been used properly. But I think there's still a smoldering fire that can relight our faith.

"The students at the *seminario* picked up Latin quickly, and art and music too. It amazed the priests so much that they praised them as being quicker, even, than young Europeans. I have to admit I was never much good at art or music, and now when I join in the hymns, I completely throw off the pitch. But I wonder what it was that allowed our community to blossom during that time. It was as if the light of the age had chosen to shine over the lands of Arima and its people.

"When the bishop visited, we'd put on plays in Latin. But those weren't the only times—we performed them during the festivals too, and when the townspeople came, we'd mix Latin lines with Japanese.

"Especially in the *mysterio* passion plays, we'd include some of the songs left to us by Lorenzo-dono, the blind monk and biwa player. At the parts where Chirisuto-sama is taken down from the Cross and Maria-sama laments, the audience would get completely wrapped up in it and start crying. Afterwards, the actors on the stage and the people who had been watching all felt as if we'd been related for hundreds of years.

"We put our hearts into those rehearsals. The actors were also the writers. We wrote the words and scripts and decided where to put in the songs and litanies for the Holy Mother. And at the end of the plays, both the actors and audience joined in reciting an *oratio*. The townspeople would wave to them as they left, sad to part. It seemed as if a pure light was shining in our midst. There was a sacred feeling about it all . . . That was back in my youth, but I'll never forget it. As the years go by, I remember it even more clearly."

Juan blinked, as if in response to a light blinking in the far-off darkness.

This was the first time they had heard him talk of such things. They blushed, and no one attempted to speak. After a while, Ukon said, "Those days of the Arima clan's rule, they seem like a dream . . . But now we have to do what we can to build a school like that—don't you think, Shirō-dono?"

"Yes, absolutely."

Shirō drew a somewhat pained breath.

"Hearing that story, I could see the light of all those souls, as if they were dancing on the waves along the shore. May our own efforts be like that."

"Yes," Daisuke said at once. "Since I've been granted life on this Earth, I'd like to be part of something like that. I've always been slow at learning, and I'm no good at this sort of talk, but I'll do whatever I can to help. My father agrees, and that's why he had me come here."

In this way, a school with ten or so members opened in secret in Nisuke's storehouse. Each of the students brought a copy of the *Tenchi hajime no koto* Bible. They read it to each other and discussed their thoughts about it.

After finishing his work, Kumagorō, who worked for the Hasuda family, came and listened from the back of the room. It seemed that Ukon had also told Takematsu about the meetings, so he, too, came and sat on the stone steps at the entrance. He looked drowsy, but from time to time he seemed to prick up his ears and listen. Perhaps he had been looking for a chance to launch into one of his inebriated talks, but he held his tongue and busied himself with shooing off a reddish dog that had wandered in.

Oume-yan served Takematsu some tea and whispered in his ear, "Well, what's this now? Looks like you've shown up to work as the gatekeeper for Ukon-sama's school."

Takematsu grinned.

"That's right. There's no one better suited for a gatekeeper than me. You sure are a wise woman. But, say, with all this talk going on—you think we might bring out a little of that 'strong tea'?"

Oume-yan immediately dismissed his request.

"Today all we have is ordinary tea. But, well, if the gatekeeper gets some good work done, then perhaps we might bring out a little stronger tea afterwards."

"Hmm. Afterwards? But if you're going to put it out anyway, I'd say the sooner the better. And I brought some nice snacks from the sea to go with it."

"Snacks? Well, how about that? It seems you've become quite the master of spearfishing—did you bring us some sea cucumbers?"

"Hey, give me a break! Even a three-year-old kid can catch sea cucumbers. They just loll around on the bottom of the sea. I don't need a spear for that."

"Well, in that case, did you spear us a whale or something?"

"I'd love to tell you I caught a whale, but even if I did, it wouldn't fit in this storehouse."

"Why not? We could all sit on it and cut it up, and we'd be done in a snap."

"All right, but a whale's just one dish. I brought some other things too."

Takematsu picked up his net bag from the stone steps and dropped it with a thud. Perhaps that woke up the creatures inside, for they started making all sorts of squeaking and creaking noises.

"They're presents—for the opening of Ukon's school," Takematsu said shyly.

"Oh, my goodness!"

In the evening darkness, Oume-yan leaned over the net, eyes wide.

"Look—there's eels, and lumpfish and, oh, some big lobsters . . . one, two, three, four—look at them. And look at this claw—it must be thicker than your arm!"

"It sure is a big one. I had to dive real deep to catch that one. And I had to take care in keeping it alive."

"You're a real faithful follower of Ukon-sama, aren't you?"

"I suppose I am. Actually, I'd like to serve Ukon-sama even more than Deus-sama. But getting back to those lobsters—now that I've shown them to you, how about if we go ahead and boil them?"

"No, no, not yet. If we boil them too soon, they'll get cold. When the people in there have finished reading the books, then we'll boil the lobsters. They'll taste much better if they're still hot."

"All right, but for a little pre-celebration, can't we just put out a sip of that strong tea? If we miss the right moment for drinking, it'll weaken Maria-sama's blessing."

"Oh, come on now—I'm a follower of Amida-sama, not Maria-sama. I'm different from you. I chant *namu amida butsu, namu amida butsu* while it's fermenting. Unless you say a prayer to Amida-sama, you can't drink from it."

"What's this now? I thought Amida-sama was full of mercy."

"Mercy? Mercy comes from Deus-sama and Maria-sama."

"But won't you just give me a little drink, as proof of Amida-sama's mercy?"

"Enough! Not until things are finished."

They had been bantering in hushed tones, but Kumagorō nevertheless threw them a fierce glare. Oume-san stood up and tapped on Takematsu's crushed topknot. Some peach petals that had fallen onto him somewhere along his way floated down from his hair.

Takematsu started to doze off. Suzu came in with a quilted cotton coat, probably at Oume-yan's request, and draped it over his shoulders. Before long, he began snoring like a crying tiger cub.

The storehouse was filled with the sound of young men's laughter. Suzu slipped past Takematsu and stood behind Kumagorō. Amidst the shadows cast on the straw mats by the winnowers and other farm equipment, she could see the backs of the young men. Juan-sama was repeating some difficult words she had never heard before.

The early buds were starting to swell on trees and other plants. The bent reeds along the shoreline were springing to life and the fresh grain sprouts were poking up in the fields.

The debris from the past year's mudslides was covered in new grass, so that you had to look closely to even notice it. The camphor tree at the top of the hill was shedding its old leaves and sending out new ones, and if you looked out towards Shimabara and Amakusa, the land shone with the gleam of fresh life as far as the eye could see.

That spring, the spirits seemed to be dozing. Perhaps the leaves and dirt washed up by the storms had nurtured the land, restoring it from the sorry state of last year's drought. The creatures in the sea flourished too, and people often said, "The clams and shellfish look good this year." The waters along the rocky coastline brimmed with *nori*, *mozuku* and other seaweeds of many colors.

In the third month, around the time of the big spring tides, people lined the shore like crabs drying their shells in the sun, chatting cheerfully. Eagerly, Okayo and Suzu followed Oume to the water's edge.

Oume, who had been brought up in Amakusa, was regarded as the best of the gatherers. She said that if you found a good spot it was better not to move around too much. True to her advice, she would be spotted bending over in one spot for hours at a time, and later her basket would be filled with shucked oysters. Neither Okayo nor Suzu could come close to matching her skill.

"Tonight, we'll make a feast of these."

Calmly, Oume reached her hand deep into a pool in the rocks, pulled up a baby octopus and plopped it into Suzu's basket. With a quick, affectionate glance, she warned, "Watch out, or it'll get away!"

Suzu bent over and watched the small creature closely. After appearing puzzled for a moment, the octopus effortlessly slipped its neck past the rim of the basket, hoisted itself out, and returned to the seaweed world from which it had come.

"Well, it figures. Looks like it didn't fancy ending up in someone's dinner pot. All right then, off you go. Off you go!"

As the tide came in, Suzu turned to look at the rocks where she had been working. Standing in the seaweed as it swayed in the waves, suddenly she looked down at her leg and gave it a shake.

"Look—that little octopus. It's back, and it's chasing me! Ah, it's crawling up my leg!"

Oume-yan watched the baby octopus, its head no bigger than a thumb, as it swayed along with the seaweed, clinging to Suzu and moving its legs.

"Now aren't you glad we let you go?" Oume-yan said to the octopus as it floated in the waves. "All right then, see you again. Suzu, tell it you'll see it again. Okay, let's go. If we waste time, we'll be washed away by the waves."

The sun was still shining at a low angle above the ocean. Gold fringed a dark bank of clouds, their color changing rapidly.

"Look, Oume-yan—those clouds are pretty black. It seems the weather's going to change tomorrow."

"Hmm. Looks like we may get the first strong winds of spring. And they may blow away all the nice blossoms."

Okayo tugged at Suzu's hand, since she seemed to want to stay. Oume-yan held out her hand to Okayo.

"Ah, Okayo-sama, be careful you don't fall in," she cautioned. "You have to take care of the little one inside."

As they had suspected, it began to rain that evening. A clap of thunder struck with a tremendous roar, and with it came a great gust of wind, and then the rain fell and continued on and off throughout the night.

Perhaps it was strange, but for Kumagorō, the thunder that came with the first spring winds was soothing, and he slept on past dawn for the first time in ages. When daybreak came, the bush warbler chicks began to cry out. It sounded as if they couldn't yet move their tongues well. Amidst these pleasant sounds, Kumagorō dozed off and slept again.

But—it was Sunday! He had heard that Deus-sama knew people couldn't live by work alone, and that they need a day just to be thankful for the day itself, and so he had created the holiday of Sunday. Yesterday, the men had finished preparing the ridges in the fields for planting and the women had finished packing the bags of seaweed they had been drying. And in any case, with all the rain, there was no way they could work in the fields.

The night before, Oume-yan had served the oysters she had brought back in her basket with some homemade millet liquor, for the first time in ages. Matsukichi, who slept next to Kumagorō, seemed to be waking up and crawling out of his blankets. But he didn't call out, *Wake up! Get up!* as he normally did. The smell of tobacco filled the air.

Kumagorō sat up in his futon, shifting his shoulders back and forth, his bones making creaking sounds.

"Those bones of yours, they sound pretty young," Matsukichi said, pulling an ashtray toward him. He tapped the bowl of his pipe.

"I must be twenty years younger than you, wouldn't you say?" Kumagorō replied, his shoulders cracking as he rotated them. He raised his fists, shook his body and turned toward Matsukichi.

"Weren't those oysters last night something? And that pickled seaweed, too."

"They were. And it's been ages since we've had good home-brewed sake like that. That millet brew was really fine, too. I heard that Taian-sama put it in his boat and brought it to celebrate the opening of the school."

"That white-haired guy?"

"He's quite a scholar, I hear."

"When he saw the sea cucumbers that Takematsu brought, he was amazed. There must've been a whole barrel of them."

"Come on, there wasn't a barrel full. Your tongue's running away from you again."

"Maybe so, but he sure did catch a lot."

"They say that after Takematsu goes diving, all that's left is sea cucumber shit."

"Yeah, but this time he went all out. And he brought us those huge lobsters for the celebration."

"Takematsu's a great fan of Ukon-sama. And by the way, you've been in that classroom with them, haven't you? Can you really follow what they're talking about?"

"I can catch parts of it. It's like they say, 'repeated reading makes the meaning clear.' When I hear things repeated over and over again, even if I can't understand at first, sometimes I start to get it."

"Well, that's good."

"Even for someone like me, what they're saying gets to my heart now and then. But how about you? How about sitting in with us at the school sometime?"

"It's not that I wouldn't go, but does Ukon-sama read the *Tale of the Heike* there?"

"Not just now, but after a while they're going to invite people and he'll do it. Seems it's quite a job."

"I hope it won't be too difficult for the rest of us. And who's doing the teaching?"

"Well, there's Juan-sama and Ukon-sama, and Shirō-sama. And Taian-sama can teach Latin."

"So Shirō-sama's teaching?"

"He's no ordinary person. Why don't you sit in and listen sometime when he's talking? To tell the truth, I haven't heard him yet, myself."

"I've heard that Takematsu comes, too, so I suppose there must be something to Shirō-sama's talks. It seems these days Takematsu has been following Ukon-sama the closest."

"It's pretty interesting to see the straitlaced scholar and the heavy drinker sitting close together. Usually, they talk about different things and disagree, but they get along well. And somehow the other big drinkers act like innocent girls and just sit there fidgeting. It's quite a sight."

"Hmm. I think I've seen him dozing off at the entrance to the school in the warehouse some evenings when class is going on."

"Well, yes, but let me tell you—he's a clever fox. The guy knows how to play the fool. He may look like just a boozer, but actually he knows a lot. That's why he gets along so well with Oume-yan. When they're both talking like fools it's fun listening to them."

"Oume-yan, she's another difficult one. I guess that's why the two of them get along so well."

Matsukichi was impressed to hear Kumagorō talking on so much more logically than usual.

Didn't Kumagorō come to the Hasuda house when he was just six years old? The same age as Suzu when she came. He must have lived with the family for twenty years or more by now. He was an orphan like her, but he was brought up in even more difficult circumstances.

Kumagorō was the orphaned child of a martyr. He was an illegitimate child and his mother had died just after giving birth. After that, his uncle and aunt had adopted him. His adoptive father was martyred twenty years ago. Kumagorō's life had been spared because he wasn't his biological son. His adoptive mother, unable to bear the fate of being tortured, had abandoned the faith. Later, she had gone insane and disappeared. At one time, people said she had gone off to Nagasaki and become a beggar, but now no one knew anything about her.

His adoptive father had had his fingers and toes cut off, his joints severed, and finally his head cut off. In order to prevent other believers from retrieving his body, it was burned and his ashes were thrown into the sea. On the evening of the execution, Kumagorō had run away from the house he grew up in and eventually hid by a stack of rice straw in one of Nisuke's fields. He was crying when Baba-sama—Nisuke's mother—found him there.

"Say there, whose house are you from?" she had asked.

"My house is where I am," he replied. That was what his parents had always told him.

"What's your father's name?"

"Father."

"And your mother's name?"

"Mother."

"And why are you all alone and crying?"

"Because my father's head was cut off."

Even though the adults had tried hard to keep this fact from him, probably he had kept his ears open and learned of it. Her voice shaking from shock, Baba-sama asked his name.

"Kuma."

"Kuma—you mean like in the word 'bear'? Well, Kuma, even bears can cry."

As she said this, Baba-sama wrapped her arms around the boy, who was sitting in tears with a runny nose.

"Just now you found your way here, by chance. That means we're going to take care of you."

And with these words from Baba-sama, the child had found a family to stay with. One of the reasons the *confuraria* had established the benevolence group was to help surviving family members of martyrs. Kumagorō was a year older than Daisuke and the two were brought up together as equals, so from time to time they tussled and fought. For Kumagorō, though, the memory of how he had come into the house remained vivid, and he never forgot his humble status as a worker. Nisuke and his wife taught both Daisuke and Kumagorō how to read, and they told Kumagorō that he should find a wife quickly and that they planned to build a house for him. Kumagorō revered the master and his wife as parents. And it was their son Daisuke who had invited him to come take a look at the school.

The people around Kumagorō knew about his early circumstances, but they didn't talk about them much and he didn't speak of his childhood memories.

Kumagorō still had an early memory of his father telling him, "Look, Kuma, open your mouth wide—like this—and say, 'Ahh.'" This was when he was showing him how to eat raw sardines after he had prepared them and dipped them in soy sauce with his fingers. He remembered how his father had rubbed his cheeks with his stubby beard. As he ate a sardine, Kumagorō had just barely managed to stand up by holding on to his father's shoulder. And now, when Kumagorō touched his own cheeks, he clearly recalled the feeling of his father's skin and beard. He hadn't known that this man had been his adoptive father—not his real father—until Baba-sama told him about it just before she died.

When he was a child, Kumagorō had only been able to imagine a beheading by picturing something like a doll's head being cut off; but even that image had made him feel as if the heavens and earth had been turned upside down. Even today he couldn't forget it, not even for a moment. Whenever he touched his own stubby beard, he felt his neck and thought about his father's death.

Sitting in the back row when he attended the meetings in the storehouse at Daisuke's invitation, Kumagorō was searching for answers. But he had never mentioned to Nisuke or Daisuke, or to Matsukichi, that he wanted to learn about the central tenets of their religion, the tenets for which his father had sacrificed his life. It wasn't because he was hiding things from them. Kumagorō hoped they would understand this, even if he didn't talk about it directly.

Now that Okayo's belly had grown visibly larger, the family had stopped her from going down to the coast until the baby was born, but she still liked to go into the fields. Whenever she went, Suzu accompanied her. Both Omiyo-sama and Oume-yan had told Suzu to make sure that Okayo didn't stumble and fall.

It was around the time when the rapeseed flower petals were beginning to scatter and their seedpods were bending over with their own weight. Along the banks of the rice paddies, the lotus seedpods were ripening and darkening. In the sky above the grassy path where Okayo and Suzu were walking, skylarks were flying about. The grain was growing well.

Omiyo had told them to snap the flower buds off the daikon plants so they wouldn't produce seeds and get tough.

"Don't go pulling up the roots because you might fall down and land on your butt," she had warned them any number of times. "Come back with your baskets filled with just the flower clusters. And don't take any sickles with you. If you slip and fall with them, it's dangerous."

And so Omiyo had sent them off, telling them that she would boil the flower buds and give some as an offering in remembrance of Baba-sama, since she had always loved their bittersweet taste so much.

"Suzu, there's a place on the stem where the flowers snap off nicely. If you do it that way, there's no need for a sickle."

For the winter crop, daikon seeds were usually planted before the autumn equinox and once they sprouted, the seedlings were thinned. After being weeded they grew up strong and healthy. Around the time of the first frosts, if you just tapped them with a knife, they burst open with juiciness. If they went to seed, though, they became overly spicy. The whole plant was used, even the greens, with nothing thrown away. The women also prepared dried daikon so that, even after the green vegetables of summer were gone, they were still able to enjoy some daikon with their meals.

"Say there, Suzu."

"Yes?"

Suzu loved working in the fields. She had become as good as Okayo at snapping the flowers from the stems.

"These days even the leopard plants have grown tough. It's kind of boring."

"You mean it's more fun harvesting daikon flowers than cutting leopard plants?"

When harvesting the leopard plants, they had to bend over and use both hands, but plucking the daikon flowers was easy.

"It seems you like this sort of work, don't you?"

"I do. How about you, Okayo-sama?"

"I do, too."

"Can you tell which ones are best to leave for seeds?"

"Well, I suppose . . ."

Feigning ignorance, Okayo pointed.

"That one?"

Suzu and Okayo pointed at the same time. It was a daikon with much larger leaves and a root that heaved up high above the soil. Its white flowers—two or three times as many as on other plants—were blooming gorgeously.

"Look how well the horse manure worked!"

Suzu rocked her jaw back and forth a couple of times, imitating Oume-yan's characteristic way of talking.

"Well, you're pretty clever, aren't you?"

Okayo bent over in laughter, but then she stroked her painful belly. The baby inside was moving. On the path that led along the banks of the paddies, Oume-yan was approaching with a woman's pack on her back. Suzu pointed cheerfully and called out:

"Oume-yan—butterflies are coming with you!"

Two white cabbage butterflies were dancing about in the air above the large farm woman.

Oume heard them laughing. Okayo-sama's child was due in another two months or so, just around the time when the wheat would be ripening. *What sort of child will it be?* she wondered.

When Daisuke-sama was born, Oume had helped with the birth. This time, for Okayo's delivery, Omiyo had again asked her to assist. Before she even heard Oume's response, Omiyo had felt at ease. Oume hadn't received any formal training as a midwife, but in the course of events that is what she had become. *Goodness me,* she thought, *this time it's going to be Daisuke-sama's child.* But in any case, for Oume it wasn't a burden. She had been looking after Omiyo ever since she was her nursemaid. Even now, she considered her a somewhat unsophisticated girl who couldn't tell bad folks from good ones. Oume thought, *Well, if I don't do it, then who will?*

In her youth, after completing a term of service with Omiyo's family, Oume had married a man from a farming family in her hometown in Amakusa. But she hadn't fit in with her husband's family and had run off, returning to Omiyo's house. Her marriage had lasted for less than two years. It was fortunate that she hadn't had any children. Omiyo was glad she had returned. Oume continued to work for her, and when Omiyo married she had become part of the Hasuda household with her. Perhaps her role as the midwife for Daisuke's birth—and now for that of his child—had been destined from a former life. Fortunately, this time Suzu would be helping care for the baby. She had already agreed to this.

Oume mused, *Okayo-sama and Suzu are laughing about pleasant things. Whenever she has time, Omiyo-sama is sewing clothing and diapers for the baby. She doesn't get out of the house so often, but her daughter-in law loves the fields and the shore and she plays there with Suzu, just like I used to play with Omiyo-sama.*

Oume had been feeling a bit out of sorts lately—perhaps it was the cloudy weather—but as she walked toward Okayo and Suzu, she felt a little better.

As Okayo watched Oume approach, she recalled something she had heard people talking about recently:

"Oume-yan has been a great help for your family. Really, she's worth as much as a whole storehouse."

Okayo had nodded heartily in agreement. Her mother-in-law Omiyo had talked about the same thing.

"Last year we managed to make it through the drought thanks to Oume-yan's resourcefulness. If it had been just me, we couldn't have done it."

Oume-yan had looked annoyed to have such things said in her presence.

"I'm a worker in this house, and that's why I'm here. The resourceful one is Omiyo-sama."

Her eyes blinking as if she had been scolded, Omiyo replied,

"Well, no matter what happens, our bellies won't be empty and we won't starve."

Okayo thought, *The paths along the fields and hillsides are covered with fresh green. It's hard to imagine that we had a drought last year. Still, we have to be careful. I'm going to be the mother of a baby.*

Last fall, Mother-in-Law and Oume-yan were talking in the storehouse, sighing as they tried to decide how much to thin out the porridge with dried daikon leaves. What will happen if that sort of thing happens again?

Okayo felt a movement in her belly. Involuntarily, she bent over and cried out. In the past month the baby had become increasingly active. Oume-yan put down her sickle and came to her.

"There's no need to worry," she said, then stopped.

"You didn't really need to come. It's just moving a little. Ah—it hurts!"

Looking carefully at Okayo, Oume asked, "Is it kicking?"

"Yes . . . it kicked here."

Clutching her side, Okayo's face broke into a tearful smile.

Nervously, Suzu came over and looked up at Oume, and then down at Okayo.

"Shall we start back for home?"

"No, it's all right. These days it's just moving around as it pleases."

Okayo let out a big sigh.

"It's practicing for getting out. Does it hurt much?"

"Not really. It's behaving pretty well."

"Well, just in case, we'd better start for home. I can't tell, since I've never been through it myself."

Oume had never given birth to a child of her own, but she knew she shouldn't get flustered. She gathered some daikon greens, placed them in her basket, and got ready to head back home.

"Well, with such good color in your face, there's no need to worry. Just walk slowly in front of me. Suzu—you'll be her walking stick, so stay right beside her. If anything happens, I'll put down my basket and help. But not yet; your belly's not that far along yet. Everything's fine."

Suzu slipped something that looked like a handful of old straw into the pocket of the small apron she had been given. She looked puzzled.

"What's that you're doing now? Come on—get your basket!"

Just as Oume was scolding Suzu for being unusually slow, Okayo called out:

"What's that? Ah—it's a skylark's nest! And, there's a baby chick in it. Let me see!"

"Okayo-sama, that's no good. And Suzu, put it back right away. Its parents are worried and they're calling for it. Can't you hear them? Put it back in the grass again, quickly."

Unaccustomed to such scolding, Suzu became flustered. She placed the nest in the grass and looked up nervously at the sky.

"Stop this foolishness. What are you doing, stealing a skylark's nest? Can't you hear its parents crying out in worry?"

Suzu nodded her head silently.

"But the little nest was so well made. How did they make it?" Okayo asked.

If she didn't think Oume would scold her, she probably would have taken a good look at it.

"When you become a parent, you'll do anything to protect your little ones. Birds are the same. You, too, will be like that."

After she scolded Suzu, Oume felt content. It's often said that grandchildren are cuter than children, and it's no different if someone else's child becomes attached to you. Oume felt sad to see Suzu, an orphan, trying to act clever in front of others, but she didn't hesitate to scold her when she had to.

Not having any children of her own, Oume regarded Suzu as a gift from the Buddha. Ever since Suzu became part of the family, Oume had gone to sleep with her in her arms. When Suzu cried, Oume had stroked her back and cried in sympathy. *Suzu doesn't know much about me. Still, she's lucky. She wasn't sold off, and she was taken in by this family, and she's learned to work, and she's become so helpful and so good at it.* Oume was determined to teach Suzu as much as she could, although she didn't know what she would do when she got older.

When the three arrived home earlier than planned, Okayo said to her surprised mother-in-law, "In the fields, I felt some cramps and Oume-yan was worried about me."

"But you must have been worried too! Are you all right now?"

Okayo nodded as she stroked her belly.

"She hasn't come to full term, but it could be early, couldn't it?"

Omiyo, who had only given birth one time herself, looked at Oume anxiously.

"Well, she didn't seem to be in labor. I'd say that when she's at term, the baby will come out all by itself."

Oume gave her prediction as if trying to convince herself.

The women of the house expected the baby would be born around when the grain was ready to harvest.

The fine spring weather didn't last. Days of sun alternated with days of rain, and the colors of the fields and hillsides turned steadily deeper.

"This year, the rapeseed plants have so many seeds, they're all bending over to the ground. Unless we prop them up, they'll get beaten down by the rain."

With this prompting from Oume, Kumagorō had come to help. He set up bamboo poles and tied the rapeseed plants to them with lengths of straw. Unless the bamboo poles were properly staked in the ground, the weight of the rapeseed plants would topple them over. The work needed a man's strength. Yellow petals still clung to some of the plants, and the tightly-packed pods drooped from their stems, some touching the ground and some bursting open.

"They sure put out a lot of seeds! If they get rained on before we take them in to make oil, they'll start sprouting."

"Perhaps we used too much horse manure."

"Well, you know, the government is saying we're going to have to pay more of the rapeseed oil for taxes this year," Kumagorō said without even being asked, as he set up a pole. Oume bent and straightened out some of the fallen plants, tying them to the bamboo.

"More, you say? Why, they told us we'll have to pay *twice* the usual amount!"

"Twice? That can't be."

"I'm not joking—twice as much!"

"Even if we take in all the seeds, there's no way we can double the amount."

Thinking of how Nisuke, the head of the household, would have to worry about this, the two looked at each other and continued their work in silence.

The fields and the rice paddies belonged, of course, to Nisuke, their owner. But when the crops—that is to say, the plants that the men and women who worked for him tended with their own hands—ripened with grain and the fields burgeoned, they all took great pleasure in it. When people said in praise, "Nisuke-sama's bean fields look so green and beautiful," they all felt immensely happy. When they saw the less well-tended, overgrown fields of some other families, they could imagine the state of affairs in those households. But now, when they heard that the fields they had tended with such devotion were going to be double-taxed, it cast a dark cloud over their spirits. Already, in their village, some farmers had abandoned their fields and fled.

Hearing what sounded like a young woman's voice, Kumagorō turned around. He thought it might be Okayo-sama, but he was mistaken. Okimi, the wife of Yozaemon's son, was walking along the path. When she saw the two people working in the field, she waved and broke out in a big smile. People spoke of Okimi as an energetic, good-natured young wife, and she was highly regarded by all. The villagers thought of her as a bright shining flower in Yozaemon's household, which of late seemed somewhat somber. Like Okayo and Oume, her family home was in Amakusa, so she liked to visit the Hasuda family on one pretext or another. Being the wife in a large farming household, she didn't have a lot of free time, but today she had probably gotten permission from her mother-in-law and was now stopping by, her joy showing in her exhilarated steps and laughter.

Right behind Okimi, another girl was walking along the narrow path. Judging from her clothing, Kumagorō supposed she was one of Okimi's helpers.

"Oba-yan," Okimi called out to Oume in a carefree voice, "If you work too hard, you'll fall over—like those rapeseed plants."

"So, it's you, Okimi-sama. You're looking well. Where are you off to today?"

"Where am I off to? We're visiting your family," Okimi replied cheerfully.

"Well, what brings you this time?"

"The coming *obi* ceremony for Okayo-sama's baby."

"Well, how kind of you."

"And I also have a request for you."

"For me? What would that be?"

"Well, my husband's grandmother, her knee's been acting up a lot."

"Ah, this is a bad season now."

"Yes, and she says it's worse than usual. And she thinks the rains are going to last a long time this year."

"Folks who have knee pains are all saying the same thing—the rains are going to last long."

"You think so? We're having nice weather now, aren't we? Anyhow, my mother-in-law asked me to see if you could spare some of your moxa, before the rains come and our feet get soaked."

"What are you talking about? I've been making moxa just for times like this."

"Well, I'm glad I found you here. If you'd already gone off to the woods and hills, we were wondering what we'd do—right, Ofumi?"

Ofumi was her helper.

"Actually," Oume replied, "I do need to go up there."

Removing her head cloth and wiping her sweat, Oume looked toward the top of the hills. The rapeseed fields there were later in blooming than those in the other fields, and their color brightly outlined the ridgeline where it met the blue sky above.

"Since we planted them late, they're still blooming."

Remembering the drought of the previous year, they hadn't planted any millet this year. Instead, they had sown rapeseed, since it can be harvested quickly. Above the gentle slopes of the hillside covered in the yellow flowering rapeseed plants, a trail of white clouds shone brightly in the sky.

"What do you say Ofumi; how about if we take a little break? It's been a hard trek in getting here. Why don't you take off your pack?"

Inside her basket-pack were some pomelos, with leaves still attached. The fruit were as big as the heads of young children. Okimi took one out casually.

"Let's eat one together. Oume-yan, could you peel this with your sickle? The skin looks pretty thick."

"But wait, shouldn't they be saved as presents for the baby's ceremony?"

"They're presents, but I brought my own, too. Listen to me Oba-yan."

Every time Okimi spoke, it was with great fun. She smiled at Kumagorō. For some reason, her upturned nose looked especially charming.

"I've got a baby inside, too—and mine's saying it wants to eat pomelos."

Talking on like this, Okimi realized that she might have been acting a bit strange, and so, placing her cheek on Ofumi's back, she began to chuckle. Kumagorō, who had been sitting a bit apart from them as if to avoid the women's talk, found himself getting pulled in and stopped his work.

"This one sure has a thick skin. Kumagorō—could you peel it for us? It seems the little one in her belly wants some. This needs the strength of your fingers."

Taking the pumelo that Oume-yan handed to him, Kumagorō sat down on the bank of the field. Ofumi giggled to herself quietly. As Kumagorō peeled back the thick, crimson-tinted skin, an indescribable fragrance wafted in the air.

Okimi split open the fruit, handed sections to each person, and dropped her own piece into her mouth.

"Whew—incredibly tart! Amazing!"

Despite her somewhat large body, when Okimi spoke with such innocence her words and actions were charming. Oume thought, *Her helpers must feel at ease with a woman like this.* Pomelos like the ones Okimi had brought couldn't be found at just any house. They started to ripen in the middle of winter, and having any to eat at this time of the year was rare. The people at Yozaemon's house must have taken great care in growing them. They had a bracing, refreshing bitterness.

Okimi rubbed her juice-covered hands and sat with a dreamy expression.

"How beautiful the sky is. It looks so close—just beyond that hill of rapeseed. It might be that the path to *Paraizo* leads on from there."

Kumagorō looked up at Okimi's face in surprise. Far in the back of his mind he heard his father's voice at his dying moment, and the voice of his mother. Their voices, however, didn't have the carefree tone of Okimi's.

Oume asked, "So when is your little one due?"

"Around the tenth month, I think."

"The tenth, is it? That's about four months after our Okayo-sama is due."

For some reason, Okimi laughed to herself.

"By then the crops should be in. Everyone in your house will be so busy."

"Well, yes. My mother-in-law says that when the baby's born she'll cook up some beautiful white rice."

"White rice? That'll be quite a celebration. Last fall the rice fields at your place were damaged badly, weren't they?"

"Yes, and my parents-in-law were really discouraged. But these days we've been working hard to ready the fields for planting."

Having eaten the pomelo and said the things she wanted to say, Okimi stood up and cheerfully went on her way with her helper.

"What a cheerful woman. Lucky from birth, I guess."

Looking at Kumagorō as she saw off the two women, Oume sighed. *What a fine woman that Ofumi is. Seems she'd be just right for Kumagorō.*

As the sunny weather continued, the ears of grain were ripening, and from their roots up, the stems began to turn color.

The rapeseed harvest was finished without trouble, and when the seeds were dried, there looked to be about a third more than in average years. When Oume placed her hands on the sun-warmed seeds, she felt soothed. The little brown balls were plump with oil and the yield would be very good. The oil pressed from them would light their lamps for a year and flavor their feasts on celebration days. In this household, in this season only, they enjoyed the custom of eating dried daikon leaves fried in rapeseed oil. Afterwards, the dregs from oil production could be used as top-grade fertilizer.

When they used it in the melon field, the fruit grew so sweet. And, Matsukichi and Oume thought, even if the governor's office should take a lot of the oil, still, somehow, they would find a way to keep some for the household.

Deep in her heart, Oume pondered: *I've never seen the faces of those government officials, so I can't judge their characters. But they're wrong if they think their little piece of paper will let them take away what the farmers have raised with such devotion, while they've never worked with their bodies.*

Nisuke and his wife are so different from those merciless officials. It may be the will of Deus-sama, but they're always working for others, hardly sleeping at night and not earning a penny for it. That time when the old folks' house was washed away, when I saw Nisuke's grief I felt for him from the bottom of my heart. It moved me so much I was almost saying amen.

Oume shook her head. She was seated in front of a straw mat, spreading out rapeseed. Just then, a shadow slipped in.

"Oume-yan . . ."

The voice was Takematsu's.

"What are you muttering about with that serious face?" he asked.

"I wasn't muttering about anything."

"But you were saying *amen*, weren't you?"

Oume looked uncharacteristically flustered.

"Nonsense! Why would I need to say *amen*?"

"Well, with that serious face you're like a female Deva god. Or like Juan-sama when he's knitting his eyebrows in thought."

"You needn't go meddling in my affairs."

"I didn't mean to meddle, but I saw you passing rapeseeds between the palms of your hands, back and forth, and then pouring them out like a child at play."

Oume was on the verge of tears, but quickly she pulled herself together.

"Well, sometimes even I like to play now and then."

"Do you? As for me, I often set traps for sparrows, and while I'm holding them, I say *amen*."

"*Holding* the sparrows, you say? And then you pluck them and eat them!"

"Well, maybe so, but first, after I take them out of the traps, I hold them and say *amen.*"

"That's just killing them."

"Is there any person who doesn't take the lives of others? Not so long ago, you were saying yourself that if I came back with a whale, we'd cut it up and divide it among ourselves!"

"Well, well now, you're speaking rather eloquently today. I'll bet you've been drinking since noon. So, did you have a reason for coming round?"

"Some question that is! I wouldn't have come if I didn't have a reason. Is Kumagorō here?"

"Kumagorō's out in the bean field."

"The one up in the hills?"

"No, the closer one. So, tell me, what are you after?"

"Well, I have a little something to talk to him about."

"Don't bother him while he's working."

"Don't worry, I won't bother him."

As she watched Takematsu walk toward the bean field, Oume sensed that he hadn't had much to drink after all. But what was his errand? Something about the school? It was strange how, when he was sober he hardly talked at all, but as soon as he had just a little to drink he could banter away and even joke at ease. But Takematsu wasn't just a drinker. He could read people's feelings. Maybe he had caught her saying *amen* to herself—was that such a bad thing?

Unusually flustered, Oume couldn't help staring from time to time in the direction of the fava bean field. A while later, the two men appeared, shouldering large bundles of beans.

Takematsu's bundle was slightly smaller and neatly tied. Probably, he'd asked Kumagorō to prepare it for him as proof that he hadn't been interfering with the work. Oume wished she could see the two men's faces as they walked toward her. But realizing that she wouldn't be able to hold back from pestering them with questions, she quickly went into the kitchen.

Tonight, we'll eat the first fava beans of the season—the first staple crop of the year. I'll boil the tender green pods in salted water and offer them up to Deus-sama and the ancestors of the household. When the beans are heaped on our plates, everyone will take special joy in these first delicacies of the season. After tonight's dinner we'll all have to wait until the pods still ripening in the field turn black before we eat any again.

Tonight, when we eat the salted beans, we'll also be happy that the loquats and strawberries are ripening, and the eggplants and cucumbers are coming along nicely, and before long the grains will be harvested. Somewhere, the god of crops must be nodding at us.

The whole village was in a flurry of activity now that the season to pick tea had come. Almost all the families planted tea bushes around their houses, and when the women were outside picking the young leaves, they called out to each other, exchanging news and gossip.

At Nisuke's house, too, extra workers had been hired to help out, and the spirited voices of the women could be heard from a distance. Since they were picking not only around the house but also in scattered distant tea fields, Omiyo and Oume were busier than usual.

The tea they picked before noon had to be roasted in a big pot before sundown. They took the still-hot leaves, kneaded them with their hands, and then quickly spread them out to cool. The women shared a common working spirit as they put the tea leaves into the pot, where they would crackle and pop, and then set them out on straw mats and began massaging them. If the work slowed at any point, the color and fragrance of the tea would suffer. And since the house always had lots of visitors, they took particular care in the process. Oume was placed in charge of roasting the leaves, stationing herself beside the pot and watching over it carefully.

Inspired by the diligence of the other women, Okayo became completely absorbed in the work. Her belly had grown larger and was showing more. She panted as she joined the women in kneading the hot leaves fresh from the pot. Okayo's hands were still tender and the hot leaves made them feel like they were burning.

"Don't force yourself. The baby's really dropping down now," Omiyo said, looking at her belly.

"You're not having any cramps, are you? And no one can roll leaves well at first."

Seated beside Okayo, an older woman they called Ane-sama, who was from a related family, was working away calmly, scooping the leaves spread before Okayo into her palms as if hauling in a net, then rolling and squeezing them with a *wasshi, wasshi* sound.

With her small hands, Okayo worked uneasily. When Ane-sama noticed that she was going slower than the others, she picked up a handful of leaves that had cooled enough to handle easily and placed them on the mat in front of Okayo.

"Try these," she suggested.

When she removed her hand, steam rose up from the leaves. They gave off an incredibly rich aroma as they released their green liquid.

Okayo's hands and legs wouldn't move as easily as she wanted them to, but she continued rubbing the leaves, inwardly chanting *wasshi, wasshi* along with her unborn child. A while later, she felt as if water were streaming down her inner thigh. She raised her legs and then stopped moving her hands and bent over the leaves. Omiyo, seated beside her, sensed that something was happening.

"What is it?"

"I think . . ." she said in a restrained voice, " . . . it may be coming."

At the same time, Ane-sama asked, "It's coming?"

The two women reached out their hands, all smeared with dust and tea chaff, and embraced Okayo. Oume, who had been seated beside the roasting pot, hurried over to her. All work came to a stop.

Oume looked at Omiyo encouragingly. Omiyo, looking over the large kitchen, turned toward Ane-sama and said quickly, "Oume and I will take care of the birth. Can you all follow Ane-sama's directions and finish the tea roasting for today?"

"Finally, it's coming."

"Isn't it a bit early?"

Amid such whispered exchanges, the work resumed as before. Slowly, with the help of the two women, Okayo started to walk, her body bent forward. She could hear the conversations continuing behind her:

"Come to think of it, the big tide should get here today or tomorrow."

"Around dawn tomorrow, isn't it?"

Although it was a month early and the wheat hadn't ripened

yet, a baby girl was born.

Daisuke apprehensively came into the room.

"Wonderful! Wonderful!" he said, gazing at the baby. "I'm so glad you're both fine, even though she's early. So she decided to come out while you were making tea! Look at her little head. And her eyes and her nose and mouth. They're all perfect!"

Gently, he held her tiny shaking hand.

"Look at her hands, and her feet, and her fingers—they're all perfect. It's incredible! And look at her tiny fingernails! Surely this is the grace of God."

Just then, the baby opened her tiny mouth in a big yawn.

"Look, she's yawning—just like a grownup!"

As he watched her yawning innocently, Daisuke was awestruck.

It seemed to him that the gift of this pure, delicate life carried with it an admonition from Deus-sama. *Chirisuto-sama told us to "treat all beings with love." I am on the threshold of that journey. Today, I begin my life as a father, entrusted with this tiny life.*

Daisuke gazed at Okayo as she lay on the futon on the tatami floor. In her face he saw her tiredness from childbirth, but also an exceptional gentleness. From time to time, she opened her eyes and gazed at Daisuke, full of reliance and trust. For him, Okayo's eyes beamed with radiance. A woman giving birth, how strange and miraculous. Holding back the apprehension welling up within, he asked, "Is our baby the one you saw in your dream?"

"I can't remember the face in the dream. I'd be happy no matter what her face looked like, because she's your child."

"She's a blessing from God."

"What name should we give her?"

"How about Otama? That sounds nice, doesn't it?"

"Otama? Hmm . . . but it might be mistaken for a cat's name, don't you think?"

"A cat? Well, maybe so. Then how about a flower? The *ayame* irises are just about to bloom. How about Ayame?"

"Yes, that's a nice name. But might it be too beautiful? Perhaps we shouldn't burden her with trying to live up to it. Why don't we ask your parents? They've been looking forward to her birth so much."

After discussing it together they decided to name the baby "Ayame." Okayo's grandmother Ofuji and father Seibei came over from Uchino to celebrate, bringing presents of soba and mugwort *mochi* dumplings. When Ofuji saw the baby, she sighed.

"Look—her eyes. They're just like Omiyo-sama's. And her mouth is just like Okayo's when she was a baby."

As she spoke, tears filled her eyes.

Within a week, all the tea was roasted and processed. From where she lay, Okayo could hear bits of pleasant conversations such as, "Ahh, the smell of new tea is everywhere."

With Okayo in her lying-in, Daisuke came to her side to tell her about the progress of the school.

"But if the government hears about it, there could be big trouble, don't you think?"

"Well, there could, and we talked about that last night. But in any case, by summer it's going to be pretty hot and stuffy in the storehouse . . ."

"Are you planning to move it into the living room?"

"Yes, but if we move it there, we'll have to keep the sacred books a secret."

"We could ask Ukon-sama to read from the *Tale of the Heike* again. And afterwards, a few people could go to the storehouse to study. That might work alright."

"How smart you are—that's just what Shirō-sama suggested."

"Speaking of Shirō-sama, has he been staying at Ukon-sama's house all this time?"

"No, he's gone back to Uto. He's been coming the day before we hold classes, and going back afterwards."

"Whenever people see him, they get inspired to do things."

"That's the truth. Yazō sure brought back an amazing young person. In Amakusa too, after the droughts and all that's happened in the last couple years, people have really been waking up and reviving our faith."

"Now that you mention it, I've heard that my brother has been holding meetings with the people he met a year ago when they prayed together for rain."

"Your brother's holding meetings?"

"Yes. My grandmother has been wondering about what they discuss."

"Are the meetings held around Uchino?"

"Yes. And my father says the young people have been getting really worked up about things."

"I heard there was quite a lot of trouble over there last year about the borrowed grain."

"They say my brother was the leader of it."

"Did he keep it a secret from your family?"

"It wasn't a secret; but although they'd been warned not to make a commotion, they barged into the magistrate's office full of spirit . . . The neighbors told my grandmother about it."

"According to Shirō-sama, the people in Ōyano and Kotsuura have been reviving their faith with great enthusiasm. Is your brother a Christian?"

"No, he's a Buddhist like the rest of my family. But they say the lord of the Amakusa area has been a lot more lenient about the prohibition of Christianity than the lord here."

"Your father and grandmother told you that?"

"Yes. And they also told me that, now that I've become a parent, I should protect my child, along with Daisuke-dono, no matter what happens. That's why they told me about what was happening there, and about all the troubles going on in the world."

"Hmm. I'd like to talk with your brother sometime."

"My father says it's no good being stubborn."

With a chuckle, Daisuke replied, "It's good for a man to be stubborn. You know, I'm a lot more stubborn than I look—more so than most people."

That wasn't what Okayo thought, but ever since the night of the big storm she had felt there was a kind of solid core within him.

In any case, Okayo wondered what her brother Sasuke was thinking about. Last summer when she went back to her family home in Uchino, her brother had been away, attending the prayer meetings for rain, and had apologized for not being with her. She remembered how kindly Sasuke had always treated her. He had carried her on his back when they crossed streams and had helped her climb trees, and when other children teased her, he had chased them away. Her brother, rather than her father, had always stayed close to her. He was like her guardian spirit.

After her brother got married, things had changed. For the most part, she had stopped calling him "Dear Brother," as she had since early childhood, but occasionally she still did. Last fall, he and his wife had welcomed a baby boy. After being away for so long, she wanted to meet her brother and talk.

It is often said that the best food for nursing women is carp cooked in miso, and so Okayo had received gifts of carp from many people. Whether it was because of this or some other reason, her cheeks and the baby's wrists had grown plump and healthy and the smell of milk filled her room.

During the day, Omiyo and Daisuke often came in to see the baby and to press their cheeks to hers. Omiyo kept telling everyone not to hold the baby too much, or she'd get used to it. But she was the one who held her the most. Even her father-in-law would sneak in on tiptoes and gently open the baby's tiny hands and coo at her. Okayo felt so happy watching them.

At first when the baby was born, Suzu was cautious about getting too near it. Quietly, from a slight distance, she would mimic the baby's expressions, scowling and grinning along with her and comparing the baby's fist with her own. It seemed to Okayo that Suzu might have been thinking about her own birth, and about her own parents. Soon, this tiny infant became Suzu's treasure.

From the birthing room where she slept, Okayo could look out over the fields. On clear days, the colors of the ripening grain radiated brightly inside the house.

"Just another four or five days and we'll start cutting it."

"Shake out the straw mats and dry them in the sun and clean up the rakes."

More than usual, this sort of talk filled the air, and once again Okayo was struck by the farmers' exuberance and feelings of abundance at this time of year. Seeing Kumagorō and Matsukichi working so energetically, Okayo wanted to get up from her bed soon and start working, too.

"Well, my little Ayame, mama is up now, so let's go out and help cut the grain."

No matter what Okayo was doing, she couldn't help talking to Ayame.

"I'm out of bed now, so I'll put Ayame on my back and help with the harvest," she said to Omiyo.

"Don't be foolish," Omiyo scolded. "What will happen if a stalk of grain gets into the baby's eyes or mouth? She can't even hold her head up yet."

Suzu rushed in and called out enthusiastically:

"I'll take care of the baby, and I'll make sure she's kept away from the scythes and the cutting work."

The adults stared at her. They didn't know that Oume-yan and Suzu had already agreed that Suzu would care for the baby. One night, Oume had promised Suzu that once the harvest started in two days, Suzu could take charge of the baby.

"When you get good at taking care of her and you can do it without too much trouble, I'll weave you a basket for picking strawberries. We can use the leftover straw from the grain harvest."

That was just what Suzu had been looking forward to the most. Once they collected the fresh straw that was left over from the harvest, they would be able to weave baskets and go out to the fields and pick wild strawberries. This was the greatest pleasure of the girls in the village.

"I'll make one for you, but when you go into the bushes to pick raspberries, make sure the vines don't get into the baby's eyes."

Oume-yan watched out for such problems. It was hot and humid on the night they talked, and sweat ran down their foreheads. Probably it was the relief of finishing the tea harvest that let Oume think about things like making straw baskets. Suzu went to bed that night with a most peaceful look on her face. But during the night it started to rain.

Oume jumped up from bed and, worrying that she might have left the straw mats outside, went out to shut the doors of the storehouse. Matsukichi and Kumagorō, too, had gotten up and were outside already, making sure that all the firewood had been piled under the eaves.

"Looks like we were wrong about the weather."

Nisuke and Omiyo, and Daisuke, too, had gotten up and were

outside under the eaves, looking up at the sky.

"If it rains all night, do you think we should put off the rest of the harvest for another few days?"

"Well, we'll have to wait for the fields to dry out. That'll take three or four days, it looks like."

Rain splashed Nisuke and Daisuke as they talked.

When morning broke, the rain grew heavier. Oume, who had dozed off again, was wakened by the crash of thunder. An ordinary rain storm was a welcome holiday for farmers. But to Oume, this rain seemed a troubling omen. *Yozaemon's mother's knee has been acting up more than usual. After the long wait since the days of starvation in last year's drought, and thanks to everyone's work, we finally made it to the early summer harvest. But now this downpour; perhaps that old woman and her knee were right.*

As the rain poured down in torrents, Oume felt trapped in the house. The working day began. With an unusually heavy feeling, she stepped onto the earthen floor and started a fire in the stove. Opening the door just enough to let the smoke out, a spray of water, like a fog, flew into the room. The fire wouldn't catch.

And the grain, so perfectly grown—has it already been soaked? Have the gullies turned into rivers? Four or five days ago I picked some grains from a few ears and crushed them in my fingers. They had some juice in them. When I chewed them, they were sweet, with a nice taste. I asked Nisuke to taste them, too.

"These look good," he said. "Nice big grains."

Thinking about it now, we should have started the harvest the next day. No doubt the others feel the same. But we'd brought the crop along so well, and in just four or five more days, the grains would have tightened up nicely, separating easily from their husks, making our work easier. Probably everyone's been thinking this, though they haven't said it. But that's the way things are and there's nothing to do about it. I'd wanted to give some of the fresh grain to the new mother, but for now she'll have to make do with the old.

As Oume was mulling these things over, Omiyo came in and said sympathetically, "Oume-yan, what a disappointment."

"It couldn't be helped . . . it's the will of Heaven and there's no way we could have known."

"Well, maybe so. It's a good thing we finished the tea harvest."

"That's true. We certainly had nice weather while we were doing it."

"To drive off the bad luck this morning, why don't we make porridge and mix in some of the new tea?"

"Good idea. It'll help us feel better and get over this."

With glum looks on their faces, the household gathered around the hearth. Oume-yan passed the pot from the fireplace to Kumagorō, and the smell of fresh tea porridge wafted through the room.

For the first time in twenty days, Okayo joined everyone for breakfast. With a normal term birth, she would have been back at work in a week, but because the baby was early, Omiyo had been strict and kept her in bed until now. It was a thrill to see everyone around the hearth.

"Ahh—tea porridge!"

Nisuke broke out in a smile. As they crunched on the pickled daikon and ate the warm porridge, somehow the anxieties they had been feeling since early morning melted away. In the miso soup were some of the first eggplants of the season.

Stretching, Daisuke sighed.

"Well, if we can't harvest today, then I can play with Ayame."

Nisuke added, "Seeing how it's raining today, why don't we do some paper work?"

"What's this you're talking about?"

"The grain quota for this year, ordered by the magistrate's office. But before we go discuss it with the village heads, we'd better make our own estimate."

"Oh, that. There are all sorts of rules."

"Well, we're going to have to count Ayame's birth in it, too."

"Hmm. I'd suspected they might tax the newborn baby, but will they really?"

Daisuke stroked the baby's hair as she nursed at Okayo's breast.

"Well, my little Ayame, it looks like you're going to help decide the land tax. So now you count as a person, understand? All right then, I'll just have to do the work of two or three people."

Daisuke smiled gently, and amidst the sound of the rain, the entire group formed a happy circle.

Stepping down onto the earthen floor, Matsukichi said, "Well, this is quite some start for the rainy season."

Matsukichi always had something to say when he started to work, perhaps to motivate himself, and on this day he had brought a wooden hammer for pounding straw. He began his work.

The rhythmic sound of pounding started. On rainy days the straw was moist, so the sound was soft. And because this was a rainy day, he had to make several extra pairs of *zōri* sandals. When pounded, the straw became pliable, so it could also be used to make rope or straw mats.

Some people were good at making rope and others weren't, and Matsukichi considered himself rather poor at such handiwork. He was good at pounding the straw, but since he had lost the middle finger of his right hand to a blade when he was cutting straw, he wasn't much good at twisting and twining it into rope. He would leave most of the finish-work of making the short straw sandals and mats to Kumagorō and Oume-yan, but he had the energy and persistence needed for the steady pounding and softening of the straw, and he considered this his own work. In the fields, he would bind the crop into bundles with the straw rope and carry the bundles, one after another, to the storehouse and sheds for threshing. Even if he wasn't particularly gifted at it, he thought he ought to help with the rope making. With such thoughts in mind, he moved his workplace to the shed.

At first, Matsukichi thought it might have been better if they had taken at least a little of the grain into the sheds. But he realized that even then, without proper drying mold would have grown on it. There was no use in fretting over what had happened; it really couldn't have been helped.

In the same shed, Kumagorō was measuring out some of the partly dried rapeseed and pouring it into bags.

"Put the fully dried stuff in the bins."

"Right."

"Where do you think we should hide them? You have any ideas?"

"Well, actually, I do."

"You do?"

"You know, I've spent some time cutting firewood. I could put the thick boards from my old boat under the firewood. I suppose we could dig a pit under those boards and store the bins there."

"That's not a bad idea. You've been chopping a lot of firewood, haven't you?"

"Well, it's hard for me to just sit around watching the grain ripen."

"Hmm."

Matsukichi's voice sounded a bit uneasy as he looked at the young man.

"When I work with my body, my mind starts working, too. I was thinking that, if the early grain harvest is really good, and if the rice harvest is good, too, I could cut a big pile of firewood and hide some bins under it."

Placing a sack on the dirt floor, Kumagorō tapped one of the bins of miso next to him. Then, like a trained orator finding his proper pitch, he started to speak.

"If there's a famine, I'll call out to our master; just like the dog of that old fellow Hanasaka in the fable who could make flowers bloom from withered trees. You know, the dog who called out to his master, '*Here it is! Dig right here!*' Just like that dog, I'll tell my master, '*Dig right here—the rice is right here!*' And then, I suppose, Oume-yan will come round and tell me I must be dreaming.'"

"Ha, ha . . . Well, maybe so."

While Matsukichi was chuckling, Sadaichi, a worker from another farm, rushed in with someone following behind.

"The rains have hit early. I thought they were letting up but now they've started again."

Sadaichi wiped his head and legs and looked at Kumagorō and Matsukichi.

"We came to see you in this rain—and here you two are looking so cheerful. Well, I suppose this is good weather for taking a rest."

"I'd hardly call this rest. Our plans for harvesting have fallen through and we're not happy about it. But how about you—don't you have any work to do when it rains? Just killing time running around?" Matsukichi said, wondering who the man standing behind Sadaichi was.

"God called us to come and check on you," Sadaichi joked, but it seemed he had some more important business.

"And what sort of conditions are you finding here?"

"Well, if you ask like that, so directly, it's hard to say."

"Come on, tell us. Oume-yan will be here soon with tea."

"Oume-yan? She's kind of scary, isn't she?"

Just then Oume-yan entered, carrying a tray with tea, and stood right behind Sadaichi.

"What do you mean by 'scary,' Sadaichi-san?" she asked.

Sadaichi yelped exaggeratedly.

"So you're taking it easy today too, are you? The harvest's gone bad all around," Oume said, placing the tea tray on top of an upside-down bin.

"Here, how about some fresh new tea?"

With that, she returned to the kitchen.

"The same as ever, isn't she?"

"Well, that's the way she talks, but her heart is God's."

"Maybe so, but she still scares me."

"But I suppose you came here to talk about something, didn't you? Have a seat."

Kumagorō pointed to a few piled-up straw mats. Still standing by the doorway, Sadaichi motioned with his jaw toward the person he had brought with him, a young man of perhaps twenty-five or twenty-six. He bowed and stepped over the threshold.

"This is my cousin Sankichi, from Arima."

Sankichi bowed to Kumagorō and Matsukichi.

"Sankichi's found a sacred painting from back in the old days, and he's been worshiping it."

"A sacred painting from the past? We don't see many of those these days. What sort of picture is it?"

"Well, it has a figure that looks sort of like one of the old padres, and a group of women kneeling in front, and one of them is wiping his feet with her long hair. The figure looks so divine—I suppose it must be Chirisuto-sama."

"Did you have it looked at by anyone who knows about these things? It's fine to worship it, but you need to find out what sort of painting it is, don't you?"

"Well, that's what we've come here to talk about. We were hoping Ukon-sama and Juan-sama might take a look at it."

"I suppose you could do that, but why take the trouble of going to see them when you could ask the master of this family, right here? In the old days, a lot of padres used to stay here."

"Then, so much the better—right, Sankichi?"

Sadaichi turned toward the young man.

"Actually, Matsukichi-don, some pretty strange things have been going on. Sankichi, why don't you tell him about it?"

For a moment Sankichi was at a loss for words. He looked up at the two men, and the whites of his eyes seemed strained. Matsukichi sensed that he had a rather nervous temperament.

"Well, last year, on the night of the big storm, my mother had a dream," he finally said.

"A dream that told the truth," Sadaichi added, holding back his anxiety.

"The winds were howling and lightning struck three times over our woodshed, and then, in her dream, she saw lightning shooting down, and she jumped out of bed and shouted, 'There's a fire in the woodshed! A fire in the woodshed! Get up! Get out!'"

"Everyone must have been in a big commotion."

"Well, yes. She'd always been a quiet person, but she was crying out frantically, so I went running out to the shed."

"And then?" Sadaichi urged. He wanted Sankichi to tell Matsukichi and Kumagorō the rest of the story quickly.

"Well, then the roof blew off the shed and just the old center post was left standing. In the rain and wind, it shone with a pale bluish-white light."

As he sipped his tea, Matsukichi's hand suddenly froze.

"Broken roof beams were twisted around the post, and bits of something—like rain, or something white—were whirling about it, giving off light. I have no idea what it was, but I saw it clearly with my own eyes."

"You think it might have been the tongue of the sea god Ryūjin?" Sadaichi asked.

No one answered. The sound of the rain grew stronger and, for a moment, the storehouse went dark.

"Then the light went out and, strangely, there was no fire. My mother collapsed."

"She was in bed for a month, wasn't she?"

"Yes . . . The next morning, when I was cleaning up the roof, this is what I found."

Sankichi untied the cloth covering around a soot-stained bamboo tube.

"It's in here."

When he removed the contents from their carefully-sealed covering of oiled paper, there was the picture, painted in vivid colors on a cloth brown with soot, just as Sadaichi had described it.

"This picture must have quite a history."

"My mother was in a frenzy and said repeatedly that, on that night, there was a cross standing in the shed, and the soul of my father was there. The next morning, when I cleaned up the remains of the shed, I found this bamboo tube . . ."

Suddenly, Sankichi choked up. Sadaichi tried to continue the story for him, but his voice faltered.

"Actually, Sankichi's father was one of the martyrs of the Arima group. He was crucified. It happened when Sankichi was a baby."

Matsukichi had never heard Sadaichi talk so gently or seriously—usually he behaved rather wildly at gatherings and was generally regarded as superficial. Kumagorō was staring fixedly at Sankichi.

After a pause, Kumagorō asked, with a catch in his throat, "That old post—did it look like a cross?"

"It could have been seen that way. It was stuck to a crosspiece, and for a while it was standing there in the blue light, so perhaps to my mother it looked like my father's cross."

Matsukichi noticed a strange, faint gleam in Kumagorō's eyes.

"After that, my mother started acting strange . . . Until then, she'd never spoken about my father at all. She was trembling all over and then she started calling out, 'Father's come to the woodshed!' It was as if an evil spirit had come over her. Then she cried out, 'The cross with the blue light—you saw it too, didn't you? That was your father's cross—I'm sure of it! And he even brought this sacred painting. We have to build a shrine here, right away!' And just like that, she was a changed person. No question about it, she'd been taken by my father's spirit. Normally, she'd been so quiet and reserved, and hardly spoke.

"So, I tried to calm her down. I told her that Father was killed mercilessly, but he died a martyr and he's surely in *Paraizo* now. I told her that if we made a big fuss, it might cause problems for people in the future. But she started shaking all over and shouted, 'How can you say such a thing? You make light of it, but do you have any idea how he died?' She said she couldn't even talk about it in words and she broke down in tears. That was the first time I'd seen my mother in such a terrifying state.

"She grabbed my chest and cried out, 'Look—I became a Christian for eternity. Go ahead, tell me you're going to kill me and run me through with a sword.' She didn't look like the mother I knew. She looked like my father when he was killed. Her face was so frightening, and filled with such sorrow."

"It seems your father couldn't get up to Heaven so easily. Maybe people who die in an unusual way can't make it up to *Paraizo* in one leap. Maybe they have to go back to the family they left."

"I guess it's like my mother said—unless I set up a place to pray to that picture, like she's demanding, she'll jump around all over the place yelling, 'The cross! The cross! It's burning! Unless you carry it, you'll go to Hell!' But even if I do build a shrine to worship the picture, I need to know its history in case people ask me about it. That's why I talked with Sadaichi-yan and decided to ask you about it."

Matsukichi worried about how Kumagorō was feeling after hearing this story. He could hardly breathe from the worry. In recent years, he hadn't heard many rumors about captured Christians, other than the martyrdom of Nakaura Julian. But twenty years ago or so, not only well-known priests, but ordinary believers, too, had been taken in and punished as examples, one after another. In all the villages, people had held their breath, as if in the wake of a battle. They whispered the names of victims to one another and prayed for their happiness in the world beyond. That was the time when Sankichi's father was crucified.

Matsukichi wasn't a particularly devout believer. His family had worked for the Hasuda household since his parents' generation and so he had become a Christian as a matter of course. But Sankichi's story struck a deep chord in him. For many years, Sankichi's mother had borne the suffering of her husband's death alone, without speaking of it to anyone, but on the night of the storm and the lightning she had reached her limit and, all at once, had released her pent-up feelings. Perhaps when her husband was executed, she had abandoned her faith and been spared. But when she saw that post wrapped in blue light, looking like a cross, the Christian soul of her husband had once again captured her. A heavy dread lodged in Matsukichi's heart.

Kumagorō clenched his fists to quiet the slight trembling that came over him. He clasped his knees and gazed at the light reflecting off the rapeseed bin. *What did my own father see in his dying hours? And where is my mother now, and what is she doing? Or has she already left the world of the living?*

Suddenly, Kumagorō felt a wave of affection for Sankichi's mother. Most likely, she had never forgotten her husband's death, not for a single day. Perhaps it was similar to the way he could never forget his own father's death. On that night of the storm, might Sankichi's mother truly have seen her husband in flames on a cross? Perhaps, taken by the spirit of her martyred husband, she had returned to being a Christian. Perhaps that was what it meant to be a Christian.

The Christian teachings we learn at the school seem to me like lessons for grownups. But we simple Christians, we're like Sankichi's mother, and maybe to others we look crazy. In his mind, Kumagorō called out, "*Mother!*"

Kumagorō noticed Sankichi's hand shaking as he held out the soot-colored bamboo tube. Their eyes met. The whites of his eyes looked pale.

Matsukichi took the bamboo tube and, asking the others to wait for a while, took it into the main house.

"Juan-sama is here now and he's taking a look at it," he said when he returned.

Then he ushered Sadaichi and Sankichi into the main house.

Juan was examining the picture with extreme care.

"This truly is rare. The seated figure is Chirisuto-sama, and the woman wiping his feet with her hair is Magdala Maria. The painting tells the story of the time Magdala Maria saw our Lord when he had returned very tired after a long journey, and she shed tears of sorrow and washed his feet with her tears and then wiped them with her long hair. You say it came from the woodshed of your house? And your father—if I may ask—he was martyred? I have no idea how it's happened, but it seems that your father's spirit may have appeared in the form of this picture. You must take great care of it.

"It would be best if you built a shrine for it, but you'll have to take great caution so the authorities don't find it. You'll have to be very careful to keep it a secret. But what you've shown me is truly wonderful. Today I just stopped by to see how things were going with the rains, but now I see they're truly going well. Sankichi, please worship this with great care."

Tears streamed from Sankichi's tough, hardened face.

"Surely, my mother . . . and, my father too . . ."

Barely able to say even this, Sankichi bowed deeply.

As Sadaichi and Sankichi started for home deep in thought, the rain stopped. After the hard downpour, a fog settled over the land, rising from the sea and the mountains. As the two walked along the banks of a rain-swollen stream, Kumagorō came running after them.

"Wait a moment, won't you? I . . ."

With the banks of the stream wet and slippery, Kumagorō skipped along as if dancing.

"I, too . . . I'd like to . . ."

Kumagorō's voice faltered, but then he caught his breath and continued:

"I'd like to pay your mother a visit. Please allow me to meet her."

Sadaichi and Kumagorō looked at each other. Sadaichi was three years older than Kumagorō. As children, they had been mischievous playmates, but Sadaichi had been prone to saying inappropriate things and he had been weak at fighting. When someone so much as raised their hand, he would burst into tears and run off, looking for Kumagorō. He would hide and cry behind the younger Kumagorō's back. Just a glare from Kumagorō was enough to make the attacker back off. Nonetheless, Sadaichi was older, and when they met, he took the part of the elder brother, which helped Kumagorō feel at ease.

Probably, Sadaichi had brought Sankichi to talk to him about the painting in part because he knew that both men had martyred fathers. Kumagorō looked over at Sankichi, the corners of whose eyes were twitching. He could by no means think of him as a complete stranger.

After staring back at Kumagorō for a moment, Sankichi said hoarsely, "If you'd come and talk to her, it might help."

Sankichi looked at Sadaichi as if seeking his agreement.

"Yes, it might," Sadaichi said, nodding. "If Kumagorō visits, perhaps it might help put your mother at ease."

"She's more to me than just someone else's mother. Today I have work to do, but if I get permission from Nisuke-dono, the next time it rains I'll be sure to go and meet her. Is that all right with you, Sankichi-don?"

"Is it all right? . . . Why, it makes me so happy."

His face flushed with emotion, Sankichi bowed his head deeply.

"When you go, I'll take you there on my boat," Sadaichi added.

Kumagorō was struck by his thoughtfulness.

For the next three days the weather was clear. In the lowland fields the furrows remained muddy and the workers weren't able to harvest, but in the upland fields they got together and harvested the grain. Since the fields were on a slope, the water had run off well and the crop had dried quickly. They would be able to take it into the sheds and then put it out to dry in small batches, as long as they kept an eye on the weather.

"If the weather holds up for just one more day, we can get the lower fields cut quickly, even if they haven't dried out all the way. We'll clean up the storehouse and the sheds and spread it out there."

"It feels like last year we didn't harvest any rice at all," Matsukichi said the night they cut the first grain of the year, looking around at the workers as they ate dinner. The conversation seemed lively enough. From now until the rice planting was finished, the kitchen would be bustling. It was during this season that Matsukichi carried out his role to the fullest. Following the directions of this leader experienced in sharpening sickles and repairing straw mats, the workers felt as if the straw bags were filling up with grain right before their eyes.

When the day's work was completed, Oume sat grinding beans and wheat with a stone mill, as she had been for the past ten days whenever she had free time.

The Hasuda household had a tradition of making dumplings with honey and salt for the workers to enjoy after they finished harvesting. It brought great pleasure to all those who had helped, and Oume's grinding work was at the center of it all. Omiyo, too, was helping, seated beside the grinding mill, using a sieve to remove the husks from the ground beans.

"Looks like we've got enough to make dumplings."

"Yes. I think this should be about right."

"Is this the end of last year's wheat?"

"I left a little to keep until planting time, just in case."

"Somehow, we managed this year."

"Yes, but I'd like to reserve more from this year's crop."

"So would I. Next year will be Ayame's *hinamatsuri* celebration."

"I suppose the folks from Uchino will come over for it?"

"Yes. They're really looking forward to it. We'll make mugwort mochi."

"I've already boiled up a lot of mugwort that Suzu's picked for me."

"It was good that Okayo's family came when we held the celebration for the seventh day after Ayame's birth. They brought us the water to have her baptized and give her the Christian name Luisa."

"Right," Oume said ambivalently. "I thought Ayame-sama was a good name."

Supposing that Oume didn't have much feeling for Christian names, Omiyo changed the subject.

"Can I leave the preparation of the food trays to you?"

"Well, if you don't leave it to me I'll have nothing to do."

As usual, Oume expressed little emotion, but she was in charge of managing all the women who would come to help with the harvesting. *I shouldn't get in the way of her preparations,* Omiyo thought. She hurriedly finished up her task and then went off to the main building.

They started the harvesting early the next morning. At break time, just when the steaming dumplings were brought out, the sky started to cloud over. Since there were lots of people working, they had been able to cut about half the grain. Everyone gazed up at the sky.

"What should we do—should we keep on cutting like this?"

"Or should we gather it quickly and take in what we've already cut?"

Everyone looked at Matsukichi and Oume.

In the end, they quickly gathered the cut grain and took it into the sheds.

The hot dumplings had cheered everyone up, and soon they started to silently bundle the grain and carry it into the storehouse. On this day, for the first time, Suzu was allowed to carry the baby on her back. She watched the adults carrying the bundles to the storehouse. Since she had been told not to let the baby breathe in the chaff from the ears of grain, she slid open the door of the living room just a bit and peeked through the opening.

Kumagorō stood in the middle of the storehouse directing the stacking of the bundles. When there was no room left in the storehouse, they began piling the bundles in the work shed. It had no walls, but straw mats had been hung from the eaves. Just when they were almost finished taking in everything, the pitter-pat of raindrops started. And just as they finished and everyone was sitting in the dirt-floored room, a steady downpour started.

The workers were still breathing hard and their eyes looked sunken as they stared at each other. It must have been around six in the evening.

"That was quite some battle we went through."

"Busier than a battle, I'd say!"

There hadn't even been time for lunch.

"I made it through on those dumplings."

The workers were hungry, but they smiled and spoke with relief at having taken in at least some of the crop.

Oume announced, "Well, anyway, let's have lunch—or rather, supper."

"This rain's no good," Takematsu said as he came in, soaked like a drowned rat and shouldering a hemp bag. With a thud, he dropped the bag in a corner of the kitchen and announced, "Here are some oysters, still in their shells. I just splashed them with sea water and brought them along."

"Well now, isn't this wonderful!"

Takematsu was embarrassed at this greeting from Oume-yan, which she made with particular respect and a rare bow.

"All right then, I'll put them in a big pot with hot water and soon we'll have a nice soup for everyone."

In no time at all, the soup was ready and the room lit up with joy. As people started to feel their bellies filling there was a lull in the rain, but they all knew the rest of the crop must have gotten soaked. Nisuke stepped in and greeted them.

"Thanks to you all for your work. Because of it, we were able to take in more than half the crop and get it into the storehouse. But those of you in families who were planning to harvest tomorrow must be worried."

Everyone sat in silence. They remembered seeing the colors of the neighboring fields as they carried in the bundles of grain.

Someone asked, "Will this rain stop?" Replies of, "I wonder" were heard here and there.

When the rainy season came, just one day could make all the difference between households that were able to take in their harvest and those who weren't. If the grain was harvested unripe, the yield was poorer and it was also more vulnerable to mildew and mold. Naturally, people were tempted to leave it as long as they could to ripen fully. On the other hand, sometimes it was necessary to cut it a bit early to avoid the risk of getting rained on. Striking the right balance was difficult. If they put wet grain into the storehouse, it was bound to get moldy. If it got rained on, there was nothing to do but delay the harvest and leave it in the fields until good weather came and dried it out.

It rained the following day, and the next day, too. Everyone worried that the rainy season had arrived earlier than in normal years. Nonetheless, they continued working hard, taking care of their tasks indoors and looking up to the heavens as if in prayer.

At Nisuke's house, they managed to thresh the crop. When that work was finished, with Nisuke's permission, Kumagorō went to visit Sankichi in Arima. And, as promised, Sadaichi took him there on his boat, in the pouring rain.

At a glance, it appeared that in Sankichi's house the mother and son had barely managed to get by and make a living after the father's death. The Hasuda's house, where Matsukichi, Kumagorō and the other workers lived, was neat, with straw mats woven by Oume and the carpentry work done by Matsukichi. But Sankichi's house had a sloping, thatched roof and its floors were covered with coarse straw mats.

Kumagorō wondered how much Matsukichi had explained to Sankichi's mother about his background. Even though it was early summer, she was sitting in a corner of her closed room with her head bowed in silence. Her white hair hid her face. She seemed older than he had imagined. When he saw her thin, bony shoulders he felt as if his heart might break. He imagined that his own mother must have looked even more pitiful when she died.

Kumagorō couldn't find words for a proper greeting.

Sadaichi called out to her, "Aunt!" In a somewhat reserved voice, he continued, "This here is Kumagorō, the son of Yasuzo-san, one of the martyrs. I mentioned him the other night."

The old woman's shoulders moved a bit, but her head remained bowed. Gradually, Kumagorō's eyes grew accustomed to the darkness inside the house. In one corner was a chest woven from vines, with a hard, thin futon placed on it. A small shelf was attached to the lintel. On it was a discolored wooden box, and in front was a sake bottle that held a small branch with some leaves. Probably this served as an altar. In the gray interior, the green leaves were the only objects that lent a hint of life. Near the wall were two small tables with some wooden bowls on top, their lacquer worn off. This was the only furniture in the room.

Her husband who had been killed had owned a little land and had worked other people's fields and woods, and they had gotten along all right. After her husband's death, she had sold their small plot of land and depended on the compassion of relatives and neighbors to bring up Sankichi. But the drought of the past two years had overwhelmed her. Sadaichi had spoken about these things while he was rowing the boat.

"And on top of that, ever since she saw that blue fire on the cross, that's all she's been thinking about. Though she still cooks, Sankichi says she often burns the food, and the house is dirty. Keep that in mind when you see the place."

Remembering Sadaichi's words, Kumagorō calmed down a bit and bowed deeply.

"I'm Kumagorō. I work for Nisuke's family in Kuchinotsu . . . I've been told that my father died in the same way your husband did, so I wanted to visit and talk with you."

The old woman coughed; it sounded as if she had a crack in her throat. The sound of rain started again.

"May I ask where you worship your father?"

Sadaichi pointed:

"Over there. Up above."

Kumagorō looked up at the shelf attached to the lintel. The woman coughed again, more forcefully than before, and tried to say something, but the phlegm in her throat prevented her words from coming out. Sankichi rubbed her back.

She heaved and then raised an emaciated arm, pointing in the direction opposite from the shelf.

"I tell you, he's over there."

Kumagorō guessed she was pointing to the ruined woodshed. In the dim light, he made out her face. Flustered, Sadaichi corrected himself:

"Ah yes, that's where he is. He's in that shed."

The mother inched her way forward and started whispering in a thin, shaky voice, "We haven't put a roof over it yet. With all this rain now, I feel so sorry."

Sankichi and Sadaichi looked at each other in surprise; ever since the night of the storm she hadn't spoken a word to other people. The word "sorry" seemed to be directed at the spirit of her husband who was living in that shed—or to Kumagorō, who had made his visit in the rain.

"All right Mother, when the rain stops, we'll cover it over with a nice straw roof. But for now, we'll just have to wait."

"I know. If your father had told us he was there in the shed, we could have repaired the roof earlier. Hiding in there, even after he died, he wanted to help us."

Her tone of voice changed.

"My dear—I'm sorry. I haven't forgotten you, even for a day. You must know how many times I've wanted to follow you and die. But you told me to raise Sankichi well, so I've held onto life. But you've been watching us! Until the night of the big storm, I hadn't realized you were here. You've been living next door and looking after us, right up until that night. As soon as the rain stops, we'll put up a thatched roof with a nice smell and it'll keep you from getting wet."

She stopped for a while, and then continued in a gentle voice, as if wringing her words out.

"Please move here to this place. I want to care for your wounds until we can put the roof on the shed. And Sankichi, you, too—ask your father to come. When I think of it now, it seems we built that shed as a place for you to stay after your death. I remember how hard you worked then. Sankichi, that shed is a keepsake of your father. It has the shape of his hands."

Although she seemed aware that there were visitors present, the mother's attention was focused entirely on the woodshed.

"Have you visited it today? We have a visitor today, so let him visit it first," Sankichi said. He seemed accustomed to his mother's ways at times like this. He bowed to Kumagorō, walked to the woodshed, and then, in a low voice, started to recite an *oratio*:

"We humbly pray. Dear heavenly Father, and Zezu Chirisuto, our true Lord, Lord of the land of the spirits who, upon the Cross, took upon yourself the suffering and sins of the world with infinite love and unfailing spirit; to you we express our gratitude. Please make this poor shed into a shrine where we may worship you and recite our *oratios*. Amen."

Kneeling with the others, Kumagorō thought about how he had often heard Juan-sama recite *oratios* at gatherings, but he had never recited one himself. Of course, he had no idea what kind of *oratios* his own father, who had been martyred, had recited. Just trying to imagine it made him feel as if the blood in his head was flowing backwards.

Sankichi's *oratio* sounded different from the usual ones. He spoke of his hope for making the woodshed into a shrine. Kumagorō thought, *Sankichi and I are very different. I've never seen things like a cross burning in a blue flame.*

Perhaps pulled in by her son's prayer, Sankichi's mother started to say something. At first, her voice was very small.

"Let's try to talk about it, Sankichi."

"All right. What should we talk about?"

"Well, who was it that claimed to be the Lord?"

"It was the One who was nailed to the Cross."

"Yes . . . that great man. Yes, your father went with him. But why?"

"Well . . . because it was the Lord on high. My father went with him."

"What does that mean, 'on high?'"

"Before he was nailed to the Cross, our Lord said, 'Although I am your Lord, my kingdom does not belong to this world.'"

"What sort of kingdom is it?"

"They say it's a kingdom with sacred *anima* spirits."

"Who told you this?"

"In my dream—Father came, and he taught me it."

"Your father? Yes, he comes to my dreams, too. But did he have to die like that in order to get to the land of *anima*?"

The mother's voice was choked with tears.

"It was so he might come back to life again, wasn't it?"

"What do you mean, 'come back to life?'"

"The Lord in the kingdom of *anima* was destined to offer his life at the tip of a spear, taking on our pain and sins. And, in return, we're granted eternal life. That's what Father said."

"That's right, Sankichi! You know the way he was. He understood things in an instant, and then he leapt right up into the kingdom of *anima*."

As Kumagorō listened carefully to the conversation unfolding unexpectedly in front of him, the vague question he had been holding in his mind ever since his parents' death started to take shape.

"Your voice, Sankichi—it's like your father's."

"Neighbors have told me the way I speak is like my mother's."

Smiling, Sankichi looked back at Sadaichi. Perhaps overwhelmed by the unusual things going on between the mother and son, Sadaichi had lost his usual quick tongue and just nodded.

"Sadaichi, we should be thankful for this rain, shouldn't we?"

Sadaichi looked at Sankichi's mother with surprise and relief to hear her speak to him in an ordinary way.

"This really is a good rain," he said.

Sankichi's mother replied in a voice that sounded almost sweet, "With this rain, the grain is rotting and the rice won't grow. It seems the whole world is falling apart and rotting to the core, just melting away."

"Aunt!" Sadaichi cried out, trying to stop her from saying too much. But he stopped himself. It was said that insane people could predict the future.

"Sadaichi, don't you think that everything rotting away in our world is just junk, and that now the true world is being born?"

Apparently not expecting an answer, the old woman looked at Kumagorō.

"You made quite a trip here. Thank you for coming. So your father was one of the martyrs? And your mother is gone? You must be lonely."

Kumagorō noticed her hand sliding quietly across the torn straw matting. She placed it on his knee, and then she stroked his shoulders and then his cheek. It was a small, warm hand. Slowly, she gripped his shoulder. The damp room smelled of rotting straw. It was as if he were being led back through distant memories. A warm tear fell on his head. Giving himself over to the old woman's caring, he muttered something. "Mother" . . . that was the word he had been wanting to say. And then, the word did come from his mouth:

"Mother."

Kumagorō lifted his head toward Sankichi's small, frail mother, this elderly woman whom people thought of as insane. Her heart beat hard and she embraced Kumagorō in her arms. They were warm arms. Slowly, tears welled up in his eyes. He felt as if he were returning to that day in his childhood when he had run along the grassy path in tears. His body shook in agony.

Astonished by what was happening, Sadaichi blinked and worried that someone might appear at the open door. It wouldn't do to have other people hear all the strange things that this old woman and her son had been talking about so freely. He was glad it was raining.

When the old woman let go of Kumagorō, she moved her fingers over her knees and started chanting, as if talking to herself.

"These rains are a blessing. The wheat is rotting and the rice isn't growing. All the roots will be washed away. Your father's blood, the river of his blood, will mix with this rain. And finally it will become clear and pure, and it will call out to the flowers of *anima* to blossom."

She sat in silence for a time. Then she pointed toward the sea and said sharply, "Sankichi and Kumagorō! An army is approaching us from the capital of the living dolls. Sadaichi—don't let yourself get caught off guard!"

Rowing his boat back home, Sadaichi apologized.

"Sorry if that was a shock, Kumagorō. She seemed quite changed today."

"It was no problem for me. Thank you for helping me make this visit."

"Somehow she seemed reasonable enough to me. What did you think?"

"She seemed all right to me."

"You thought so? But if that's her real character, we need to be even more cautious."

"Me, I don't remember what my mother was like, so I felt almost jealous of Sankichi-don to see that a parent and child can talk to each other like that."

"For me, it was frightening. The two of them seem possessed by spirits. Hearing them talk, they weren't like ordinary Christians. They must be possessed by a truer Christianity. It really makes me wonder."

"It's natural that things like that happened. You say that after her husband was martyred she became very docile and stopped talking. But that was just a temporary state. Now she seems to have returned to her real self."

"So even you are telling me this? I suppose everyone has a true self. But we don't show it to other people. What would happen if we showed our true selves to everyone? The world goes along as it is because no one shows their true self. That's how you and I do things too."

"Sadaichi-yan—" Kumagorō burst out, "if I were possessed by a true Christian spirit, what would you do? Maybe I *am* possessed."

"What? Enough nonsense! If that's what you're thinking, you'd better get off this boat and swim back."

The two laughed so hard their bodies shook along with the swaying of the boat.

After that, the rains would let up for a half a day, or during the night, but no longer.

It was a time for reading books, and the young people gathered in the storehouse. They got so wet coming and going, they started bringing changes of clothing. They set up poles in the kitchen to dry their wet things. The smell of the young men's bodies mixed with the smoke from the stove, nearly choking Oume and Matsukichi. Still, they continued working silently in the kitchen.

CHAPTER SIX

The Sacred Painting

Kumagorō spoke about Sankichi's mother to no one. Even when Nisuke and Juan asked him what had happened to the picture, he seemed to sink into thought and gave no clear answer.

Since Kumagorō was a household worker, when he attended the school meetings with so many children of samurai families, he sat quietly at the back of the room. Although he didn't ask questions, his teachers noticed his look of determination, and they knew that this young man was the orphaned child of one of the martyrs.

Daisuke's decision to invite Kumagorō to join the school at his home had come naturally, since they had grown up there together. But when he saw how impressed the teachers were by him, he realized how meaningful that decision had been. He felt a deeper bond with Kumagorō, who was a year older than he.

"That Kumagorō—he doesn't say much, but he has a clear look in his eye."

Hearing this from Juan pleased Daisuke greatly.

"Fate led him to our house that night after what happened to his father, and our family wouldn't be the same without him."

"Hmm. Is he still single?"

"Well, my father says that if he can find a good woman, he'll help arrange the marriage and then he can start a family. But for now, he doesn't seem interested."

"He looks like a reliable fellow. Some of those samurai's sons are weak-minded, but Kumagorō seems tough."

"I'm glad to hear that. It's good we got him to come."

When Juan gave Yamada Yomosaku the silk canvas that Yazō had brought back from Nagasaki, he asked him about the painting in Sankichi's woodshed.

"I can't say for certain without seeing it, but it might have been done by someone at the *seminario*—or even by me," Yomosaku replied. "I'd like to see it with my own eyes. If I did paint it, it would have been in my younger days, an immature work. I'd be interested to see how I painted it."

"All right then, I'll talk to Sankichi soon and ask him to bring it over."

"I'd be grateful if you would. Recently, I've been wanting to try my hand again at religious painting. Perhaps I'll be able do a little better than I did back then."

"I'm glad to hear that. If we're going to provide the right kind of education at our school, we ought to have some religious paintings there—as long as we don't attract the attention of the officials. If you would paint them for us, we couldn't ask for more. By the way, is this the kind of canvas you wanted?"

"It certainly is. When I see canvas like this, I feel I've been given divine grace. The spirit of the painting just rises up."

"I can imagine that's so. I envy you."

The painter dismissed Juan's remark with an exaggerated wave of his hand.

"Actually, Juan-sama, I envy you for the way you prepare such fragrant tea. I wish I could do it as well. I can't hide the truth that my poor skills are a mere façade."

"Enough flattery. For me, it's good just to hold the dipper in my hand, with the steam playing about it. But then the *matsubori* slips in through the doorway and reminds me of past battles."

"The *matsubori*?"

The *matsubori* was a wind that swept in unexpectedly from the high plains of Mount Aso now and then.

"Yes, it has a way of haunting a place."

"Hey, don't try to scare me away. I'm just a painter, and this sword at my side is only for show. If a wind like that blew in, the tip of my brush would start shaking."

"Maybe so. But your brush is a lot more help to the people around here than my sword. When I see farmers praying in front of one of your sacred paintings, it really moves me. You don't need manners or rituals to pray, like you do with the tea ceremony—just sincerity."

"This sort of talk embarrasses me. I paint because I enjoy doing it. As for my faith, it's really quite shallow."

"There's no need for modesty. It's enough simply to like it. And as for my tea—well, I do that because I like it, too."

Juan smiled with an impish twinkle in his eyes. Yomosaku mused, *I'd thought of this old fellow as rather inscrutable, but now it seems I can talk with him freely about painting and tea.*

When Nisuke asked Kumagorō to help put up a new thatched roof on Sankichi's woodshed and to fill the boat with as much of this year's straw as needed for the job, Kumagorō quickly intuited his master's underlying intentions.

Probably Nisuke wanted him to check on the painting. Nisuke had no real obligation to send straw for thatching the roof of a house in another village, but he was likely keeping in mind Kumagorō's feelings about Sankichi.

"Please tell Sankichi that he'll be helping us out by using that straw," Nisuke added. "Tell him we don't have a place to store it here, what with all the rain. That way he won't mind accepting our help."

And so, in the space of two days, between the rains and with help from Sadaichi and neighbors, they were able to put up a new thatched straw roof. They also filled the woodshed with firewood. On an altar, sheltered in a narrow space amidst the firewood, they placed the sacred painting, after removing it from its bamboo case. Sankichi showed his mother their work.

"My goodness! You've fixed things up so much here I hardly recognize it. What a beautiful shrine you've made. Now I suppose we'll have to invite the Holy Spirit to come in. But where did you hide the painting?"

They pulled away some firewood from along the wall, revealing a small, dark space in the back where they had enshrined the painting.

"I see—that's a good place for it."

Gazing at the altar in the darkness, Sankichi's mother prayed for a long time, casting aside all other thoughts.

The figure in the center of the picture was Maria Magdalena. Her black hair, covering half her body, fell over Jesus's feet as she tried to wash them. Her downturned eyes were clouded with tears, so she could hardly see his feet. Kneeling in the dark space in front of the painting, Kumagorō joined Sadaichi, Sankichi and Sankichi's mother in prayer.

"It was an unexpected honor to be there when they celebrated the entrance of the Holy Spirit into the shrine," Kumagorō reported to Nisuke when he returned.

During the long period of rains, only the apricots continued to ripen and show fresh color.

The plump grain in the fields started to blacken. When Nisuke heard that Yozaemon had managed to store about two-thirds of his crop, he was relieved. When he talked to families in the community about their situation, there were some differences, but most were worried about the crops they had left in their fields.

Nonetheless, as soon as the rain stopped, people hurried off to the upland fields, hoping the crops on the hillsides could be saved. Wet grain is heavy, so no one laughed when workers slipped and fell along the paths that wound through the hills. They knew that the cows and horses would be happy to eat even swollen, soggy grain.

As they went along their way their words were few, even when they happened to meet someone. They left any spoiled grain standing in the fields and tilled the places they had harvested early. Then they began making seedbeds and taking care of other preparations for the rice planting. But the more rice they grew, the more they would have to pay as taxes to the local lord. Now, even more than in other years, their work in the rice fields brought an unrelenting sense of futility.

Looking up at the sky, people began to pray. Since they weren't holding a formal ceremony about the rain, they didn't use any gongs or hand bells, but the spirit of their prayers resounded throughout the villages.

Although Shimabara and the Amakusa Islands were separated by straits, the two areas could almost be spoken of as a single connected region. Yazō traveled frequently between the islands and the peninsula, and he reported that Amakusa had been facing the same extreme weather. The islands of Ōyano and of Upper and Lower Amakusa had all suffered long, heavy rains, and the people were united in their fervent prayers. Especially in Kōtsuura, the town on Upper Amakusa Island where the Christian churches had once stood, people walked in processions, carrying crosses.

Shirō was away from the school in Kuchinotsu in Shimabara for some time. Yazō brought back news that Shirō and his father had been visiting people on Ōyano Island and holding discussions about religious matters.

One day around this time, Shirō was walking the grassy pathways that skirted the seaside on the way to Kōtsuura on Upper Amakusa Island. Tarōsuke, a young relative from Ōyano, accompanied him and showed him the way. Both were wearing straw raincoats. The ground was wet and soggy and the paths had become channels of rainwater. Along the pathways, tufts of grass swayed back and forth and wild red strawberries bobbled in the currents. The rain striking their umbrellas formed a mist that covered their faces.

"If the rains continue like this, even the fish will drown."

Tarōsuke was a relative on Shirō's mother's side of the family. His comment was not a joke.

"During the big rains and floods the goldfish at Amamiya-sama's pond lost their way and ended up stuck on the branches of the azalea bushes around the *torii*. Some children picked up a few and brought them to me."

"Really?"

Tarōsuke looked carefully at the bushes along the pathway.

"Look—here's a carp. This is where it escaped to. Or is it a crucian carp? No, it must be a regular one, since it has whiskers."

And, sure enough, in the shade of a wild rose bush submerged in a pool of water was a small black carp. It was about fifteen centimeters long and was opening and closing its mouth, having escaped the swift current.

"Rain like this is hard on the fish. It's no good for them. What do you suppose is going on with this weather?"

Shirō looked back toward Shimabara and Kuchinotsu. He couldn't even make out Mount Unzen. All he could see was the vague play of light and shadow streaming down from the scudding rain clouds. What, he wondered, were Ukon, Daisuke, and the others doing?

At a meeting at the school, Shirō had met Takematsu, the man reputed to be such a heavy drinker he had nearly been expelled from the *confuraria*. Shirō had expected a rowdy sort of character, but, on the contrary, had found him to be a gentle, kind man.

"Some people only pretend to be foolish, so we have to be careful," Juan had commented with a look of amusement as he plucked a hair from his nostril.

At Nisuke's home in Kuchinotsu, Shirō had gotten to know a number of other people. Among them was Oume, who had been drying clothes in the kitchen that faced the storehouse. They had exchanged greetings. Although she said she wasn't a Christian, he had never met such a hearty and utterly kind person. She acted a bit brusque, but her heart was humble and respectful.

"Thanks for your help," Shirō had called out to her, but she said only, "It was nothing."

That was all. Thinking back on it now, he fondly recalled her manner and tone of voice. As Shirō followed after Tarōsuke, his feet got splashed and soaked.

In the old days, Kōtsuura had been the site of the church led by Father Mamacos. For the past two years, people there had been holding out through bad harvests, and they all had been looking forward to this year's harvest with high hopes. But now, on account of the unusually long rains, the grain they had tended with such care was rotting in front of their eyes. Kōtsuura was not the only area where this had happened, but since their town had a special identity as the place where the churches had held out to the very last, when the skies opened and turned red, the people took it as a warning that God had become outraged at the evil ways of humans, and rumors went around that it was an omen; likely a foretelling of the coming of *zuiso*, the final day of judgment. With his father Jinbei's support, Shirō had set out to visit this area to see for himself what was happening.

Jinbei had advised him that on his first visit, he should meet with Umeo Shichibei, the village headman of Kōtsuura. Shichibei was an in-law of Watanabe Kozaemon, at whose house on Ōyano Island Shirō and his father had been staying. Kozaemon's aunt Osato was Shichibei's mother.

Shirō's father had told him, "It's not far from Miyazu to Kōtsuura if you go by boat. Since old times, among all the Amakusa parishes, the Ōyano parish has had a particularly close and important relationship with the one in Kōtsuura. Remember that when you go."

The document that Kozaemon had shown them a while back—the one addressed to the Society of Jesus in response to a request from Padre Couros—had listed the members of the congregations of Kōtsuura and Ōyano in the Higo Domain. At the top of the list was Shichibei's name. His Christian name was Migeru. It moved Shirō deeply to realize that he was now among some of the same people who had sent this impassioned letter to Europe some twenty years ago, before he was born.

When Shirō entered the village of Kōtsuura to call on Shichibei, he came to a prominent house with an impressive gate. This was the village headman's home. He walked around to the garden and, holding his rain gear, called out a greeting to the woman standing behind the open *shoji* screen.

"Hello, I'm Masuda Shirō, from Uto. I've come at my father's request."

"Well, well, then, come right in. What a pleasure it is to see you again! I've been wanting to see how you look, and—my goodness, what a fine young man you've become."

The elderly woman who came out so energetically and extended both hands to him was Osato, Shichibei's mother. He remembered her from visits to the Watanabe house with his father and grandmother on ceremonial occasions. She had been at the center of all the women, giving out instructions about what needed to be done. A good friend of his grandmother's, she had maintained a special fondness for Shirō. Now, just from the warmth of the old woman's joy, Shirō felt as if his wet clothing were already drying out. He entered the guest room and took out the letters written by Watanabe Kozaemon's father Denbei and his own father, Jinbei.

Five or six men were gathered in the guest room. Umeo Shichibei, the head of the household, appeared to be around sixty years old. His silver hair was gathered at the back, rather than tied in a topknot. Although short, he had a dignified bearing. When Shirō was introduced, everyone started to speak at once.

"Well, how fortunate we are to have Masuda-sama's son with us now."

Nodding in agreement, Shichibei spoke with a joy that sprung straight from his heart:

"Since old times, we here in Kōtsuura have been like one family with the Ōyano parish and we've never forgotten our close ties, so we're delighted by this young man's visit."

All the men vied to speak first.

"We've heard that Masuda-dono and Ōyano's headman Watanabe-dono have pledged an oath of brotherhood, so now we're like family members."

Everyone agreed to these words from a middle-aged man who was apparently a former retainer of Lord Konishi, and Shirō was immediately treated as a family member. He began to understand the friendliness of these island people.

"Knowing that Umeo-dono has a relative like this, we can look forward to our future with pleasure."

"Please excuse us. With all the rain, the talk tends to be a bit gloomy when we get together these days. Having a new face in our midst really cheers us up."

Shichibei was apologizing for the men's somewhat excessive exuberance.

"To tell the truth, wherever we look, things are rather depressing. But then, how are things over on Ōyano? Do you have any good news?"

"I wish I did, but I'm afraid there's not much good news to report from over there, either."

Shirō was sitting formally as he replied. Shichibei, preparing some tea for him, responded with a smile:

"Shirō-sama, there's no need for such formality with these folks. We're just saying all these things to let you know how glad we are to see you. That's our way of welcoming a person. So, please, sit back and relax."

For a moment, Shirō was unsure what to say, but then he remembered the purpose of his visit.

"In regard to the continuing rains you've been talking about, on Ōyano, too, they've been discussing it at every meeting. And on my way here, as I walked along the different roads, I took a hard look at the condition of the fields. It was truly painful to see all the toppled grain, soaking wet and already sprouting."

Shirō let out a long sigh. All the men stared at him. The faint bluish tinge around his eyes gave him a rather anguished appearance.

"We're getting all this bad weather on the heels of two years of bad harvests," he went on. "The farmers all prayed to the heavens, but it didn't seem to help much, and now everyone seems to be simply waiting for the end of the world. Kozaemon-dono and my father have been worrying that terrible things are happening, even among family members, because of the food shortages. While they're chanting *amen*, people have been gripped by the ghosts of starvation. They're afraid our faith is being eaten from the inside out."

Shichibei gazed into the eyes of those seated around him.

"They're right. To tell you the truth, recently an entire family living near here died by strangling themselves. We're meeting here today to talk about their funeral."

"A whole family strangled themselves? How could such a thing happen?" Shirō asked.

"It started with a theft," a man who appeared to be a local samurai farmer answered.

Shirō glanced at Shichibei, who was placing a tea whisk in a tea bowl. He resumed the story in a mournful tone.

"Well, it was nighttime and a thief came into a squash field. A man caught him and found that it was a young boy, about ten years old."

Since Shichibei seemed to be having a hard time continuing, a kind-looking man, probably in his forties, continued in his place.

"The man who caught the boy was the owner of the field, a blacksmith, and everyone knows he's bad-tempered. He grabbed the hands of the boy, who was sobbing in apology, and thrashed them with a rod, shouting, 'These are the hands that stole!'"

"The punishment was excessive," the samurai muttered, "but the rumors that spread afterwards were far worse."

All around, other voices erupted:

"Some people said the parents made their child steal it."

"So then the whole family shut its doors and stayed inside."

"Their next-door neighbors felt sorry for them. They called to them from outside and left some summer beans they'd cooked, but the next morning the beans were covered with ants and they could hear old Kichizō-san's tearful voice inside."

"People worried that they were starving to death. When they didn't hear any sounds from inside for three days, they broke open the door and went in. They found that the three children had been strangled, and the grandfather, grandmother and mother also were dead. It was a gruesome sight, and none of them could bear to keep looking. The father had died two years before."

"As for the blacksmith, he probably regretted punishing the boy so harshly; after all, he was just a child. The man went crazy. His eyes started darting about like a bird's and he was speaking deliriously. He shouted, 'I'm a goblin!' After that, he ran off somewhere with his family."

"Everyone said the dead took them away."

"Some people said that one night they saw six floating spirits leading off the blacksmith's family."

When the men finished recounting these events, a dark mood fell over the group.

"We conducted an improvised burial, but we've all felt bad about it," Shichibei added. "Some people have been saying that our whole village will be haunted, since this was no ordinary matter. So we've decided to hold a proper funeral tomorrow, conducted by the *confuraria*. We feel awful, but at least we still have our last comfort; we haven't forgotten our prayers."

Even though it was early summer the room was chilly, so they built a good-sized fire in the hearth. The damp room had taken on the smoky colors of charcoal, which suited it well. Shichibei stirred to stirring the ashes from time to time, as if by habit.

At dawn the next morning, Shirō followed Shichibei to the house where the family had died.

"I never came by to see what sort of life they were leading," Shichibei had said. "And now, after what's happened, we can't expect that anyone else will live in the house, so we'll have to tear it down. But before the funeral, I need to take one more look around the house. Otherwise, I'll bear the shame for it. This, too, is my responsibility as headman."

Shirō had decided to go with him.

The house was the bare-bones sort of place that Shirō had imagined. Entering the dirt-floored room, they saw a large earthenware water jug. Near the cooking stove was an old pot, caked with the remains of a soup broth. On a bamboo shelf beside the water jug, it pained them to discover several dishes that had been nicely washed and turned over to dry in a basket. Shichibei picked one up and examined it.

"Bush clover flowers . . ." he muttered, handing the dish to Shirō. It was decorated with an attractive design of flowering bush clover.

"What do you suppose they ate on this?" he asked, agitated.

The elderly silver-haired man glanced up at Shirō. Then, with a mixture of fear and respect, he slowly, quietly approached the cooking pot and removed its cover. He bent over and stared for a moment into the bottom of the empty pot.

"Look—hijiki," he said in a low voice. "They were eating just hijiki seaweed. Kichizō. . . you . . ."

Shichibei's voice became strange. Shirō wondered if old Kichizō, whose tearful voice the neighbors had heard, had been a childhood friend of Shichibei's. Shichibei grabbed hold of Shirō's hakama trousers and, staggering, knelt before the cold cooking stove.

"Forgive us, Virgin Maria-sama. Forgive us."

It seemed he could barely put the words into his mouth.

Holding the dish in his hands, Shirō copied his motions in silence. Some neighbors, probably having noticed the arrival of the village headman, had gathered and were looking into the house. From the dirt floor, Shichibei picked up a child's straw sandal. Its thong was broken and it was muddied, but the straw sole was still in good condition. His hand trembling, Shichibei passed the sandal to Shirō. From the doorway, a young girl said, "That's Jirō-yan's half-foot."

Such sandals were called "half-foots" because of the way they were made to cover just half of the foot, in order to save on the use of straw. Holding the little half-foot in his hand, Shirō approached the young girl.

"This was Jirō-yan's?"

Nodding, the child looked up at Shirō and the old man.

"How can you tell it's his?"

"That field over there—that's where I picked it up."

The girl was pointing to the squash field where Jirōkichi had been caught. It seemed she had picked up the sandal from the field and then thrown it into Jirōkichi's house.

"You picked this up? Well then, you did a good thing, didn't you," Shichibei said, standing in front of her.

Shirō accompanied Shichibei as he staggered along, for some reason still holding in one hand the small half-foot sandal with the broken thong. Shirō held the dish in his hand and glanced down at it occasionally. Following behind them were the young girl and three boys. As they walked along, some adults tried to signal to the children, urging them not to follow the men, but the children ignored them and continued walking. As if following after itinerant monks or entertainers, they made their way along the shore in single file.

Shichibei stopped at the site where the family had been buried. As they marched along, more children joined them. Death seemed to draw children from everywhere in the village. Somehow, they, too, seemed to hear a voice from beyond. In silence, the procession entered the yard of the village headman.

Shichibei's yard was larger than those of most other houses. With its imposing gate that was also so different from the gates of most homes, normally the children might have felt it improper to enter. However, they continued walking all the way to the garden. Perhaps they thought that, since a funeral was a special occasion, they wouldn't be scolded. The children were intrigued by the unusual plants in the garden and played at hiding among them. They looked with amazement at the *shikimi* trees sculpted into tubular shapes.

The women neighbors who had gathered there were talking together in hushed voices as they prepared the meal for the memorial ceremony. They had decided to make soba and serve it in a soup of vegetables. Under the current strained conditions, even the headman found it difficult to provide such food, but everyone felt that it was necessary to serve some kind of meal for the memorial ceremony. So finally, the women had settled on a soup with soba dumplings.

The children flocked around Shirō. For some reason, wherever he went children seemed to gather around him. It wasn't that Shirō had a particular liking for children, but somehow, like iron filings attracted to a magnet, children were drawn to him.

"Today's a day to remember the impermanence of life, right? So let's all wash our hands and faces really well."

"The impermanence of life" was the phrase people used when they spoke of death. Following Shirō's suggestion, the children ran over to the well, then rushed right back to him displaying their clean hands. They gathered around him again and busied themselves with various tasks such as picking up stray stones.

More people joined them. At the proper time, when enough people had assembled, Shichibei began his remarks.

"Thank you all for coming today, in spite of the bad weather. A sad event has taken place, the likes of which we've never seen before in our village. By now I think Jirōkichi and his family, all six of them, must be up in Heaven together. But because of the way they died, well, they may have some lingering thoughts about this world. Somehow, it seems they're still with us, still here in this world, perhaps over there in the shadows of that rock, or that tree. Theirs was a tragic death. As head of this village and of our parish, I feel I wasn't sufficiently concerned about them. Although I recited *oratios* morning and night, I feel that my prayers haven't been true prayers, and that's why this kind of thing has happened."

From the front of his kimono, Shichibei took out the straw sandal with the broken thong, wrapped in a white cloth; the one that had belonged to Jirōkichi. Reverently, he raised the sandal high with both hands, showed it to the assembled group, and then placed it on an altar.

"Early this morning, I went to Jirōkichi's house. A young girl who lives nearby gave me this half-foot sandal. She said it had fallen on the squash field and its thong had broken. The boy must have been wearing this sandal when he was caught. It was made of last year's straw, so it was still new. Since he was such a small child, probably he could have worn it for quite a while longer. It breaks my heart. The straw is still new, but the boy who wore it is no longer with us."

Shichibei looked up at the sky, as if trying to steady himself.

"Our children are the treasures of this village. These treasures were destroyed so easily. In our religion, taking one's own life is the most serious sin of all. What unbelievable determination it must have taken to strangle the entire family, knowing this. Such outrageous determination, who could have summoned it?

"Who was it, really, that strangled this entire family? . . . Well, first on the list must be me . . . me."

Shichibei's neck slumped in dejection. After a pause, he raised his face, as empty as if all but the light in his eyes had been erased from it.

"When someone steals, it's natural that they should receive punishment. But it's hard to imagine that Kichizō, the grandfather, would have strangled all six people in his family as the punishment for the actions of one grandchild. There's no reason to think they assumed they could not go on living because they had run out of food, either. No, it was a problem of spirit. The coldness of our spirit took away their strength to go on living—was this not so, everyone? What does our religion teach us? Let love guide our lives. Love thy neighbor as thyself. But when we recited our *oratios,* our thoughts weren't with the sufferings of this family. With the bad harvests and everything else, we've come to think only of our own families; as if things would be all right if we, alone, should go on living. And whose fault is this? My own. As the head of our parish, I failed to see the desperate situation of this family. Even when I heard about the theft, I let it pass through my ears too casually. Because of my weak, hypocritical faith as a leader, it seems that God has forsaken our *confuraria*."

Shichibei knelt down and raised his clasped hands above his head, like a man who had fallen through a crack in the world. He cried out:

"Dear Lord in Heaven, forgive us our sins."

A silence fell over the gathering. Suddenly, Shichibei's hands, extended toward Heaven, seemed to grasp the necks of those who had overstated the truth and spread the backbiting rumors. They had attended the funeral, feigning innocence, because they wanted to escape the wrath of Heaven. Some of them glanced fearfully at Shichibei. Was he not digging up the past and stirring up the bitter feelings of the dead? The little half-foot straw sandal that he had shown them sparked unexpected fear and remorse in their hearts.

Most of the families in the village had children around Jirōkichi's age, and in most houses they made straw sandals about the same size as his. The half-foot sandal that Shichibei showed them must have been made of straw beaten by the children and woven by Grandfather Kichizō and his wife.

The image of the little half-foot that had been violently pulled off even though it still could have been used was superimposed on the image of Jirōkichi's dead face, with his bluish-black swollen eyelids, and on the image of his swollen hands. A profound sense of the death of the entire family sank into the hearts of everyone present, leaving them trembling and disoriented. Shirō sensed a silent panic grip them as they stood bolt upright.

Completely exhausted, Shichibei opened his eyes and saw Shirō standing close by his side. In his hand was the white dish he had brought from the basket at the house. As soon as he saw it, Shichibei was seized with a vision of Shirō carrying the spirits of the family members above the dish.

"Shirō-dono, since you still have that dish, I have a request for you."

"Yes. What is it?"

"I'd like you to say a prayer. My strength has left me. Would you say a prayer for the *anima* of Jirōkichi's family?"

"All right."

Shichibei looked around at the villagers, hoping to calm their spirits.

"As I just said, I am a sinner. My prayers haven't been strong enough. But fortunately, a special visitor is with us. Masuda Shirō-sama has come over from the Ōyano parish. We in Kōtsuura have had a strong relationship with Ōyano since old times. He's come back to Amakusa after finishing his religious studies. This morning he went with me to Jirōkichi's house. We brought back with us a dish from that house. We don't know exactly what they ate at the very end, but we saw that they left their dishes all nicely washed and set out to dry."

As Shichibei spoke, the group's focus shifted toward Shirō, and to the white dish he was holding. Slowly, Shirō stepped forward and introduced himself.

"Today, I'm grateful that we've been brought together by these unprecedented events. In spite of my youth, I've been asked to share a prayer with you. Before I begin, I'd like to invite the souls of those in the departed family to join us."

After saying this, Shirō called to the young girl. Her face was filled with astonishment. He handed her the dish and whispered something to her. Then he called to five other girls and boys and, as if reeling them in on a string, had them stand in a line.

Suddenly, in the gloom of the day, a gleam of light flashed from the cross on Shirō's chest. The crowd was startled. In recent times, on account of the government's strict prohibition, they hadn't seen anyone openly wearing a cross on their chest. And the light from the cross was brighter than usual. *That must be what people call "gold,"* they all thought.

Shirō knelt in the midst of the hushed group and recited a prayer in a barely audible voice. Then he rose slowly and stood in front of the girl who was carefully holding the dish. He removed the cross from his chest and held it in his hand. All eyes were fixed, unblinking, on the movements of his hand. A gleam of light shone from between his fingers—long, slender fingers that moved with a grace not of this world—as he touched the cross to the girl's forehead and then quietly placed it on the dish.

Amidst the drizzling rain, sunlight broke through the clouds. At that moment, a bright, blood-red spot appeared above the white dish. As the crowd strained their eyes in wonder, a pomegranate flower appeared, newly opened and quivering, surrounded by fresh leaves.

Shirō whispered into the ear of the girl, who was watching in astonishment, "That's Jirō-yan's *anima*. Don't drop it."

A commotion arose among the people standing near the girl, but soon it settled down.

Reciting a prayer, Shirō stood in front of the eldest of the boys and repeated what he had done with the girl. After receiving the sign of the cross on his forehead and listening to some words from Shirō, the boy opened his hands. In them, people saw another bright red pomegranate flower appear. In the damp, rotting air of that brief pause in the long rains, the light that shone from the crucifix in Shirō's hand and from the bright red pomegranate flowers seemed extraordinarily fresh and beautiful. Shirō made flowers appear in the palms of all six children. To each he said the name of one member of Jirōkichi's family. In words that only the children could hear, he said, "This is a soul. Take good care of it."

Seeing the children become suddenly respectful when they heard Shirō's words, the adults tried to guess what he had said to them. They felt as if they were being swept from their feet into a vortex in the depths of the ocean. As this dizzying feeling continued, they realized that, in their deep remorse, their hearts had reached a breaking point. Instinctively, they all knelt down and joined together in asking, from the depths of their hearts, for forgiveness:

"Virgin Maria-sama, save us!"

Voices layered one upon another. Before long, everyone felt that souls were hovering above them. Their eyes were fixed on the beautiful flower that floated on the white dish. The face of the girl who held this spirit in her heart was the face of an angel.

The golden light that had shone from the crucifix in the fingertips of the quiet young man, and the flower that had appeared in front of their eyes, hovering on the dish used in the last meal of Jirōkichi's family, who had died so pitifully—they took these as signs of the beginning of a spiritual rebirth.

Ah—that's a soul! That's the flower of Jirōkichi's anima*!* Their eyes filled with tears. They entered a liminal space between this world and the world beyond, feeling they were redeeming their souls, along with Jirōkichi's family. Remembering how they had been taught that those who committed suicide would go to *Inferuno*, they prayed to Maria-sama with all their hearts, imploring that the family would not be sent there. And at the same time, they prayed that they would be forgiven for their own sins.

Standing before the line of children holding the flowers in their hands, Shirō straightened his posture and began reciting an *oratio*, intoning it clearly so that all could hear.

"Dear Lord who cares for us so deeply, we humbly beseech thy unfathomable mercy. Thou who hast, time and time again, taken on the suffering for our sins and overlooked our behaviors which so deserved punishment, and who hast forgiven our past sins, we ask thee to bestow thy grace upon us so that we may not return to such fallen ways and we may never again commit such sins.

"Grant us the light in our eyes such that we may escape from the sickness of our souls and be guided by the vision of thy suffering on the Cross, and that we may taste of the sweetness of the flower of life, and, as thou hast taught us from thy death on the Cross, grant us the grace to care about those who are going to kill us. *Amen.*"

As Shirō recited each verse of his *oratio*, the group that had gathered for the service followed along and became united in a feeling of rapture such as they had never before experienced.

For Shirō, this unexpected event made him grateful that he had received the golden crucifix as a keepsake from Okattsama in Nagasaki.

Following her advice, Shirō had carried the crucifix as a protective object, not on his chest, but in a leather pouch at his waist. This was the first time he had ever shown it to other people. At Jirōkichi's house, when he had seen the child's straw sandal and held the dish from which the family had eaten its last impoverished meal, he had felt as if a firm hand had been placed on his shoulder. He had decided then to use the crucifix at the funeral. Okattsama had told him that he should use it as sacred object at such a time. When he walked away from Jirōkichi's house along the grassy pathways by the sea, he had been absorbed in these thoughts. He had thought that the situation was altogether tragic, and that the *anima* of the six people wouldn't be comforted by an ordinary ceremony. Until then, he had never called out to the spirits of the dead, but he thought that perhaps now was the time to make use of the magic he had learned from Yang on that Chinese ship. *In the back of Shichibei's house, pomegranate flowers are in bloom. They're such humble, beautiful flowers. When they grow into fruit and split open, they make us think of new life. Those flowers could send off souls. This should be no mere parlor trick like the ones I performed for the girls in the Nagasaki pleasure quarter. I must lead the people in pure light. Let me gather my utmost efforts and present my magic to the souls of the dead. Above all, I'm being tested by God, and by the dead. Perhaps my path forward is opening in this moment.* Shirō concentrated his spirit and assessed the moment.

His prayer came to an end.

Shirō realized that a feverish state was developing in the crowd. He had dared to do what he normally forbade himself to do in front of others. Okattsama had spoken of "the pleasure of the Highest Paradise," and told him that she had enjoyed learning magic tricks. He didn't know the details of the daily lives of the family that had died. All he knew for certain was that this family had led a life completely different from the lives of people who can think of the "Highest Paradise." And on top of that, they had killed themselves, and parents had killed their own children, acts that their religion forbid. The members of their own faith had driven the family to that state. It would not be strange if the entire village were cast into *Inferuno*. He had witnessed the villagers trembling in fear.

With the recent rains coming after years of bad harvests, people had lost their direction. Their eyes had become hazy. Shirō thought that perhaps the dead family had been sacrificed like sheep in order that the wayward spirits of the people might return to them. After their deaths, the villagers had become confused and had remained silent, and the deaths had become like a curse they imposed on themselves. Shirō thought that if the spirits of the sacrificed could be purified, and if the villagers could see the process in front of their own eyes, their feelings of shame might lift. Without this, there could be little hope for their religious revival.

Shirō realized that he had been placed at a point where he needed to push himself to take a step forward. *Compared to the lives and deaths of that family of six, my own sixteen years of life have been a mere trifle. In their house, all I saw was that one pot, with the traces of the last meal they ate. And Shichibei cried out in shock, "They were just eating hijiki—just seaweed!" But really, wasn't the last thing they tasted humiliation? I've never experienced anything like that. I know nothing about my fellow human beings.*

A dreadful feeling of emptiness had been welling up within Shirō. But when he saw the unblinking eyes of the young children looking up at him, a fire was kindled in his heart, like the seething volcanic mud of Mount Unzen. *These children are in greater danger than any of us; they're closer to the Devil—and closer, too, to God. In which direction should I step?* The hot mud seething in his heart reached the boiling point, and an electric charge surged through his body. He had the feeling that his self was being replaced with that of another being.

Shirō stepped forward slowly and pointed toward the sky.

"Today I held the cross like this—in front of Deus in Heaven, and Chirisuto the Son, and Maria-sama the Blessed Virgin. And I made a vow with you in my *oratio* that we would swear upon the flowers held by those children to remain faithful. O Lord, I beseech thee, if I should become unfaithful, take me first."

The wind stirred and a faint, violet-tinted stroke of lightning flashed through the clouded sky. Shirō remained standing with his eyes closed and his arm raised, pointing to the heavens. Restrained murmurs spread among the people gathered in front of him. When Shirō opened his eyes, it seemed as if he had grown in stature. He was no ordinary youth of sixteen years.

As he faced the sky, Shirō's voice was filled with dignity.

"O Lord, we beseech thee. With our continuing years of poor harvests, it has become hard for us to go on living. In our poverty and want, parents have come to doubt their children, neighbors have come to despise their neighbors, and we have fallen into the ways of the Devil. The blood and the oil of our bodies has been squeezed from us as if we'd been shoved through an oil press until the spirit of our religion has run dry, and we've been driven to the edge, gazing into *Inferuno*. Will our entire village starve to death together? Or will our bodies be burned in the fires of *Inferuno*? Before long, we will have no place in this world to live.

"O Lord, we ask you to witness our suffering. Grant thy mercy to those who have killed themselves, disobeying your commandments. For a long time our religious faith has been persecuted by the fire and the swords of the feudal lords with their fierce and cruel hearts, and already many people have died on the cross for praising the work of our Lord. O Lord, who gave his only beloved Son on the Cross, we who have for such a long time kept your teachings amidst our persecution, we realize that our spirits have become weak and that we are sinking into the valley of death."

Sobs rose up all around.

"O Lord, receive in *Paraizo* the souls of these six people to whom we have offered flowers today. We ask thee to show us who are wandering in the valley of death the path to the country of *anima*. Have mercy upon us, O Lord. And even if we should cease to exist on this Earth we have now vowed to return to the spirit of our faith, which has been protected and saved by our blood, and to arrive in the land of *anima*, which is filled with light, without leaving anyone behind. O Lord, grant thy strength to us who are weak in our faith."

While Shirō stood as motionless as a statue, it seemed that the people around him had been struck with awe and forgotten the passage of time. After a long silence, Shirō turned his gaze toward them. Suddenly, his face broke into a smile and he began speaking cheerfully. Once again, the pure, young sixteen-year-old boy was there among them.

"How could our sincere prayers fail to reach the Lord? Our Lord in Heaven, I believe, has taken into his hands the pitied souls of these six people. Already, they're at peace in the land of *anima,* where they've come back to life, like these beautiful flowers. They've become heralds, preparing for us the way to live together in the land of *anima*."

A voice from the congregation, neither moaning nor bellowing, cried out:

"He must be the Archangel Michael! Our Lord is sending us an angel. We are awakening! From today we will return to the true principles of our faith and prepare ourselves for the kingdom of *anima*."

The person who had cried out this oath, shaking his clenched fist, was one of the local samurai that Shirō had met the previous evening at Shichibei's house.

"We were all about to get kicked down into Hell, weren't we? But the Lord has not forsaken us. Now is the time for us to return to the teachings of our religion.

"We have to stop praying secretly and do it freely, under the sun. Don't you all agree?"

Immediately, Shichibei stood up with the others facing Shirō and pressed his hands together in prayer.

Cries for forgiveness sprung up all around.

Shichibei's mother Osato came forward, carrying several white dishes. She knelt reverently in front of the children and had each one place a red flower in a dish. One by one, she had them hold the plates and raise them to their chest.

"We beseech thy glory," she called out and then made the sign of the cross.

Shaking in agony, not comprehending what was happening, people shuffled their feet and looked at each other imploringly.

Someone said, "A cross—we must make a cross and lead a procession of atonement!" At that, four or five men rushed off to a nearby cedar grove, chopped down a tree, stripped it of its branches, and quickly fashioned a cross. A line formed behind the hastily-constructed cross and the procession began to move. At its head were the children with their pomegranate flowers, the leaves still attached, on the white plates.

Passing down the grassy pathways of Kōtsuura, the frenzied procession headed toward the grave mounds along the sea, chanting the litany for Holy Mother Maria. People living in the lower hills came out to watch the procession, and soon, many of them joined in.

At times, the man carrying the heavy cross staggered under its weight. When it appeared that he could no longer bear the burden, other men cried out, "Tsunekichi—let me take over for you!"

But Tsunekichi would not give up the cross.

When Shirō returned to Ōyano Island and told his father Jinbei—who had been staying there in Miyazu at the home of Watanabe Kozaemon—what had happened, Jinbei was shocked. Since Kōtsuura, on Upper Amakusa Island, had once been the distinguished home of the foreign churches, he could see how a fervent rekindling of faith might take place following the tragedy of the joint suicide. But every event bears fruit in its own time. Jinbei had not expected that he would send his son to check on the state of affairs in Kōtsuura only to have him reawaken the community's faith. But what must happen will happen. Perhaps the opportunity had already been ripening. In any case, Jinbei was amazed by the profound power hidden in his own son.

Throughout the Amakusa Islands, efforts to obtain emergency rice from the government had been continuing. The year before, they had gone to Tomioka Castle and petitioned Miyake Tōbei, the new administrator of the Karatsu domain, and had been granted 370 *koku* of rice. This year, too, representatives from each area had been sent to ask for assistance, but Tōbei had ordered them to first ask their local leaders.

Lord Terazawa, who had built the main castle in Karatsu, had appointed the administrators of Tomioka Castle and set up three local districts under them in Sumoto, Hondo and Kawachinoura. The district leaders were local samurai. Accordingly, the farmers had gone to their respective district leaders, but these officials had a reputation for ignoring the farmers' painful appeals when they took in the land taxes. In addition, they had expressed their great anger at the farmers for skipping over them to appeal directly to the upper office, without observing proper procedures. Their anger was compounded by their animosity toward the new head of the Tomioka administrators who had been sent in from Karatsu.

Masuda Jinbei had come to a decision:

A tragic famine has come over the Amakusa lands. Receiving rice and grain assistance will only provide a temporary solution. I don't wish to disparage people's efforts, but even if, after appealing time and time again to the local administrators and the Tomioka magistrate, we should receive a little assistance again this year, it will be just a pittance, and soon it will be gone. It will be like throwing water on red-hot stones. The story that Shirō brought back about the family in Kōtsuura that committed suicide was only the beginning. He saw that the people are facing a catastrophe from which it will be very difficult to be rescued.

Catastrophe—Shirō wasn't just referring to the hell that will appear in this world when there's nothing left to eat and families fight each other for food. What he saw in front of him was the hell on earth of a ruinous war. Shirō said he saw the cosmos-devouring flames of Inferuno. *Perhaps he was seeing what the rest of us haven't been able to see, and hearing what we haven't been able to hear. A catastrophe—it means that the faith we've held until now, amidst our oppression, is being trampled in the mud. Shirō has seen that we who have lost our faith are about to be burned up in the fires of* Inferuno.

The people of Kōtsuura aren't the only ones whispering about the coming of the end of the world. With the years of bad harvests and the taxes that haven't been eased even a bit, people have lost their hopes for the future. Desperation has set in. Even our faith, which we have clung to despite persecution, is on the verge of dying.

People may think that if they pretend to abandon their faith but still hold the teachings in their hearts, one day they'll be saved, but aren't we just going through the motions? Ever since the bakufu *appointed Terazawa Shimamori as lord of the domain after he served as magistrate in Nagasaki, it was clear that they weren't going to leave our religion alone. In recent years, we've been caught in their net without even noticing it, and we've lost hope. We're stumbling into an abyss of self-destruction.*

Since the death of Lord Konishi Yukinaga I've come to understand how empty the lives of the samurai are. As a former samurai, my path must be devoted solely to justice. Like Christ our Lord, I must wager my life to save thousands of souls by going in valor to the battlefield. Now is the time for us to raise our religious flags openly again. We have to escape the rule of our cruel lords and make our way to the joyous land of anima. *Grain assistance will be of no use. The rice and grain stored in the clan lords' storehouses was a gift from Heaven to us, the farmers. Looking to Christ our Lord, let us break open the lords' storehouses and establish our own country, here in Amakusa. There is no other way for us to live.*

O Lord, we ask thy blessing . . .

Night after night, Jinbei bowed his head in deep contemplation.

Jinbei asked Kozaemon to send a message to Kozaemon's father, Watanabe Denbei, the headman of Amura Village.

Denbei had gone by the name Kozaemon when he was headman of Ōyano Island, but he had passed on both the leadership of the parish and his name to his son, the present Kozaemon. Nevertheless, people still came from all around to seek advice about difficult matters from not only Kozaemon the son, but from Denbei as well.

"Denbei-dono, what do you think we should do?"

"Well, since I'm retired now, I'm afraid I can't be of much help."

He would say this, but nevertheless he would offer some advice. His opinions were always right to the point, and for this reason many people felt comfortable asking his help.

In his free time, Denbei would walk about with a hatchet on his belt, looking at his favorite trees, or take a boat out fishing at sea. And since he was darkly suntanned and his movements were brisk, if his hair hadn't been arranged in the formal "tea whisk" style, he might have been mistaken for a woodsman or a fisher. When people were looking for him, they would ask, "Is our retired leader off in the mountains today, or is he out at sea?"

Jinbei had great respect for Denbei, who was six years his elder. Jinbei was aware of the severe conditions surrounding them, and of the famine that was likely to become a reality soon. In the midst of this, he was trying to restore the spirits of a people at the bottom of an abyss, and he was determined to stake everything on this effort. But he needed kindred spirits. At the top of his list was Watanabe Denbei.

Shirō's elder sister was married to Kozaemon's younger brother Satarō, so there had been occasional comings and goings among the in-laws, but beyond that there hadn't been much contact.

Dark clouds are gathering over the land. I'd very much like to meet and consult with you. I will wait for you to come.

This was the message that Jinbei had sent to Denbei.

When Denbei arrived, his eyes gleaming even more brightly than usual, Jinbei guessed that he had understood the meaning of his invitation.

The day was already growing dark when Jinbei, Kozaemon, Denbei and Shirō gathered in a room detached from Kozaemon's house. At Kozaemon's request, the other members of the household stayed away. Jinbei was unusually quiet and, like still water, Shirō waited patiently at his side. Denbei and his son sensed that difficult matters were about to be brought up.

"Yesterday I heard some news from Umeo Shichibei in Kōtsuura," Denbei said, getting the discussion started. "Shirō-dono, it seems you really did some auspicious work there in Kōtsuura. Shichibei told me he was moved to tears. The people there are fired up with emotion and returning to the principles of our faith."

Leaning on his cheek in the shadows, Shirō replied, "Well, that may be saying too much. But that family died because we've lost the strength of our religion, and now we are all being tested. The incident in Kōtsuura was an omen. I fear that from now on, we're going to see many more scenes from Hell."

"This is why I've asked you here today," Jinbei said in a firm, low voice, as if shoving aside rocks. "What's happening now isn't a problem in Kōtsuura alone. We're all approaching the limits of what we can do. As you both know, lots of people in the villages are talking about the end of the world, even here in Ōyano. How long can we go on like this? I've been thinking about how we can survive, but we've exhausted every means. Now that things have come to this, I'd like to confide my thoughts to both of you."

One of Kozaemon's cheeks was quivering.

"I've made up my mind—I'm going to rise up in rebellion."

Jinbei stared at the two men in front of him. Denbei and his son stared back intently.

"If we're going to start a rebellion, simply capturing the local office and the Tomioka guard house where we petitioned for grain won't be enough. We'll have to drive out the lords from Amakusa completely and establish a Christian country. We'll march together under the banner of Deus with an army of God, and we'll smash the granaries of the local lords and create a land of people who reside in the glory of the Lord. If we aren't tough and disciplined enough, we'll end up fighting each other and falling into a hell on earth. Right now, the farmers are like dry grass ready to erupt in flames at the least spark. This is the time when our long-standing Christian alliance will come to the test. I, too, am a poor Christian, but if it's for our people, then—like our Lord who, on the Cross, showed more courage than any other person in the world—I'm ready to become the toughest of warriors."

Though Jinbei was dressed in plain clothing, his entire being expressed dignity, and in this brief speech he gave voice to all the feelings he had long held in his heart. For a moment Denbei just blinked his eyes, but then he sat up and replied formally:

"Jinbei-dono, you and I have known each other for a long time, but now you have laid before us your deepest feelings. I honor your determination. And, to tell the truth, I too have been thinking things over and wondering when I should speak out. As you've said, if we go on like this, we'll bring on our own destruction.

We've reached the border between life and death. We must make up our minds with complete resolution. I, too, have decided. We Christians cannot keep dragging ourselves along like this forever. Throughout all time, our headmen have worked for the people. And we have also been given the religious responsibility to work for our neighbors. Now, I realize, this is what our Lord has been telling us. Now I've awakened."

Denbei's deep-set eyes shone and energy radiated from his small body.

"Thanks to having lived this long, I've received the grace of Maria-sama. And thanks to her, I've found my place of work. Jinbei-dono, even though I'm just an old sack of bones, I pledge to work with you until the end. Unless we're prepared to face the worst, our religion will have no future. With the grace of Maria-sama, I hope to go on to the next world without worries. Whether I end up in *Paraizo* or *Inferuno* is up to Deus-sama. And that's fine with me."

Jinbei was roused. For some years he had been holding back from speaking his deepest feelings. He realized that he had come to his decision in the twilight years of his life. Now he had spoken his true feelings in front of his closest friends, and he had been prepared to part ways if they didn't agree with him. The sound of water flowing outside cut through the tense atmosphere in the room.

"I'll never face such a grave matter again in my life. I'm going to make the most of Jinbei-dono's decision. I, Kozaemon, to the best of my ability, will follow after and support my father."

"If you will do this, then I have no fears for our future. If it's time to die, then let us die together. All right then, it's decided."

Breaking into a smile, Denbei glanced at Shirō, who had been sitting quietly beside his father. "I'm glad to see that you've become such an honorable young man," he said. "It's only natural that Shichibei was so impressed by you."

Nodding vigorously, Kozaemon sat up straight.

"All right then, how about exchanging a few cups of sake to seal our pledge?"

"That sounds good to me. We're about to make a once in a lifetime decision among men, so let's drink the night through, for the first time in ages. What do you say, Jinbei-dono?"

"But first—"

Jinbei fell silent and placed his hands on the tatami. Then he continued:

"I, Jinbei, wish to express my thanks to the two of you. This matter I've brought up—this plan—is truly terrifying. It's earth-shaking. A rebellion; such a thing reaches far beyond our own private concerns, and beyond the bounds of our families as well. It draws into it all the innocent common people, and it may well drag us all to ruin and destruction. Just thinking of it makes me tremble. We've worked together for many years, and now you are consenting to this on the spot. I, Jinbei, am deeply moved. My gratitude will last forever."

"Enough of this formal talk. It doesn't suit you. My feelings about a rebellion are just like yours. This outrageous government makes my old man's blood boil. Let's raise our hands!"

Denbei moved next to Jinbei and grasped his hand.

"Jinbei-dono, let us prepare to face the hangman, the cross and the crucifixion. Whether we live or die, we're in this together."

In silence, they prepared for a drinking session. In the stillness of the night, Jinbei contemplated the fate of Denbei's large household. *Just because my daughter married into his family, am I destroying his family line? But no—it will not be the end.* As he took his first drink, his body trembled.

In an instant, memories of Jinbei's entire past flashed through his mind.

From my parents' times, my family served the Konishi clan and we were able to lead our lives as members of a religious group. But now, as I think about what it means to be a samurai and a Christian, I realize that I haven't understood either. The samurai farmer-soldiers of Ōyano who came from Hyūga worked for the government and held decent positions, but that time is long past. In light of the sad downfall of Lord Konishi Yukinaga and all the plots and schemes that arose afterwards, I haven't missed the military life. But with the countless changes of recent decades, where have I found the spiritual sustenance to go on living?

Now, at last, I understand. To live as a samurai warrior means to live for the cause of justice. Everything I've experienced has been for justice. I served Konishi-sama and I saw his tragic death with my own eyes. I travelled to Nagasaki so many times and met with people there to earn money for the clan lord. And now I'm witnessing the unprecedented crop failures of recent years. All of this has prepared me to understand what it means to live for justice as a samurai and a Christian. Even if I have to face a row of spears ready to pierce me, it will be my duty to march forward, striking out against the peril facing my companions, as did my Lord, Christ. This is my path to justice.

God must have decided to bless me with a son like Shirō. Thinking back, Shirō must have started out on a path that I never imagined, long before I realized it. His ears must have been hearing voices from the world beyond. It seems that he is both my child and not my child, and that he has been entrusted to me by the Lord from that world beyond. At my age I've made this fearful decision, perhaps because the Lord who entrusted me with bringing up Shirō has pushed me along a road of no return.

Jinbei glanced at his son Shirō. A slight smile played about his cheeks, almost like a fog.

"Shirō, do you suppose you could do a Noh dance for us, in celebration of the beginning of our journey? I'll sing."

"Yes, a dance! This old timer would love to see you dance."

Denbei smiled and beat his hand in rhythm. Without hesitation, Shirō stood up. He closed his mouth tightly and held a white fan.

Denbei began reciting a verse from the Noh play *The Pearl Diver*. It was a part he had sung back in the days when he served under Lord Konishi, a section he remembered his lord having a particular liking for:

> *How sad that your body is aching from the weariness of travel and overcome with hunger. This is the end of our world, living here humbly in the country. How miraculous to meet you, a person of such lofty rank, in this place. Please eat of this sea staghorn, this already-cut sea staghorn.*

Watching Shirō move with sliding steps onto the veranda with the blackness of the night sky behind him, as if he were dancing in the deepest reaches of the ocean, Denbei sighed.

"His dancing, it's almost not like that of a human. It's—like a flower. It's a gift for my aging eyes."

Having been asked to stay away, the other members of the household had kept a distance, but now they gathered nearby, straining their ears to listen.

"That must be Jinbei singing now. Something important must be going on."

The lingering rains lifted, but in almost no time the wet weather turned to drought.

The fields where the unharvested grain had rotted were planted to rice, but the seedlings were poor and most of the fields dried up.

Children played, digging in the ground with hoes and piling up mud in the parched fields. In the moisture at the bottoms of their scoops of mud they could find fifteen or more loaches at a time, some small and some big. When exposed, they wriggled about together in lumps, trying to avoid the sun. In the previous year, during the drought, swarms of carp, frogs, and loaches had piled up and died around the roots of the rice plants. At planting time, when people turned over the earth in the ruined fields, it had brought them some cheer to find the loaches still surviving in the depths of the mud.

This year the farmers figured they should dig up their fields soon in order to have something to put in their soup pots. All around, in every paddy, they could see big mounds of mud, bigger than the ones made by moles. Often, they heard gleeful shouts such as, "Look, I got a big catfish!"

When summer came, they weren't able to gather as much food from the seaside as in normal years. They used oyster pickaxes to dig among the rocks and gathered shellfish like the "demon's claw," things they usually wouldn't look for. In August, Mount Aso erupted and they could see its smoke and ash billowing across the Ariake and Shiranui Seas. Many people were burned to death and there were rumors that the people living at the base of the mountain were in great confusion.

"Now I see why this scorching heat is so different from usual."

After gazing at the sky in the east, people spread rumors.

Following the eruption, the sky remained a stagnant yellow and the rice plants were covered with ash, and then started to whiten and wither. When late summer came, it seemed that the skies burned red for days on end. These were not picturesque sunsets but a uniform red, without any bands of coloring.

Everyone found it hard to concentrate on their work. Sometimes, a person would stare up at the sky in desperation and cry out, "The Day of Judgment has come. The end of the world has come!"

In Kōtsuura, there was talk of a young woman who had become deranged.

"A woman who married into a family in Sumoto just gave birth and she's been acting strange. The road of blood sickness has come down from the sky and it's taken her with it. She's been going back and forth to Kusatsume Pass, clawing at the sky and shouting, 'Pull that sickness down to the earth!' It's really troubling."

"That red sky is frightening, too. But giving birth to a baby in a time like this, without enough food, that's really too sad."

"And they say she hasn't been eating enough, so her breast milk has dried up. I hear she's been walking around holding her baby in one arm and crying out, 'Let the sky fall! Let the sky fall!'"

In this time of unrest, rumors circulated that, all around Kōtsuura on Upper Amakusa Island, people were returning to Christianity and that they were lining up in front of a cross, scourging themselves with bamboo branches, and calling for redemption as they sang sacred songs. And there was word that a remarkable young man had made the flowers of *anima* bloom with his golden crucifix.

Stories about the processions in Kōtsuura also reached people on Ōyano Island.

"Sure, everyone's talking about Shirō-sama over in Kōtsuura lately, but it all started right here on Ōyano. Masuda's father was one of the old Christians. It's no small matter that we've stayed close like this since old times."

"Yes, our relations go way back. And now we're planning to build a chapel like no one else has."

"We accepted Shirō-sama as our religious leader before anyone else, and our momentum is really growing."

"We may not have the same history as Kōtsuura, but I don't see them rebuilding their old churches."

"All over Kyushu, Christianity's been falling into decline. But here in Miyazu, on Ōyano, we're building a road to the country of *anima*."

Such was the sort of talk going around.

Deep into the night, the four men continued their secret discussions.

"Our plan is not to rob the daimyo of their land. And it's not to start a peasant revolt against the lords. It's a heroic undertaking to establish a kingdom of God on this Earth. It's essential that the people understand this," Denbei said.

"We're planning something that has never been attempted in the history of Japan," Jinbei said, picking up the thread. "We may be farmers, but we've been given grace as Christians. It's essential that we stay aware that we're responding to God's call. And unless we have the spirit to serve as the force of Deus, we can't expect to be victorious in this struggle."

Breaking his silence, Shirō said quietly, "The crucified martyrs have become gods of war, and they will lead our forces."

He gazed up at the sky as if the martyrs were right before his eyes. Kozaemon was trembling like he had been seized by a fit of ague.

"That's right! All those who've gone to *Paraizo* already will surely join us."

Kozaemon's face was flushed with excitement. Denbei glanced at him, deep in thought.

"But what about the farmers and fishers? Who's going to talk to them and inspire them with the spirit? Jinbei and I aren't suited for it, since we're too close to them," he said, gripping his thigh.

"Shirō's the one to do it," he continued. "We're going to build a chapel here on Ōyano. That may be the best way to restore our religion."

"Well, that sounds good to me," Jinbei responded. "We've been hiding our religious practices from the officials and reciting our *oratios* in fear, but how can our spirit rise up if we go on like this? If we stop hiding and come together to build a chapel, we'll all feel more committed to the cause—don't you think?"

"In any case, there's nothing more awesome than complete devotion. A chapel will be the foundation for bringing people together and uniting our faith. What do you think, Shirō-dono?

Since there aren't any padres left around here, it looks like you'll have to take over as our spiritual leader."

With Denbei looking on so approvingly, Shirō realized that this was not a time for modesty.

In a remarkably short time, a chapel was constructed in Miyazu on Ōyano Island. It was located at the end of a small inlet where boats were harbored. The project, in clear defiance of the prohibition, became widely known among the people and created unusual excitement.

Behind all of this work, Masuda Jinbei's family had, of course, been active. And Watanabe Denbei, an old hand at organizing, cajoled the village headmen in the area to gather funds and materials. On the day of the dedication ceremony, believers gathered from all over the region, rowing over on boats from the coves and inlets and walking the paths along the coastline.

People looked at the modest, unadorned building. With hushed voices, they entered.

"What a wonderful chapel! At last, our church is seeing the light of the sun."

The people had not forgotten the government's strict prohibitions against their religion. They knew that they had been able to enjoy a period of peace by pretending to apostatize and keeping their beliefs hidden. But those who traveled by boat to attend the dedication were impressed by the determination of the Christian group in Miyazu, so evident in the chapel they had openly built and the flag they had raised to proclaim their faith in defiance of the ban on Christianity.

"It's no good, no good at all. It's terrifying," some had said at first. But when they saw the chapel with the cross on top of it right in front of their eyes, everyone, including the naysayers, felt their fears and hesitations vanish. There stood the very chapel they had longed for in the depths of their darkness.

Inside, the fragrance of wood filled the chapel, and the light from the candles in a large stand shone on the red berries and green leaves of a holly tree growing in a large pot.

People whispered in awe when they saw the two large sea breams that had been placed on a small stand above the altar. For these people, whose families had long lived by fishing and farming, the sea breams imparted a special intimacy, and seeing them placed in front of Deus-sama brought them great joy. A small white-pine bonsai sat to the right side of the sea breams, and on their left was a beautiful bonsai of bamboo. A crane and a tortoise made of gold and silver paper strings were beside them. The whole display made a most welcoming and festive sight.

The women whispered, "Those cranes and tortoises—who do you suppose made them?" But it was the young man at the center of all the rumors whom they waited for most eagerly, standing on tiptoe to catch a glimpse.

The headman of Miyazu arrived and expressed his appreciation to all the believers who had worked so hard and made contributions, and then a thick curtain was opened to the inner sanctuary. A girl who looked about six years old raised a cross, the crimson sleeves of her gown swaying to and fro. Surprised at being observed by so many eyes, the girl froze for a moment, but soon she remembered her responsibilities and took her place at the side of the altar. Shirō, the young celebrant, stepped up to the altar after her. With all eyes fixed on him, he felt as if shafts of light that extended back thousands of years were striking him. The short sleeves of his white kimono were decorated with a flower motif, and his deep green sleeveless *haori* jacket had a flower pattern that gave the impression of light sinking into a deep green sea. With them, he wore *hakama* trousers. This was the formal clothing that Okattsama had given him in Nagasaki.

Shirō took a candle from the altar and carried it to the back of the inner sanctuary. Seven more candles had been placed there, and when all were lit the altar seemed to float. On the far side of the candles, a sacred picture of Maria-sama holding the infant Jesus was hanging on the wall.

Shirō knelt in front of the painting and began an extended meditation. Soon, the rest of the congregation joined him. As the light from the ocean side entered and filled the chapel, the meditation came to an end. The young girls in front stood up, all wearing the same white gowns. They began to sing:

How clouded are my eyes
I ponder after my tears run dry.
The dear ones of deep compassion
are now away from me.
Beyond the border, where even birds don't fly,
the *anima* birds, at least,
understand our hearts
and fly over the distant reaches of the heavens.

With the older girls leading the verses, the younger ones joined in and followed along.

Some in the congregation recalled having heard the song before. Some remembered it as a lullaby sung by an old woman who used to live by the seashore and had now passed away. This woman had learned it from a blind monk and biwa player named Lorenzo. If the padres had heard the song, they might have recognized the melody of the Good Friday Elegy.

The song was repeated two times. The congregation listened with heads bowed. The song sounded so pure that they felt moved, unexpectedly, nearly to tears.

The "dear ones of deep compassion"—that must mean the beloved people who used to be close by, but are now far away. But, no, above all, it must refer to our departed parents.

As they listened, they realized how deep the sorrow hidden in their mothers' hearts must have been as they silently and lovingly embraced them as children. With what spirit did their departed parents and grandparents raise them? When they thought back on it, they realized they had been ignorant of their parents' true thoughts and feelings when they were alive. They were filled with affection for their dear ones.

When Shirō opened his eyes, he immediately felt drawn in by the congregation's sorrowful expressions. Old and young alike were praying fervently, their hands interlocked in prayer. Their eyes showed that they had found a hand to lead them to the place beyond this world. He realized that it was at such times that people used the expression "*grant us the grace of the afterlife.*"

With this unspoken entreaty deep in his mind, Shirō proceeded toward the sacred painting. A small purple velvet box had been placed near it. Setting it on the altar, he removed the lid with a slender, wax-like finger. He then took the golden cross from inside the box and hung it on a holly branch. With the small cross swaying among them, the green leaves and red berries stood out vividly.

Shirō turned to face the congregation, and as he sang the last two lines of a hymn, he reached out slowly with his right hand. A round form covered with white feathers appeared within it. The form expanded into a dove that looked out at the people with tilted head.

"Now—here!" Shirō cried out.

Slowly, the dove flew around the congregation. Not understanding what had just happened, they watched with mouths agape. The dove circled the chapel once and then flew off into the sky.

"It's the *anima* bird! The bird of *anima*!"

All at once the children pointed, stamping their feet and gazing up to follow the bird's flight into the clear autumn sky.

Shirō watched the bird fly off, and then, moving forward slowly, took the cross that the young girl had been holding and placed it in front of the incense stand. He then moved a few steps back and recited the prayer of Santa Cruz. The entire gathering joined him.

He opened the Bible that had been placed on top of the incense stand.

"For the infinite mercy of our Heavenly Father who has saved us sinners and who, in his sorrow and benevolence gave his only Son on the Cross, we offer our eternal gratitude."

After reciting the *oratio* and holding up some incense, Shirō began speaking to the congregation.

"Today, in this beautiful chapel, we have been blessed with a glory such as is rarely granted. Thanks to our ties to the world of the past and to the grace of our Lord and the Blessed Mother Mary, the time has now come when we may meet each other.

"I am so grateful to see you all here at long last. In arriving at this place today, we have passed through darkness for a hundred years; or for two hundred years; or perhaps for a thousand years. From whence have we come? And through what joys and sorrows have we passed in coming to this island? This chapel, which was built thanks to all of your great efforts, has been completed as the long-cherished wish of people of previous lives. Perhaps we can call this moment *Paraizo*."

Shirō's voice harbored a deep sadness.

"We don't know what life was like during the thousands of years that we humans have passed through. We don't know if we lived as ogres or as beasts in the earlier world, but we were able to make our way here and to meet each other, longing for the distant light and voices of people. And so we realize that our next-door neighbor may be unfamiliar, like a stranger, or that a stranger may be familiar, like a long-time friend. Therefore, to us, all people are beloved.

"How blind I have been, for such a long time. But now the grass, the trees and the face of each person here appear to me in the light as if for the first time. I am telling you this because of the song that the children and all of us were singing together just now. Perhaps some of you remember it from the past. The song was composed by the blind monk Lorenzo who played the biwa, the one from Bizen who was a disciple of Saint Xavier. One of its verses went:

> How clouded are my eyes
> I ponder after my tears run dry.

"Those words of lamentation were spoken by our Lord Chirisuto on the Cross. They express his deepest feelings when the spearhead of evil was about to pierce him. How utterly alone and forsaken he must have felt."

Shirō caught his breath and then continued.

> "The dear ones of deep compassion
> are now away from me.

"When our Lord was facing his death, his disciples were not with him. The disciples had been the consolation of our Lord, who had renounced the glory of this world. And it was not only the disciples but also all of the people he met along his path who comforted him during the sufferings of his life. Maria Magdalena, who washed his feet with her long hair, gave him the utmost compassion during his short life.

"When Chirisuto-sama was about to be nailed on the Cross, every comfort he had ever known was far away from him. How utterly alone he must have felt. When I think of this, something comes to my mind."

As Shirō gazed out at the congregation, he seemed to be trying to control his emotions, yet the people could see he was on the brink of tears. They held their breath at the sight of his unexpected expression and contorted mouth.

"Such great sorrow and compassion—that was what was in his mind before he was crucified and rose up to God. This has great meaning for all of us who were born after him and who look up to him now. I am talking about the sadness of our ancestors who gave us our existence; their sadness at the times of their deaths. I am talking about their irrepressible compassion for the remaining ones, and about their voices in their dying moments, which perhaps were suppressed in their hearts. I can't help but connect these things to the voice of our Lord. We are always at the side of the people who have lost their lives.

"The cherished image of those we have loved, whether we are related by blood or not, becomes the light in the far distance that shines on our path. Was it not our Lord's final message that we should reflect deeply on these bonds?"

Sobs filled the chapel.

"However, in the midst of his agony, the Lord prayed:

> The *anima* birds, at least,
> understand our hearts and
> fly over the distant reaches of the heavens.

"What are these birds of *anima*? They are the birds that lead people like us to the land of salvation. Even in the depths of our sorrow, the Lord cares for us—we who have forsaken him—and shows us the road to salvation.

"The birds of *anima,* released at the borders of life, are flying up right here in the skies of Miyazu. Although our Lord Chirisuto-sama called us his 'beloved people'—which is more than we deserve—we have been losing the spirit of Christianity for a long time, through our fear of the cruelties of our local lords and officials. And yet, never forsaking us, our Lord has released the birds of *anima* to lead us on to the land of salvation.

"When we think about it deeply, these years of bad harvests, too, may have guided us back to the true path. Have not these continuing rains and droughts been signs from our Lord, calling on us to repent and change our ways? Can we not hear his voice resounding throughout Heaven and Earth? Today we have hardly anything left to eat, but now is the time to depart for the land of salvation.

"This year is the one thousand, sixteen hundred and thirty-seventh year since the birth of our Lord, and he is watching over us here in Amakusa. He is telling us that he came not in peace but rather to light a fire on Earth. This fire will spread to our souls. With the fire of resurrection, we will burn down the halls of the devils who oppose God, and by building the land of *anima* here in Amakusa, we will carve a path to salvation."

The chapel fell silent as ripples of emotion spread through the congregation.

"Many years have passed since people raised crosses high in Amakusa. Today, in this chapel, we have forged an extraordinary bond and returned to our true brothers and sisters. Brothers and sisters—look carefully. Look at today's godly autumn sky. You will see no trace of that bird, for it has flown to the land of our salvation. Let us go to that land where we are free from the oppression of the government rulers and free from hunger and thirst. Let us go there with deep repentance."

The sounds of the believers reciting *amen* resounded above the incoming tide that swept along the seashore.

Among those invited to the dedication ceremony were Umeo Shichibei, his wife and others from Kōtsuura. Shichibei and his wife stood with Watanabe Denbei, whom they had not met as a couple for a long time, and waved to the people who had started rowing for home in their small boats.

"Today's ceremony was truly a great event. It stirred my soul," Shichibei said, his voice filled with lingering emotion.

"Well, it happened because faith is surging again in Kōtsuura. We have you to thank for everyone's determination and hard work."

Denbei looked up impishly and smiled.

"Not at all. If Shirō-sama hadn't come, I would never have made up my mind to act."

"That's certainly the truth."

At his side, Shichibei's wife Okiku looked up at him.

"Lately, my husband's been telling me that one life isn't enough so he'll have to live a second. He's been so active," she added.

"Yes, but that young man—what sort of a person is he? When I heard him speak again today it sent shivers down my spine. I never thought I'd meet such a person in all my life. He's no ordinary person."

"His father Jinbei-dono has said that although he is his son, he's also *not* his son."

"Well, perhaps that's so. But in any case, he's a rare person. Usually when I see him, he looks like a pure, unaffected young man, but when he speaks in public, he's completely different . . . and speaking of Shirō, where is he now?"

Shichibei looked around. Okiku, too, scanned their surroundings curiously.

"Everyone wants to see him up close. Where do you suppose he could have gone?"

"He's a bit different from most people. He often goes off to the hills to think. He's probably off in the woods right now. I imagine he'll be back once he's settled down a bit."

"Really though, when he got the spirits of those six dead people to rise up above the white dishes, I felt we were being led forward to the gates of the next world," Okiku went on emotionally. "That's what I came here to talk about. I feel absolutely sure that my spirit was freed from my body in that moment. It was like the bird that flew off today."

Her voice rising, Okiku gazed at Denbei, whom she hadn't seen in ages, and then turned to pray to the sun as it settled over the sea.

Denbei watched her and nodded, and then invited the remaining group from Kōtsuura to the porch of the chapel. The candles on the stand were still burning. Catching the sea breezes, the curtains that had been drawn shut to close off the inner chapel billowed and fluttered gently. Several children who didn't seem ready to go home yet peeked inside.

One of them asked, "Where's Maria-sama?"

An older woman who was sweeping the floor answered, "She's gone now."

"Why?"

"Well, if the sea winds blow on the baby Yesus, he'll catch a cold. And you mustn't catch cold either, so it's time you hurry off and get back home."

The men standing on the porch smiled. Noticing that the boy who had asked the question was clutching a small paper packet, the old woman asked:

"Didn't you eat your present already?"

"I want to take it back to Grandma."

"Oh, I see. I know your grandma has been in bed."

"Well, Grandma wants to be blessed by Maria-sama too, so she asked me to get two of them. One for me and one for her. So, I'm taking this present to her."

With a rustling sound, Shichibei's wife took a small paper package from the bottom of her kimono sleeve pocket.

"Take this to your grandma, too. It's a present from Maria-sama."

The women had managed to prepare small packets containing two slices of chestnut sweets as gifts to be handed out at the end of the ceremony. With peach-colored grains of rice mixed in, the cakes looked dainty enough to be eaten by a princess. Everyone responded with joy and gratitude.

Originally, they had hoped to prepare auspicious red and white mochi cakes as the presents. But, despite their efforts, they hadn't been able to find enough mochi rice to make them. Jinbei was deeply moved when he saw how both young and old responded with such lively, happy looks when they received the chestnut cakes.

Jinbei sat on the porch looking perplexed, his arms crossed over his chest. He was glad his son had done far better than he could have imagined on this crucial day, but he was concerned about his own tasks moving forward. In addition to the work of reviving the congregation's faith, he had to find believers who could become central figures of the rebellion.

His back bent slightly and his *hakama* swishing, Watanabe Kozaemon served the guests.

Jinbei had been impressed by Shirō's speech, which seemed to have moved the congregation even more than the words of the catechism. *What a joy it would be if we all could farm the fields on these islands as sacred lands, spending our days praying and receiving the spirit of God's blessing. But how can we ever realize such a hope?* The thought of Shirō's troubles to come gnawed at his father's breast. Although Shirō was his own child, he was already standing in a territory that Jinbei himself had never reached.

Jinbei looked for his wife Oine, who had come over from Uto on the mainland to attend the ceremony. She had been feeling badly about her inability to do all the things a mother should do, but that day, in the back of the chapel, she had taken pleasure in assisting Shirō and the young singers in changing their clothing for the ceremony. She disliked crowds, so she had stayed in the shadow of the chapel's doorway. But she had poked her head out because she had wanted to see her son. It was a lovely scene.

"That's your son—go on in and see him in his hour of glory. Now, go down in front and listen to him."

One of Oine's relatives had pushed her forward, but she waved her hand and backed away. She whispered something to Shirō's grandmother, who was sitting beside her, then placed a rosary over her wrist and whispered to a woman relative nearby. The woman led the grandmother to a seat in the front so she might see her grandson. Together with the rest of the congregation, she knelt in prayer and broke into tears.

When Jinbei saw her in this state he was overcome with emotion. Shirō had spoken of the light of this day as the light of resurrection. But for how long, he wondered, could that light shine over this land? Dark thoughts filled his soul. For how many years had those beautiful churches in Nagasaki lasted until they were destroyed? And for how long might this little chapel hope to survive?

The light that Shirō had delighted in streamed into the chapel directly from the west, illuminating the people gathered there. With the rays of the evening sun sinking slowly before them, they had sighed in wonder. Slowly, the sun dropped closer to the surface of the sea and the day grew cooler. It seemed to Jinbei that the sacred world he had just been a part of was now returning to the reality of the swishing treetops. The remaining group gathered around him, Denbei and Kozaemon.

"I never imagined we'd be able to pray to Deus-sama in a chapel in my lifetime," Shichibei said with deep emotion. "I can't find the words to express my feelings about the speech your son gave."

From the rear, a man with his hair tied back in samurai fashion said, "In any case, Shirō-dono has traveled thousands of leagues farther than any of us. He said our relationship today is the kind created only once in a thousand years. There is no deeper bond than ours. It sent shivers down my back."

"You know, there's something mysterious about Shirō-dono," Shichibei answered hesitantly.

"Yes, but what do you think it is? We've heard about so many strange things already."

As Denbei urged Shichibei to continue, Jinbei grew more anxious.

"You remember Father Mamacos, who used to be at the church in Kōtsuura?"

"Certainly, I remember him. He was expelled from the country around the end of the Keichō era. That must have been some twenty or more years ago by now."

"Well, when he departed Kōtsuura, he shared some parting words. It was on the night of his farewell party. He said that twenty years or so after he left Kōtsuura a young servant of God would appear."

Denbei stared in amazement at Shichibei.

"His words are still etched in my heart. And there must have been five or six others who heard him. Now they've all passed away and I'm the only one left."

"Can you remember his exact words?" Denbei asked calmly. Shichibei closed his eyes and spoke as if reading from a written text:

"After twenty years have passed from my departure, he will appear. The skies will burn red hot and the fields and mountains and the people's dwellings will be burned. After a flood, any remaining seeds of grain will die. At that time, a young servant of God will appear. He will be able to read, even without studying, and he will bring many auspicious omens. Soon after, this young servant of God will walk through flames. He will lead the believers on and open the way to Heaven. He will raise white flags on the mountains and fields and the people will place crosses on their heads."

The entire gathering fell silent.

"Around the time when Father Mamacos was ordered to leave, he started behaving rather emotionally and saying and doing strange things, perhaps because of all the stress he'd been going through. I didn't listen so carefully, and after some time I forgot most of it, but in recent days his words have flashed in my mind at unexpected times. I'm serious, Denbei-dono. It must have been a true prophecy; a burning red sky, seeds of grain dying, a young servant of God . . . The other day, when Shirō-dono was at the funeral in Kōtsuura and called back the spirits of that family that killed themselves, my senses awoke. It was like a revelation telling me that Shirō was the prophesied young servant of God. And now with his sermon today, I have no doubt about it—the servant of God that Father Mamacos prophesied must be Shirō-dono."

Denbei's eyes met Jinbei's.

The samurai farmer with long tied-back hair who had been sitting quietly next to Shichibei placed his hands solemnly on the tatami mat.

"It's rude of me to cut in after Shichibei-dono, but my name is Kamimisaki Daizen and I would like to speak. For some time now, I've had a deep wish. My wish has been that we would appoint Shirō-dono as the leader of all of us Christians. Jinbei-dono and Denbei-dono, I ask for your assent."

Kamimisaki Daizen placed his hands back on his lap and looked around at the group.

"We have returned to true Christianity and built this chapel. We can't turn back. Not only the Tomioka clan, but Karatsu, too, will surely send their armies. Soon a battle will start. Without a leader, we won't be able to fight. When I met Shirō-dono for the first time in Kuchinotsu, my soul lit up. After that, as I watched him and listened to him, I realized that he is without a doubt the servant of Deus-sama. We can't take lightly what our village leader just told us about Father Mamacos's prophecy. Everyone, I tell you: Shirō-dono is the young servant of God who has been prophesied. If we make him our leader, we Christians who have lost our spirit and have been pushed to this desperate point will be able to begin our struggle. Jinbei-dono, I ask that we appoint Shirō-dono as our leader."

Once again, Kamimisaki Daizen placed both hands on the floor. The people who had come from Kōtsuura seemed completely absorbed by his words. Jinbei's face showed conflicting emotions. In silence, he clenched his hands into fists and fixed his eyes on the darkness outside.

And so, on this night, the leaders of Miyazu on Ōyano Island, joined by representatives from Upper Amakusa Island who had come over for the dedication ceremony, met in the house of the Miyazu headman and pledged to make Shirō the leader of a rebellion dedicated to restoring their religious faith.

As they began to discuss how they might take these plans back to their villages and start preparations, a young man in the back stood up. He spoke in a low voice, as if not accustomed to speaking.

"My name is Tsunekichi, from Kōtsuura. I ask you to let me serve as your messenger. I'm a fast runner, and that's about all I can do. Just give me the word to go somewhere and I'll be off in a flash. I can run ten leagues at a time with no trouble at all."

Lowering his voice, he added, "But I can't beat a horse."

A burst of laughter broke the strain all were feeling from the work of making such difficult decisions.

"All right then Tsunekichi—you're the one!"

Shirō remembered this man well. He was the one who had carried the heavy wooden cross during the march of atonement in Kōtsuura and who had continued to carry it, without letting go, even when he had seemed on the verge of collapse. *For innocent men and women like Tsunekichi, I can rise up in action*, Shirō thought. When he returned from meditating in the woods, he learned from his father that the congregation had chosen him as the leader of the rebellion. He responded quietly, with no sign of his feelings, leaving his father puzzled and anxious. For him, it was not so important that he should become a leader. While in the woods, he had seen a vision of a dry white road that led to Calvary Hill. He would have to travel that unknown road. He believed that he would go to any place the Lord asked him . . . With this decision, his mind became clear and emptied.

CHAPTER SEVEN

Divine Flute

The decision made on this night came to be known as the "Pledge of Miyazu Chapel," and later, when they moved to Hara Castle, it was often spoken of.

Yazō brought the stories he had heard about Shirō's visit to Kōtsuura and what he had done in Miyazu to Nisuke, Takematsu and Suzu in Kuchinotsu. Other household workers also gathered around him, eager to hear the news.

Yazō was out on his boats constantly, working as if he were trying to pull together his life's work. He sent his boats, large and small, to places all along the coast, from up around Umegae in Nagasaki and Mogi, Chijiwa and Kuchinotsu on the Shimabara coast, down to the Amakusa Islands and even as far as Takase and Kawajiri in the Hosokawa domain on the mainland, and to the port of Chikugo. He supplied provisions and exchanged marine products from the coast for grain from the inland areas, helping to stave off the famine that had been pushing Christian communities to the brink of starvation. He did this, of course, at fair prices. Although the veteran *benzashi* didn't have much formal schooling himself, he helped fund the operating expenses of the Christian school.

From Yazō's stories, the people who gathered at the school learned that the situation around them was quickly becoming far more serious than they had foreseen, and they sensed that the time had come to prepare for the worst.

For days on end, the sky remained scorching hot and the cherry trees started to blossom out of season. The villages in Arie and Arima in particular were known for their cherry trees, and recently the young people who passed through them had been remarking on this strange occurrence.

"Cherries blooming at this time of year—it doesn't seem right."

"It must be a sign of something."

"They're like ghost flowers."

Henmi Juan and Ninagawa Sakyō and his son Ukon stayed out of such talk and appeared deeply engaged in planning. Oume, working in the kitchen, listened to the news about Shirō with evident pleasure, but of late she had seemed wrapped in her own thoughts and hadn't spoken much.

One evening, a rugged-looking man named Senzoku Matsuemon showed up at the Ninagawa house, introducing himself as a messenger from Masuda Jinbei and his son Shirō. He was from Senzoku Island, next to Ōyano Island, and for the past month, whenever he made trips back and forth between Ōyano and Shimabara he had been staying with a friend in Kita Arima on Shimabara Peninsula. He, too, was a former samurai of the Konishi clan, and he had come to deliver a personal message from Jinbei regarding the situation in the Amakusa Islands region.

Ukon eagerly opened the letter from Shirō that Matsuemon had brought.

Ukon-dono, I hope you've been making progress in your reading of the Psalms. And I wish I could hear you read from the Tale of the Heike. *My life now is like a snowflake floating on the wind. How I would like to see you again.*

As he read the letter, Ukon was caught up in thought. *He's only sixteen, yet he feels his life is like a snowflake floating in the sky. I hope that soon I may be able to work with him.* Ukon held back a rush of emotions.

Worrisome, yet vaguely expected events were steadily approaching. Could it be that Shirō could hear the horses of God pounding through the red-hot flames of the heavens, a warning of things to come?

Ukon focused his gaze on the flame burning deep within his spirit. They had opened the school, but perhaps it, too, would be short-lived. A vision flashed before him of the remains of the earthen storehouse they had made into their schoolhouse. It had turned into an empty field of plume grass. Other visions continued to assail him. A rent appeared in a corner of the sky, and through it a woman dressed in red, a child, and dogs, cats and other sorts of things rained down, one after another. In the sky, one by one, pages of the Christian writings were being peeled off and scattered. For a moment, the sky turned blue. Then it changed to gray, and then it was filled with falling snowflakes. He thought these must be spiritual messages from Shirō.

My dear brother is trying to stand in a hopeless battlefield, bearing the undeserved weight of our troubles. A transparent sadness swept through Ukon's body. *Whatever may come, I have to protect Shirō. But even if something happens that brings the school to an end, I'll have no regrets. For what purpose have I been studying, and for what purpose have we made this school? Hasn't the true purpose of my studies been to link my fate with Shirō's? Even if all trace of this school vanishes, the seeds we have sown will send up sprouts that reach to Heaven.*

Matsuemon's message confirmed Yazō's reports. The believers in Kōtsuura on Upper Amakusa and in Miyazu on Ōyano had formed an alliance and were sending representatives and messengers back and forth between Miyazu and the Shimabara region, on opposite sides of the Ariake Sea. There was no telling how much farther the flames would spread.

Kita Arima, where Matsuemon often stayed, had been a stronghold of Christian believers since the days of the Arima domain. It was important to realize that, if Matsuemon was using the home of the headman Matsushima Sadonokami as a base, it meant that practical discussions between the Miyazu and Kita Arima groups had already advanced to a certain point. But Sakyō worried that, with all the secret comings and goings, Kita Arima might not be sufficiently removed from the Matsukura daimyo's base at Shimabara Castle, and he also believed that the Christian groups on Ōyano Island were particularly brave. Sakyō had not yet met Shirō's father Jinbei. Jinbei, however, had sent Matsuemon, who had gained everyone's confidence with his sparkling eyes and direct way of speaking.

"If you took Yazō-dono and tidied him up a bit and dressed him as a samurai, that's how he might look," Sakyō's wife had remarked.

Sakyō had first met Sadonokami the previous fall, at the magistrate's office. After that, a number of former samurai had gotten together at the Ninagawas' house. They had hoped to dispel some of the rancor they felt toward the magistrate's office, and it was Sadonokami who had spoken the most persuasively.

One of the samurai insisted that if they were going to rise up in action, they needed to work together with the other ronin and prepare for a battle that could overthrow the country.

"But can we really do such a thing?" Sadonokami had retorted. "Already, it's been twenty years since the Toyotomi forces were defeated in Osaka. Think of how Lord Katō was exiled and you'll see that the *bakufu* government is rock-solid. Even if all the ronin got together, we'd just be throwing straws against the wind. We may be quick to talk now, but look at what's happened to us, the former samurai of the Arima clan. We're all just struggling to survive—even the bravest of you, like Chijiiwa-dono. Our swords are rusting.

"I'm not telling you to give in to cowardice. We can't expect to get out of this without big trouble. If Matsukura's tyranny continues, the farmers will reach a point where they won't keep quiet any longer. And if rebellion breaks out, I don't want us to die like dogs. If we make a mess of things, we'll just end up in the trap of the Matsukuras—or rather, of the *bakufu*. It would be a disgrace for us to be held guilty for not paying the land taxes. If we're going to rise up, then I want us to do it for the Christian cause and fight with honor. This is a time for patience. I know it's been hard putting up with our treatment from the Matsukuras for so long, but we need to take our time preparing a response."

The Kita Arima headman had looked around at the group pointedly.

"There are a thousand sacks of rice sitting in the Kuchinotsu grain warehouse. Rations like that could feed our forces for quite some time. Don't you think we need to start making that kind of calculation?"

Sadonokami's talk, and his mysterious, audacious smile, remained fixed in Sakyō's mind.

Not only had Matsuemon brought a letter from Shirō to Ukon, but, as Sakyō suspected, he had been informed of Jinbei's secret plans and was charged with helping to forge an alliance between the Christians in Amakusa and Shimabara. After talking at length about the believers' group formed recently in Kōtsuura, the chapel built in

Miyazu and the "Pledge of Miyazu Chapel," Matsuemon continued:

"All of this has not been the work of the Amakusa group alone. We know how important the support we've gotten from you here in Shimabara has been. Since old times, Shimabara, like Amakusa, has been fertile ground for our Christian faith. We're brothers and sisters in our beliefs. However, with the ongoing bad harvests and heavy land taxes, we've barely managed to stay alive. Nothing has improved. We've already made a pledge with Matsushima Sadonokami-dono in Kita Arima. Kuchinotsu is the stronghold of the Christians in Shimabara. Today, at Matsushima-dono's request, I've come to meet with you, Ninagawa-dono."

Sakyō gauged the depth of Matsuemon's piercing glance. Already, he had for the most part predicted what he would say. What, however, would the implications of an uprising be? Of course they would have to bring their religion into the open. This meant that things would not be easy.

Sakyō felt torn by all these thoughts.

Publicly reviving their religion would stand in direct defiance of the edicts of the Matsukura clan, and of the *bakufu* government as well. What would happen once they began to act openly? No doubt, people would be crucified. Were they not just rushing themselves off to the crucifixion posts? The people of Amakusa had made a momentous decision. They had declared their determination to fight against the government and its allies.

Had the time come, at last? He would be lying if he said he hadn't expected it. How many times had he talked about it with Juan, Hyōgo and Bannai, after all? Words, however, were not the same as reality. And now that they finally were becoming reality, Sakyō felt somehow deflated. It wasn't a feeling of emptiness; rather, it was a strange sensation, as if he had left his body and was secretly watching his own conversation with Matsuemon.

Sakyō was a levelheaded man and held no illusions that his people could easily prevail in a fight against the *bakufu* and its allied forces drawn from the entire nation. What they were doing now went far beyond organizing a protest to demand a reduction in land taxes from the local Matsukura clan. If that were all they were doing, then they might claim a victory even if the protest leaders ended up being killed. But openly raising the flag of Christianity would strike directly at the roots of the *bakufu*. The government would likely gather its forces from all over Kyushu and bring them to Shimabara. The battle could well lead to death for everyone, including the elderly, the women and the children.

Sakyō pictured the faces of his wife and daughter. *Would that be all right? Or not?* Questions like this hounded him.

Perhaps taking Sakyō's silence as a sign of hesitation, Matsuemon spoke up again:

"Ninagawa-dono, the grace of Deus-sama is with us. Masuda Shirō-dono is, without a doubt, a child of God sent to us from Heaven. Any number of us can attest to that. We have seen things with our own eyes. We from Amakusa have decided to stand together in serving Deus, and in raising the banner of battle without doubt of our victory."

Intentionally ignoring Matsuemon's crazed stare that seemed to press hard for a decision, Sakyō smiled calmly.

"Certainly . . . We know Shirō-dono's character well, since he's been an esteemed guest in our house. And Senzoku-dono, we understand the purpose of your visit. As for myself, I share the spirit of the Amakusa group. However, this is an extremely serious matter for the people of Kuchinotsu, and not one for me to decide alone. Very soon, I'll discuss this with our leaders. As for tonight, I apologize that I can't offer you much with the times being hard as they are, but please make yourself at home here."

Matsuemon took a deep breath and released the tension from his shoulders.

As Sakyō headed towards Juan's house, he had the feeling he was watching a fire spread underground along roots that connected the *confuraria* groups of Amakusa and Shimabara.

Soon after Matsuemon's departure, and after Sakyō, Juan, Nisuke and Kuchinotsu's other leaders had met and confirmed their agreement, all the village headmen were summoned to the magistrate's office. The stated business was the coming year's tax assessment, but the actual details proved far beyond anything they could have imagined: they were told they would have to make up for all of their previously owed rice payments, and on top of that they would have to pay an additional amount for the current year, beyond that of previous years. They were also told that a Matsukura boat carrying three hundred *koku* of rice to pay for repairs to the Babasakimon horse riding grounds at Edo Castle had sunk, and to make up for that loss, an equivalent amount of rice was to be sent from the grain stores in Kuchinotsu.

The local magistrate had been changed from Tada Kurōbei to Matsuda Gonzaemon. Kurōbei had been bad enough, but at least he had some reasonable points. Gonzaemon, however, was harsh and unyielding. He held up his nose like a wild pig and conducted affairs recklessly and by force, and he spoke without consideration for anyone's feelings.

"Last year you had some losses from wind and rain, so we eased up a bit, but as for this year—well, don't go looking for that kind of treatment any more. Any losses from drought or water damage—or from whatever—you're going to have to make up for them with back payments. No mercy now. I know all about how you village headmen work. All we're interested in is the number of sacks of rice you bring in—that's how we'll judge what you're up to now. To carry out your responsibilities, you're going to have to act as our agents in dealing with whatever the farmers are grumbling about. This year I'm not listening to any sob stories. That's how I see things. And if payments fall short, I'm going to hold women as hostages. I'm not like Tada-dono. I hear they call me 'stubborn Gonza' at the castle, on account of my detesting when people neglect their duties. Well, just as magistrates have our own work, farmers have theirs. And that work is to make sure the taxes come in, and to take care of the lords. Now is that sufficiently clear?"

Magistrate Matsuda Gonzaemon stared at the group as if he were licking each person's face. Then he emitted a short dry cough as if belching up a poison gas and rose from his seat.

The village headmen stared at each other in silence. Sakyō was among them, but he felt neither anger nor hatred. The government officials seemed to think that if they treated people severely, the people would pay their taxes. But Sakyō found that way of thinking ludicrous. Perhaps it was an ingrained habit of many years, or perhaps it was their basic nature. It made him want to laugh. Huffing and puffing and browbeating like Gonzaemon had done was childish. For them to think they could simply rake in the taxes at this point was pitiful.

As Sakyō left through the gate of the magistrate's office, Nisuke appeared at his side. Nisuke seemed to feel the same way Sakyō did, and they shared a wry smile.

"Ninagawa-sama, that was quite some threatening look he gave us, wasn't it? It seems we don't know which way our hearts are going. Better just to let it go. With all of us there—and all of us not saying a word and not showing any expression—that guy must have been an imbecile to not see what was going on with us. It's almost funny."

Sakyō stared intently at Nisuke's face. Nisuke's expression seemed bright, unshadowed by gloom. Although not a samurai, Nisuke gave off a deep sense of calmness and energy. Perhaps this was owing to the great responsibility he felt toward the farmers. Sakyō vowed to himself that he would die alongside this man, if things came to that.

When Juan heard from Sakyō about the Amakusa group's proposal, his first thoughts were about what it would mean for the school they had just started. Of course, given the tyrannical Matsukura administration, there was no telling how long the school would survive anyway, but the pace of recent developments was far beyond what he had ever imagined. Nevertheless, the stalwart old warrior was ready to act, whatever the course of events might be.

Juan was encouraged by recent news from Ukon about Sankichi's work. Accompanied by his friend Kakunai, Sankichi had taken the sacred picture to Miyazu on Ōyano Island and, in the chapel there, he had been baptized by Shirō. When he returned, the dignity in his face had been evident. At last, he had become a true, devoted Christian. And in the shrine in his woodshed, the *anima* of his father was being honored and the sacred picture was being displayed openly. Rumor had it that Sankichi was calling on relatives and neighbors to meet there and pray. Kumagorō had told all of this to Ukon.

I should have warned them to be more careful, Juan thought to himself.

Or maybe not. He shut his eyes. *Maybe this is what the moment of decision feels like. While we samurai have been biding our time and endlessly thinking things over, people like Sankichi have received God's affirmation and slipped into a world the rest of us have been unable to enter.*

After thinking for a while, he remarked to Ukon, "That young Sankichi, he's about to get drawn into a blood bath. And Kumagorō, is he still at Nisuke's place?"

The image of Kumagorō sitting at the back of the storeroom schoolhouse and looking on intently was deeply fixed in Juan's heart. As he looked at the calm, composed faces of Sakyō and his son Ukon sitting across from him, Juan thought, *Even if the Ōyano group hadn't come to us, we could hardly have expected life in Shimabara to go on as usual, now that Sankichi and his fellows have started to act.* When the elderly samurai opened his eyes again, a smile spread across his face, as if he were smelling the sweet scent of plum blossoms.

"Well, in any case, we have to make some decisions. Don't you think we should call on young Shirō? It seems he's received the divine flute and he's the one to lead us. We have to be ready—don't you think, Sakyō-dono?"

Messengers were sent out to all the young people who had attended the school. Three days later, in the evening, more than twenty people came in from the villages of Kuchinotsu, Kazusa, Chijiwa, Obama, Minami Arima, Kita Arima, Kushiyama, Futsu, Fukae, Nakakoba and Antoku.

Since Nakaō Jian, the elderly leader of Arie, was hard of hearing, they had sent him a letter from Juan. The white-haired former student of the *collegio* showed up finely dressed, carrying two swords. After exchanging greetings, he grasped the hands of his old friend Juan and broke into tears.

"I made it here while I'm still standing to do my part for the Christians."

First, Ninagawa Ukon briefed the group on the tense situation in Amakusa and the response from Shimabara. The young people listened attentively, yet they didn't appear particularly surprised, as if they'd already heard about most of it. Seeing Kumagorō sitting in the back as usual seemed to reassure Juan. He turned to Nisuke and whispered in his ear that they should ask Kumagorō to join them for a drink afterwards. And since it had been decided that on this night, because of the special circumstances, women, too, would join them, Okayo and Oume were present, sitting in the back. Suzu had been told that she could sleep there with the baby, so she was already asleep on the floor. She was, after all, still a child and she had worked hard all day, so she had fallen asleep early.

Since Oume was a Buddhist and all the talk that evening would revolve around the Christians' return to their faith, Nisuke had worried that it might be uncomfortable for her to listen. He told himself he'd talk to her about it later and let her take some time off to visit her home in Amakusa, but for now he asked her to join the meeting.

When Ukon finished speaking, his father Sakyō continued. He stressed that the return to their religion was to be the final decision of the people of both Amakusa and Shimabara, who had been deprived of their path in life. He reminded them that the *bakufu* and the daimyo were determined to destroy them and that, even if they remained patient amidst their fears, the years of oppressive taxes were robbing their strength, leaving them to wait to die of starvation. As he neared the end of his lengthy talk, Sakyō opened his eyes wide.

"Although our *collegio* has only existed for a short time, it does not seek glory in this world. Our school draws from the well of true life. May we—each one of us—dedicate our lives to the glory of the Lord."

Spirited young voices cried out "Hurrah!" Then Juan, who had been waiting beside Sakyō and Ukon, stood up slowly. He looked around at the faces of the young people and began to speak.

"It's a bit chilly for viewing, but outside there's a full moon. While I was watching your faces here inside, some words sprung up in the depths of my mind:

"Cry of the cuckoo—the mountain bamboo splits.

"A Zen monk once spoke those words to his young students, but strangely, they come to mind now."

Juan paused.

As the night deepened, moonlight spread over the mountains of Shimabara, as if pressing down on them.

"What do you think—are we the cuckoo? Or are we the split bamboo?"

No one spoke to answer.

"I have lived long enough. I'm soon to become compost for the next generation. But all of you—you are the flowers of the Shimabara Christians. You must continue your work."

Serving in the role of priest for the first time in years, Juan led the prayers. The smell of the incense burned on this night was completely different from that used at regular Masses. When the *oratio* came to an end, everyone closed their eyes and breathed in its fragrance. Juan had used the treasured incense that Shirō had brought back from Nagasaki. The full moon rose higher and higher in the sky.

Breakfast the following morning began in silence.

"Okayo, go ahead and eat some for Ayame, too. What do you say Ayame? Mama's milk tastes good, doesn't it?" Omiyo urged.

Ayame smiled as she listened, as if she understood her grandmother's words. The ponderous mood in the room lightened a little. The breakfast porridge was made of barley and rice mixed with lots of steeped, dried *kusagi* leaves. Daisuke glanced at Okayo, perplexed, as a gentle smile spread over her face. After hearing the talk the previous night, he understood how things were likely to unfold. He would have to discuss difficult matters with his wife, but he wondered how he should go about this. It seemed to him she had better go back to her family home in Uchino, but he hadn't had a chance to talk to his parents about it. No doubt, Nisuke and Omiyo had been thinking about it, too.

Oume devoted herself all the more energetically to her work. When lunch was finished, Nisuke and his wife called her in to the living room.

"You heard the talk last night with your own ears, didn't you?"

"Yes."

"You've always been essential to our household, and not only for Omiyo and me, but for everyone here."

"What is it you're getting at now, Danna-sama?" she asked, addressing the head of her household with utmost respect.

"Oume, you are like a sister, or a mother, to us . . ."

Omiyo's voice became choked with tears and she couldn't go on. Nisuke continued for her.

"We'll never be able to return all the kindness you've given us."

"But, Danna-sama, what are you saying? It's quite the opposite."

Oume regretted not having been quick enough with her words. *Why wasn't I the first one to use the words that Danna-sama said just now?*

"We talked about this last night, but as you know, there's going to be a fight."

"Yes."

"The reason why things have come to this is—well, you're a follower of Amida Buddha, but you understand, don't you?"

Oume's throat tightened.

"Yes, I understand," she said quietly.

"It's still hard to believe, but we can't expect this household to escape the troubles. The revolt against the shogunate will come to us all."

Oume lowered her head.

"Omiyo and I are Christians. As headman of our village, I've also served as the leader of the benevolent association. Your religion is different from ours, but you helped us with the old folks' house, and what you said at the funeral made me think very deeply. And you've been so kind to the young people studying at the school. I want to express our gratitude to you once again."

Oume seemed at a loss for how to deal with the situation. With her head bowed, she looked up slowly.

Nisuke remained silent for a moment, but then said decisively, "Oume, all I can say is that if you stay here as a member of the Hasuda family, you'll likely die with us. You aren't a Christian and you've done more for us than we can ever tell you."

Her eyes glimmering, Oume broke in.

"Are you telling me that you want me to go now?"

"Oume, what are you saying?"

Omiyo's voice trembled.

"Well, if you're telling me I'm too old to be of use, and if you're telling me to go back home, I suppose I could just go quietly back, even though I don't have a home to return to. But if you're telling me to escape because it's too dangerous here, I don't have the legs to escape with. At a time like this, who could desert their family? If I were forced to leave this house, I'd hang myself."

Oume's eyes were wide and sorrowful, looking off somewhere else. Nisuke and Omiyo were taken aback.

"Yes, I chant the *namu amida butsu*. That's because my parents taught me to chant the *namu amida butsu*. But there's another reason why I don't say *amen*. I've never mentioned it before, but now I will."

Nisuke and Omiyo caught their breath, wondering what Oume was about to say. They had often wondered if Oume might have more to say about her past, but they had never asked her about it.

"My father was a man of deep faith and he worshipped Kannon-sama. I'm told that when I was a baby and almost died of the smallpox, he prayed to the Iwato Kannon-sama at Kazusa and I was saved. He carved a statue of Kannon-sama from a yew tree and put it in a boat, between my mother and me, and rowed us from Fukuro Inlet to Kazusa.

"My parents heard that the padres and some of the young Christians burned the statues of Iwato Kannon-sama, calling them objects of heresy. It happened shortly after my parents made their boat trip. The padre-samas chopped up every last Buddha statue they could find—they said they made a nice bonfire. Although my father's carving of the Kannon-sama was roughly hewn from a yew tree, people said that it looked a lot like the baby—me. My father spoke in tears of how he wished he hadn't carved it to look like me.

"Danna-sama and Omiyo-sama, this is the first time I've spoken of this. You've never said anything to me for not joining in your prayers, and you've always taken care of me . . . so you see, I really didn't want to tell you this story. I never wish to speak badly of Deus-sama."

Oume looked directly at Nisuke and Omiyo, an unfamiliar expression in her eyes. The couple sat motionless.

"I know there are Buddhist monks who expect to get lots of money from people when they recite the *namu amida butsu*. And

I know there are some bad ones among those who chant *amen,* too. I've never believed that Deus-sama would tell people to burn a Kannon-sama.

"In coming to this family, I've seen the true face of Deus-sama, and the true face of people. If the Kannon Bodhisattva-sama my father prayed to could meet Maria-sama, they would get along well and be even kinder. It's been my intention to stay here serving both Maria-sama and Kannon-sama as long as my body can work. You may wonder what this old woman is saying now, but last night, when I heard the talk, I knew that I'm of the same spirit, even if I'm not a Christian."

Oume's voice took on the tough manner of a warehouse worker. "We'll need more than swords and rifles for this fight. We who do the grinding with stone mortars, we'll gather the pots and pans and knives and we'll be ready. I'm better at that sort of thing than Omiyo-sama."

Realizing the oddness of what she had just said, Oume chuckled, but then her lips twisted and she began to weep.

Nisuke and Omiyo stared at Oume in bewilderment.

"Oume . . . forgive us."

Omiyo bowed and placed her hands on the tatami.

"Please accept our apologies to both your father and your mother that such things have happened."

"Enough of that. I'm sure my parents are happy I've had such a good life with you."

Oume remembered how she had felt, more than forty years ago, when she first held little Omiyo in her arms and carried her on her back and bathed her. She knew just about everything there was to know about Omiyo.

"That we may die together—that is my hope."

After that night, the school in the warehouse did not open. The young people who had gathered formed a group, and before going back to the quickening whirlpool of activity in their villages, they promised to meet again.

Even though people realized that a rebellion was in the making, deciding exactly what to do and how to prepare would take time.

Still, there was no doubt that the day of reckoning was coming. Almost everyone expected the approaching deadline for paying the yearly land taxes to be a crisis point.

One thing they worried about was Sankichi and the recent activities surrounding him. Word of the sacred painting had spread, and there was talk of people traveling to pray before it. So far, the magistrate's office didn't seem to have heard about it, but it was only a matter of time before they did. Through Sashiki Sukuzaemon, the elder brother of a student at the school and a close associate of Sankichi's, Juan sent Sankichi a letter expressing his concern and urging him to lay low until the time was right.

When Senzoku Matsuemon, Yama Zenemon, and the others returned home from Shimabara, Jinbei and Denbei were surrounded by a swirl of activity.

In Kōtsuura, with the continuing drought, Tsunekichi and his young friends hadn't been able to work in the fields. And when they dived in the sea, they hadn't been able to get many shellfish or sea cucumbers. The young people were bored, and their spirits were dulled, as if their hands and feet were no longer touching the ground. They just milled about, occasionally going to dig bracken fern and kudzu roots.

"In times like this, I'd have been better off born as a horse or a cow."

"Okay, but you should see how much Gosuke's cow eats. You'd think its mouth would get cut up, eating all that sedge weed."

"Yeah, they sure can stuff a whole lot of grass into their gut."

"And everywhere you look, it's grass and more grass."

"I sure wish we could eat it ourselves."

Everyone laughed over such talk.

As long as we can still laugh, we're all right, Tsunekichi thought. He racked his brain for some way for them to get enough food.

"If we're desperate enough to consider eating grass, maybe we should ask the guys in Ōyano to take us out whaling."

A chorus of surprise rose up.

"Whaling? That sounds good!"

"Tsunekichi, you've been going to Miyazu over on Ōyano a lot lately—are the whalers over there Christians?"

"Well, that's what I heard."

"All the better, then! Next time you go over there, would you ask if they'd take us whaling?"

"Well, I'll try to bring it up, but the talk might not go so easily."

"Come on, at least let us hope!"

"Sorry. But I'll give it a go. No harm in trying!"

Tsunekichi and the other young people knew there were highly detailed rules and agreements about net fishing in the inlets, and that taking things from another group's area without permission was strictly forbidden. But they also thought that in the current tough circumstances, some people might be open to talking about the idea. Several of Tsunekichi's friends in Miyazu came to mind. Still, reality might not live up to the young people's hopes.

When the Ōyano whalers went out, they used proper boats fitted with special equipment to take them into the ocean beyond the Ariake Sea and the Straits of Hayasaki, where the waves were very different from those in coastal waters. What would they think when the people of Kōtsuura, who had never gone out in anything but small boats, asked to be taken along? Even if they were allowed to go, they would have to be taught everything; from how to row and steer with a tiller to how to use nets and harpoons. They'd only get in the way. Tsunekichi felt he had been a fool to suggest such an idea, and he regretted it. Nevertheless, he brought it up with his friends on Ōyano Island. But the big storm last fall had damaged many of the boats in Ōyano, and this year they were still being repaired. Although they had sent out a few crews, they had only been able to catch one small sperm whale.

Nevertheless, the people of Ōyano gave them some of their meat. It was a small amount of salted tail fin, and arrived with a message from Masuda Jinbei in Ōyano urging Tsunekichi and his friends to keep up their good work as go-betweens for the two communities.

Their manner of working was impressive. When the tides were high, Tsunekichi and the others dashed out through the thick bushes along the coast making rustling sounds, and at low tide they hopped briskly over the rocks on the shore. Handling oars came easily to them and they made a rash, spirited group. Whenever they met others, they asked them, "Have you heard about Shirō-sama?"

To the ones who hadn't, they spoke with enthusiasm:

"He's like a god come down from Heaven. If you doubt it, just go and see the chapel in Miyazu. And you can listen to him talk, too. He's a blessing from above, right while we're living."

Quite apart from Shirō's own thoughts about himself, rumors had started to spread about him being a child of Heaven. People began to think that the energy of Tsunekichi and his friends also came from Heaven.

Feeling their strength grow, some of them cursed and threatened others, venting their pent-up energy.

"If you don't become a Christian, you'll be punished and sent to *Inferuno*. You know what *Inferuno* is? Well, compared to the Buddhist Hell, it's many times worse."

Already, many had lost their fear of the samurai in Tomioka Castle and the government officials in Sumoto and Hondo. As the young people's fervor increased and cries for blood mounted throughout the villages, they took up positions at crossroads and watched for government spies. An outcry arose after word got out that some young men had seized a horse dealer who had come to buy horses. Mistaking him for a Tomioka spy, they had nearly killed him. People were even talking about forcing their way into the government office in Sumoto and threatening bloodshed unless the officials helped the Christians.

There were also reports of an Ikkō-sect Buddhist monk at a small temple in Kōtsuura who had expressed sympathy for the Christians. He was said to have come from Hiroshima and to have an impressively strong physique, like a fighting monk from the days of old. He had started to tell people about his thoughts and experiences:

"Even as people suffer thirst and starvation, Buddhist monks with full bellies are spouting off from high in their pulpits about doing good deeds and casting off desires, but actually they're mercilessly preying on abandoned people's desires and trying to appear like the noblest beings of all. They're cold-hearted people totally incapable of casting themselves into the fray for mankind's salvation. I've come to despise such monks and their society. I ask you to allow me to join with you Christians."

Using Watanabe Denbei's house as a base of operations, Shirō's father Jinbei kept informed of developments throughout the region. Former retainers of the Konishi domain and provincial samurai who had held onto their spirit through the long gloomy years often visited him. Some spoke as if they were fulfilling an old dream, but most calmly accepted the fact that things could not continue as they were and prepared themselves for whatever was to come, realizing that events might not turn out well.

Yanagi Heibei, who liked military planning, asked, "What kind of strategy do we have?"

Jinbei faced questions like this every day, and had to be very careful about how he responded.

"We're not just making drunken boasts anymore," Heibei added. "Our biggest problem now is how to gather the farmers and fishers together to fight with us as a single unit. Women and children who have no swords or spears will be caught up in this fight. For more than ten years, we've been living as samurai in name only, and we've started to take the feelings of the farmers and fishers more seriously. Now we can finally be of some use, yet at this crucial time, we still have no real strategy. Jinbei-dono, we need you to make good plans."

Jinbei realized that despite his outward appearance, Yanagi was sincere, and possibly a person he could rely on.

Jinbei's big worry was how Lord Hosokawa, the daimyo of the Higo domain on the other side of the inland sea, would react to an uprising in Amakusa. One day, when Senzoku Matsuemon and some other samurai were present, Jinbei brought up the question. More than twenty years ago, Matsuemon had taken part in the Battle of Osaka when Toyotomi Hideyoshi was attacked in Osaka Castle. He had also been on close terms with some of the missionaries in Osaka and Kyoto.

"The Hosokawas are rather hard to figure out," was how Matsuemon put it, shaking his head.

"As you know, ever since the time of the first lord Hosokawa Yūsai generations ago, the Hosokawa family has been good at surviving wars, and they've also had close ties with the Christians."

"Are you talking about Lady Hosokawa Gracia?" another samurai asked.

"Well, in part. The padres all praised Lady Gracia as an exemplary Christian. And although her husband, Lord Hosokawa Tadaoki didn't end up getting baptized himself, he had deep connections with the Christians. He was particularly close to Takayama Ukon-dono, and when Ukon-dono was exiled, Tadaoki found a good position in his service for Takayama's retainer, Kagayama Hayato-dono."

Matsuemon paused and grimaced.

"Lord Hosokawa Tadaoki kept a big store of armaments, but after the Battle of Sekigahara, he just sort of followed the Tokugawas. And although the Tokugawas gave Kagayama six thousand *koku* of rice at Kokura, Kagayama refused to renounce his Christian faith, so they ended up beheading him."

"And I hear that just last year, the whole Ogasawara family was beheaded for some reason," Yama Zenemon said. He was a local farmer and former samurai from Senzoku Island who was known for his ingenuity and was well-liked by the farmers.

"That was Ogasawara Genya-dono and his family," Jinbei said. "When Gracia's residence in Osaka was surrounded by Ishida's forces, the person who protected her from the enemy and assisted her in dying honorably at the end was Ogasawara Shosai. Shosai's third son was Ogasawara Genya-dono, a devout Christian. Since the Hosokawa family owed a debt to the Ogasawaras for taking care of Lady Gracia, the Hosokawa Lords Tadaoki and Tadatoshi had protected them until two years ago. But Genya was condemned by the Nagasaki magistrate and sentenced to death. He had nine children, and it's said that they, too, were all beheaded. They say Lord Tadatoshi kept urging Genya to send his children off for adoption in a distant place. Tadatoshi had hoped to avoid tragedy falling on the whole Ogasawara family. Nevertheless, Genya and his wife refused to give up their children for adoption. I heard this story from one of Tadaoki's retainers named Sansai, who's now retired at Yatsuhiro Castle."

"Lord Tadatoshi was Lady Gracia's child, wasn't he?" Zenemon asked.

"Yes, he was Gracia's son. And the reason the Hosokawas protected Genya-dono was out of respect for his mother. But that was a private matter for the Hosokawa family. Lord Tadatoshi had intended to protect the family, but, as Matsuemon-dono said, the Hosokawa daimyo was looking for a chance to gain favor with the *bakufu*. In any case, since Tadatoshi was appointed daimyo in the wake of the Katō clan's exile, now he has to show his loyalty to the shogun, so it looks like he'll come and fight against us."

Jinbei thrust his hands into the sleeves of his kimono, searching about inside and pulling out some scraps, which he threw into the fire.

In Kuchinotsu, Nisuke and his son had understood that when the magistrate warned them he would hold their women hostage if they were late in paying the land taxes, it wasn't an empty threat. And the story about the sinking of a boat carrying three hundred *koku* of rice for the reconstruction of Edo Castle, too, appeared to be no mere rumor. With this additional burden added to the already heavy pressure from the *bakufu* to pay the land taxes, it would be almost impossible to pay them back.

At first, the previous Shimabara Lord Matsukura Shigemasa had protected the Christians. But after he was summoned by Shogun Iemitsu and reprimanded for it, to set an example he had gone to the sadistic extreme of calling for the execution of anyone who wouldn't renounce their Christian faith, women and children included.

When the new Lord Matsukura Katsuie took over, he increased the cruelty of the measures. The people had already faced merciless assessments for land taxes, and now there was no telling what extremes his outrageous demands might reach. The local magistrate knew that all the village headmen also served as leaders of their Christian communities, so Katsuie must have thought his harsh measures to suppress the Christians would strike two birds with the same stone. People could only assume that their own families would be subject to the same treatment.

Above all, the new regional magistrate Gonzaemon—unlike his predecessor Kurōbei, who had been willing to bargain—was the kind of person who would act immediately once he made up his mind. Although old Kurōbei had threatened to hold women hostage, he had never actually done it. He had accepted that some things couldn't be accomplished immediately, and had allowed some payments to be put off. It seemed the new magistrate Gonzaemon was willing to take extreme measures to get both the increased taxes for the current year and the unpaid back taxes. Holding women as hostages would be a quick way to show the people just how serious he was.

Nisuke had decided to send Okayo back to her home in Uchino with Ayame. Knowing what was likely to happen from now on, he couldn't very well let the magistrate take his daughter-in-law hostage, and so this had seemed the best plan. He had heard the stories of how so many Christians, including young children, had already been martyred, and when he watched Ayame moving her hands and feet about and heard her calling out so gleefully, he couldn't bear to think of her getting involved in the coming fight over religion. If he sent her to Uchino with Okayo, at least the Hasuda line would survive. Of course, there was no assurance that the winds of war wouldn't eventually reach Uchino on Lower Amakusa Island, but he guessed those winds would be gentler than the ones raging in Shimabara, the seat of the erratic Matsukuras' tyranny. And Okayo's family were Buddhists, not Christians.

Nisuke called in Omiyo and Daisuke and informed them of his decision. Omiyo agreed without hesitation. Daisuke thought it over for a while, but then, concluding that there was no other alternative, he nodded silently in assent.

"We don't know for certain that all of us will die," Omiyo said to her husband and son. "We have Deus-sama on our side, and we may prevail. If that happens, Heaven and earth will shine in the light of Christianity. If they can stay in Uchino for a while, in time we may all be together again."

Nisuke listened sadly to his wife's words. He wished that, if there were a land free from war, he could leave everything behind and flee there, together with his wife and children. Or at least the thought crossed his mind, but in an instant, he felt ashamed. *For generations our family has led this village and the* confuraria. *How can I think of running off and leaving the farmers behind?*

Nisuke wanted to take this chance to give vent to his pent-up thoughts.

"During these past five or six years they've held off on executing us Christians, but instead, they've been raising our taxes relentlessly. It's like the torture method where they force Christians to dance around in straw raincoats they've set on fire. They might be hoping that we Christians will die off without their having to dirty their hands. For too long, too much blood has been shed without mercy. I've never said this out loud, but the grass and the trees here are growing on the blood of our people. The land of Shimabara is crying out. My heart can hardly bear it."

Temporarily at a loss for words, Nisuke stared for a while at the large persimmon tree in the corner of the garden. People said it had stood there for some three or four hundred years. The fruit on the branches was turning orange even now. Would they have time for making dried persimmons this year? As Omiyo looked out along the same line of sight, her thoughts were the same as those of her husband.

"At the meeting the other day, the headman of Nakakoba Village said, 'That Matsukura, he thinks that if he cuts off the heads of the farmers and burns them to death, rice will sprout from their open throats. But even if he hangs us all upside down, he's never going to get rice or anything else out of us. And if anything does come from us, we'll snatch it up and eat it before he can get it.'

"And then another headman asked, 'Why were we born into this world? If we have nothing to hope for, why even grow any grain next year? We're going to die, so let's be quick about it—with a rebellion that rings out so loud they'll hear it all the way up in Heaven, and they'll know we fought with our swords and we punished the foes of Deus-sama. Then we'll be called up to Heaven. Otherwise our lives will amount to nothing.' That's the way the farmers have been talking. So, let's hope our souls may depart quickly from this world, and let's pray that we may go to *Paraizo*.

"Omiyo, you and I are together, and we have our son Daisuke with us, and we've gotten to see the face of our granddaughter. We've led full lives here. Together, we've had a happy life . . . But for generations, our family has served as village heads and leaders of the *confuraria.* We have to serve Deus-sama by carrying out these responsibilities. From now on, the magistrate's office will determine when things start heating up. I'm ready for the fight to begin, even if it's tomorrow. I know it won't be easy, but Omiyo, please stay by my side until the end."

"My dear . . ." Omiyo said, then paused for breath. "You've spoken well, my husband, and I'm happy to hear your words. Even if I'm a hindrance, and even if it comes to hell or high water, I ask you to take me with you . . . From now on, we're going to be very busy."

Quite unexpectedly, Omiyo broke out in a confident smile.

After several discussions, Okayo was persuaded to go back to her family home in Uchino. Suzu went with her. Suzu considered it her responsibility to take care of Ayame, and when they left, she carried her on her back. Daisuke accompanied them to Uchino.

Nisuke, Omiyo, Oume and the other farm helpers saw them off, carrying their baggage as far as the harbor. When they passed through the front gate of their yard, everyone instinctively turned around to look at the old house where they had been living.

Suzu rocked Ayame on her back and gestured with her shoulder toward the house

"Look, Aya-sama, let's say goodbye to our house. Goodbye and good wishes!" she said.

Okayo patted the baby's wrist. Imitating a baby's voice, she called out, "We'll be back soon, everyone!"

Suzu looked back at the house and garden. They made her think of how old the home was. From the stable, Ine the horse gave a high-pitched whinny, perhaps because he saw that everyone was going out together. Suzu and Ine were kindred spirits and she had often fed him hay and rubbed his neck, and whenever she had the chance, she had called out, "Hey there, Ine!"

Calling this out again by habit, Suzu looked up at the faces of the adults. Her eyes begged to bid farewell to the horse. Everyone nodded quickly. She looked as if she were about to run.

"Don't run—you'll fall," Daisuke called to her.

Oume prayed quietly as she watched Suzu walk, with the baby strapped to her back. Together, Nisuke and Omiyo nodded deeply.

This, perhaps, would be their last time with her. It seemed that whatever happened to Suzu, she would always stay with Ayame. Just like Oume had stayed with Omiyo. Okayo and Daisuke sensed what they were thinking, but when Suzu ran back after saying her farewell to Ine, they thought they shouldn't show their tears.

"Did you take Shirō-sama's cross with you?" Oume asked.

Suzu nodded and pointed to her chest.

"Well, you mustn't show it to other people—it's so important," Omiyo added.

Nodding, Suzu looked back intently at the adults, and gradually her eyes filled with tears.

"For quite a while, there's going to be a lot of trouble here. It's better if the women and children are away. Until we can take care of things, it'll be better for you to be at Grandma's house in Uchino where you can look after the baby. You know how to do everything now, so you can help Grandma, and she'll take good care of you. But above all, take good care of Ayame."

That was the way Nisuke and Omiyo had made their request to Suzu on the previous day, with bowed heads, when they called her in. Perhaps overwhelmed by their serious looks, Suzu had reacted with surprise, but since she was still a child, she had seemed to accept it, and without saying anything had bowed, even more politely than usual. She hadn't cried.

Before Suzu's departure, Omiyo called her over once more and placed in front of her knees a package wrapped in a *furoshiki* cloth.

"This is the figured satin obi my parents brought back from Nagasaki for me when I was fifteen or sixteen. It's for you, for taking care of Ayame. I hope you'll like it."

Removing the covering, Omiyo showed her the contents. On top was a folded obi, light blue and embroidered with plum flowers that shone brightly in the light. Beneath that was a light bluish-gray kimono, woven with a design of plovers and waves. When Omiyo spread it out, the sleeves showed their lining of brilliant red.

Suzu seemed puzzled and uneasy. Even when she saw Omiyo's warm smile, she remained disconcerted. Omiyo touched her shoulder and had her hold the bundle to her chest. Suzu didn't look particularly happy. She seemed conscious of holding something of great importance. But when she put Ayame on her back, her face recovered some of its usual cheer.

What will happen to our family from now on? Omiyo wondered. *It's likely that Nisuke and I will die. If that happens, we can expect that Daisuke will meet the same fate. Who, then, will raise Ayame? We were thinking of her when we asked Okayo to return to her family in Uchino, but if troubles arise in Kuchinotsu, Okayo is likely to worry about Daisuke and perhaps she'll try to return to be with him here in Kuchinotsu. That was part of our thinking in having Suzu go with Okayo and Ayame, of course. There couldn't be a better guardian for Ayame than Suzu. Although she's only eight years old, she already understands the hardships of the world and has a clear spirit.* Omiyo gave thanks to Maria-sama and prayed for her continuing divine protection.

At the wharf, as he caressed the baby, Nisuke bent over and said, "Back at the house, you said something to Ine, didn't you?"

Speaking for the baby, Suzu replied, "We told Ine we're going to see Grandma in Uchino, right, Aya-sama?"

"That's right. That's right, isn't it?"

Nisuke wrapped his arms around Suzu and Ayame and said in a deep, muffled voice, "Tell Grandma in Uchino that we're well. Tell her the Hasudas are all getting along well."

Nisuke pressed his cheek to Ayame's and Suzu's cheeks and stood with them.

Oume stood in the shade of the big banyan tree by the shore and wiped her eyes again and again with the fringe of her apron. Before the boat left, Daisuke took Ayame from Suzu's back, held her in his arms, and then stepped on board.

"We'll be back soon . . ." Okayo said to her parents-in-law, then began to cry. Daisuke remained silent, rubbing her back.

On this day, the waves were somewhat rough. Later, in her dreams, Suzu would often see the adults standing beneath the big banyan tree, waving on and on. Even in her dreams, the waves rose and fell, and amidst the crests of the dancing waves she would see the smiling faces of the people she loved most. In all the rest of her life, Suzu never once wore the beautiful kimono she received from Omiyo. It was too precious, and it had come from the realm of sadness. She regarded it as a treasure, or as clothing for a god.

In Uchino, Okayo's family rejoiced at having their daughter and her new family back home, but they immediately realized the danger of her situation. Daisuke was surprised at how well-informed Okayo's family was about the activities of the Christians in Ōyano, Kōtsuura, and the Shimabara region.

"Until the disturbances settle down, I'd like for Okayo to bring up Ayame here with you. So that this won't be too much of a burden for Grandmother, Suzu has come with them. She will look after everything for Ayame. And here is a written request from my father."

Daisuke handed a letter from Nisuke to Okayo's father Seibei. As Seibei read it, anguish crept across his face. Closing his eyes and rolling up the letter, he remarked quietly, "So thoughtful and gracious . . ."

With great concern, Seibei passed the letter to Sasuke, Okayo's older brother. Sitting up straight, Sasuke began reading. The letter was, in effect, a message of farewell. With an anguished face, Sasuke raised his head, looked at his father gravely, and nodded. Okayo noted their looks.

As she watched Daisuke, Grandmother Ofuji tried to imagine his feelings. Compared with the first time she saw him, when he had come to meet Okayo as a prospective husband, he seemed to have matured considerably.

"Ayame, of course you're my grandchild, but if I may say so, you're such an adorable baby. Your mother found a very good husband, didn't she? We're so glad you're all happy," Ofuji said, lifting Ayame. A smile spread over Daisuke's face as he watched Ayame's great-grandmother playing with his child. Everyone put aside their downcast feelings and brightened up.

"Grandma, she's your great-granddaughter!" Okayo's sister-in-law said as Ofuji hugged Ayame.

"Well, yes, I suppose she is my great-granddaughter, not my granddaughter. I never imagined I'd even get to be a grandmother. I guess I've been around for quite a while."

Taking Ofuji's words as a compliment for Daisuke, Okayo was overcome with emotion.

According to Sasuke, there was unrest in Uchino and the Jokiba area as well. Last year, when they petitioned for emergency grain, he had gone with a group of young people to the government offices in both the Hondo and Tomioka Castles, but the district deputy in Hondo was a miserly lout. In the end, they had received only a token amount of grain, which left them feeling as if they had received nothing at all besides lingering distaste for the official. Sasuke said that with a man like that in charge of their affairs, they felt like they were facing the end of the world.

"The struggle this year is very different from last year. This time, there's almost no chance of getting any grain assistance, and the Christians in Futae have held many meetings about it. The people along the coast are all worked up, and even if we're of different religions, we're all from the same place and we're all wondering how we can get through these hard times. My father and I talk about it all the time."

Sasuke's eyes were clear, perhaps taking after his mother's. But anger flickered in them as he gazed at his father and Daisuke. For the first time, Daisuke felt a deep bond with his younger brother-in-law Sasuke. Despite their different religions, they were united. He had learned that from Oume. He only wished that they could have become close sooner. He felt with relief that, as long as Sasuke lived, the hopes of their people would also remain alive.

"You know, actually, we have some connections with your Christian family," Seibei said. "Okayo and her mother Onobu both have Christian names, and I'm sure Onobu must be very happy about that, even though she's passed away. And Ayame has been given the beautiful, unusual Christian name Luiza. Surely her Grandma Onobu is delighted. Ayame, won't you come to Grandpa?"

Okayo handed his granddaughter to him.

"Now don't you count me out yet as being too old and useless. When the time comes, I'm ready to shake this old white-haired head of mine and spring into action, right, Ayame?"

Everyone turned and looked at Seibei. His eyes, blinking rapidly and close to tears, were gazing up at the sky. His eyelashes were flecked with white.

"Well, this is a surprise—Grandpa getting into the action. The thunder gods, too, must be surprised."

"Well, Grandma, if Ayame should ever be in danger in our house, you'll see me brandish my sword."

"Your sword? Don't be a fool—a sword's nothing. As for me, if the time comes, I'll be out there with our shooting iron."

Everyone refrained from laughing because she looked so serious.

In fact, the family had a firearm made by a local master gunsmith in Noda. Everyone in the house knew that Seibei oiled it regularly and kept it in good working order. Daisuke was especially grateful to them. Their words showed their concern for his safety and peace of mind.

Okayo brought out an *ama-gatsu* guardian doll, a present from Omiyo for Okayo's younger sister Nana. Ofuji held the doll in her hands and told Nana to sit down. Seeing how it was made of such fine material, Ofuji sighed.

"This doll has Omiyo-sama's spirit in it," she told Nana. "It's a living doll. You must always treat it carefully."

Actually, there were two dolls. The other one was for Ayame. Nana hugged her doll joyfully and moved closer to Suzu. Suzu listened to all that was going on, with Nana as her companion.

The next morning, Seibei, Sasuke and Okayo, with Ayame on her back, went to see Daisuke off at the inlet in Futae. As they walked along, the stories that Daisuke told about Oume and Suzu seemed to make a deep impression on Seibei and Sasuke. When they reached the mouth of the river and came to the familiar Igawa well, they drew some water. Respectfully, Okayo poured the water into a large flask that Sasuke had brought.

Handing it to Daisuke, she said, "This water is for when you say an *oratio*."

"That gun we talked about last night, could you use it?" Seibei asked calmly.

"We most certainly could," Daisuke replied immediately.

"In that case, we'll get it ready and Sasuke will bring it over to you as soon as he can."

The three men looked into each other's eyes. Okayo held on to the gunwales of the boat until it left. She looked down, biting her lip for a while until, at last, she looked up and saw her husband facing her with a serene expression. With his fingertips, he brushed away some hair at the back of her neck that the sea breeze had been blowing into the baby's face.

One night shortly after Daisuke returned to Kuchinotsu, Sasuke showed up with the gun, as promised. Sasuke hoped to deepen his ties with Nisuke and the Hasuda family while he was there. He had traveled at night in part because of the tides, but he had also been wary of going out in daylight with a gun. Omiyo, who had been doing needlework late at night, stepped down into the earthen foyer and welcomed the visitor. Overcome with emotion, they stared at each other for some time without speaking.

"Ayame is so beautiful, and my boy's already playing with her like an older brother," was the first thing Sasuke said to her.

Omiyo had wanted to remain calm, but when she heard her granddaughter's name, tears streamed from her eyes. Flustered, she ran to call her husband and Daisuke from the back of the house.

"Oh, I'm so glad, Sasuke is here with news of Ayame!" she said.

Daisuke and Nisuke were still up, deep in conversation.

"We will never forget your incredible kindness," Nisuke said when he received the gun from Sasuke. "Your family has cared for this so well, and now it will give us courage."

Nisuke was deeply moved. Never could he have imagined that his daughter-in-law's family—a Buddhist family—would present him with a gun. It was reputed to be a masterpiece, made by the famed gunsmith Kinuya Tanji who had lived near Noda. Seeing the barrel of the gun gleaming in the lamplight and noting how well it had been kept polished, Nisuke realized how much daily attention the patient old Seibei must have put into maintaining it.

"I hear it's no short trip from your house to the wharf in Futae," Omiyo said. "You must be starving. I'll have some food ready for you soon." She hurried off to the kitchen.

Until now, Nisuke's family hadn't had a chance to talk with Sasuke. After Daisuke had returned from Uchino, he had said he wished they had gotten to know each other sooner. As Nisuke looked again at Sasuke, he wondered how to express his feelings. If they were to miss this chance, there likely wouldn't be another opportunity to exchange words freely from their hearts. When Oume brought in the food and drink and was about to leave the room, Nisuke and Omiyo asked her to stay. And so, in a departure from ordinary customs, Oume sat down and joined the group.

"I'm glad we have this time together, thanks to this gun," Nisuke said. "Since Daisuke never had a younger brother, it's a great fortune for him to have you."

Sasuke was two years younger than Daisuke.

"I, too, grew up not knowing what an older brother was," Sasuke answered, lost in thought. He sat up straight and continued. "In terms of our relationship as in-laws, I suppose I might be called Daisuke-dono's elder brother, but I think of myself as the younger. And so, to celebrate this great night, if we could share a cup of brotherhood, nothing could make me happier."

"Sasuke-dono, that's how I, too, have felt, all along. Father, could you pass Sasuke-dono and me sake cups? From this night on, we are true brothers."

"With pleasure. Omiyo, would you pour the sake so they can drink to true brotherhood?"

"Why, yes, with pleasure!"

Omiyo rose on her knees and picked up an unglazed sake flask from the table. Daisuke called out to Sasuke, who had emptied his cup, "To my brother!" And, with nothing more to say, he kept filling his cup.

Noticing that Sasuke was in tears, Omiyo said, with a lump in her throat, "Sasuke-dono, you know, Oume is from the Amakusa Islands, like you. She's from Fukuro no Ura."

Sasuke had recently heard about Oume from Daisuke, when they had been walking along the road to Futae no Ura.

"I hear you've been very kind to my sister Okayo."

Flustered, Oume waved her hand in protest.

"And hearing that you're from Fukuro no Ura, well, my mother, who's now passed away, she was from Shiki, the next town over. So it brings back good memories."

"So it does. When I was young, I loved my hometown, and I used to think of my parents' island just across the waves from here. I'd put Omiyo-sama on my back and walk along the beach, looking in the direction of my old village. But now this has become my home."

Oume had never talked of things like this before.

"When we're talking together like this, our spirits are so close, even though the world around us is so troubled," Nisuke said. It seemed that he was speaking of more than religious differences.

With deep emotion, Daisuke added, "And there are also some people who are so close to each other, yet whose hearts are far apart."

It seemed to Sasuke that this meeting marked a point of destiny. *In the past, what sort of people came to visit in this well-built old house? And who will remember it and pass on its stories?* For this was no ordinary house. Its history was now on the verge of disappearing. What would become of the stories of these old households and families with roots that reached back to the times long before the current government and its policies of "one-domain-one castle"? Overcome with emotion, Sasuke held up his sake cup to Oume.

"You've become a guardian god of this house."

Oume shook her head as if to dismiss such an outlandish idea. But it seemed to Sasuke that the shaking of her head was like the gentle waving of the great camphor tree at the top of the hill. The image of that camphor tree had come to Sasuke from the stories Okayo had told him about Oume when she visited Uchino the year before.

"It seems your father-in-Law Nisuke is always so busy," Ofuji had remarked to Okayo.

"Well yes, Father-in-law is always busy, but he's always calm and steady, like the the Igawa well with the hackberry trees. As Oume-yan has said, he's a blessing from above," Okayo answered.

Sasuke remembered that his father had looked at Okayo in amazement for some time. Back when Sasuke had seen Daisuke off from Uchino, they had stopped by that same sacred well with the hackberry trees. And now, in front of him, he was seeing Nisuke's face. The face seemed to be floating, reflected on the surface of a bluish, bottomless well.

"Even my own thoughts are all twisted, and everything is heading in the wrong direction. When I think back, it seems the main battlefield has been the one in my heart. How many times, I wonder, have I been attacked and nearly died?" Nisuke said, picking up the gun.

"Whoa—it sure is heavy!"

Groaning, he gripped the muzzle and breech of the firearm.

"Why don't you try it and see how it feels?" Nisuke asked as he passed the gun to Daisuke. "It's really been looked after well. I've never actually used one of these but . . . here, Daisuke—you take it."

Nisuke rotated his shoulders and took a breath to rid himself of his heavy thoughts. Everyone remained silent, as if listening to the passage of time, and watched as Daisuke held the gun in his hands. Through what seemed like fissures piercing the world of silence, crickets chirped. Surrounded by the multitude of voices of those tiny creatures, Nisuke reflected, *We are like those insects.*

Deep in the imagination harbored within Omiyo's eyes, countless flowers were swaying in the breeze along the pathways. She thought about how this scene was probably similar to the last landscape the martyrs had looked on. *Someday, when Ayame grows up, will the day ever come when she, too, is able to look on the sights I have seen?*

Cups of sake were passed around, again and again. For the first time since she had come to this house, Oume joined in drinking the homemade sake, and without hesitation.

"I've been wondering, how's Takematsu doing?" she asked as her face started to redden.

Everyone seemed pleased. Sasuke looked a bit puzzled, so Daisuke explained, "Takematsu is our scholar who can't read. Isn't that right, Oume?"

"It sure is. He's been teaching me things right from the start."

"Don't try to fool us, now. Takematsu says there's no one in the world scarier than Oume-yan," Nisuke said. He almost never teased her like this.

Although Sasuke had attended his younger sister's wedding and exchanged greetings with her family, he hadn't had the chance to visit again and get to know them, since they were separated by the Hayasaki Straits. He felt this short visit now might be his last opportunity to talk at length with everyone in the household, including Oume.

Even back in the mountains of Uchino, daily life wasn't all that calm, and Sasuke had heard all sorts of stories from the local people about what was going on across the bay in Shimabara. When he heard the rumors about Christians being slaughtered in the hellish hot springs of Mount Unzen, he had wanted to cover his ears. He had heard that the brutality stopped for a while after Lord Matsukura Shigemasu, the one who started it all, went crazy and died in Obama.

"For heaven's sake, his was no ordinary death. It was divine retribution! He was damned and punished!" the local people whispered amongst themselves.

Christians had been tortured. Their ears and noses had been sliced off, leg tendons severed, fingers sheared off and scattered, and bodies tied to horses and hauled off to the hot springs at Mount Unzen, where they had been tossed in and boiled until their lives finally slipped away. As an added taunt to farmers who hadn't paid their land taxes, the tormentors had tied them up in straw raincoats and set them on fire. As their bodies burned in excruciating pain, the executioners had laughed and called them the "dancing straw coats." Taga Mondo, the chief counselor, had often appeared on the scene and, with bulging veins, goaded the executioners whenever they started to slack off in their tasks. The young Lord Matsukura was off in Edo, not wanting to be in Shimabara, so no one around the castle saw him.

The Buddhists, too, talked despairingly about what was happening.

"Can you believe it? Humans doing such things to other humans!"

The Christians had faced their deaths with acceptance and prayed that the sins of their executioners be forgiven. The Matsukuras' cruelty knew no bounds, and even pregnant women and newborn babies were sacrificed. It was rumored that the blacksmiths who made the instruments of torture went insane. There were reports that some had escaped from this terrible region and were begging for food and clothes around the Nagasaki harbor. Sasuke reminded himself that it was because of these atrocities that Nisuke had quickly sent his daughter-in-law off to the house in Uchino for protection.

While bound and burning in the flames, the martyrs had quietly chanted prayers to Maria. In the end, they met their deaths and were swallowed up in the womb of the hell-springs of Mount Unzen and belched out with its volcanic gasses. The people of Shimabara could not very well stand back and ignore these horrors.

Back when his younger sister left to get married, Sasuke's family had discussed the issue of her marrying into a Christian family. Both her father and grandmother, and Sasuke too, had been happy about it, in part because Okayo's departed mother had been a Christian. But if they had known that circumstances would become so dire, would they have agreed to the marriage? Where they lived in Amakusa, events were beginning to take a similar turn as those in Shimabara. When Okayo married, the fact that her father-in-law was the leader of a benevolent association had reassured her family. As the two families sat facing each other, they had trusted that this fact, along with the couple's faith and love, would keep them together through the ups and downs of life.

The sounds of cricket calls filled the night air. Sasuke, along with the others in the house, listened to their voices, feeling present in an eternal moment.

Sasuke had announced that he would leave the next morning at daybreak. When morning came, two men he hadn't met the night before came to see him off. They introduced themselves as Matsukichi and Kumagorō. Sasuke had the feeling that Kumagorō's strong, earnest eyes would be fixed on him forever. As he looked around at the house and its grounds, he noticed the cracks running along the walls of the main house and the two old storehouses. Yet those very cracks, along with the large posts and beams, gave him the sense that the structures had been rooted in the land for many years. As he looked around, wondering where all the insects of the night before could be hiding, he noticed that the leaves of the red spider lily plants, whose flowers had fallen away, were shining brightly.

Four or five days after Sasuke's departure, a messenger from Yozaemon, the region's leading farmer, arrived out of breath.

"Are things here all right?" he asked.

Since the runner's face clearly indicated something out of the ordinary, Nisuke asked what had brought him.

"They took Yozaemon-dono's daughter-in-law."

"What? Okimi-dono?"

So what he had feared had finally happened. In part, he was relieved that he had acted quickly in sending Okayo and Ayame to Uchino, but he was also shocked to hear that the authorities had already come to Yozaemon's place.

"Tell us how it happened."

The messenger explained that, among the fields that Yozaemon farmed, there was one section owned by Tanaka Sōsuke, the now-retired chief counselor, and some of the land tax for this section had not been paid. Sōsuke had told Yozaemon that, because of his own difficult financial conditions, he was requiring complete payment, before autumn, of all unpaid taxes for the past five years. He had come again and again demanding payment. "You gave priority to filling the daimyo's storehouses but you put off paying me," he had complained. He had made it clear that he would show no leniency regarding the payments.

"Last year, that red rice with adzuki beans from your field was quite tasty," he had added. "This year, when you make your rice payment, add some adzuki beans to it."

After inquiring at length, Yozaemon had learned that a big celebration was being planned for Sōsuke's seventieth birthday. His entire family and all his retainers would be invited, and there would be all sorts of festivities, including a Noh performance, and it was very important that each of the guests' dining trays include the traditional celebratory dish of red rice with adzuki beans. For this reason, no delays or excuses would be permitted.

It wasn't true that Yozaemon had made no payments at all during the past five years. He had paid as much as he could. Only thirty sacks of back payments had accumulated. But Sōsuke had decided to get tough on account of the planned celebration. He claimed that he had brought up the matter many times to no avail, and therefore he could no longer trust Yozaemon. And so, he said, he had decided to take Yozaemon's daughter-in-law as a hostage. Sōsuke claimed that he wasn't happy about having to take her, and that he hoped Yozaemon would pay up quickly and completely so that he could return her. Five men had come and taken her away, without saying a word. Yozaemon and his son had been away from the house when they appeared. Only the women and helpers had been at home.

That wonderful, warmhearted young woman had become like a wild, fleeing animal who had lost all place of refuge. She had suddenly thrown herself against one of the samurai, and then had been shoved down to the ground by the enraged men. They had kicked her, although her mother-in-law clung to her and begged for mercy. Finally, when the leader saw her belly and realized that she was pregnant, he had ordered them to stop. Although her mother-in-law and the head of the workers had run over to help her stand up, the men had tied Okimi's hands behind her with a rope. The leader snarled:

"You're mighty lively for someone expecting a little one. See, this is what you get for resisting."

"I wasn't resisting, I was trying to escape."

"That's resisting."

"Okimi has done nothing wrong!"

When the mother-in-law rushed toward them, she was shoved away by the leader. He said right to her face, "If you love your daughter-in-law and you want to get her back, you'd better pay your rice tax soon. The retired councilor, himself, said that."

Okimi had called out to her husband, who wasn't there:

"My love!"

When they dragged Okimi away with her hands tied behind her, her belly was hanging out and she had looked on the verge of falling to the ground, the messenger told them.

At the time, Yozaemon and his son had been away from the house repairing the banks of a dried-out field near the sea, but when Yozaemon learned what had happened, he and his son had run straight to Tanaka Sōsuke's place. The messenger said that they had not yet returned, but requested that Nisuke go to their house right away. When the messenger finished reporting all of this, he dropped to the ground in exhaustion.

Tea was brought out, in hopes of reviving him. Daisuke stared at his father's face. It was tense and tinged with a look he had never seen before.

"All right, I'll go check on the situation," Nisuke said. "But since there's no telling if something might happen at our place too, I want you to stay here."

Daisuke nodded with determination.

"So, I'm off for a while. Otaki-dono must be getting worried. I want you to just do your regular work here and not go anywhere else."

Nisuke said some words of encouragement to the messenger, and then they went off together. But how could Nisuke's household simply continue with their regular work? Their tasks this fall would be different from those of other years. Oume was stocking up on provisions for the rebellion and Matsukichi and Kumagorō were cutting firewood and making lots of torches. While young Kumagorō was busy going around the area as a messenger, Matsukichi was collecting sickles and hoes and removing their handles. They took them by boat to Yushima Island and had the blacksmith there rework them into spears and knives.

Soon after Nisuke arrived at Yozaemon's place, Yozaemon and his son returned, looking pale and exhausted. The son's eyes were narrowed and his face marked with despair. They said they had taken Sōsuke two sacks of red rice they had managed to collect from the upland fields, the grain so small and poorly ripened it could hardly be called rice. They hadn't meant for Sōsuke to make do with that so much as to show him the grim reality.

In front of Sōsuke's residence was a small river that served as a moat. Yozaemon and his son had arrived at its gate and crossed over a bridge. Their helpers who were carrying the straw sacks of rice followed. As the guards questioned them, the steward had come out yelling, "Hey, what's all this noise about?"

It was the same steward they had faced many times in the past when they paid their land taxes. They remembered how he would always pat the sacks of rice with his palms and then, for some reason, place his ear against them and listen. With a cringing feeling, Yozaemon had made his appeal to the steward:

"Suyama-sama, may we ask your assistance with something?"

"And what would that be, Yozaemon?"

Of course, Suyama knew full well what had happened.

"Suyama-sama, we have a request."

Yozaemon's son stepped out from behind him and prostrated himself, placing both hands on the ground. Along the way, Yozaemon had cautioned his son:

"When we arrive at Sōsuke's residence, you shouldn't say much. You've got a quick tongue, and you might upset them. I don't know what's going to happen."

In spite of this, he seemed to have already forgotten his father's warning.

Suyama shut his eyes like the mythical giant toad of old.

"Your name—what is it?" he asked, his eyes still closed.

"My name is Chōichi."

"Chōichi? Ah, yes. And your wife's name?"

"Her name is Okimi," he said, then burst out passionately, "Please, I beg you—give me back Okimi! Where is Okimi . . . ? Okimi, Okimi!"

Chōichi stood up, clinging to Suyama's neckband and grasping his chest as he called through the gate, as if he believed his words might somehow reach his wife.

Several samurai came running over.

From behind, Yozaemon restrained his son.

"That's no way to act! Don't be foolish! Please forgive us. My son is terribly upset now. Please accept our apologies."

With his shoulders heaving, finally Yozaemon found his voice. Normally, he was poor at expressing himself, but in his desperation to help his daughter-in-law he had managed to speak.

"Well, your son and his wife are certainly full of energy."

Yozaemon was stunned. Okimi was a cheerful, warmhearted woman, without a cloud in her soul. When people who were feeling depressed met her, she restored their spirits like a whiff of fragrant incense on a spring day. Perhaps her character was working against her now. When she was tied up and taken away by the samurai, she had struck out at them physically. Yozaemon worried that even here, she might resist orders.

Looking at the straw sacks of rice, Suyama asked, "Now what is *this* supposed to mean?"

"It's red rice that has failed to mature. May we ask you to take a look?"

Suyama's face changed color.

"Unripened rice? Now why would you ever bring such a thing here?"

"If you search our storehouse, this is all you will find."

It seemed as if the legendary giant toad was slowly lifting his eyelids.

"Have you brought this here to mock us?"

"Certainly not. We've been searching everywhere for something we can use to pay the tax, but this is the reality now. We've come to tell you the truth about the situation."

"And do you really think we'll be able to prepare red rice for the banquet with this unripe grain?"

"Well, no, we don't."

At a loss for how to answer, Yozaemon struggled on:

"I'm not saying it can't be done, but it's wet . . ."

"What was that you just said?"

Yozaemon wished he had said nothing at all.

"Probably it's not possible."

"You're telling me it's not possible because it's wet?"

"I'm sorry, but the rice harvest wasn't good."

"Bringing trash rice like this—it's an insult to this house!"

"Please, we would never do such a thing. We came here to ask you to return our woman. She's with child."

"We know that. We aren't treating her rough. But weren't you saying you've been trying to find some rice somewhere?"

"That's what we've been trying to do."

"Well, the Noh performance to which our retired counselor Sōsuke-sama has invited the entire household is scheduled for the end of this month."

"Could you allow us a postponement?"

"Absolutely not! We've already invited the whole family and the household. We're going to serve them this year's new red rice, so make sure you get it here by the fifteenth of the month—no excuses. If you fail, well . . ."

Suyama's eyes grew menacing.

"Our retired councilor has said that if you pull any tricks and try to delay your payment, the hostage will be treated to drinking the river water. He's always exacting about people meeting their obligations."

"River water?"

Chōichi groaned. Groveling, Yozaemon grasped Suyama's *hakama* trousers.

"Please, I beg you—take me as your hostage, but set his wife free!" he implored.

"*You* as a hostage?"

Suyama opened his eyes wide.

"Your role is to find better rice for the payment!"

Although the samurai guards standing behind them had maintained blank expressions, there was, nevertheless, an eerie feeling. Glancing around the estate, they saw no sign of where Okimi might have been taken to.

"Please, allow us to meet Sōsuke dono-sama."

"Even if you were to meet him, just what do you think you'd do?" Suyama asked dismissively. Then he shrugged and turned his back on them. Taking this as a sign, the guards came over and threw the two men out from the gate.

Yozaemon and Chōichi had then run along the bank of the river that flowed past the wall of the estate. Soon they came to a place where the water supplying the household flowed in. Since it was a tidal river, at high tide the sea water backed up into it. Because of this, a tall stone wall had been constructed. An opening for taking in fresh water had been cut into the base of the wall in order to give the household a pond and a place for washing. As Yozaemon and Chōichi knew well from past visits to pay their grain taxes, there was a storehouse near the pond. Perhaps, they thought, Okimi was being held there. They stood in front of the place where the water entered, the light extinguished from their eyes.

When Yozaemon and Chōichi arrived back at their house, the people who had been waiting for them saw their faces and for a moment were silent.

"Whatever happened?"

Yozaemon's wife began to sob convulsively.

"And with her carrying a baby!"

The people who had gathered hesitated to say anything, finding the situation so shocking. After thinking for a long while, Yozaemon managed to say, in a voice that caught in his throat:

"I never imagined our house would be the first to get hit. Old Tanaka seems to have had his sights set on us for quite some time. In fact, we've always paid him a lot, because we produce a lot, but that's why our unpaid taxes are also so high. I'd heard that the magistrate's office recently issued orders to take women as hostages, but I never thought old Tanaka would go after us. He must have thought that hitting the house that has the most would shake up the rest of the people."

Scuffing the ground with his toes, Chōichi cried out, "I just pray he returns Okimi unharmed!"

Yozaemon recounted their story to all the neighbors and workers who rushed in.

Although Yozaemon was the leading farmer in Kuchinotsu and played an important role in the Christians' affairs, he did not often take part in their meetings. People supposed he found it difficult to speak in front of others. Yet, whenever the benevolent association needed help, he opened his storehouse for them. For this reason, his place was known by the local farmers as "Yozaemon-sama's Benevolence Hall."

Now it seemed as if Yozaemon's usual reticence to speak had left him. On the other hand, Chōichi just fixed his eyes on one spot and said nothing. Normally, he would cover for his father's silences by speaking out energetically.

"We were told we'd have to find some way to pay by the fifteenth, but there isn't much chance we can do that. All I can think about is getting Okimi back . . . But no matter where I go, no matter who I ask, there's no way we can come up with thirty sacks of red rice. Even the other government storehouses seem to have taken in only fifty or sixty sacks so far. All I can do is laugh in desperation. That's an absurd number of sacks."

Realizing Nisuke was present, Yozaemon pressed on like a child too young to understand logic, "Nisuke-dono, I'm glad you're here. You've helped us a lot. And, well, do you think we might get Yazō *benzashi*-dono to help us find some red rice? At least five sacks of it? I'll look around for the rest."

"But Father," Chōichi cautioned, "I don't think that's going to be enough."

Pulled back to reality, Yozaemon's face darkened again.

"I realize that, but at least it's something."

Groans slipped out from the people gathered at Yozaemon's storehouse. Listening to him talk, they realized that even this storehouse, at the largest farm in the area, was completely empty of rice. Some people had harbored hopes that perhaps, as in the past, Yozaemon might somehow open it and provide them with food.

According to Nisuke, Yazō was away on a trip, so he couldn't help in this crisis. However, even if Yazō could help them out temporarily, they would have to pay money for rice. And even if Yozaemon still had some money to buy rice from Yazō, the smaller farmers didn't have any. They had even been forced to eat the wheat and millet set aside for next year's planting. All they could do was stare vacantly into space.

"Our parents and grandparents never faced such brutal conditions . . . We always had faith that, as long as we devoted our hearts fully to working our fields, we could rely on the spirit of Deus-sama. But now it's come to this. I don't understand what's happening."

Yozaemon covered his face and broke into tears. Everyone looked glumly at his slim, solitary figure.

"Nisuke-dono, my faith hasn't been strong enough. I haven't understood other people's true feelings. I've heard about the martyrs any number of times, but my ears and my eyes have been closed, and I haven't really heard or seen. And now they've taken our daughter-in-law . . . There's hardly another woman like her in this world. Such a wonderful woman."

"Come now, Yoza-dono, you're mixing things up. This isn't about our faith in Christianity. It's about our payment of taxes."

"I know that, but they'll torture her just like those Christians were tortured. Like they said, she'll be 'treated to drinking the river water.'"

"What? River water?"

"I can't bear to think how much she must be suffering."

Their voices faltering as they said goodbye, one by one the visitors began to leave.

When night fell and even the insects quieted down, a bright, nearly full moon shone in the sky.

The day for paying the taxes arrived. There was a stillness and quietness in all the villages.

At Yozaemon's house, Okimi's parents and her brother and sister had come over from Amakusa, so that her whole family was there. Like beads in a rosary, they filed along the narrow pathways of reddened grass between fields on their way to the estate of the retired councilor.

Through the cracks in their doorways, people in the villages along the way watched them pass. When Okimi was taken hostage, some of the farmers had sent their wives and children to live with relatives in distant places. But most people couldn't do that, so they shut themselves in their houses and prayed for Maria-sama's protection or chanted incantations.

Yozaemon's group sat down in front of Tanaka Sōsuke's gate. To the guard who came out, they presented a bundle wrapped in straw, filled with lobsters, turban shellfish, and dried fish from Amakusa, along with the small amount of red rice they had managed to find, at great effort. They humbly begged the guard to accept it. The guard quickly shut the gate and left them outside waiting for a long time. Unable to bear this treatment, Chōichi knocked on the gate. A guard rushed out and struck him with his staff.

"Listen up! If you want Okimi to be punished, then go right ahead and make trouble!"

They blanched and hung their heads at these violent words. Suyama the steward appeared. He said that Okimi wouldn't be released unless they received the full tax payment. However, he would allow one person to meet with her.

Okimi's mother-in-law Otaki was a gutsy woman. She overcame the fear that held back the others and quickly slipped inside the gate alone. She followed the guard to a small structure surrounded by reeds next to the pond. Another guard was standing there. He motioned to her with his chin.

"In there—she's in there."

Otaki peered inside the open door. In the darkness, beyond some wooden bars, she saw a human shape moving. Okimi's face was visible in the light that filtered in. Her eyes were puffy and her lips were pale.

"Mother-in-Law!"

Okimi edged closer and, with difficulty, extended an arm through the bars.

"Okimi, be patient. Just a bit longer and we'll get you out. Everyone is there at the gate."

Choking on her words, Otaki grasped Okimi's hand and hugged it tightly to her chest.

"After all that's happened to you, your parents from Amakusa shouldn't have to see you like this. Soon I'll take your place in there."

"No, I can take another four or five days of this."

"What are you saying, Okimi? We all came here to get you out. Your mother from Amakusa, too."

Fretfully, Okimi grasped her mother-in-law's chest.

"My mother—she came over from Amakusa . . . ?"

Otaki nodded again and again. Her whole body trembling, Okimi shook her head.

"And my husband?"

"Chōichi came too. On our way here, he was at the front the whole time. He comes every day."

"Why isn't he here now?"

"These guys would never let him in."

"You better not talk like that," the guard cut in. "You're the only one we're letting in. If you complain too much, we'll kick you out. Look— those samurai are running over here now. Ready to go?"

"Just a bit longer."

Otaki gripped the wooden bars firmly.

"Are you all right? As soon as we get you out of here, you'll be sleeping on a soft futon. We're all working to get that red rice. And when we give it to the master of this place, you'll come back with us and we'll cook up some of it for you to celebrate."

"What about my husband?"

Okimi turned her head and opened her eyes slightly. She seemed to be smiling.

"We've all come to take you back. Soon you'll be back home."

Writhing in pain, Okimi shrieked, "My darling!"

Otaki saw two samurai rushing around the pond toward them.

"Look—you've made us run. What's all this shouting?" one said to her with a sigh. "You'd better deliver those sacks of rice soon, while she's still got some life in her!"

A guard who had arrived after the other two yanked her away from the bars and slammed the thick wooden door shut.

They led Otaki out to the front gate, opened it, and shoved her out.

She threw herself to the ground in the midst of the waiting family.

"It's too much! It's just too much!" she sobbed, kicking the ground with her now-bare feet and striking out at the air.

Yozaemon's sister noticed that her kimono was soaking wet below the knees. Thinking she must have lost control of her bladder from shock, the sister whispered:

"Look, your kimono is wet. Let's get you home quickly to clean up."

"Ah—what's happened?"

Otaki noticed for the first time that the wet skirt of her kimono was sticking to her ankles.

"How did it get wet?"

Realizing that it must have happened in the prison hut, shivers ran up her spine. The floor had been flooded. When she was kneeling in front of the wooden bars, the hem of her kimono must have soaked up the water. At the time, she had been too agitated to notice.

"It's water . . . that water."

She clung to her husband, unable to go on. The guard's words, uttered with a sigh, "soon, while she's still got some life left in her," echoed in her ears. Perhaps, moved by Okimi's spirit, he had let his concern show. How many more days could Okimi, with a child in her womb, survive in that prison flooded with pondwater? There was no time to lose. They did everything they could think of. They sent a messenger on a fast boat to meet a rice merchant in Nagasaki with whom they had conducted regular business. His reply, however, was that it would be impossible to get so many sacks.

In the meantime, they received word that the daughter of the

Kushiyama headman had also been taken hostage. They heard she was being held in the magistrate's office.

As they were reeling from this news, a messenger arrived from Sōsuke's place.

"A child has been born at the retired councilor's residence. We ask you to come and take back the mother and child."

Chōichi didn't know how he got there so fast. They had rushed off carrying a door with a futon draped over it to serve as a stretcher. Six or seven people went, including Okimi's parents from Amakusa.

On the way, Chōichi had pictured how Okimi, with a woman servant by her side, might say something to him sweetly like, "My darling," as she placed her head on his chest. He was frantic to be with her. He knew that when his mother met with her, Okimi's eyes had been swollen nearly shut, no doubt from crying day and night.

The gate was opened quickly.

A stretcher covered with straw matting lay on the ground. Beside it was an elderly woman. Chōichi stared at the matting, petrified. There was no movement.

"It was stillborn. We return it to you."

The elderly woman looked down and pressed her palms together in prayer.

Stillborn . . . If the baby was dead, then where was the mother? Just then, Chōichi noticed Okimi's clenched hand sticking out from the matting. In an instant, he understood what had happened. He could neither scream nor weep. He simply gazed at her white hand, hanging like a stone.

CHAPTER EIGHT

SIGNAL FIRES

On the road leading south along the seacoast from the castle town of Shimabara, at a distance of three leagues was the village of Fukae. At four leagues were the villages of Nunotsu and Dōsaki; at five and six leagues were Arie and Arima; at eight leagues was Kuchinotsu, with Kazusa another league beyond; and from there on, dotted along the Bay of Chijiwa in the southern half of the Shimabara Peninsula, were the villages of Kushiyama, Obama and Chijiwa. In the center was Mount Unzen, from which the hot springs of Obama flowed.

Rumors were beginning to reach the Matsukura clan that in Minan, as they called this southern part of the peninsula, some sort of trouble was brewing, and that it was spreading stealthily throughout the entire region. A group including the chief counselor of the Matsukura clan, Okamoto Shinbei, went to inspect the area with Taijima Kudayū, the local magistrate of Arie, as their guide.

The officials and their men searched the coast in boats, making stops here and there and going inland near Kuchinotsu to investigate the situation. Surveying the main road from Arima to Kuchinotsu from their boats, they noticed a steady stream of people, including women and children, traveling in small groups as if coming and going to a festival, or sightseeing. Unaware that they were being observed, their expressions were enraptured, and to the officials this seemed suspicious.

All of this activity was going on just when the land taxes were due, when the farmers should have been busiest at work, so the officials decided to visit the village headman's home to investigate.

"Chief Counselor Okamoto Shinbei is carrying out an inspection of the Minan area. Be careful you don't make any blunders," people warned Nisuke.

Hearing these words, he felt tense. The deadline for paying taxes was upon them, and Yozaemon's daughter-in-law had just died in captivity. It was unlikely, however, that the chief counselor would come all the way from Shimabara Castle just to demand the taxes. After having made the difficult agreement with the Ōyano group, Nisuke was uneasy.

From what he had heard, the officials wanted to question him about why so many people were out on the roads of late. Nisuke sent messengers to summon two other village leaders.

In fact, in the past few days, many people had been coming from the mountains and seaside and traveling up and down the road, through the dense thickets of autumn wildflowers. Nisuke guessed that most of them were visiting Sankichi's shrine.

Counselor Okamoto dismissed Nisuke's invitation to come into his house, instead sitting down on the porch by the garden. As he sipped the green tea that was quickly served, he stared menacingly at Nisuke.

"It certainly is suspicious that so few farmers are out in the fields at harvest time, and so many people are coming and going along the roads when there aren't any festivals going on. The women and children look mighty happy, even though they shouldn't be out playing in the mountains. You must know what's going on. Tell me now—I want to hear the straight truth."

"As you say, people are out and about, but I'm not sure what's going on. It's quite unusual."

Nisuke looked for a nod of assent from the village leader Jinshichi, who was well known for his skill at feigning ignorance.

"Yes, it certainly does seem odd. These past few days I've heard stories about a powerful god coming over from Amakusa, and I hear it's attracted a following pretty quick. No doubt the people are trying to find out where it's enshrined."

"I, too, have heard such talk," Nisuke said quietly. "I hear people have even been coming from other villages."

"I wouldn't doubt they've been taken in by fairies or goblins. They probably think they can get some special blessing from that god if they find out where it's dwelling. I suppose they're not themselves, plagued as they are by hunger and thirst."

Nisuke refrained from commenting while Jinshichi was speaking, but his face expressed due concern.

"Since it's harvest time, we've been quite annoyed by the situation. We've warned them, but a lot of them still seem to be out in the fields and hills. It's no easy task to make them stop. I'm at my wit's end."

Jinshichi was feigning severe concern about a made-up god coming over from Amakusa. But Nisuke wondered how long it would be possible to maintain this deception.

Okamoto appeared to have listened to their account very carefully.

"I'm not sure I understand what you just said, but for now I'll let that go. However, this matter of people walking about festively on the roads all over the place, and right at harvest time—that's a real affront to the government. I shouldn't have to tell you that village leaders have responsibilities to carry out. You must warn everyone in the villages that there is to be no unauthorized roaming about. As long as this disturbance goes unchecked, you'll be held responsible—you understand?"

To their surprise, Okamoto Shichibei concluded his remarks and stood up, as if stressing the importance of his affairs and his need to move on quickly with the inspection.

As the officials made their way back to Shimabara, they couldn't stop thinking about the joy they had seen on people's faces, as if they were either possessed, or their souls had been totally liberated. The constant stream of people leading children along the roads remained in their eyes. What, they wondered, was going on? It was hard to believe that farmers would leave their fields untended. As the group returned in their boats, they eagerly discussed these questions. They could round up some people and question them, but what sort of trouble would that stir up? Even five or six years ago, when the horrible executions were going on, there hadn't been such large numbers of people traveling about the southern part of Shimabara.

"What do you make of all this talk about the arrival of a sacred god from Amakusa?"

As he sat huddled in the hull of his boat, avoiding the spray that was blowing in on the evening breeze, Okamoto asked his men for their thoughts. For a while, no clear answers emerged, but then one man spoke up:

"What that village leader said about people not being themselves because of their hunger and thirst—that worries me."

The men continued rowing their boats past Arima. At this time of year, the sun set early over the sea. As they scrutinized the coast, someone called out, "What's that over there—those lights?"

"You suppose it could be will-o'-the-wisp?"

For a while, the men in the boat remained silent. As they watched the lights flickering about on the land in the distance, they recalled the seemingly possessed faces of the farmers they had observed earlier in the day and wondered what to make of the situation. The lights might be torches, or perhaps lanterns. But in any case, there were far too many of them.

Looking more closely, they could see there was one line of lights moving up from the south, and another coming down from the north, and where the two lines converged, the lights were flickering.

One of the retainers suggested anxiously, "They do say will-o'-the-wisp lights come and go."

"First what we saw in the daytime, and now these suspicious lights . . ."

Might they be seeing the same people they had watched earlier in the day, now walking about with lanterns? *Could they be the ones with those same enraptured faces, the ones who have come to find the dwelling place of a god from Amakusa?*

Okamoto harbored an eerie feeling, in spite of himself. Perhaps sensing this, one of his main footmen said a bit more loudly than usual, "If those are the people we saw in the daytime, then . . ." he began, but cut himself off. "Anyhow, we shouldn't be fooled," he muttered and then turned silent.

"Sir, do you think it's all right for us to return without going up into the hills and checking out what's going on?" one of the samurai asked.

"If we go up there in the dark, what do you think is going to happen? If there's trouble, there aren't enough of us to do much," Okamoto grumbled.

Some of them recalled hearing a story about a boat bobbing

about on the waves all night, having been led astray by phantom lights. Okamoto called out to his oarsmen:

"Don't lose sight of the land!"

The following day, the source of the mysterious lights was revealed. The news was sent to Shimabara Castle by fast horse and boat.

Around the same time Chief Counselor Okamoto Shinbei's boat was heading north past the strange lights, the main Christian leaders from Amakusa and Shimabara were rowing unlit boats to Yushima, an isolated island about five miles from the shore of both areas. Nisuke was one of several leaders from Kuchinotsu on the boats. According to a letter from Juan, their first joint meeting to plan the rebellion was to be held that night. As the sea breeze blew over him, Nisuke reflected, *So this is how it begins.*

As the boats carrying the band of rebel samurai from Kita Arima headed for Yushima, they, too, saw the lights burning on the Shimabara mainland.

"Look!"

Holding back their pent-up feelings, they all gazed in silence.

"Those torches—they're heading to Sankichi's place. I hope nothing happens up there tonight," Sashiki Sakuzaemon groaned.

"I'm worried about that too," Matsushima Sadonokami replied. "For the past five or six days, more and more people have been going up there to pray. When I walked the pathways around Sankichi's house I saw many people sitting quietly, knee to knee, waiting their turn to enter the shrine in the woodshed. If you include all the people spilling onto the village roads, there must have been five or six hundred of them."

"How do you suppose they heard about it?"

"And they came not only from along the seacoast, but from inland, too, from villages like Obama and Kushiyama, crossing over the mountains with their families."

"They had to show themselves in public to do it, too."

"I suppose the local governor's office will get wind of this soon. I imagine it's already been reported. Given that Counselor Okamoto has been inspecting the whole Minan region, they must already know something's going on. But just look at all those lights. There must be twice as many as last night."

"Sado-dono, there can be no stopping what the farmers are doing. Juan-dono from Kuchinotsu has told us to keep Sankichi under control, and I've often cautioned him and the others not to act too boldly, but the fire has already spread to the dry grass, and now no one can put it out."

Cross-waves hit their boat, sending sea foam high in the air. Wiping their faces with their sleeves, the men kept their eyes fixed on the lines of fire receding into the distance. Someone shouted:

"Those are the farmers' signal fires, going up to Heaven!"

"When the time for action comes, the farmers move faster than we samurai."

"They put their bodies into it instead of endlessly thinking. We'd better stop dragging our feet."

Listening to the conversation on the boat, Sadonokami said brusquely, "That's why we're gathering tonight. Everyone—are you ready?"

Suddenly, the dark shadow of Yushima Island rose up in front of them.

They stepped onto the wet rocks of the harbor and walked up to the home of the village leader.

One of the men asked, "What kind of person is Masuda Shirō? I'm really looking forward to meeting him."

In the discussions the night before, they had agreed to ask Shirō to serve as leader of the rebellion. Their decision had been prompted by a few brief words from Sadonokami:

"When a young leader appears like a blossom floating in a clear blue sky, we should receive it as a sign of God's blessing for success in our cause."

Yushima Island sat between Arima and Ōyano Island, as if dividing the Hayasaka Straits in two. It was home to just under twenty families. It had a good harbor and friendly people, so traders and fishermen often stopped there.

In the dimly lit home of the island's headman, the Christians squinted to see who was present and pricked their ears to hear each other's thoughts and plans.

The former retainers of Lord Konishi in the Amakusa region were surprised to learn the extent of the resentment the former retainers of Lord Arima in the Shimabara region held toward the present Matsukura clan. The former Konishi retainers had also lost their stipends and had been stripped of their status as samurai, and they shared the same grudges; yet there was a subtle difference in the histories of the two groups.

Although the local samurai in Amakusa had been retainers of the Konishi clan, they had only received stipends for a little over ten years. However, in the case of the Arima fief on the Shimabara Peninsula, there had been a long history of strife with the Ōmura and Ryūzō clans. The Matsukura clan had entered the Shimabara Peninsula as outsiders, on behalf of the Yamato central government.

In addition, the Shimabara region had a tragic history of gruesome persecution of Christians. In light of the horrendous treatment the former Arima vassals had received at the hands of the Matsukura father and son, their deeper and more lasting resentment was understandable. In contrast, the Amakusa samurai had long been divided into five smaller areas that were governed according to the so-called "Five Amakusa Groups" system. Their bonds with the Konishi clan had been weak. However, when Lord Terasawa came in from Karatsu after the fall of the Konishi clan, there had also been resentment.

But the current problem isn't about these animosities and hostilities, Masuda Jinbei thought as he gazed at each of the faces in the dim light. *Their pride as samurai won't get them anywhere now. Among the men here tonight, many are simply farmers. What is crucial now is that each of us overcome considerations of status and position and join together with a burning sincerity as Christians, like one great pillar of fire.*

As Shirō listened to the earnest talk, from time to time he made eye contact with Ukon, seated diagonally across from him. It was their first chance to meet in some time.

As the urgent discussions continued, Ukon, in his usual manner, carefully recorded their comments, and so a large candle had been placed at his side. In the flickerings of its light and shadow, his sedate, refined looks were impressive, like those of a statue. He reminded Shirō of a slender bodhisattva. *Perhaps it's thanks to Ukon's presence that I feel at ease now, even in a place and time like this.*

And, come to think of it, just before in the darkness outside, I was surprised to hear that familiar voice greet me. When I looked carefully, I realized it was Takematsu, the famous drinker. At first I thought he'd simply followed Ukon again. But then I realized, even if he's a drinker and he can't read, the fact that he's here tonight may mean that his special talents and character are starting to be recognized.

"Thank you so much for coming."

Takematsu seemed embarrassed at being greeted so politely by Shirō.

"Well, actually, I'm here tonight because I was asked to help out with the cooking."

Takematsu was known not only for his skill as a diver but also for his talent in preparing his catch. So perhaps what he said was true.

The lines of fire on Shimabara that Shirō had seen were still burning in his eyes. According to reports from the Arima group, the reputation of the shrine at Sankichi's place had been spreading day by day and worshipers visited it at all hours. The Arima group was prepared for the government's intervention and knew it was a matter of time until they would have to put the rebellion into motion; their flags, rifles, swords, spears and other materials were ready. Shirō recalled Sankichi's serious expression when he was baptized.

Sankichi and Kakunai had brought him the ashes of their martyred fathers, wrapped in tattered cloth. They said they had been keeping their fathers' remains until an appropriate person could recite an *oratio* for them. The two young men's eyes had filled with tears.

It was the first time Shirō had faced the ashes of a martyr. Naturally feeling tense, he had recited an *oratio* that he was still learning and, at the request of the two men, had taught them how to conduct the rites of baptism. Sankichi and Kakunai said there were tens—or, rather, hundreds—of others who wanted to be baptized. *Those two men, their transformation clear even in their faces, went home and ignited the fire that is burning all along the banks of the peninsula across the water. It seems the people are becoming signal fires, starting with Sankichi and Kakunai, and one after another, they're lighting the way.*

Juan's deep voice pulled Shirō from his ponderings back to the present.

"We've discussed just about everything regarding the situation in the villages and coastal areas, and the preparations we need to make. But there's one thing we haven't yet talked about, and that's our commander in this battle. The people from Amakusa have already made their decision, I believe. And the groups from Shimabara are of the same mind as those in Amakusa. And so, our leader—"

When Juan paused, the rippling of conversation suddenly ceased and the group became tense.

"As I hardly need tell you, this struggle will be different from any other in this world. This will mark the start of a battle for our Lord Chirisuto, who will appear among us again. We all know the names of many leaders of past battles, and some of you are here now among us. However, the commander who will lead our army of farmers will not be a usual one. Unless our commander is the servant of God who has come down from Heaven to act as our leader in this struggle, our task will be most difficult."

There was one listener—crossing and uncrossing his legs impatiently—who seemed particularly impatient for Juan to announce the chosen commander's name. About to call out to Juan, his mouth was half open.

Juan turned toward Matsushima Sadonokami of Kita Arima.

"Sado-dono, would you tell us your thoughts?"

From the dim back of the room, Sadonokami looked out at the gathering, his eyes shining like those of a crab poking out from the shadows of a cliff.

"We in Kita Arima have already decided. Masuda Shirō Tokisada-dono is God's servant. We look to him as our leader. There is no one else for this task but him."

A stir rose up among the many people who had grown impatient from waiting.

"Yes! Our leader will be Shirō-sama!"

"This brings me great happiness. Nothing could please me more," Umeo Shichibei, headman of Kōtsuura, said, his voice choked with tears.

Jinbei waited for the commotion to settle and then asked permission to speak.

"I thank you all for your good wishes; however, my son is still young and he is not qualified to be the commander of a rebellion. He isn't well-informed about worldly affairs and it would be far beyond his ability to lead a battle. In our Shimabara groups, we have many with experience in fighting on battlefields. We also have among us the religious elders Juan-dono, Matsushima-dono and Ninagawa-dono, do we not?"

"We understand your concerns, but Shirō-dono's duty will not be that of a warrior," Juan answered quickly. "Among our Arima group, there are quite a few old samurai with battle experience, and in the groups from Amakusa it's much the same. You yourself were a Konishi retainer and surely acquired military skills. If you look around, you will see we have no lack of military leaders, but we're all more or less the same. Telling you this is like teaching a fish to swim, Jinbei-dono, but in this rebellion, our military strategies and tactics aren't the main concern. Rather, it is our commitment as Christians of the Western Shore that will decide this fight. And who among us can summon this passion? No one other than Shirō-dono. The proof is in the commotion we heard just a few moments ago."

Jinbei said nothing.

"Jinbei-dono, you have to make a decision at this critical juncture," Denbei said sympathetically. "Shirō-dono has already been chosen by our Lord. As you said long ago, he is partly your child, and partly not your child."

Filled with difficult emotions, Jinbei hesitated. The fact that people had come to look up to Shirō as a servant of God accorded with the plans he had in mind, and he accepted the saintly nature of his son even though it kept him at a distance. Yet he remained reluctant for him take on the leadership position because of his concern for the Shimabara group, and compassion for his son, who was only sixteen.

The entire gathering fell completely silent.

Taking this pause as an opening to speak, Sadonokami said emphatically, "I'd like to speak to all the people from Amakusa once more. We from Shimabara have chosen Masuda Shirō as our leader. If anyone has an objection, I ask you to speak up."

A general excitement spread throughout the room. Together, everyone raised their fists, and the tatami mats creaked.

With his eyes shut, Shirō looked like a solitary white sea god standing on a reef. The hair on his forehead looked wet in the candlelight. The sound of waves constantly breaking on the rocky coast of the small island surrounded them.

Shirō opened his eyes. His face marked with agony, he asked, "Would you mind opening the shutters?"

Surprised by his voice, the people sitting near the windows stood quickly and opened the shutters. A sea breeze blew in, freshening the air inside the room that had become stale with body heat, and then passed outside and up the slope behind the house. The flames above the candle stands placed around the room flickered and sputtered. With one hand, Shirō drew the nearest big candle stand closer and then, staring at it as if drawing in his gaze tightly around a single point, he blew the candle out in one breath.

"Would you please put out the other candles too?" he said. In the dim light, his voice carried well.

Pale moonlight filtered into the room. Beyond the dark rolling sea, around Mount Hidake on Ōyano Island, a thin, clear sliver of moon was rising in the sky. In the yard around the meeting house, shadows scurried about in silence. The islanders who had worked so hard to prepare fish and shellfish for the visitors were now setting out straw mats in the yard to seat them.

The gentle sound of waves breaking along the island's coast seemed to reverberate in their knees. It was a small island, just over two square miles in area. Southern banyan trees served as natural buttresses protecting its embankments. In the daylight, the exotic red flowers of tiger's claw trees shone brightly. With bated breath, everyone waited for Shirō to speak.

"Tonight, under the stars of the arching sky, our ark, chosen by Heaven, is floating over the sea. With all of you, I bless this ark of Yushima."

The first time Shirō had come to Yushima, at the request of the people of this island of only eighteen households, he had spoken to them about Noah's Ark and told them the story of the destruction and revival of the world. The islanders now thought of their island as the ark that would carry their hopes as fellow-Christians. His words evoked among them that image.

For the others, Shirō's unexpected metaphor struck them powerfully and they raised their heads.

"As you know well, at the time of the great flood, the people who escaped on the ark that Noah built went on to start the next world of humans. For us now, as Christians, there is no way we can continue living in this present world, and so we are about to meet the end of this world. On this evening we have pledged to work together, and this island of Yushima is the ark carrying our hopes. We believe in the Second Coming of our Lord, and on this night, as we prepare ourselves to set off to the garden of the battlefield, I, Shirō, inexperienced though I am, call on Santiago, patron saint of war, and enshrine him on this ark."

Standing, Shirō concentrated on his prayer, overflowing with pathos. The entire room became a space of silent prayer.

"Everyone, Santiago, the patron saint of warfare, has now come down to our battlefield. He has granted us fortune in our struggle."

He paused for a moment, and then continued.

"Look at the moon over Mount Hidake. We can see the moon wherever we are in this world; however, the moon tonight is not a usual one. In this noble, slender moon I can see the body of Maria-sama. She is looking down on us with compassion, as we have experienced all the sufferings of this world and are now taking up our swords and beginning our struggle, trying to enter the country of God. And even if we should fall in our struggle, she will hold our souls in her arms, just as she did when her beloved Son died on the Cross, and she will restore us to life."

The distant sound of the waves resonated within the pauses in Shirō's voice as he delivered his revelation that transcended words.

In the moonlight, the sea swelled gradually, so that it looked like the land. For a moment, Shirō was silent. When he spoke again, his voice was softer and calmer.

"When Moses led his people, whose spirits had grown so tired, across the desert sands, I imagine that what he saw must have been similar to what we are seeing tonight on the surface of the sea. When he stood on the banks of the sea and prayed, his pursuers at his back, the waters seethed, rose up, and parted, and a passageway was opened, through which his people passed. In the old Christian stories there are many such amazing occurrences."

Shirō turned toward the west and pointed.

"Look at those lights moving on the land over there. Those lines of torchlight stretch from Sukawa to Kita Arima."

"Yes, I see! I can see!"

In the darkness, the congregation strained their eyes toward the flickering light of the distant torches. The wind fluttered over the flat top of the small island.

"As we talked about earlier, those lights are coming from people traveling to the shrine that Sankichi, a farmer in Kita Arima, built in his shed. Those lines of flickering light in the distant darkness are mysterious. Sankichi and the others have set their own bodies on fire and are burning themselves up to make those signal lights. As it was with the passion of the Christians of old, Sankichi and the others are heading for the Kingdom of our Lord, without qualms or confusion. This is the passion of their religion. The intensity of that passion can part the seas and cleave the mountains."

Shirō's voice pierced the night air like a sacred arrow. Ninagawa Ukon stood, as if that voice was lifting him up.

"Hurray! Hurray! Santiago!"

Ukon was astonished to find his own throat crying out the name of a European saint of war. Then a group of men stood at once, raising their fists and roaring out the name Santiago, again and again.

Throughout the island, the plants, cows, dogs, cats, chickens and all the other beings cried out and trembled, while the constellations swept brilliantly around the moon.

After the discussion ended, and just before the meal began, the island headman offered a message of greeting.

"Nothing could be a greater honor than having the distinguished presence of all of you from Amakusa and Shimabara on our island tonight. For many generations, our ancestors have lived on this small island. We are most thankful to hear that, as Shirō-sama tells us, God has chosen this place as the ark that will lead us on to His country. It brings tears to our eyes. We have only eighteen households here, but we are honored to join you in the coming fight."

Speaking with the dignity of a veteran minister of state, the bearded elder held back tears as he concluded his greeting:

"For the past few days, our men have gone out to sea and our women and children have gone down to the shore, and we've brought back all the fish and shellfish we could gather for this meal. We've also prepared a little sake as a token of our gratitude. We hope you will enjoy this banquet for our joyous departure to the fullest."

With deep respect and tears in their eyes, the islanders brought out plates of seafood and placed them in front of their guests. At first, the well-tanned children couldn't understand why the adults were crying, and they looked up at them anxiously, but soon, as pleasant voices began to fill the room, the children broke out into laughter.

Shirō, even more humbled than usual, felt deep ties with the people around him who had provided the place for this evening of discussions. After meeting with the leaders from all the regions, Juan, Sakyō and his son Ukon, and Nisuke and his son Daisuke from Kuchinotsu gathered around him. Their faces filled with emotion, they practically hugged Shirō's shoulders. When Ukon saw the change that had come over Shirō, whom he had always regarded as a younger brother, he was deeply moved. But he couldn't put his feelings in words, so he just smiled quietly with muted shyness.

"When I first heard Ukon-sama yelling out that war cry, it stunned me. It sounded like the roaring of a lion," someone said, and everyone started laughing. It was Takematsu. He was busily passing around food and pouring sake, and he was already tipsy.

The person who had roared like a lion was the same quiet, proper Ukon who gave lectures on Christianity and the *Tale of the Heike*. Usually he spoke clearly and properly, but he had responded to Shirō's talk with a spontaneous bellow that roused the entire gathering. No doubt, it had come naturally from within him, but his affection for Shirō had made it happen. Shirō was glad that Ukon regarded him as a younger brother, and it deepened his sense that this was a person to die with.

Juan gazed at the two young men through half-shut eyes.

"Being alive on this day brightens my many years of sorrow," he said. "Our leader Shirō and Ukon-dono are the flowers of Christianity. We are old soldiers, but to set off to the battlefield with these blossoming young warriors is truly the glory of our lifetime. Hyōgo-dono, both of us are old timers, but in our own ways, let this be our final blossoming."

"Come on now Juan-dono, I'm ten years younger than you—I'm far from an old warrior."

Normally, Kazusa Hyōgo was an awkward speaker, but now, perhaps because he'd been drinking, he spoke with ease.

"I feel a lot lighter now, in body and mind, and a lot younger, too. Going off to battle with like-minded people, and under the protection of an *Espanya* war god, that excites me. My only regret is that I never taught Ukon-dono how to catch crabs. But that will just have to be."

Hyōgo noticed that the two young men were smiling and nodded at them, then turned to the bleary-eyed Takematsu.

"Say there, Takematsu—"

"Who's that calling me?"

"You need to ask who?"

"Ah, it's you—Hyōe, from Kazusa."

"Not Hyōe, Hyōgo."

"All right then, Hyōgo-sama, did you get enough to eat and drink?"

"Maybe not as much as you, but I've had my share of drink."

"Well then, please excuse me."

"Takematsu, this might be a good chance."

"What? Hyōgo-sama, are you going to teach me how to use a sword? My legs are a bit shaky."

His sake cup still in hand, Takematsu attempted to stand, but his legs gave out. Ukon reached out and supported him before he fell.

Hyōgo chided, "Have your legs gotten so weak? You won't be of much use like that. I've been thinking of handing over my secret crab-hunting spots to you, but with legs like that, there's no point."

Ukon, who rarely laughed about such things, watched Takematsu with amusement.

"What secret spots, Hyōgo-sama? Why, I know all about them. Like they say, set a thief to catch a thief. Anyone who knows the shores knows where to find the big crabs."

"Well, maybe so, but since last year, I've been hoping to teach your master Ukon about them."

Hyōgo cast a serious glance at Ukon.

"What? Teach Ukon-sama?"

When Takematsu heard the words "your master," he was greatly pleased. He placed his sake bottle in front of him and sat up straight.

"That's right. I was all set to teach him my secret methods for catching crabs as the finishing touch on his education," Hyōgo said, grabbing a big red crab claw from a plate and holding it up excitedly. The crabs from Yushima Island were considerably larger than those from the Kazusa coast.

Ukon remembered the night of Okayo and Daisuke's wedding, when Hyōgo, Bannai, Juan and others had stopped in at his house. They had talked about how it wasn't enough for him just to study academic things; he had to learn how to catch crabs, too. That was when the real meaning of the words "to eat" had first struck him. He hadn't forgotten, but his plans for becoming Hyōgo's disciple in crab-catching had been put on hold while they set up the school. He pressed his hands solemnly on the floor.

"Please excuse my rudeness. You offered me the chance to learn such important secrets, and I intended to do it, but I've been so disorganized and caught up in studying the Christian books. As a result, I didn't have the chance to receive proper training from you. Please forgive me."

Ukon apologized so much that the people around him sighed tensely.

"No need for apologies. You're suited to reading. As for catching crabs, that's our line of work. Right, Takematsu?"

"Right. If we teach Ukon where to find crabs, he'll probably go there and teach them how to read. But, Hyōgo-sama, to tell the truth, I, Takematsu . . . ."

Feigning ignorance, Takematsu glanced at Chijiiwa Bannai, who had been quietly slurping down the innards from a crab shell at his seat beside Hyōgo.

"Hey, Bannai-sama."

Takematsu was being unusually sociable. *This must be a great night for him*, Bannai thought, looking up at him.

"Actually, I've been meaning to tell you something, and tonight I don't want to miss the chance," Takematsu continued, swaying back and forth.

The people around him were concerned about how drunk he was. But they need not have worried, for, just as his head seemed about to droop down, he turned it toward Shirō and asked in a dignified manner:

"Shirō-sama, if a person confesses the things he's done in all honesty, is it true that Maria-sama will forgive him?"

"Have you done something wrong?"

Shirō had been wanting to talk with Takematsu, but when he had tried, he had found him strangely sensitive. Takematsu smiled bashfully.

"Well, actually, I've been going out at night to Hyōgo's secret crab holes and taking them," he said in one breath.

"So *that's* what's been going on! This year it's seemed there were only little ones out there—like their growth had fallen off. You lout!"

"Forgive me, forgive me, Hyōgo-sama. I did it for Ukon-sama's school. Ukon-sama and all the young people have been working for the future of our religion. I, the unworthy Takematsu, wanted to do something to help . . ."

Takematsu looked up with a pointed expression.

"I've launched night attacks on Hyōgo-sama's secret headquarters. I grabbed the crabs and threw them down and twisted off their heads—I mean their claws—and raised an advance cry of victory."

Takematsu's eyes became glassy.

"My arms may be thin and weak, but when it comes to the battle in the sea, those Matsukura samurai are no match for me. Me and the other divers along the coast will kick the asses of those cowards who pour in from Yamato. Shirō-sama, my commander, let me take care of the sea. I can round up two or three hundred men with harpoons any time you need us."

Takematsu was trying to show off, but as he sat there, his eyes narrowed like crescent moons, and then, smiling absent-mindedly, he drifted off to sleep.

As he slumped down, Nisuke and his son lifted him and were about to move him to a less crowded space, but everywhere they looked was crowded with people.

"It'll be all right, don't you think?" Shirō suggested. "He's sleeping happily right there." The people around him made space for

Takematsu to lie stretched among them. A woman brought in a wooden pillow and slipped it under his head. He began to snore. Juan gazed at his sleeping face.

"If you imagine his snoring is the soughing of the wind in a pine forest, it's quite poetic."

Takematsu was breathing peacefully. Everyone looked affectionately at his sleeping face.

"What do you say, Daisuke? Why don't we just carry him on our backs to the boat. He looks pretty light," Nisuke said thoughtfully.

For how many more nights might people sleep in this house? Nisuke had become acutely aware of how things were changing. *Perhaps the fate of all things, from the destiny of humans to the stirring of the plants, was decided long, long ago. In my farming and in my faith, I've always lived as if I were putting down roots in the earth; but now here I am with my son, meeting in the middle of the night on a small island to plot a war. I never expected this, but my life must have been destined to end like this. I've wanted to talk about these things with Shirō-sama, who's sitting in front of me now.*

We humans love things of beauty. We're always hoping to meet beautiful spirits. Such people are right here in front of me. With them, my dreams in the afterlife will be good ones.

As if urged on by something, Nisuke looked up at the moon.

"It was a fine banquet, wasn't it?" Daisuke remarked.

From time to time, they could see the heaving of the waves. To Nisuke, Takematsu's breath as he slept and the pressing winds of war seemed to be coming together as one.

"Deus-sama has called upon our family, and the family of the Yushima village chief, too, to carry out essential responsibilities. It was all decided ages ago. For father and son to be called together to this duty is a divine blessing."

His son looked up at the moon silently and nodded. He placed his hand on the shoulder of his father, who was slightly shorter than he.

Everyone listened carefully for the incoming tide. Before long, it would be time to send off the boats. Here and there, people joined hands and exchanged words to reaffirm the bonds among them.

Deep in thought, Juan stood up and gazed at the group.

"Soon the tide will be high. We are reluctant to leave, but the time has come to head out in our boats. May the things we have agreed upon this night be inscribed in our hearts, and may we never betray them."

Among the people gathered on the rocky shore where the boats were tied, Matsushima Sadonokami's tall figure stood out. Sadonokami turned away from the boats to face the others, as if overcome by emotion. His rough beard swayed in the night breeze.

"People of Yushima, as our leader said earlier, this is a special island. It's an ark that will carry us to the land where we will be reborn. I believe this is the truth. Your hospitality tonight will remain deep in our hearts. Seeing your pure faces and reverent manners, I felt this must have been what faith and love were like back when Chirisuto-sama and Maria-sama were in the world. With Shirō-sama's guidance, I've come to remember the things I had forgotten and lost. We samurai from Arima, our mirror of *anima* had become rusted. Tonight, the fog has been cleared away.

"While we were fussing around, talking about a rebellión without ever acting, we almost forgot the people of our villages who were waiting to go up to *Paraizo*. People of Yushima, we from Arima will take up our swords for people like you, who have such beautiful souls. This is the joy of our new tomorrow.

"People of Yushima, Ōyano, Kōtsuura, Shimotsuura, Senzoku Zōzō Island and Sumoto, let us meet again on the field of battle."

Amidst cries of "Santiago!" the mooring lines were drawn back into the boats. The branches of banyan trees chafed against the ropes, their fragrance floating over the waves that caught the first rays of dawn.

Under the guise of fishing, the people from Miyazu rowed quickly back to Ōyano Island. To those watching from Arima, Arie, and Fukae, it seemed unusual that so many small, fast boats from Shimabara should be out on the water.

When those with relatives in Arima arrived back on the Shimabara shore and asked what had been happening there, they were met with worried expressions. Late the night before, they learned, thirty or more samurai from Shimabara Castle had raided

Sankichi's shrine and arrested him and his mother, along with ten or so others from Minami Arima who happened to be there, including Kakunai and some other men and women of different ages. As usual, a large number of people had gathered to worship, and the officials had questioned them and raided the homes of Sankichi's and Kakunai's relatives.

The officials had thrashed people at random with their clubs, yelling, "Are you so inspired by that barbarian heresy? Defying the prohibition is absolutely unpardonable. You may as well consider yourselves dead!"

They had torn down the sacred painting, ripped it to shreds, and trampled it again and again. People recounted all of this, trembling as they spoke.

Everyone was worried about those who had been taken away. They would have to meet to discuss how to get them back. If this should lead to a battle, perhaps the pilgrims from Amakusa would help them. They talked distractedly, but weren't able to stay gathered together for long because government boats were passing up and down along the shore.

For the past week or so, day and night, people had been traveling back and forth from the mountains to the sea and from the sea to the mountains, their heads in the clouds; they had already abandoned their normal way of life. Searching for their still-unseen God, their spirits had begun to float away from their bodies. When they finally found their way to the chapel at Sankichi's place, the pilgrims had been told that they could receive holy water. In the evening, they had waited in line, holding torches. They had sat in the chilled evening air, listening to the sound of the waves. The light from the immense number of torches seemed terribly precious. Joining their voices with those of Sankichi and Kakunai, the ones in front had begun reciting an *oratio,* and then, little by little, others had joined in and repeated the short verses over and over, until all were pulled into an ineffable state of rapture.

People had cast off their farm clothes, and throughout the villages everyone had arranged to meet in this place, leaving their homes almost empty. They had come after leaving behind all the troubles of this world. *Paraizo*, the pure land promised by the foreigners, seemed close at hand.

Everyone was well aware that Sankichi and his mother, and his friend Kakunai were the surviving family members of martyrs.

"After all, it looks like whatever they've been possessed by is real."

While everyone was pressed together, feeling each other's warmth and whispering together, the government officials had made their raid. Sankichi and his mother were pushed out in front of the others and tied up with thick straw ropes. They put up no resistance. Lit up by the jostling lights of the torches, their faces had looked joyful.

"All of you—we'll go first."

They had looked so calm and self-possessed that, for a while, people were left in a daze. Watching them as they were led away along with their relatives toward the place by the dock where the officials were assembled, the people's rapture finally cooled and they moved toward the beach like a surging wave. Then, in a flash, the boat carrying Sankichi and the other captives was gone.

"Now it's going to start," those who returned from the Yushima meeting told the others. That was on the twenty-fifth day of the tenth month of the year. On the morning of the following day, a fast boat arrived from Arima carrying a circulating notice from Yama Zenemon, from Senzoku Island, and the Arima Village leader Sashiki Sazaemon. At the Yushima meeting, Sazaemon had explained in detail the activities of Sankichi and those around him. Zenemon had been sent to the meeting by Masuda Jinbei and others who were worried about the urgent situation in Arima. Their message described a grave state of affairs:

> *This is an urgent announcement. Today, Hayashi Hyōzaemon, the magistrate of this village, was beaten to death here for opposing Deus-sama. Masuda Shirō, our messenger from God, has taught us that killing is a grave matter. However, in the current circumstances, we must order you to put to death every last one of the heretics, starting with the village magistrates. This is the time when the Last Judgement is to be put into effect throughout the entire land of Japan. It is imperative that we, at last, as members of one religion, be steadfast in enforcing this judgment.*

Further details will be issued when we meet, and we have sent notices to all the villages.

Sashiki Sazaemon
Yama Zenemon
25th day, 10th month

After reading the notice, Shirō thought, *Well, at last, it's started.* In silence, he handed it to Watanabe Kozaemon, who was seated next to him. The words "we must order you to put to death every last one of the heretics" had not been among the things they had decided at the meeting two nights ago. That sentiment must have been sparked by the killing of the magistrate.

According to the people on the fast boat, Magistrate Hayashi had been killed the day before. It had happened after Sankichi and the others were arrested, and after the villagers had met and put up a painting of the Lord. When Magistrate Hayashi heard about the unrest, he headed toward the place they were gathered and was killed by the outraged villagers.

One after another, fast boats from Shimabara arrived at Shirō's headquarters in Miyazu on Ōyano Island. Magistrates were being killed in Kushiyama, Kazusa, Kita Arima, Fukae and other villages in that part of Shimabara. Already, ten had been murdered. It seemed that no one could put an end to the killings. Shirō was struck with a vision of a cyclone wrapping itself around a column of gigantic black flames and descending on the sea, sucking him up and swirling him about, upside down.

Watanabe Kozaemon greeted Shirō and his father.

"So, finally, it's started. I'm going to bring your mother and grandmother and sister back from Ebe right away. On my way there, I'll call on the commissioner in Sumoto and see if I can get him to help us."

Kozaemon's expression was grave.

Since the consecration of the church in Miyazu, Jinbei and Shirō hadn't had time to see their family in Ebe. Given the critical state of affairs, Shirō didn't want to leave his mother and grandmother, and his elder sister who was visiting them, in the village of Ebe in Uto, which was in the Hosokawa domain. Kozaemon had offered to bring them back, since Shirō and Jinbei could not leave the headquarters. Shirō's elder sister was married to Kozaemon's younger brother.

"I should have taken care of this earlier, but my plans fell through, so I must apologize for asking you to go in my place," Jinbei said, bowing deeply. Everyone understood that in these circumstances Jinbei could no longer leave the headquarters.

"Tell them we can't wait to see them!" someone called out. Kozaemon turned and smiled.

"I'll bring them back safe and sound."

"It's a lot of trouble for you. Take care, my brother, and look out for the Hosokawa forces who are watching the coast."

As he bowed respectfully, apprehension welled up in Shirō's chest. He felt the vision of the strange cyclone returning. He shook his head, trying to rid himself of the image. With some other family members, he accompanied Kozaemon as far as the shore, where they boarded a small boat.

"We'll be back in three days," someone said.

"Three days? We don't even know what will happen tomorrow."

None of them, including Shirō, had any premonition that this would be the last time they would see each other.

That evening, Shirō and his father received a letter from Kozaemon, written in Sumoto.

I'm writing this in haste. I just spoke with Ishihara Tarōzaemon-dono, the Sumoto commissioner. I argued with him head-to-head, but I couldn't get him to help me. Even after pleading with him as a family member, it came to nothing. And since Tarōzaemon didn't agree with us, it seems the number of our supporters here may not be as great as we believed. However, we have a rather enthusiastic group and, gradually, they should join us. I'll go on to Ebe tomorrow and quickly prepare a boat to take back your mother Oine-sama and your sister and the whole family."

The Karatsu clan had divided the Amakusa Islands into three regions and had chosen one samurai from each area to serve as commissioner. One of them, the Sumoto Commissioner Ishihara Tarōsaemon, was married to Kozaemon's younger sister.

By the time Kozaemon and his party arrived in Uto, the situation in Shimabara had changed rapidly.

On the day the Arima magistrate Hayashi Hyōzaemon was killed in Minan, all thirteen villages in the southern half of the Shimabara peninsula had suddenly risen up in rebellion. These included Nakakoba, near Shimabara Castle, and Fukae, some three leagues beyond it, along with other villages along the coast of the Ariake Sea: Futsu, Mie, Dōsaki, Arie, Kita Arima, Minami Arima, Kuchinotsu and Kazusa. As the unrest boiled over, the rebellion had spread northward along the coast of Chijiwa Bay to Kushiyama, Obama and Chijiwa. People had declared openly that they were returning to Christianity, reciting the *Yaso Sutra*, the Hymn of Jesus Christ, as they rose up.

The Shimabara authorities were in shock to learn of the murder of Magistrate Hayashi, and with every ensuing report, their astonishment deepened. Starting with Yasui Saburōemon in Kuchinotsu, murders continued throughout the region. Shinto shrines and Buddhist temples were burned and their monks and priests killed. Believers captured and crucified officials and Buddhist monks and buried them alive or decapitated them, after dragging their bodies through the villages with horses—just as had been done to the Christians in the past.

When evening came, the government sent Okamoto Shinbei and Taga Shusui as commanders of a fleet of twenty boats headed for Arima. But since all the rowers were Christians, word was leaked to the Christian headquarters:

"The agreement made on Yushima Island is now being put to good use. Seeing those officials in such a frenzy was quite a sight. We set off for Arima, and after we'd rowed about two leagues and were near Futsu, the officials could see the fires burning on the land. We were excited, wondering if they were temples or officials' buildings that were burning; but the samurai stood up at once. It seemed that people had lit fires in all directions, and the land glimmered with flames and light from their torches. The reflection of the endless flames on the waves was truly magnificent.

"The samurai gnashed their teeth and stared ferociously at us rowers. They seemed to have noticed we weren't surprised at all . . .

"And then there was a big discussion on the boat. Some of them thought they should go up onto the land and start fighting, but others said no, they should be patient and wait, since to land and fight with such small numbers against the people who were prepared and eagerly waiting would surely lead to their dying like dogs—and, in any case, they should go to Arima and investigate the situation. Finally, a few words from Okamoto Shinbei settled the argument."

According to the boatman, Chief Counselor Okamoto had said to them:

"All those fires—that's no small matter. They might be able to attack close to the castle. We'd better get back right away."

Okamoto had reasoned that, if the attackers had already gotten inside the castle, they would have seen an explosion from the gunpowder in the main keep, but since that hadn't happened, the castle must still be all right. The samurai were reassured by this explanation, but it showed that Okamoto himself had been quite confused, and for a moment had imagined the worst possible scenario.

Chief Counselor Okamoto and his men were able to make it back to Shimabara Castle in part because they happened upon an unexpected person out at sea.

While debating what to do, they had been approached by a small boat. When they called out to it, they learned it was carrying Honma Kurozaemon, the magistrate of Kita Arima.

According to Honma, one of the peasants—a man he had helped out in the past—had told him that the farmers were planning to kill him, and warned him to escape quickly. He had just barely gotten away. He had taken one of the small boats left along the shore by people from Amakusa who had come over to pay homage to the sacred picture at Sankichi's place.

"Arima is already in the hands of the Christians. Around the place called Kitaoka, they're waiting with eight hundred or more rifles. We're no match for numbers like that. We all need to get back to Shimabara Castle as soon as possible and take measures to defend ourselves."

Perhaps joyful at having escaped the clutches of death, Honma Kurozaemon did not conceal his excitement.

Okamoto's fleet of twenty boats rowed hard toward Shimabara Castle. Here and there along the shores, fires were burning and people were carrying lighted torches. It was impossible to distinguish allies from enemies, so it seemed unwise to call out to them. At last, they made it back to the harbor by the castle.

Before they moored their boats at the dock, they ran into further trouble. In anticipation of their return, numerous lights had been set up around the docks. When they saw all the lights, they feared it could mean that the castle town was already occupied by the enemy. They hesitated to enter the harbor and dock their boats. Finally, a small boat was sent out to them from the coast, and Okamoto's men learned what was going on.

As they walked from the harbor up into the castle town of Shimabara, they found it strangely dark. Usually, on special occasions, people lit lanterns; however, the town now was completely silent and lightless. What had actually happened was that, while Okamoto's boats were out on the Arima Sea, the authorities had taken some Christians hostage and put them in the castle. Non-Christian families had also put their women and children inside the castle for protection, so the whole town outside the castle was mostly deserted. In the past few days, some families had even gathered up all their household goods and sent them off on boats.

When Okamoto's group entered the office of the magistrate, they found the leaders of the castle town gathered there. The moment they saw Okamoto's face, they said, "We must be strong allies in this situation, so we ask you to lend us some weapons."

Okamoto didn't fully trust these people, since they had previously been Christians.

"I can't do that," Okamoto replied curtly.

The leaders countered that if he didn't trust them, he could take hostages from their families. And so, it was decided that Okamoto would put the wives and children of the local leaders in the castle and provide the men with guns and spears to protect the town. Already, the sky was beginning to turn light.

The rebel forces had set up bases in the homes of village headmen. They had also hidden some of their soldiers in the nearby mountains, woods and bamboo thickets they knew so well. They drew the Shimabara clan forces nearer and repulsed their attacks, broke through vital checkpoints and barriers, and gradually made their way toward Shimabara Castle.

During the early stages, it was often difficult to tell enemies from allies, and even when they met people whom they had known well enough in regular life, it was hard to be assured of complete safety. An incident happened in which, pretending to be a Matsukura ally, Genemon, the powerful leader of Mie, a village north of the castle, had led a group of thirty or more rebels into the castle and had been carrying out missions and conducting secret communications with other rebel forces. But because some monks and their followers from a temple in Mie had also been inside the castle, their scheme was exposed. Sano Yashichizaemon, one of Matsukura's vassals, left an account of what had happened. It was dated the twenty-seventh of the tenth month.

The monks and their believers told us in secret about the situation, so I managed to summon the farmers' groups, and they came in and laid down their weapons. Shinbei said that people who were loyal had come in even from distant places and that they had tried to get into the castle quickly. He criticized people from the nearby villages for arriving late and said it was suspicious. The believers made all sorts of unsuitable remarks, like a bunch of crows fighting. When the samurai leader announced, "You're all going to be executed," the rebel farmers stood up suddenly and tried to grab their hatchets and swords, but they were held back by the samurai guards. They ran around, outraged that their scheme had been exposed. They were chased down and killed to the last man.

In Sano's account, the name "Shinbei" referred to Chief Counselor Okamoto.

Apparently, in addition to Genemon and his followers, many other farmers from Mie had entered the castle falsely claiming to be on the Matsukura side. After their scheme was exposed, some of them were able to flee the castle and meet with other rebels—after having taken with them sixty stolen rifles, spears and other arms. The written account stated that upwards of two hundred villagers from Mie were executed in the castle, and that their heads had been publicly displayed on gibbets.

Doubts remained about the loyalties of some people who had worked for a while inside the castle. Driven by these doubts and fears, the government officials killed anyone they deemed suspicious and tossed their bodies out. At the time, some thirty blacksmiths summoned from local villages were in the castle. The officials looked into their background and, using information from their home villages, determined that all of them had reconverted to Christianity. And so, on the twenty-seventh of the month, the officials executed them all. Not knowing who to trust, the Matsukura samurai began to panic, but in the end, they eliminated all the traitors inside the castle and strengthened their defenses. Their success was attributed to the careful arrangements made by Chief Counselor Okamoto.

Sankichi, Kakunai and the fourteen other people arrested with them were also executed on the twenty-seventh day of the tenth month. Sankichi's mother was of course among them.

It remained difficult to distinguish allies from enemies for a number of days. Early on the morning of the twenty-sixth, Counselors Tanaka Shōfu and Taga Shusui were appointed as field commanders. They led an army of about five hundred soldiers as far as the bridge in the village of Imamura and sent an emissary to the village of Antoku to deliver a message:

"Is Antoku our ally or our enemy? Depending on your reply, we may have to advance with our troops and crush you."

However, the headman of Antoku Village was away in Fukae checking on the situation there, so the emissaries took his brother and the village subleader back to the castle as hostages. In other words, the officials were in considerable confusion over the fundamental question of which villages to target as enemies and where to send their troops.

Okamoto rushed to the scene, most likely because he was worried about Tanaka Shōfu's ability to command. It was decided that Shōfu would return to the defend the castle, while Okamoto reorganized the forces and advanced as far as the plains of Fukae. But even then, he was unable to determine who the enemies were. So Okamoto summoned the headman and leaders of Nakakoba Village, between Fukae and Antoku, and ordered them to try to convince the headman of Fukae to join his forces.

The Nakakoba headman delivered a message from Okamoto to the Fukae headman:

"Because you have served the clan up to this point, if you continue to be our ally, we will save your life."

The Fukae headman replied:

"The situation has changed, and we cannot be your ally."

"And how has it changed? I have not forgotten how everyone begged to renounce their faith after your forebear refused and was thrown into a roasting cage and burned to death. How can you join this rebellion after that happened?" the Nakakoba headman said, sighing.

"We have heard the word of Heaven directly from Shirō-sama. There can be no defying it. We want to work earnestly to establish a Christian country. Thank you for delivering the message to us, but please don't come again. If you do come again, our answer will be the same."

There was no point in the Nakakoba headman saying anything more. Disappointed, he returned to Okamoto.

It was about mid-day, and word had come in that rebel forces were in a field in Fukae called Hirohata. In haste, Okamoto led his troops there. The rebel forces, scattered across the open field, started to shoot at them with their rifles. Okamoto held back, waiting for the enemy to discharge its ammunition and need to reload. When he judged that the moment was right, he ordered his troops to fire, charging the nervous rebels.

The rebel forces were immediately thrown into confusion and scattered. The castle troops chased down and killed eighty-five rebel soldiers. Some of the rebels, however, stood their ground and kept firing, resulting in heavy injuries and deaths among Okamoto's troops, including his artillery commander.

While Okamoto's troops were taking a break, four or five farmers appeared from the nearby pine woods.

"To repay the kindness you've always shown us, we've left our wives and children behind and come to join your forces," one said. "You should know that some rebels have gathered in the house of the village headman of Fukae and are waiting there. We'll show you a secret path to get there without being seen by the rebels."

Pleased, Okamoto ordered, "Have our men on horses dismount and we'll all advance in silence. The rebels may have soldiers hidden in the bushes along the way, so we'll have to be careful. They outnumber us, so if we do run into them, it will be a tough fight and we mustn't lose our concentration."

At the time, Okamoto was impressively attired in a helmet decorated with ox horns, but the other men had thrown on their armor haphazardly and could hardly have been said to make an imposing impression. In an effort to compensate, Sano Yaeshichizaemon had cut some nearby bamboo for a pole and hastily fashioned a banner.

The troops marched along behind the farmers. Eventually, they arrived at a large residence surrounded by a dry moat. According to the guides, this was the home of the Fukae headman, and quite a large number of people appeared to have gathered inside. Beyond the moat was an old stone wall, about five feet high, covered with ivy. Beyond that was a thick grove of bamboo, softly rustling in the wind. The circumference looked to be about 250 yards. An old bridge spanning the dry moat was the only entrance. An eerie silence hung about the residence. The restless foot soldiers advanced uneasily. Okamoto, thinking such behavior improper, shouted out, "Hurrah!" three times in a battle cry. The foot soldiers, however, only moved their mouths as if chewing on paper, hardly making a sound.

Gnashing his teeth in anger, Okamoto yelled, "You think you're samurai, do you?"

Then, from beyond the bamboo grove, they heard the voices of what sounded like two hundred or so people chanting the *Yaso Sutra*; the Hymn of Jesus. The soldiers thought, *Just as we figured—they've been hiding in there, preparing to defend themselves.* Okamoto jeered at the rebel group and then crossed the bridge. The gate opened with ominous ease. It was unclear whether the people in the bamboo grove were aware of Okamoto's advancing soldiers, but their chanted hymns continued to float softly through the whispering bamboo without the least sense of alarm or disarray. The attackers could see, in addition to the large main house, a storehouse and some sheds, but no sign of people. It sounded as if the hymns were coming from the main house. Strangely, no shots were fired, nor stones thrown from inside the house. Uncertain about what kind of machinations might be awaiting them, Okamoto hesitated as to whether he should attack and break in. After a few moments of careful thought, he made his decision.

"Move 'round to the windward side and torch the place."

Okamoto's soldiers hurried around the yard, and soon the sheds were billowing with flames, which then spread to the thatched roof of the main house. To their surprise, only thirty elderly women emerged from the burning building. When asked what they were doing, they answered that, since they couldn't help with the fighting, they had decided to shut themselves inside and recite *oratio*. They said they had no idea where the headman or any of the others were. They appeared ready to die. Together with the women, there were also three elderly men. Showing no fear of the samurai, they came to the front and spoke, offering their heads:

"We've been Christians since way back. Against our will, we've fallen away from the true teachings, but now we have returned to the faith to die in peace. We wish to be reborn in *Paraizo* soon. So go ahead, get on with your business. Slash away and take our heads, and get your credit for it."

Although Okamoto detested what they had said, he couldn't help being moved by their utter composure. He imagined that, having decided that they could not be of service to their fellow villagers in battle, they had prepared to give up their lives. But when Okamoto saw the look in their eyes as they spoke of *Paraizo*—a look that burned with a fanatic devotion—it repulsed him. Beheading these elderly farmers wouldn't be a proud achievement. His samurai exchanged reluctant glances and watched Okamoto. As if trying to rid his mind of unpleasant thoughts, Okamoto called out his order:

"All right, since that's what they want, take their heads."

Okamoto's soldiers abandoned the executed bodies and moved on. Here and there, they came upon trenches, and in the fields above them, rebels were waiting. The rebels hurled stones and, to everyone's surprise, they even split open Okamoto's ox-horn helmet. But the most they could accomplish was a series of guerrilla attacks, and in the end, they retreated into the mountains, so a real battle never developed. Okamoto's young samurai, fired up with the taste of their first battle, cried out, "Let's chase them down—let's crush them in their bases!" When Okamoto heard this, he ordered them to return to the castle for the present.

Above all, Okamoto was concerned about the lack of clarity surrounding the situation. He was worried that Shimabara Castle might be attacked while he and his men were away, and that they might be made fools of by the enemy, who seemed so elusive. Moreover, he didn't have enough faith in his men. He realized that some of his foot soldiers were related to the rebels. In addition, some had been killed or wounded.

As Okamoto and his troops headed back to the castle, some farmers from Antoku loaded their horses and oxen with luggage and followed after them, holding their children tightly. They hadn't supported the rebel forces and had asked for protection inside the castle. When Okamoto and his men entered the castle town, they found it in an uproar. Having heard the rumors about a rebellion, those who still remained in town were in a state of confusion and panic, and were seeking refuge inside the castle grounds. Looking out from the castle walls, people could see fires raging in distant villages to the south. It appeared that temples and shrines were being swept up in flames. Okamoto could clearly see that the rebellion was swelling like a great tide.

As he had feared, the violence spread quickly to the castle town, where the rebels started to set fires in various places. The soldiers he had sent out as far as Fukae returned to their homes to bathe and eat, but when they saw the fires burning everywhere, they were unnerved and hastily returned to the castle.

Back in the castle, Okamoto assigned tasks to the men who had returned. Above all, he needed to secure the various castle gates; but in addition, the castle's stone walls had been damaged, so he stationed his artillery forces near the breaches in particular. Okamoto's worries were endless. He was haunted by the image of suspicious people appearing among the buildings and in the thickets of trees, which he had been seeing for some time. He wondered if rebel forces had already broken into the inner castle and were waiting to set fires again. Okamoto had his young samurai thoroughly search the castle, and when they found several suspicious men, he had them executed immediately.

While this was going on, a war cry suddenly rose up, as if shaking the heavens and earth. An army of several thousand rebel troops was storming the main castle gate. In front, flags emblazoned with crosses and the words "Lord of Heaven" were being waved about, leading them on, and loud strains of the Hymn of Jesus resounded in the air. The rebels quickly toppled the notice boards proclaiming the prohibition of Christianity and trampled them to bits, then began shooting and making an all-out attack.

At that time, the inner castle was minimally manned, and its main gate was guarded by only eighteen samurai and six rifles, along with some townspeople who had been brought in to assist. The attackers used axes and rods and started to break down the gate, soon making an opening about a yard wide through the doors of the main gate. The Matsukura samurai thrust their spears through the opening and tried to defend themselves with a counterattack. A volley of rifle fire felled some, but still the attackers didn't lose their nerve. Among them were some women. Their disheveled hair tied back with headbands, they set fire to woven rush mats and hurled them into the guard house beside the gate. The castle forces had to pull the mats out, stamp out the fires and hastily mount a defensive strike.

The main gate, however, remained solid and the rebel forces were unable to destroy it. The battle went on for two hours or more, it seemed. Then a commotion broke out among the attackers. The fires they had lit had spread to the houses in front of the main gate and were burning fiercely, such that the attackers, too, were being threatened by the flames. Finally, after raising a war cry, they retreated from the castle gate. They left behind eighty-four bodies.

The rebels also attacked other places around the castle, including the rear gate and the third gate. They fought hard, but in the end, they were barely able to fight off their enemies. The castle forces, too, suffered heavy losses. Some of the samurai who hadn't been able to enter the castle were killed in the town.

After the rebel forces left, the people inside the castle retained a great fear of the ill-equipped, stubbornly determined farmer-soldiers who had made their way over dead bodies while fervently singing their heathen hymns. Reverberating like the moaning of a tsunami, the hymns remained in their ears. It seemed the attackers had no regrets about dying. Of course, the Matsukura samurai, too, had been prepared to lose their lives, but when they saw the intense zeal that was so different from the samurai's customary determination, they felt there was something uncanny about the rebels' spirit and resolve.

The rebels surrounded the castle from a distance, set fire to every one of the Matsukura clan's boats, and then retreated. They hid out in various places, setting up a base in Arima, and from time to time appeared around the castle, showing their high spirits.

With the castle so crowded with people seeking refuge and not even eighty armored samurai stationed inside, it was all the Matsukura forces could do to protect the three gates of the inner keep. They feared it would be difficult to defend the inner keep if it were attacked again. With their scant emergency food rations also running low, Counselors Okamoto, Tanaka and Taga sent out a joint appeal to neighboring domains for assistance.

Starting on the twenty-sixth day of the tenth month, people in the Hosokawa domain noticed signs of something unusual happening across the bay in Shimabara. At the home of Chief Counselor Nagaoka Kenmotsu, while he was playing a game of *go* with a guest, disturbing sounds, like the crackling of distant thunder, were heard from the southwest. Fearing it might be rifle fire, he immediately sent scouts to the seaside. Soon after, a swift messenger arrived from Kojima on the Ariake coast, warning him that fires had been sighted and rifle shots heard coming from Shimabara. On the same day, refugees from Shimabara started to arrive on the coast near Akita. Non-Christians had fled before being forced to escape.

When the Hosokawa clan learned from the refugees what was going on, they sent Michiie Shichirōemon, whose yearly stipend was 300 *koku* of rice, to Shimabara Castle to investigate early on the morning of the twenty-seventh.

When he got into the castle, he heard that the rebel forces were claiming that their uprising was not the work of humans, or of Japanese, but of an angel in Heaven. They were saying that their young leader, named Shirō, had come down from Heaven because God was angry at the Christians for not following the principles of their faith. They claimed that they would soon be taken up to Heaven and that they had seen a vision of a flaming cross above the sea, and that the farmers had bowed down and worshipped it. They had planned their rebellion earlier in the year and had prepared themselves to die, and therefore they had stopped growing their crops. For farmers to cease farming showed the extreme seriousness of their commitment. When Shichirōemon heard these stories from his informants, he understood how the Christians had been able to resolutely face their deaths when they attacked the castle. The defenses inside the castle were extremely weak, meaning reinforcements were urgently needed. Michiie Shichirōemon hurried back to report that Shimabara Castle appeared to be just barely holding up.

Emissaries had also been sent to Shimabara Castle from neighboring domains, and on the following day, the twenty-eighth, two representatives from the Ōmura domain arrived. Christianity had flourished in Ōmura in the past, and officials knew the flames might soon spread to their own homes. When the envoys reached the castle, they were shocked to see the scale of the rebellion and the extreme state of affairs. When they returned to the wharf on the eastern coast intending to sail for home, they found that their boats were gone. Although the eastern coast did not appear to be under the control of the rebels, villages had been burned and here and there black smoke was trailing across the southern sky. The boats' crew had been seized with fear and abandoned the emissaries, fleeing for home in their boats. As a result, the emissaries were forced to travel back along the roads to the north; however, Mie, on the north side of the castle, was under rebel control.

The Ōmura emissaries requested guides, and Okamoto Shinbei sent about sixty men to accompany them, equipped with guns and spears, along with a courier from the Nabeshima clan who happened to be there. The area that extended some two leagues to the north of the castle was under the rebels' control. Along the way, they met a group of about thirty farmers, armed with spears and long swords. A man who appeared to be their leader said they would like to be allies, but since they had heard that people trying to get into the castle might be punished, they had hesitated. Sano Yashichizaemon, the head of the guards, thought the man's words sounded a bit suspicious, but, wanting to hurry on, he gave them a noncommittal reply, thinking he might escort them on his way back. Sano was the same leader who, at the battle at Fukae Village, had cut the bamboo for the battle flag and led the fight. He was the leader of a group that received an annual stipend of 400 *koku* of rice.

The villages farther to the north had remained loyal and shown no sign of rebellion. If the envoys could get that far, they would be safe. With a sense of relief, Sano watched the group of farmers finally go on their way. He worried that, on his way back, these same farmers might attack them, but fortunately nothing happened. It seemed that, instead, the farmers had hidden themselves and kept a protective watch over the envoy's group.

While Shimabara Castle was under siege, the area to the south around Kushiyama and Kuchinotsu echoed, like the rumbling of the earth, with the high and low voices of people reciting *oratio*. Farmers, carrying flags with crosses painted on white backgrounds and accompanied by women with headbands tied about their combed hair, emerged from along the grassy roadways bordered with swaying bush clover. Heading for the magistrate's home, they joined ranks with others along the roads that led to Kuchinotsu.

In the magistrate's residence, for the past three or four days, Yasui Saburōemon, the second in command, had sensed something strange going on with the villagers. When he looked outside, he was horrified. Before he knew what was happening, his residence was surrounded by flags with crosses on them. Quickly, he grabbed his sword and spear and jumped down into the yard. The sounds of heavy breathing approaching from both sides only increased his fear.

The unfamiliar sounds of religious hymns sung by large numbers of people grew louder. Then, suddenly, the march halted in front of the gate and one man's powerful voice rang out:

"We're here to ask the magistrate's intentions. I am Kazusa Hyōgo. I've come with the people of Kazusa."

Then, in turn, Murakami Gen'ya of Kushiyama Village, Ninagawa Sakyō of Kuchinotsu and others announced their presence. It appeared that Christians from all the nearby villages had shown up in full force. There must have been several thousand of them.

Chijiiwa Bannai was charged with energy as he stood in front of the gate and shouted:

"Open the gates, immediately! Already, Kuchinotsu belongs to our religious group. If you don't answer, we'll break down the gate."

Listening to Bannai's high clear voice ringing out, Jinbei had the feeling that Bannai-dono had lived his entire life for this day. Some time ago, he had said that his sword was crying out in the night for action.

A battle cry shook the air, and quickly the gate was broken down. To Yasui, the cry sounded like the word *santiago*. The question struck his mind, *What on earth is "santiago"*?

With Bannai leading the rushing crowd, the magistrate's officials backed away, holding their swords and looking as if something had been thrown into their eyes. The magistrate wasn't present, but Yasui, the second in command, raised his sword and stood pale-faced and stiff, like a rock.

As he unsheathed his sword, Bannai cried out:

"No needless killing—just the leader. I'm taking your head! Step forward now!"

Behind him, Ukon led an *oratio*.

"We offer our hearts; first to you, our Lord, and to Santa Maria, San Miguel, San Juan, San Paulo and to all the blessed saints, and we confess the many sins we have committed in our words and our thoughts."

Ukon's voice was strikingly clear, completely different from usual. Then the entire gathering joined in chanting the prayer, pausing together after each verse.

Yasui smiled with wry resignation.

"None who accept life can escape death," Ukon intoned. In the morning, do not wait for sundown, and in the evening do not expect tomorrow to come."

At that moment, Yasui's neck was severed. Blood sprayed over the wall, tracing a rainbow through the clear sky. Ukon's voice wavered.

A scream rose up as the group outside the wall realized that someone had been killed. Ukon's voice was drowned out by the overpowering force of the people singing the *oratio*.

Bannai, holding his bloodied sword, and Hyōgo appeared outside the gate. Then the people saw that the head of the Kuchinotsu headman's son Daisuke was covered with blood. Suddenly, the singing stopped.

His face pale, Kumagorō rushed to Daisuke and wiped the blood with a white hand towel.

"Stay with us!" he cried as he tried to clean the wound.

"It's nothing, I can take care of it," Daisuke answered, pushing Kumagorō's hand away; but when he saw the blood on the towel, he, too, was shocked and placed his hand on his neck again. He had been watching, aghast, as Yasui's head was cut off. He vaguely remembered hearing Ninagawa Sakyō yelling for him to get out of the way. Blood had spattered his body.

At the gate, Juan stepped forward slowly. His white hair was tied back by a headband.

"Just now we executed an official who has long been one of our worst enemies. Now let us march to the rice storehouses by the harbor."

A tremendous cry rose among the rebel forces. It was almost as if they had forgotten how to speak. Just as they were about to run off to the storehouse, Juan's powerful voice called them back. From what part of this elderly man, they wondered, had this voice come? It stopped them in their tracks. "Wait! Wait! Listen closely to what I say," he cried.

Suited in armor, his white hair waving in the autumn wind, Juan dashed about lightly in a parched rice field. He looked like a veritable demon, and the crowd stepped back instinctively as he spoke.

"The sacks of rice piled up in that storehouse were taken from us, at the cost of our blood and sweat, while we endured starvation. Those sacks of rice belong to us."

Wails rose from the crowd.

"However, when we see those bags of rice, we must not lose control of ourselves. No matter how great our suffering has been, we've followed the teaching of helping our neighbors and living together in peace. We must not eat this rice until we achieve victory in the coming battle. We must come together and decide how to distribute the rice, with everyone's assent and with fairness for all. We must think of the sacks of rice we are about to see as gifts from Maria-sama. There must be absolutely no sense of greed or theft in what we do."

"Yes! It belongs to everyone!" the crowd answered immediately.

"And what should we do if anyone gets greedy and steals some of it?"

"Take their heads! Their heads! Cut their heads off!"

"Tear them to pieces!"

"I think you've talked about this at your *confuraria* meetings, but let us all agree here and now—we are the war force of our Lord and of Santiago, the patron saint of war. If anyone dishonors the name of God, he or she will be beheaded. Do we all agree?"

Stamping their feet, young and old, men and women all expressed their consent. If they didn't seize the rice storehouse, they would not be able to wage their rebellion. In fact, Juan and the leaders of all the villages had been worrying that when the rebels broke into the rice storehouse they might fight over the rice like starving wolves and might even end up killing each other.

Not all of the people with them were followers of the Christian faith, and the majority could not be expected to recite from memory the words of the *oratios*. Some were close to the gates of Heaven in piety, but the truth was that some in both the rebel and the government forces were motivated by mercenary considerations.

Once again they gathered in groups according to their villages, and this time they advanced quietly toward the harbor. As they came so close to setting their eyes on the treasured sacks of rice, most were too nervous even to chant *oratios*. When they surrounded the rice storehouse, the guards stationed there lost the will to fight and quickly opened the gates. Two or three samurai drew their swords and stood in the way, but soon they were beaten down by the clubs and hoes of the rebels.

When the attackers saw all the bags of rice piled up in the storehouse, bags filled with such bitterness, some began to cry.

There were also stores of soybeans, adzuki beans and sesame seeds. On that day too, their stomachs were empty. As a temporary measure, a few sacks of rice were distributed to each of the villages, and men chosen from each village were appointed to guard the storehouse. The others returned to their local villages.

At Nisuke's house, Oume was working. She had instructed the women to cook rice porridge in a large pot.

Takematsu was with the women, helping out by counting the number of people present and other small tasks.

"Well now, this is quite something—a celebration without any drinking," the women teased, noticing he was sober for once.

"Yes, I suppose some celebrations don't involve drinking," he answered, feigning indifference.

"This is the first time I've seen you looking like such a man. Look at that handsome smile!"

"I think I'm falling in love. Need a wife?"

Takematsu seemed embarrassed. But, in truth, his lean, gentle face did look manly.

Wiping away her sweat, Oume joined in the teasing:

"Takematsu, are you drunk on the smell of the porridge today?"

The other women broke into laughter, and Takematsu nodded humbly.

"Ah, rice porridge . . . how could I not get drunk on this delicious smell? I only wish I could share some of it with my dead parents."

Takematsu's jaw quivered, and then the women witnessed something unexpected. A tear shone on his sober face. They fell silent and joined in reciting an *oratio*, which they had forgotten to do before beginning their meal.

Nisuke's house was large, and with all the leaders from Kuchinotsu gathered there, it looked like an army headquarters. That night, they received news from Arima and learned more about what had happened in the attack on Shimabara Castle. According to Yazō, people were rising up throughout the Amakusa region across the straits, including in Kōtsuura.

Juan and Sakyō were encouraged by the fact that all thirteen villages along the southern Shimabara coast had also joined the insurrection. Still, they couldn't help feeling deeply anxious about the future. It seemed that the northern villages might not move against the government. For the time being, Matsukura's samurai were locked up in the castle, but surely, before long, supporting troops from neighboring clans would arrive. Even if the people in the villages kept their spirits high and chased off or killed some of the castle forces, no one knew what would come next. Perhaps they could blame the failed attack on Shimabara Castle on their lack of equipment. But still, what had happened there was highly regrettable. Since the Kuchinotsu forces were responsible for gathering fighters from all along the coast of Chijiwa Bay to seize the government rice stores, they hadn't taken part in the attack on the castle. Even if they had, the castle wouldn't likely have fallen. It was, after all, the great and formidable castle built by the Matsukuras.

The main concern of Juan and the other leaders now was the expected approach of the *bakufu* army. The rebels had forged an agreement on Yushima Island, but they had no unified strategy to implement it. A chain of command, centered around Shirō, hadn't yet been clearly established.

"It won't be hard to take care of the Matsukura samurai. Some of them may slip out from the castle, but we'll rout their forces. But, Sakyō-dono, before long, daimyō forces from all over the country will begin pouring in. How will we fight all of them?" Sakyō asked.

Juan gazed calmly at him.

"That's the question, isn't it. You and I may be satisfied to have our last hurrah on the battlefield, but I feel so much for the farmers, and especially for the women and children."

"Our ranks include people from all the villages. Even if we make the big decisions by consensus, we can't easily work out the details. Even at Yushima, we only managed to make a temporary decision. It won't be easy to wage war against the *bakufu* armies like this."

"I suppose our only choice is to hole up inside the castle. We'll have to bring down Shimabara Castle."

"Hm."

For a while, Juan remained deep in thought.

"But even if we did, who would give the commands and get the village leaders to obey? At Yushima we chose Shirō-sama as our leader, but now he's over in Ōyano, on the other side of the bay."

"We have to send a messenger to Shirō-sama right away."

"I agree. That's the only way. Could we ask your son to do it?"

"I'm afraid Ukon isn't ready for that yet."

"Sakyō-dono, you can't keep thinking of your son as a child forever. We need Ukon-dono's thoughtful and clear spirit right now."

Juan shut his eyes. Filled with distressing thoughts, Sakyō stared at Juan's deeply furrowed face.

The Hosokawa domain was located just across the Ariake Sea from Shimabara. Beyond the Uto Peninsula, which jutted into the

Ariake Sea, lay the string of the Amakusa Islands. As soon as the Hosokawa officials grasped what was happening in Shimabara and set up a tight warning network along the coastline, they began reporting all incoming information to the Bungo overseer. This official oversaw the affairs of the entire Kyushu region and reported directly to the central government.

The Hosokawa clan had already received a request from the Matsukura clan leaders for assistance, and planned to send their troops to Shimabara Castle whenever necessary. However, the *Buke shohatto*—the central government's strict Law Governing Military Households—stated that, no matter what the situation, all local forces throughout the country must "act only upon orders from the Edo government." The Hosokawa clan's Lord Tadatoshi was currently in residence in Edo. His three chief counselors, Matsui, Nagaoka and Ariyoshi, were in charge during his absence and had sent several messengers to the Bungo overseer requesting reinforcement troops. But since the counselors were constrained by the Law Governing Military Households, they were unable to dispatch any forces and were growing increasingly impatient.

After thirty days passed, on the thirtieth of the month, unexpected news arrived from the regional office in Uto. Watanabe Kozaemon, the leader of the Amakusa Christian forces, had landed at Kōnoura, near the end of the Uto Peninsula—and he had been captured.

This was defeat. Looking back, Kozaemon had realized this the moment he was captured by government officials.

That was ten days ago. If the shame and suffering were mine alone to bear, I could endure anything; but Shirō-sama's mother and elder sister have also been captured. Our fight has hardly begun, and now our allied forces have been defeated, right at the outset.

It was my mistake to stop at the house of the village headman Hikozaemon after I landed in Kōnoura. Although Hikozaemon isn't a Christian, I've always been friendly with him, and I hoped he'd help me out with some advice about what roads to take in bringing Shirō's family to safety. But that was naïve. I knew the Hosokawa clan would be keeping a close lookout for enemies along the coastline, but I didn't imagine how thoroughly the village officials would be involved. I regret my mistake bitterly. Perhaps it couldn't have been helped, but now it seems such poor judgment to have exposed our plans by asking a member of the Masuda family for assistance.

Fortunately, when Kozaemon was captured at the headman's house, the others on the boat had realized what was happening and managed to escape back home. The news of Kozaemon's capture probably reached his father Denbei and Masuda Jinbei and Shirō the day it happened. They had been planning to integrate all of the Christian forces and take Tomioka Castle as soon as Kozaemon returned. Meanwhile, the rebel forces in Shimabara would try to take Shimabara Castle. If they could take both castles, the Amakusa and Shimabara forces would be united and able to move on Nagasaki next.

At the northwest end of Chijiwa Bay, the villages around Nichime and Mogi were Christian. Just recently, the son of Mogi's headman had come to Shirō-sama to be baptized. From there, they had only to cross the mountain pass for Nagasaki—the "Rome of Japan"—to be in sight. Kozaemon had talked to Jinbei-dono about the many people who would likely join their forces there, but he had never imagined he would commit this kind of gross blunder.

Because of my poor judgment, Shirō's family has been taken by the enemy, and on top of that I've gotten Jihei-dono into trouble—Jihei, the headman of Ebe, who helped protect the Masuda household before the rebellion. Such is the cruelty of war, but now I've been captured and there's no way I can apologize. How can I bear the shame?

Now the Hosokawa officials are scheming to use me as a decoy to trap Shirō-sama and his father. I don't intend to go along with it, but I don't know how many more days of interrogation I can stand. I keep telling myself this is nothing compared to the boiling springs of Mount Unzen, but the mental torture is just as bad. If I should fall into such a trap, my anima*, too, will be weakened. Somehow, demons have invaded my body. I never imagined my own flesh would become the nectar to sustain demons . . .*

I've taught others about religion, but how deeply were those teachings rooted in my own body? I have called myself the commander of two thousand Christians from Amakusa, and believed I shouldered that responsibility alone. But have I fallen into their trap?

After so many days of harsh interrogation, Kozaemon's pride as a headman had been completely stripped away. The words and looks from the Hosokawa officials showed that they regarded him as nothing more than a rebel and a traitor. *For generations, my family have been headmen, and unconsciously, as the leader of the Ōyano Christians, I became arrogant. I never even realized it—not until falling into captivity . . .*

Kozaemon felt his heart might break from the weight of self-reproach.

But Chirisuto-sama himself had a crown of thorns placed on his head and was crucified with thieves. This thought brought Kozaemon deep solace.

Surely, sharing the condition of the poorest, most humble of the world has brought me closer to the Christian teaching of humility. My present state is a gift from God.

All I can do is have faith that my Amakusa brothers and sisters will be victorious and continue earnestly on the path of the Lord. For a Christian, to die honorably like the martyrs who achieved heroic death is the greatest joy.

Kozaemon tried his best to soothe his anguish. Yet phantom images kept passing before his eyes. He saw the profiles of Shirō's mother and sister. What were they feeling now, imprisoned in jail? The thought made him tremble.

Time after time, the officials forced him to write letters to his father Denbei. He tried to write exactly what they ordered him to write.

> *Please talk with Shirō-sama and persuade Jinbei-dono to return to Ebe as soon as possible. The government officials have said that if he does this, Jihei-dono and his family will be cleared of suspicion. Since they helped Masuda-dono and his family for many years they are now suffering this misfortune—and this is all because of my poor judgment. I've heard rumors that the government forces in charge of conquering the Christians will be going there soon and I'm worried about it.*

At the end Kozaemon wrote:

It's difficult to write to every one of you, but although I know we all must pass away, I'm worried about Mother's condition.

Jihei, the headman of Ebe, had also sent Denbei many letters indicating that there had been trouble:

As a person of responsibility, what made him do such a thing? I hope that Shirō and his father will come back here as soon as possible. I hope you understand how much this troubles me.

Denbei wrote polite replies to each of Jihei's letters:

I would like to do as you ask very soon, but unfortunately, Shirō-sama is now suffering from a skin ailment and has gone to Nagasaki for treatment. In any case, he will likely stop here on his way back, and at that time I will certainly follow your wishes.

Denbei wrote in this manner to both Jihei and Kozaemon. In a postscript sent to his captured son Kozaemon, he added:

Your mother is quite fine, so you needn't worry about her. And your wife is doing very well.

Riding on Yazō's boat, Ukon left Kuchinotsu for Miyazu on Ōyano Island. Kumagorō and Takematsu insisted on accompanying him.

Kumagorō had hardly spoken a word since learning that Sankichi and his mother had been executed. His expression had been solemn when he asked Ukon to take him to Miyazu. Juan, Nisuke and Daisuke understood Kumagorō's feelings and saw the group off with heartfelt wishes for their success and safe return.

Bannai went along to protect them, in case they came across any enemy boats along the way. Fortunately, all the boats they passed belonged to Christians, who looked excited and held up their rosaries as a sign that they were allies.

"Even on land, people are separating themselves by village. Halfway measures won't be enough to bring us together," Yazō said. It was unusual for him to share his feelings like this.

"You're right. You can't lead people who are on edge all the time," Bannai answered calmly. Ukon was impressed that he wasn't getting worked up like he usually did.

Along the coast of Ōyano Island, they could see people with white flags stationed on the pathways and in the shady forests.

When they landed in Miyazu and asked for Shirō's headquarters, they were immediately taken to the village headman's house.

Shirō and Denbei were there. The visitors were told that Masuda Jinbei had gone on to Kōtsuura. When Ukon saw Shirō in the back room, surrounded by Denbei and the other leaders, the joy he had felt in anticipation of meeting his close friend, who was like a brother, suddenly deflated. Already, Shirō seemed to be a different person from the boy he had first gotten to know.

Seated in the back, Kumagorō looked at Shirō. He hadn't seen him in a long time, and he was shocked to see him looking so gaunt and haggard, as if the haze of some horrible sadness was hanging over his noble features. Shirō had always seemed so bright and serene back when Kumagorō attended the school. Kumagorō remembered how radiant Sankichi had been when he returned from being baptized by Shirō. The sadness that was now overflowing from this young person would surely draw people to the pure realms of Heaven and earth.

He has such a kind and gentle nature, Kumagorō reflected. *If I asked him to die with me, I'm sure he'd bow his head and do it.*

Takematsu, seated next to him, watched Kumagorō's head slump slowly down. He could well imagine Kumagorō's feelings. After having been raised as an orphan, Kumagorō had finally found a brother in Sankichi, and now he was probably thinking he would follow him in death.

"You may already be aware of this, but . . ." Ukon began, and then summarized the events following the murder of the magistrate. He spoke frankly of his father's and Juan's concern that the rebellion was unfolding impulsively, without a broader vision.

Ukon wanted to hear Shirō's personal reaction. Shirō, however, only stared at him silently, perhaps feeling the question at hand was beyond his own abilities.

"We deeply appreciate your taking such trouble to come here," Denbei answered in his place. "In fact, we were just talking about sending a messenger to you. The villagers that make up our forces on Amakusa have been returning to the faith, even beyond our expectations. We're pleased, but uniting them is very difficult. Some have been stirring up useless violence . . . Strangely, when Shirō-sama holds religious services among the people, they settle down. But even five of him wouldn't be enough to keep up with everything."

Denbei stopped speaking, as if reluctant to say more. Senzoku Matsuemon, who had been sitting quietly at his side, noticed this and said what Denbei could not. This was the man who had visited the Ninagawas previously, urging people to rise up.

"We have to tell you that Watanabe Kozaemon-dono has been captured by the Hosokawa's men at Kōnoura. He went to Uto to bring Shirō-sama's mother and other family members back to safety. Kozaemon-dono, as you no doubt know, is Denbei-dono's son."

Ukon remembered how Kozaemon had looked the night they were introduced on Yushima Island. Certainly, Kozaemon had the dignified bearing of an important headman; and yet, compared to his disciplined, determined father Denbei, he had seemed a bit too easygoing. According to Matsuemon, Shirō's mother and sister were now being held in a prison in Kumamoto. Ukon gazed mournfully at Shirō's calm face.

Across the bay from Amakusa, the Hosokawa clan had set up new lookout posts at strategic points and strictly cordoned off the coast, sending out patrol boats to keep a careful watch over its coastline. Kozaemon's letters—which clearly had been written under duress, following the officials' orders—indicated that Hosokawa forces would soon advance on Amakusa to crush the rebellion. They could hear the urgency in Matsuemon's voice as he told them this.

Chijiiwa Bannai, who had been sitting quietly beside Ukon, cut in impatiently.

"That's why we shouldn't be doing things this way. Senzoku-dono, you used to be a samurai for the Konishi clan and you know how to fight a war. If the Hosokawa forces show up, how are we going to fight them off? What about our Kuchinotsu forces?"

Ukon raised his hand, signaling for Bannai to stop. Already, Matsuemon's face was showing pent-up anger.

"We can all imagine your distress over the misfortune of Kozaemon-dono and Shirō-dono's family, not to mention how Denbei-dono and Shirō-dono must be feeling. But as we make strategies for future battles we need to keep two basic problems in mind. First, the Shimabara and Amakusa forces are now fighting separately, and second, the Shimabara forces are not likely to act coherently without orders from our commander. And so, Commander, I'd like to ask your thoughts."

Ukon had questioned Shirō boldly. Shirō stared back at him gravely. Once again, Denbei answered in his place:

"The plans of the Amakusa forces have, for the most part, been decided. Kanzaki Daizen-dono, please tell us about them."

Denbei turned around to face a man in his forties who had been sitting quietly until then. Ukon recalled having seen him before, at the Yushima Island meeting. Then, too, he had maintained a silent but rather distinctive presence.

The man gave a slight nod of greeting, and then began:

"I am Kanzaki Daizen. Until three years ago, I worked in the service of the Matsukura clan. I came to detest everything the Matsukuras were doing, so I cut my ties with them as a retainer. I had some connections in Kōtsuura, so I started living like the farmers and fishers."

Ukon heard Bannai mutter, "Oh," in a low voice.

"If we're going to take on the armies of various clans, we need a base of operations. Since Shimabara Castle hasn't fallen, I think it's most urgent for us to take Tomioka Castle. Tomioka Castle is under the control of the Karatsu clan. It's the pivot point for us to gain control over the entire Amakusa region, so we must seize it and raise the flag of the Christians. In addition, the castle is located at the tip of the peninsula of Lower Amakusa Island, and that will make it difficult to attack. The castle is at the entrance of a harbor, so if we can control the sea with our naval forces, we'll be in a strong position. From there we can send forces over the sea to launch an attack on Nagasaki.

"In any case, we from Amakusa have discussed this and decided to move ahead with attacking Tomioka Castle. With this as our objective, and if our commander will join us in person, then the disruptive uproar from the villages will surely calm down at once. I believe that if we march on the stronghold of the Terasawa clan, who have for so long opposed Deus-sama and oppressed the common people, then the Christian forces all along the coast will joyfully join our fight."

Since the people from Amakusa had already set their plans, what were the Shimabara Christians to do? Ukon, feeling somewhat pushed aside, looked at Denbei.

"In any case, Ukon-dono, that's the way things are," Denbei said gently, probably guessing Ukon's feelings.

"We plan to vacate these headquarters in Miyazu tomorrow and move to Kōtsuura on Upper Amakusa Island. Here in Miyazu, we're too close to Hosokawa territory. In Kōtsuura there are lots of old Christian families and it will be easier to bring together our allies throughout Upper Amakusa. Jinbei-dono has already been working on advance preparations there."

"In that case, do you think Shirō-sama could go back with me to Shimabara?"

At this point, Shirō spoke for the first time, his voice charged with emotion:

"Ukon-dono, I would very like much to go and remain by your side, but the white banner of the cross is calling me now, so I must go on to Tomioka Castle. You will return to Kuchinotsu and inform the people there about the attack on Tomioka Castle. After that, I want you to decide the strategy of the Shimabara forces. Once we take Tomioka Castle, certainly I'll join you. We're of one spirit."

Ukon tried to hold back the tears welling up in his eyes.

"The Hosokawas have been talking big about crushing us, but unless they get orders from the *bakufu,* they can't move out on their own," Kanzaki Daizen continued. "An express message to Edo and back takes a month, even on the fastest boat. So for a while at least, we won't have to worry about naval forces coming to the Ariake Sea. But we can't waste this time. We have to use the strength of our surging rebellion to attack Tomioka Castle."

Hearing Kanzaki Daizen speak with such evident confidence, Ukon realized that he had become the military strategist of the Amakusa forces.

"That's why I'm planning to request that the Shimabara forces join our attack. You've come at a good time. In your area of Shimabara, Matsukura's samurai are still bottled up inside their castle, and they don't appear strong enough to make any sorties. I ask you to send as many troops as you can when we attack Tomioka Castle. Shirō-sama has been designated as the commander of God's army, but military strength is what wins battles."

Daizen glanced at Shirō as he spoke. Faint creases were gathered between the young man's closed eyes. Sensing Shirō's solitude, Ukon almost forgot to reply.

Noticing Ukon's distracted state, Bannai moved closer.

"What you've just said will remain deep in our hearts. Here at Shirō-sama's headquarters we have heard your plans and feel greatly reassured. As for the matter of joint forces, as soon as we return, we will inform all the villages, and we, the Kuchinotsu forces, will certainly go to assist you. You can rest assured about that."

Bannai turned toward Ukon as if seeking his confirmation. But even as Ukon nodded deeply, he remained concerned about Shirō's look, which was so filled with sadness.

In Kōtsuura, Tsunekichi had developed a close relationship with Osato, the mother of the headman Umeo Shichibei.

Having volunteered for the role of messenger, Tsunekichi regularly travelled from village to village carrying news, but recently Shichibei had been very busy and often was not at home during Tsunekichi's many visits to give him reports. At those times, Tsunekichi asked Shichibei's mother Osato to pass on the messages. Shichibei had told him to deliver the messages to his elderly mother because his wife Okiki was usually busy in the kitchen. Osato was hard of hearing, so Tsunekichi often had to explain everything to Shichibei again on a later visit; yet whenever Tsunekichi saw Osato, he wanted to talk with her.

"You know, ma'am, I just heard something terrible."

"Yes? Well, what was it that happened?"

Since the old woman's hearing seemed better this day, Tsunekichi gave her a summary of the main events.

"Well, some people wearing straw sashes and carrying a white flag with a cross on it broke into a wealthy household in Kyōragi. After the family fled, they took all their rice and other grain and set the place on fire and made a big ruckus. I hear they cooked the stolen rice and carried on like crazy. It's caused big trouble."

"Is that so?"

She opened her eyes wide and nodded energetically.

"Of course they went crazy at the sight of the rice, and no wonder they cooked it, too. They're all starving."

"People do go crazy from that. I wonder when they ate the rice. But I'm afraid they'll be punished by Deus-sama."

"Well, maybe so, but perhaps at a time like this it's all right."

"You really think so, ma'am?"

"I do. At a time like this, I think it may be acceptable. And how about you? You had some of that rice, didn't you?"

"Don't say that—I came running here right away to tell you the news."

"Well, come whenever you can and bring us news. Our remaining days in this world are few. I'll take this memory to the next world."

She told Tsunekichi to take some dried octopus and other things to eat, since he must be starving himself.

"What happens from here on out will be quite a sight to see. Let's take a good last look so we won't be sad to leave it behind," she added, as if imparting a secret.

The next day, a great commotion started up, so big that the old woman walked out past the gate with her cane in hand to see what was happening. The old people said that even forty years ago when they built the Christian church on this land, there hadn't been as many people as they were seeing now. Shirō's headquarters had been moved from Miyazu to Shichibei's household. Troops from all across Upper Amakusa Island had been summoned to assemble here. Although Shichibei's house was a large one, it was packed. Osato had repeatedly said that she wanted to meet again with Shirō, who was like a grandson. But, because of all the commotion, there hadn't been time for a leisurely talk.

In the small world of Kōtsuura, all across its rippled hills, the frenzied mood of the people spread to the fields and forests, so that the trees seemed to be waving their branches and chattering with excitement.

When Tsunekichi entered the house, Osato grabbed him by the shoulder and led him into the room where Shirō was sitting.

"Excuse me, Mother, but just now we're in the middle of a discussion."

Osato didn't seem to hear Shichibei. Noting her determination, the group opened a space where she could sit. Then they remembered that she was the real head of this household, and that she was Denbei's elder sister and one of Shirō's in-laws.

"So things are finally heating up. This will be our last banquet in this world," she said to Shirō in a strong, excited voice.

The gathering was shaken. What she said was true: they were now stepping into the boundary between life and death that transcends everyday life.

"Well, that *anima* boat is coming for us from the seas beyond."

The assembly listened silently to the sound of the old woman's voice. They became aware that their boats, anchored along Kōtsuura's coastline, were, in fact, boats of war headed for the realm of the dead.

"Tsunekichi—"

Surprised by the change in the tone of her voice, he looked up.

"When we go to the country of *anima*, I'll get on the same boat with Shirō-sama. And Tsunekichi, I want you to row the boat for us. We're going to need a good rower for that *anima* boat."

The room returned to silence. Osato held onto Tsunekichi, using him as a walking stick, and together they left the room, leaving behind the swishing sound of her kimono.

Osato may have grown hard of hearing, but her body sensed the presence of the people all around her house, as if they were sending out seismic tremors. With her household in such a commotion, at times she may have been neglected, but she knew very clearly what was happening.

She also knew that Shirō's family had been captured. *No doubt it's only natural that the war has led to some people taking hostages and others being taken. But that this should happen to my own dear ones, of all people . . .* She had been brought up in the same village of Nakamachi on Ōyano Island as Shirō's grandmother, and they were like sisters. When she first heard about their capture she had cried bitterly, but now, after some time had passed, she held her head up and didn't complain.

The fact that she had stayed at home alone, unattended, had given her a good opportunity to reflect on the past and on what was yet to come. *What does it mean that people who die are reborn in* Paraizo*? In any case, now it looks like we're all going to die. When that happens, will we all be born again together in that world? Shirō's grandmother and her family are certain that Maria-sama will be one step ahead of us, holding our hands and leading us forward . . . I've heard that, in Buddhist reincarnation, people are reborn separately, one by one. But if we die and go to* Paraizo, *what sort of world will we find? For as long as I can remember, I've never lacked for anything in my life. Now it seems the time for decision has come.*

A few days earlier, Tsunekichi had asked her, "Even if someone's parents fall down into *Inferuno*, can their children go to *Paraizo*?"

For a moment, she had been at a loss for words.

She knew that Tsunekichi's parents had been poor. She had also heard that he lost his wife and baby. Rumors had gone around that the baby died from a lack of mother's milk. But some people had also gossiped that the couple may have killed the baby by smothering it.

Tsunekichi's wife had been a woman of loose morals, and rumors of her infidelity often circulated. One day, suddenly, she had died.

When Shirō had come for the atonement procession and people saw Tusnekichi pick up the cross, shoulder it and stagger along at the head of the procession, some made unkind remarks.

"He must be thinking he can escape his sins by doing that."

"Can a person be granted atonement just by carrying a cross?"

"How depressing to think of going to *Paraizo* with him."

Shichibei's mother had heard and understood these cruel comments.

What am I hoping to hear from this old woman? Tsunekichi wondered. *I'm not really expecting any particular answer. It's just so lonely these days going back to my cold, solitary shack. I need her company.*

"When I was running errands here and there for Shichibei-sama, I heard lots of stories. . . It's hard to talk about them."

"What happened, and who was doing those things?"

It wasn't the first time she had asked him this, but he wondered how to begin explaining the many things he had seen and heard.

"In Sumoto, people are getting all worked up."

"You mean in preparing for the battle?"

"Right. Already things are on the verge of catching fire."

"The village magistrate took the side of our enemies, didn't he?"

"Yes, and that's made everyone even more angry."

"Well, that may be so. So then what happened?"

"Well, they say that someone named Ushimatsu—he was a man who had a sick child—had drowned the child at the Kimigafuchi trench, and everyone got all stirred up about it."

The old woman was silent. After a while, she looked at Tsunekichi and encouraged him to continue.

"Someone said it was better not to talk about it."

"Tell me what that person said."

"Well, someone had said to Ushimatsu, 'You have a sick person in your family, so you can't possibly take part in the rebellion.' They were going to dismiss him from the forces. The next morning, he showed up with a pale face at the place where they were preparing the flags and spears. He told them, 'Although my son was sick, he did his part by praying for our victory in battle. Last night, at Kimigafuchi, he asked me, "Papa, where is *Paraizo*?" And then he went there—ahead of us. So now, no one can complain about whether I'll be useful or not.'

"When he said this, Ushimatsu raised both of his hands toward Heaven and jumped about.

"Then he snatched a flag decorated with a cross and shouted, 'I'll be the flag carrier! Last night when my sick boy asked me, "Papa, where is *Paraizo*?" I told him, "You just take a leap and you'll be in *Paraizo*. Don't be sad—soon Papa will be coming to you. I'll have a flag with the cross, and soon I'll be on my way for you."'

"When he said this, Ushimatsu rolled on the ground and cried out, 'Torakichi, my Torakichi—I'm coming!'

"So, tell me, ma'am; will Ushimatsu—this murderer of his own son—will he be going to *Paraizo*? Or to *Inferno*?"

The old woman listened to Tsunekichi's story deep in thought.

"The people in this world who have led the hardest lives and who have no hope will be the first to go to *Paraizo*," she said.

Suddenly, her tone of voice changed.

"For a person like me who's spent my life without many troubles, an ordinary afterlife will be enough."

"An ordinary afterlife?"

"Yes, an ordinary one—can't I have that?"

The old woman looked at Tsunekichi as if amused.

"If we ask for *Paraizo, Paraizo,* too much, might it not be a kind of greed? I feel reluctant to ask for it."

All the way home, Tsunekichi thought about this.

That woman seems to know a lot about me. She must know things about my wife that I don't want others to know. But even if she saw what happened, she acts as if she'd never seen it.

In the Commandments it says we shouldn't take another person's wife, but I didn't take anyone's wife—she was taken from me. At that time, I thought of killing them both, and I took her to the shore and I shoved her into the waves and I pushed her down with my feet. She was so submissive. When I pulled her out and kicked her in the belly, she started crying:

"Maria-sama! Maria-sama!"

I said, "What's this crying for Maria-sama about?" How could an adulteress like her speak of Maria-sama? She didn't even apologize or ask me for forgiveness; she just cried out, "Maria-sama." So, what could I do? Maria-sama, a virgin, gave birth to Chirisuto-sama without ever having known a man. Her carpenter husband raised their son with love and care, even though he knew the child wasn't his own. But me, I couldn't do a thing like that. That child who died of poor health probably wasn't even my child.

I started to think she would die, and that's a fearful thing. So, I picked her up and carried her, half alive and half dead, on my back to our home. She lived for seven days. I was writhing in agony. Just before she died, she said the words, "Please, forgive me."

Hearing those words, all my strength failed me. I'd been planning to kill the man, and if she'd lived, I'd have done it.

I had no idea why I was living, and I still don't. I hope my soul will find peace. I don't need a next world when I die. I want to receive judgment here and now, in this life.

When I carried that heavy cross, I was thinking, Chirisuto-sama, I beg of you, please pass judgment on me. Shirō-sama and Shichibei-sama have said that they, too, are sinners. But how could they be sinners?

What about such an ugly guy like me? Go ahead, tear me apart or burn my body right now.

But after carrying that heavy cross more people got to know me. Wherever I went, they started saying nice things like "We've changed our thinking about you" and "That was such a nice memorial service." But I wanted to cry out, "You're wrong! That's not it!"

Tsunekichi believed that all people kept something like a viper within themself.

When we don't see eye to eye, even about something small, the viper raises its head and bites. A poisonous feeling remains in the person who's been bitten and, even if they bite someone else to transfer the poison to them, the throbbing pain can't be soothed.

That time when I carried the cross, the snake must have been at work. Would Deus-sama give his grace to a snake? Would Maria-sama give it her compassion? I could recite the Commandments thousands of times, but if I don't cut off the head of that viper, is there any hope for me to be saved?

Thanks to carrying that cross, even a person like me could join the forces of Deus-sama. I want to become a snake charmer who can charm the snakes inside every person so they can raise the battle cries and slither out to the enemy's forces.

I'll confess my sins before Maria-sama and I'll ask for her help. And I'll ask for her help in the next world. But that viper is still in my heart, and none of that matters if I can't drive it away.

And that burning sky—it seemed like some kind of a sign. After we saw it, we were hit by rains, and the ears of grain got all spiky and rotted, as if we were being slowly punished. Everyone's been talking about the coming of the Day of Judgment, and that day seems to be coming soon. We'll see the sky fall down, flaming red, and we'll all die.

How strange that the end of the world is coming and the headman's mother is showing me her kindness, and she's even given me flowers. There's plenty of wild bush clover and plume grass blooming in the fields, but she took the trouble to go down to her garden and cut some for me there. She asked me, "Tsunekichi, do you have any flowers for the Buddha? Even just one flower, or two—flowers are your soul."

I took the bush clover flowers and it seemed it would be wrong to tell her I could have picked any number of those same wildflowers along the roadside.

It's not at all that I have a merciful Buddhist's heart, but for the first time I realized, a flower is a soul. I took the flowers home. When I got back to my shack, where no one was waiting for me, I realized that even if I wanted to put them on the altar for the Buddha, I had no vase to put them in. So I put them in a sake bottle. When I sat down, a sea breeze blew in and I felt the deep loneliness of my life. It was so frightening. I threw away the sprig of bush clover flowers she had so kindly given me. It was so light it felt as if throwing it away meant nothing at all. Then, for the first time, the words "I am sorry" slipped from my mouth.

Surely, it's no good for people to be alone. Even with a wife like mine, I'd be better off now if we were together. If it hadn't been for my jealousy. She made our dinner, and warmed our bed, and she kept the fire going in the hearth. I miss things like that hearth fire now that I live alone. Ah, I sound like an old man. Better not let anyone hear me.

Shichibei's mother had made up her mind. *I've lived enough. I'm not waiting for someone to call me to the next life; I'm going on my own.* And she had taken care of her affairs.

The incredible assemblage of forces that had been brought together in Kōtsuura, made up of farmers, fishers and even women, was a marvelous spectacle. *Many of them know me by sight, and when they see me, they bow and show their appreciation. Everyone looks like they're possessed. Finally, the time seems to have come to attack Tomioka Castle. We can't expect to come away unscathed. The lord of the Karatsu domain and the shogun up in Edo will no doubt send armies to crush us.*

She was fully aware of the events that had led them to this moment. Almost all the discussions, plans and decisions had taken place in the house of the village headman—her own home. Back when she was a young girl and was baptized at Rimōji temple in Sumoto, neither she nor the priests could ever have imagined that her people would come to fight against the forces of the Edo government. Back then, the lord and lady and everyone else would dress in formal clothing and recite the Christian *oratios* led by Padre Floris. Those had been joyous days, almost like a festival. She wondered if the fields and mountains would remember those beautiful days forever.

But now, of all things, we're hated by the ruler of the country and we're heading into a battle against his forces. If I were just a bit younger,

I'd take a sword and join the fight, even as a woman. But at my age, my parting gift is to ensure I am not a burden in their battle of rebellion.

When I see Tsunekichi, I wonder if he's just waiting for the Day of Judgment. Does he wish the sky would hurry up and catch fire? Maybe he thinks it would be better if the end of the world would come quickly. Somehow, the look on his face tells me that. Some people speak of him as a rough man, but he seems to accept what is coming, and he doesn't make excuses for himself. There are so many people in this world who can't see their own soul. Such people often value themselves the most highly of all, without shame. When Tsunekichi went to the head of the procession and carried that cross, he didn't do it to show off. It was just something he had to do. He's not a man who shows off by praying earnestly in front of others. And as for shame, no one knows it better than he. That's why I get along with him. I'd like him to be the one to help me along to the world beyond.

But that wouldn't be right. Once the battle for Tomioka Castle starts, they'll need every extra body they can get. If he were to stay and help me die, he might miss seeing the end of the world. I'd like to see it myself.

Osato looked around the big house that she knew so well. What time was it? Chilly night air was sweeping in. The people from other villages had been busy setting up temporary shelters, but now it seemed they all had fallen fast asleep. She had heard that more troops from Kuchinotsu would be arriving the next day. The young man that Shirō thought of as an elder brother would likely be with them. Shirō was their commander, but he was only sixteen. What did his face look like when he slept? What sort of dreams did he have? She smiled and then, quietly, she stood up.

In the morning of the following day, reinforcements from Shimabara arrived, led by the Kuchinotsu forces. The massive rebel army gathered on a hill near the remains of an old castle and in the fields around an old Christian church.

As Ukon and his forces marched beneath the Kuchinotsu flag toward the headman's house, villagers welcomed them joyously. Ukon, however, noticed a somberness in their faces. At Shichibei's house, people were coming and going in great haste. They seemed to be preparing for a funeral.

Someone had looked into Osato's room after noticing that she had missed morning prayers, which she had never done before.

They found that she had taken her own life. On the top of her prayer desk was a farewell message:

I am happy about the battle we are now engaged in. I have been in high spirits, like everyone else, but my knees have become weak. By becoming an agile anima *spirit, I'll be able to lead all of you on. Don't waste time with a burial. Just toss my bones to the fields and start fighting. I have written this letter in haste.*

Our religion forbids taking one's own life, and I fully realize that I may be sent to Inferuno *for this, but I have been so fortunate in my life and I don't yearn for* Paraizo. *I give my thanks to our Lord, and to Maria Kannon-sama, and to all of you who are joined to me with deep ties.*

The news that the headman's mother had ended her life as a gift for the departing army soon spread to all the rebel forces.

"Mother, we won't allow you to be eaten by the crows and beasts."

In tears, Shichibei and his wife placed her body into the grave that had been dug for her. They could hear someone chanting an *oratio*. In an inconspicuous spot, Tsunekichi was praying. Amidst his grief, he also felt peace and beatitude well up in his body, such as he had never known before. This beatitude came to him because for the first time, he had experienced pure human affection.

Ushimatsu's son and Shichibei's mother were not the only souls who departed while the rebel army prepared to advance. In some of the villages people had sorrowfully drowned their own babies and children in order to join the fight unhindered. They knew there was no path back to their old lives now, and they set off for the rebellion with thoughts of the dead borne deeply in their hearts.

Clouds of dust rose up as the troops trampled through the dry grassy pathways that led to the shore and then on toward Tomioka Castle. A floating bridge of clouds stretched to the distant heavens beyond the castle.

At last, on the morning of the thirteenth day of the eleventh month, they began the siege of Tomioka Castle. The Ōyano forces under Shirō's command led the attack, followed by troops from the villages of Lower Amakusa Island. The advancing army swelled visibly as it was joined by the forces from other villages.

Among the Shimabara forces, those from Kuchinotsu went with Shirō while those from Arima, Kita Arima and other villages stayed at the Kōtsuura headquarters. The leaders weren't particularly concerned about the Matsukura troops shut up back in Shimabara Castle, since they were still under siege by people from Fukae, Mikai and other nearby villages. They worried much more about the Hosokawa clan forces. If the Hosokawas were to send their soldiers from the Uto Peninsula, that would immediately put the islands of Ōyano and Upper Amakusa in danger. The rebel leaders had therefore kept the majority of the Shimabara forces stationed at Kōtsuura, under the direction of the village headman Umeo Shichibei.

First, one group of the rebel forces who were heading for Tomioka Castle marched toward the town of Hondo on Lower Amakusa Island, where the local government was headquartered. In that area, the coasts of Upper and Lower Amakusa Islands almost touched each other. Hondo was where the local villagers had petitioned for relief rations of rice and conducted other business, and where they had seen the government officials so often that they even remembered their breathing. As they passed, the villagers held their heads high, thinking of how they had always bowed them to the officials in the past. They continued along the seaside, passing Oniike on the way to Futae. In Futae there was a large Christian population, and beyond it, once they reached Shiki, Tomioka Castle would lie right in front of them. Another group of rebel forces went by sea.

When the overland troops had reached Shimago, before coming to Hondo, they had encountered some soldiers from the Karatsu clan. There they fought a quick battle. They were disappointed to find so few clan forces there, and so little will to fight among the soldiers they did find.

The fight had taken place along the seashore, where the fresh white flags of the rebels were waving. Evidently just the sight of so many white flags had been enough to scare them away.

The Karatsu clan had sent some 1,500 soldiers on boats, and by the tenth day of the eleventh month they all had entered Tomioka Castle. Miyake Fujibei, the officer in charge of the castle, had been informed of the government's defeat at Shimago. He rode out with fresh troops, who ran into the rebels at Hondo. However, since the rebel forces had swollen to around 10,000 soldiers—many of them with firearms—his troops hadn't been able to put up much resistance. Fujibei was killed in the fighting at Hondo and the tattered remnants of his forces retreated to Tomioka Castle. From the beginning, Hondo had been one of the main Christian strongholds. Many of the Christian farmers in the area had been serving in the Tomioka army and, although the Tomioka forces hadn't expected them to switch sides, when the chance had come, many had rushed to join the rebels and had started setting fire to houses and creating havoc among the Tomioka forces.

The government then sent Namikawa Tazaemon from Karatsu to take over command in Tomioka. He struggled day and night to revive the sunken morale of the troops in Tomioka Castle. His men set fire to the brush all around the castle to make the approach of any attackers visible. By lottery, they assigned armed men to various positions. They brought arms and provisions into the castle and carried water to fill all the buckets.

The samurai had shut their women and children inside the castle keep. Just before dawn, as everyone was resting and wondering if they had done enough, they heard wild sounds coming from below the castle. Inside, the people waited tensely for the arrival of rebel forces as they heard footsteps rushing toward the castle. When Tazaemon looked down from atop the ramparts, however, he realized that the sounds were coming from the remnants of the clan's army that had been sent to Sumoto. He let them into the castle and asked them what had happened. When they told him that the farmers from Sumoto had all revolted, he was at a loss. This influx of soldiers should have been encouraging, since they needed all the troops they could get inside the castle. But if Karatsu troops from all over the area were fleeing to Tomioka Castle, that meant the entire Amakusa region was up in flames. Filled with such thoughts, the soldiers inside the castle felt their spirits darken. Tazaemon decided that the situation was untenable and sent the war boats from Sumoto back to Karatsu, removing his own means of retreat, and reinforced his defenses.

How many days had passed since Okayo was sent back from Kuchinotsu to her parents' home in rural Uchino? At least on the surface, she had been able to spend some peaceful time there, but everyone in her family worried that troubling news of war might arrive any day. They avoided speaking of it directly.

While Okayo and her grandmother Ofuji were busy preparing dried persimmons, a young man from Futae Inlet came rushing in.

"Is Sasuke-san here?"

"He's gone out to get firewood. Is something wrong?"

The two women rose partway, still holding some persimmons they had tied together with straw cords to hang up.

"Yes. There's big trouble in Kuchinotsu."

Okayo turned pale and dropped the persimmons from her hands.

"The battle has finally started, and the Hasuda house has become the headquarters."

"Who told you this?"

"One of the boats from Futae stopped in at Kuchinotsu and brought back a message from Yazō-sama. He wrote that everyone in the Hasuda family is safe."

"Ah—I was so frightened."

Ofuji sat down again and looked up at the young man.

"You say there's big trouble in Kuchinotsu? What do you mean by 'big trouble'?"

"The rebels broke into the rice storehouse there."

"Well, yes, I'd say that's big . . ."

For a moment, Ofuji was at a loss for words.

"I'm sure the magistrate won't be silent about this."

"I heard that the people cut off the magistrate's head before they went to the storehouse."

Ofuji shrieked, then planted her hands behind her on the floor and sighed heavily.

"So, the Hasuda house is serving as the headquarters of the rebellion . . . that certainly is serious. And they've taken the magistrate's head . . ." Ofuji repeated to no one in particular, but then she recovered her focus and spoke directly to the young man.

"We understand. Thank you for bringing us this news. We'd be very grateful if you could take the trouble to run just a little further, to our woodlot."

Ofuji told him how to get to the woodlot in the hills where Seibei had gone with his son Sasuke and Sasuke's wife.

"It's a hard trek for a woman's legs."

Ofuji turned around and looked at Okayo, whose face had turned pale.

After seeing off the young messenger, she said to Okayo, "We mustn't get too upset about this. When they sent you back here, we knew that a time like this might come. You understand, don't you? If the Hasuda house is the headquarters, it means that Nisuke-dono and Daisuke-dono are considered leaders in the magistrate's assassination and in the taking of the rice. This is a critical time in our lives. You have to be ready for whatever happens. I'm ready for it."

Seibei and Sasuke, who had returned from the woodlot, ate dinner in silence before they headed out for a meeting.

"When I was about your age, there was a battle near here," Ofuji told Okayo and Sasuke's wife. "It was a fight between two lords. Back then, the best thing was for us villagers to just run off and hide, but that won't be possible this time. We'd better be ready for it."

The normally quiet mountain village was thrown into a frenzy. People set aside their work and met at Seibei's house. Since he was the village leader, people gathered there at such times. Everyone had heard about the uproar in Kuchinotsu and Shimabara and the situation in Amakusa.

"Some people from Futae went over to see what's happening in Kutchinotsu. They say it's hard to stop the young people from rushing off in boats to join the fighting."

"That's not surprising, since the people in Futae are all Christians."

"But it's not just Kuchinotsu—our island is catching fire, too. The people of Futae are strong, and they're the best rowers in the whole western part of the country, but they tend to be quick-tempered."

"Before we think about Futae, we have to think about our own village. Here in Uchino, Christians are in the minority."

"At this point, it doesn't matter if we're Christians or Buddhists. When we went to ask for rice assistance, we went to Tomioka together, didn't we?"

"Well, that was about the rice petition, wasn't it? But this time, the mark on the flags is clear. People have gone back to being Christians. If we're going to help them, we'd better understand we're joining a Christian army."

"I suppose you're right about that. Now that you mention it, some former Christians in our village who'd been forced to convert to Buddhism have started gathering to pray in front of the cross."

"If that's true, then the battle's going to come to us soon. It's hard to decide whether to fight with the Christians or not. If we don't join them, then Christians from other villages may come burn our homes."

While this discussion was going on, Seibei had returned unnoticed and was standing at the doorway, listening in silence. When the others noticed his presence, he sat down by the hearth in the spot reserved for the master of the house.

"As for whether we decide to be their enemies or allies, we'll have to watch what happens next closely. What's important right now is that we all work together and don't separate ourselves into friends and enemies. The Christians and Ikkō Buddhists here have always helped each other peacefully. As a fellow farmer, I feel like I can understand how this rebellion came about. It's just that our religious beliefs are different."

The people around Seibei sighed, as if breathing together with him. He felt there was no reason to keep secrets any longer. He glanced at Okayo, sitting behind Ofuji with her face cast downward.

"The family my daughter married into has gotten pulled into this, too . . ."

"You must be worried," several elderly women said.

None of them, of course, knew that Seibei had sent his son off to them with a rifle.

"This is just my own thought, but it seems that back in my parents' time there were a lot of Christians around here. I hear that now the rebels are raising the flags of their old religion. Seems to me they've taken a pretty drastic step."

No one said a word.

Seibei continued, "I've thought about this, and I'm not planning on going over to that religion, but if there are some in our village who want to, I won't blame them at all. No matter what our religions are, we've always helped each other in the past. We went together to Hondo and Tomioka to petition for rice assistance, and we've shared whatever scarce food we had. Despite our different faiths, in this village we've always lived together and I think the differences have been no obstacle. But this is true only when there are no troubles. Now that people are all worked up, things have become difficult."

The villagers blinked and sighed, and it was hard to judge their feelings. Ofuji thought that Seibei, who usually didn't talk much, was speaking out now because he sensed this was such a critical moment. She listened to him intently.

"Christianity tells people to treat their neighbors kindly, as kindly as they treat themselves, and this is an admirable teaching. But as for practicing a religion that's prohibited, that's hard for me to accept. Christians worship a Lord who was nailed to a post, and that's really something. It seems that some people have been thinking about desperate situations for a very long time. The unrest now is to make Amakusa into a Christian country. If that proves impossible, they're ready to become martyrs and then pass on to *Paraizo*. So what are we to do? Together, we've gone through starvation and survived, but this time . . ."

The villagers looked at each other.

"The people in Futae are extremely fervent about their faith. Soon, they'll come here to Uchino to ask our assistance. If we refuse them coldly, they might set our houses on fire, like someone said a moment ago. I'll have to give them a proper reply. Anyhow, we've always lived together peacefully in this village, and it seems essential that we don't let the spirit of this place die out."

A resolute expression settled on Seibei's face.

That night, Sasuke returned home late. In the morning, when they looked at each other, Seibei sensed that Sasuke had decided to go. The night before, some of the young people had gone to Futae. Seibei could pretty well guess what they must have talked about.

People on Lower Amakusa Island tended to get excited easily, and since it had been a meeting of young people, Seibei knew it wouldn't have been acceptable for Sasuke to appear weak. Plus, Seibei himself had told Sasuke to take the rifle to Okayo's family, which in a way had pushed his son into the rebellion. He felt conflicting emotions as he looked at Sasuke. Relatives had told him that back when they made the petitions for rice, Sasuke had also been especially active.

"Are the young folks planning to join the group in Futae?"

"Yes. We haven't become Christians, but we're going off, as men, to join the rebellion," Sasuke said in a more restrained voice than usual.

Ofuji took a deep breath and let it out.

"So, you're going off to join the fight, are you?"

"Yes. I've thought it over a lot. Daisuke-dono from Kuchinotsu and I pledged ourselves as brothers. I can't just ignore my brother who's risking his life in this war."

Seibei had wanted to say, *The Hasuda family is the Hasuda family, and this is our own family, and also, you are our heir*. But in the back of his mind, he also had other thoughts. If the people from Futae were going to fight, then he had a responsibility to send them a sufficient number of people, didn't he? And if they helped with the fighting in Futae, their fates would be tied together until the very end.

"So you have to go, do you? Well then, if you're going, give it everything you've got, and make sure you come back alive."

"Just come back without getting yourself killed, for the sake of this child," Sasuke's wife said in a strained voice.

Holding their child in his arms, Sasuke said, "Don't get too upset now. We're not saying a final farewell to each other, and we're not going to be separated forever. Even if I go and fight, I might not die."

Seibei could tell that Sasuke was hiding his true emotions, and he was taken aback. Sasuke glanced at his wife and sister with a still, calm look.

"Just be patient for a while. I'll be with Daisuke-dono and I'll come back after we win this fight. Both of you have babies to take care of, and it won't be easy, but please look after Grandma and Father—"

Suddenly, he stopped talking.

Suzu was trying to calm Ayame, who had gotten fussy. He had just noticed how worried she looked as she listened to the adults' conversation.

" . . . Suzu, I'll just be away for a while, so please look after the baby, and Grandma, too."

Suzu nodded, her eyes expressing her strength of will.

"And besides, I'm not going off just yet."

Although Sasuke grinned as he said this, no one responded.

A large number of boats had assembled in Futae Bay. Some had come from the Amakusa Islands and others had rowed across the Hayasaki Straits from the Shimabara Peninsula.

"I've never seen such a thing," people from the nearby villages said, leaning forward from the roadways along the coast to see.

Sasuke wanted to let Daisuke know, by any means possible, that he was there. A large flag was waving prominently above the war boat of Yazō—the man who had introduced Okayo to the Hasuda family. Sasuke guessed that Daisuke might be on that boat, but since Sasuke was in the middle of a different group of boats heading for Shiki, his boat from Futae was separated from Yazō's by quite a distance. Shiki was not far from Tomioka Castle. The rebel forces landed on the shore near Shiki and fell into ranks as an army.

As soon as Sasuke stepped onto land, he rushed to the Kuchinotsu encampment. The names of each village had been written on flags marked with crosses, so he was able to find the place easily.

As he ran, he called out Daisuke's name. Surprised, Daisuke jumped up. He had never expected to see Sasuke. The two embraced firmly.

*When we die, we'll die togethe*r, Sasuke thought. *It doesn't matter if one of us is a Christian and the other is an Ikkō Buddhist, we're united by our vow of brotherhood.* Tears filled his eyes. What spurred Sasuke on, however, was not only their vow of brotherhood. Back on that night, amidst the chirping of insects in the garden, Sasuke had heard the voices of his distant relatives calling to him. The sorrows of those who had lived and died had taken root deep in his being. He believed that his bond with Daisuke had sprung from the voices he heard that night.

Shortly afterwards, Daisuke took Sasuke to the headquarters to introduce him to Shirō. Dressed in a white figured outer garment and a gold-brocade coat with violet embroidery, Shirō nodded with an ethereal look that seemed to draw him in. Sasuke would never forget that gaze as long as he lived.

His entire body energized like a spring, Sasuke hurried back to the Futae quarters. Just then, a battle cry rose up and Sasuke joined in, crying out "Santiago!" It never occurred to him that this was a very unusual sort of battle cry. Sasuke, too, was wearing a new white cotton robe. When his family had accepted the fact that he would be going off to war, his grandmother had asked him what kind of clothing he would wear. He had answered that his clothing should be the same color as the flags—white. She had sighed and, under her direction, the women had hurried to sew him the new white clothes.

"When a woman gets married, her bridal veil is white, isn't it? Well, this is white clothing for fighting, so it, too, will be clothing for a special occasion. Let's put our hearts into sewing these clothes. Make two complete sets—underwear and all."

Sasuke wore his usual old clothes as far as the village border, but when he entered Futae he put his new white clothing over them. And with a rifle on his shoulder, he joined them as a soldier.

The battle started in a flash.

"Remember, the castle is our only objective. We'll need the same strength we used to cross the straits at Hondo."

After leaving the inlet at Futae and following the coast to Shiki, they could see to their right the long spit of sand extending into the sea. At the tip of this spit was a steeply sloped hill, shaped like a hump. The castle was built on the top. The rebel forces discovered that Tomioka Castle was far more secure than they had imagined. At first glance, it had appeared that an attack by a large number of soldiers could take it at one go, but when they actually made their charge, it proved extremely difficult. In order to attack the fortress at the summit, they had to pass along a narrow road leading up the slope, and only a limited number of soldiers could scale the stone walls, while the men inside the castle shot down on them, picking them off.

The attackers burned down the samurai's houses and the guardhouse at the base of the hill, but those buildings had already been vacated, so they didn't meet any resistance.

Sasuke advanced in a cloud of dust. The attackers seemed to think of themselves as old hands at climbing hills, and so they threw themselves into reckless charges up places that had no paths, grabbing onto the roots of camellias and *isosakaki* plants as they struggled to climb. But rocks were hurled from the upper reaches of the castle walls, knocking them back down.

"This is a far cry from collecting firewood," Sasuke grumbled.

When the rebel army moved up the narrow road toward the castle gate, too many men tried to advance at the same time, and in the confusion many were felled by rifle shots. Not sure whether the blood-stained bodies they saw were alive or dead, several men picked up bodies and carried them to the rear, yelling, "Let us through! Let us through!" In spite of all this, the rebel forces were not discouraged, and continued to send in new fighters. But no matter how hard they fought, they could gain no ground and, in the end, they grew desperate.

"They say we lost about two hundred of our men," the soldiers whispered, and quickly the news circulated through the headquarters.

In spite of the large army they had sent out, their men had died in vain. Sasuke had imagined that the fighting would be done with spears on a wide-open field, but in real warfare no one could predict where, when or how a battle would unfold. And here he was in the middle of that reality, shouting things even he didn't understand. Weren't they marching straight into the muzzles of their enemies' guns? And because of the way they were firing their guns randomly at the castle walls, their own shots were ricocheting back at them.

The castle seemed to be quietly holding its breath, even as it was surrounded by the angry roar and gasping voices of the rebel army.

The sun was about to go down. On this first day, the rebels had given the forces in the castle a great scare. While the troops were wondering if they should withdraw for the day, a message was sent around from their leaders. They were to retreat to their base at the landing spot, where they would make preparations for the next day. Many soldiers complained to one another that they had left themselves too vulnerable, right in front of the enemy rifles.

CHAPTER NINE

Cherry Trees at Twilight

Spurred on by their early success in the battle at Hondo, the rebel armies had launched their reckless attack on Tomioka Castle. The Tomioka forces, however, had realized the futility of fighting a battle in the open, so they simply shut the castle gates securely and aimed at not losing a single soldier.

Despite the danger of falling headlong into the sea in some places, the rebel attackers scrambled up the steep slopes around the castle, only to be shot down from above by the rifles and arrows of the castle forces, who did not need to venture outside the castle walls. The rebels stamped their feet and shook their fists in frustration, shouting, "Come out and fight, you gutless bastards!"

But it was to no avail, for the soldiers inside just waited quietly. As the day of fighting came to a close, the rebels were left with a sense of the utter futility of having risked their lives.

At the Futae encampment, Sasuke sat by the fire thinking back on the events of the day. The rebels grilled dried fish they had carried on their backs and passed around boiled beans. As Sasuke handed out the dried persimmons his grandmother had given him, he sighed deeply.

"Fighting's important, but so is eating."

"You can say that again. After all, this whole war started from our troubles about eating."

The men grinned at each other, but their cheeks were twitching nervously. They had to clasp their knees to keep themselves from wobbling.

A man stepped up to the fireside supporting an injured soldier.

"He's still breathing, but he's been crying for Maria-sama to take him quickly," he said.

The evening chill crept along their backs. The men sat in silence, and as they fed the fire with wood and embers accumulated, here and there heads nodded and men dozed off. They posted guards to keep watch in case the castle troops should mount a night attack. They all wanted to lie down and sleep soundly, but the sight of the towering dark fortress in the distance kept them restless. Even those who did manage to fall into a deeper slumber sometimes jerked their heads up, betraying their awareness of being on a battlefield.

Sasuke's body, and his thoughts, too, were stiff. For brief moments he nodded off, but soon woke up again. Visions of blood-soaked, unmoving men flashed in front of his eyes.

It was said that more than two hundred of their men had been killed that day. And when the injured were included, the number was much larger. Why had they attempted to storm the stronghold of that castle without sufficient plans and preparations? Shirō must have had the advice of his tactical advisors. What had they been thinking?

Some soldiers had boasted, with eyes gleaming, "Their bullets can't hit us Christians—and even if they do, we'll bounce back to life right away."

Believing themselves invincible, they had charged forward and been needlessly sacrificed. The leaders couldn't have believed such things, could they? But after the battle at Shimago, where they had seen the castle forces fleeing in confusion from the white flags of the cross, perhaps they had become overconfident, counting too much on divine protection from the Lord.

Around him, Sasuke could hear the deep breathing of the slumbering men. One by one they had laid down and succumbed to sleep. Occasionally, in the dark of the night, women's wails rang out from beside the dead and injured. At times, their voices drowned out the sounds of people reciting *oratios*. Sasuke couldn't help feeling he was in an army bound for the land of the dead.

When morning broke, word came from the headquarters in Shiki that there would be no attack on the castle that day. The troops were ordered to make shields out of bundles of bamboo to protect themselves from bullets. This idea may have been prompted by the great number of casualties. Sasuke was deeply troubled by the state of affairs, but he cut bamboo from the grove and busied himself with binding it up to make shields. He wondered how Daisuke was getting along, but he couldn't leave his work to go looking for him. He forced himself to get through the day.

The men's work wasn't limited to making bamboo shields. They also had to melt lead to make bullets, set up a bamboo stockade around their camp and take other defensive measures. They also had to tend to the wounded and requisition food from the kitchens of local people to feed the troops.

As the day came to a close, Sasuke was taking a brief rest when several men entered the bamboo stockade in high spirits.

"You can find good stuff if you look in the right places."

"Tonight, we'll have porridge with adzuki beans."

Sasuke asked what they were talking about. They told him they had found some grain and beans in a burned-out shop near the base of Tomioka Castle.

"So, you've been out looting?" he asked, half jesting

"There wasn't anyone in the house. They've all fled in panic."

"They left everything behind, even their wooden sandals."

The soldier who said this was holding a sandal in his hands.

"What are you thinking, stealing shoes in the middle of a battle?"

"I'll take them home as souvenirs."

Doing things that were normally unthinkable—Sasuke realized that this was what happened in war.

On the following day, the twenty-first, there was also no attack on the castle. The troops were reorganized, drawing on solidarity within each village, and instructed in how to advance and retreat on a battlefield and make a show of force. No one wanted to attack the castle in the haphazard manner of two days earlier. All the men felt this strongly.

Because Sasuke had come with a rifle from his house, he was assigned to the newly-formed artillery unit. It was a great comfort to be put in the same unit as Daisuke, about whom he had been so worried. Daisuke was carefully holding the rifle that Sasuke had brought him before the fighting started.

In the assault on the castle two days earlier, amid the chaotic screaming and yelling as the rebels tried to scale the slope, Sasuke hadn't been able to use the rifle strapped to his back even once. His father had taught him the basics of how to use it, but with his limited skill he might have ended up shooting one of his own allies.

A man named Sagebari Kaneshichi was put in charge of the unit and drilled the soldiers in rifle practice. It was said that he could hit a suspended thread of cotton from four meters away.

"Look—you shoot a rifle with your waist. First, you have to plant your feet firmly on the ground, with your legs well apart. You aim for the target with your waist dropped down a bit. Your bullet's going to fall somewhat as it goes forward, so if you're aiming for a spot a hundred paces away you have to raise the barrel slightly above your target."

Sasuke wasn't a complete beginner at using a rifle. He had shot at wild boars plundering his fields. But that had just been to scare them off, not to kill them. This was his first experience in practicing to kill.

Sasuke was dealing with the problem of the rifle's muzzle jerking up with each shot. Daisuke, standing at his side, commented, "It's not so easy, is it?"

But after practicing all day, until dusk, the two improved their marksmanship enough that their bullets were for the most part landing near the targets.

Early on the morning of the twenty-second day of the eleventh month, the rebel forces launched a second assault on the castle. Their bamboo shields afforded them at least some measure of defense, and they made a strong attack on the castle's rear gate. But the castle forces had added cannon shots to their defensive arsenal, along with flaming arrows that set the rebels' bamboo shields on fire, and by the end of the day, more than three hundred of the attackers had been killed. In contrast, the castle forces lost not a single soldier. Although the rebels—supposedly the invincible army of Deus—had outnumbered the castle troops by several ten-fold, they were unable to make their way into the small castle stronghold. At camp that night, the men couldn't hold back their tension and unease.

As Shirō and the military leaders inspected the encampment, the soldiers stared questioningly at him. He wondered how to respond.

In this one day, the allied rebel forces had used up most of their gunpowder, but the castle forces seemed to have more rifles than expected, and plenty of ammunition. That had been the case at Shimabara Castle as well, but this time it wouldn't do to simply shoot their rifles up at the strong stone ramparts and brandish their swords in a futile attempt to storm the castle gates. The situation called for much better attack plans, but at this point they had neither the time nor the supplies to succeed. In addition, they had a nagging sense that the Hosokawa forces were rapidly approaching. According to reports, a sizeable fleet of war ships had already assembled along the coast to transport their troops.

The military tacticians and most of the village leaders felt strongly that, at least for the time being, they should retreat to Kōtsuura and see how the situation developed. Shirō raised no objection to withdrawing. What worried him most was the possibility that they might lose faith in themselves as the army of Deus. Only if this spirit burned in the hearts of the farmers and fishers could they face the forces of the daimyo, for whom battles were a routine matter. Shirō worried that continuing to attack the castle would rob his soldiers of the morale essential for fighting. As he sat with his war council that night, he announced his carefully thought-out decision.

Shirō had no intention of interfering with battle strategies. For that purpose, there were, in addition to his father, a number of military leaders. Shirō knew he wasn't well suited for the role of a military commander in chief and that he acted mainly based on his own sense of how to do things. He simply believed in the divine revelation given to him. God was whispering in his ear.

"For the time being, I have no objection to retreating. It may not be a bad idea to pull back to Kōtsuura and rebuild our forces there. However, my feeling is that we should take our Shimabara forces to Hara Castle. We'll make it our Spring Castle. Our Lord has prepared this place for us as our base. As for our Amakusa forces, for a short time they should return to their villages and families, and then cross over the straits to Shimabara and join us in the castle."

A vision from his past trips to and from Nagasaki, of the castle ruins surrounded by cherry trees in full bloom, flashed before his eyes.

A commotion rippled through the gathering.

"Where is this this 'Spring Castle'?"

"Hara Castle is where the lords of the Arima clan lived in the old days," one of the men from Shimabara answered with an indignant glance. "It's on a headland in Minami Arima, and even today you can see its stone walls rising high above the sea."

Shirō had never talked to the army about military plans before. This was the first time he had spoken as their military commander in chief and announced a decision. For this reason, it had a striking effect. After a moment of hushed silence, groans and shouts of irrepressible joy welled up, filling the camp.

A bright stream of light broke through the overcast sky. According to the people from Shimabara, Hara Castle was very large, with extensive stone walls enclosing the ruins of its three inner keeps and its outer keep. Matsukura Shigematsu had removed most of the usable construction materials when he built the new Shimabara Castle, but the stone walls had been left largely intact. If the rebel forces could occupy this castle, they would gain a strong base of operations. Not only would they no longer have to fight minor skirmishes around the region, they would also be able to provide safety and shelter for their families, who had been left behind in their villages. The men's faces showed their relief and hope.

They were not without doubts as to whether holing up in an abandoned castle was the best strategy, but they knew that in order to wage an aggressive battle they would need a secure base of operations. Having failed to take the Shimabara and Tomioka Castles, they urgently needed something to take their place.

After the meeting broke up, Ninagawa Ukon remained sitting. He had been appointed head of the group that would accompany Shirō and look after his safety and general affairs. In recent days, Ukon had come to recognize the difference between war as he had imagined it and war as a reality. He had become very tense, but when he heard Shirō speak, he felt the blood start to gush through his entire body. Until now, Ukon had worried about how this young person who seemed so otherworldly and free from normal concerns would be able to take on the responsibilities of commander in chief. He had watched over Shirō's every move as if they were part of his own being. Now, at last, Shirō had revealed his full self. A deep joy and fear spread through Ukon's body.

Shirō's father Jinbei was now in a difficult position. He had been at the head of organizing the rebellion and now, along with Denbei, Matsuemon and others, he was one of its leaders. But ever since his son became commander in chief, it had become difficult for him to speak at these sorts of meetings. He didn't want the label "father of the commander" to be hung on him.

Seeing how the samurai such as Kanzaki Daizen from Kōtsuura, Matsushima Sadonokami from Arima and Yanagi Heibei from Senzoku Island were so actively engaged in the fighting as well as the planning and directing of battlefield affairs, Jinbei felt it would be better to leave these matters to them. His own role was to advise and assist Shirō, and even serve as a shadow commander. Because he had started this fight, he had a responsibility to see it through to the end.

Jinbei's feeling of closeness to the elders Henmi Juan and Watanabe Denbei made him somewhat uneasy. The two of them would nod to each other happily as they watched the rugged leaders like Sadonokami and Daizen working so hard. Judging from their expressions, they seemed to feel acceptance, or even resignation about how things were developing. Battle strategy seemed to be of secondary importance to them.

An image of Amakusa appeared in Jinbei's mind, writhing and twisting as it adjusted its heartbeat to that of Shimabara, just across the straits. The thought struck him, *The spirits of our ancestors who inhabit this land must be urging us to run on, carrying the flame forward. How far can we run? Only God knows.*

As Jinbei sat in a corner of the headquarters absorbed in such thoughts, someone tapped him on his shoulder. He looked up and saw the smiling face of Henmi Juan, holding a bowl of tea in each hand.

"Won't you have some tea?"

Even on the battlefield, Juan never forgot about preparing tea. Like Jinbei, he had been assigned to the headquarters, but for the time being he had no particular duties. After Jinbei thanked him and took his bowl, Juan sat down beside him.

"What did you think about your son's decision tonight? I thought it was brilliant. A commander should remain quiet most of the time and then, at the very end, present his plan in a few concise words. Where did he learn that from? It must have been the upbringing you gave him."

"No, no. I've always been so indecisive. I'm a dullard who ponders things too much and avoids making decisions until the last moment. I can hardly be said to have educated him. I was surprised at what he said today myself. But in any case, Juan-dono, what do you think about his plan?"

"About Hara Castle—our Spring Castle, that is . . . ? Well, to tell the truth, I've had that castle in mind since the beginning. But I figured no one would want to hole up recklessly in that place. Only after we attacked Shimabara and Tomioka Castles did its importance become clear. Our commander has chosen exactly the right moment."

A gentle smile spread over Juan's face.

After the war council was concluded, Shirō stood alone on the beach, gazing up at the Pleiades in the night sky. He heard a beautiful sound reverberating from the depths of the heavens. Sensing that it did not come from ordinary reality, he listened intently and realized that it sounded like a multitude of voices singing old hymns. There were no words. The voices were filled with prophecy. Suddenly, an enormous figure appeared above him. It embraced the constellation in its outstretched arms and entered into meditation. *Perhaps it is a revelation from Heaven.*

But as he gazed upward, the vivid figure seemed far too real to be a mere illusion, and he had the feeling that it was somehow different from the Lord as he had imagined Him. *It might be a manifestation of the Trinity; yet it also looks like a bodhisattva.* Its skin was brownish and its upper arms were decorated with bluish bracelets that looked like tattoos, and when its arms moved, they gave off an enchanting light. *Perhaps it's an unnamed angel.*

Why, Shirō wondered, *at such a time, am I conjuring up an image of a heathen Buddha?* But soon his misgivings cleared away. The depths of his being were filled with a sweetness like the most excellent of wines.

Although his face showed no trace of hardship, a teardrop settled on his closed eyelids. He looked as if he had been released from suffering and, by entrusting himself to the solace of Heaven, had entered into a peaceful state of meditation. He held a dialogue with the being in the night sky who neither spoke nor lamented. It seemed to say:

Be not separated from the land.
Look to the movements of the constellations behind you.
In this way must you understand the meaning
Of the red ball in the palm of my hand,
And the blue flame that wraps around it,
And the meaning that hangs like a rainbow over purgatory.
The time of Heaven is impressed upon the land.
From this ball are the seeds of words sown,
Cut off, along with their outer husk.
You must know that they, too, may dry up
Because they are cut.
If you wish to see the eternal ball,
Be not separated from the land.

Although he heard this voice for but an instant, Shirō felt as if, behind his back, many years had passed. But he didn't feel that those years had been wasted; rather, he felt that time had now come around to him. A being who had meditated and embraced the real star-filled sky had taught him this.

Shirō felt as if he had become a tree that was transmitting the sweet voices of the heavens to the ground below him. When he looked up, with his feet planted on the plateau of a trembling island, the image disappeared and he saw in front of him the stars of the Pleiades, shining brightly in the sky as they had before.

In the evening wind, too, real time moved on. As the rebellion unfolded, Shirō faced a time of trial. It seemed that the island beneath his feet existed in the eyes of God; or perhaps in the arms of that being. God, too, must be suffering along with him. And for that reason, it was likely that everyone in this rebellion might have to suffer together, in the way of the martyrs.

If that was the case, then what was his mission to be? Even as he pondered these things, injured women and children were dying. Was there any way to turn back? Was there no place where people could live in peace and prayer? But if such a place existed, the villagers wouldn't have rushed here with their families, right in the midst of this rebellion.

The voice sounded in his ears again. *You must understand the meaning of the red ball in the palm of my hand, and the blue flame that wraps around it . . .* Hearing this voice for the second time, he felt as if he had been wrapped in that blue flame. He lifted his head in the evening air and made a deep vow. *In a place without peace, in a state of deep suffering, prayer becomes a flame. Go forward, wrapped only in the intuition of the believers. My feet, compared to those of the farmers and fishers, are far softer. For that reason, they feel the tremors of the earth with greater sensitivity. I must stand firm, with my body like a tree. May I become the axis that balances Heaven and earth. The world has started to revolve around my own feet. Look—the earth is bathed in the tears of the heavenly being.*

Shirō looked up, as if his soul were breathing in the incense of the heavens.

When the news that the rebel forces had withdrawn from Tomioka Castle reached people in the Shiki region, there was a great commotion. Since the arrival of the rebel army, not only had the local people been supporting them with food and lodging, but twice they had joined in battles. Since old times, Shiki had been a center of Christianity, but recently many there had abandoned their faith. They now faced a situation where, after the withdrawal of the rebels, the castle forces would surely pursue and punish those who remained with a vengeance. Nevertheless, many were reluctant to pack up their families, leave their homeland, and take part in the struggle to occupy Hara Castle. At first they had begged the rebels not to abandon them, but soon they were claiming to have been deceived. In the end, some cursed others for being cowards, and even shouted that they should die.

On the morning the rebel troops left, some of the remaining villagers stood on the shore, hurling stones at the boats and yelling curses. And from the boats, curses were thrown back:

"False Christians! Why don't you try going back to that castle army and let *them* take care of you?"

Sasuke could hardly bear to hear such hostilities being cast about by his fellow farmers. He didn't have any particular attachment to the villagers around Shiki, but he felt bad about what was going to happen to them after he and the other rebels left.

However, Sasuke wasn't responsible for the fate of those who stayed. After the boats left, the people left behind quickly apologized to the government forces and claimed that the rebels had threatened to burn their villages, and so they had unwillingly pretended to cooperate with them. In the end, they were pardoned.

Shirō's boat was buoyed on swift currents toward Kuchinotsu. As he waved to the boats heading for Kōtsuura, he thought about his captured mother, grandmother and sister. The people going to Kōtsuura would return briefly to their hometowns and then take their families to Hara Castle. But now, he had only his father to go there with him.

As had happened during the disturbance at the beach, some people might want to abandon the rebellion in this coming time. They would return to their homes and see their families. Which way would they go? It would be up to each person to decide. Shirō believed that this was as it should be. Ultimately, everything would depend on the will of the Lord.

Shirō looked up at his father, standing by his side. All of his deep emotions seemed bound up in his stern expression. He hadn't spoken a word about his anguish since his wife, mother and daughter were captured. To Shirō, it seemed he had sacrificed them to the cause. Eventually he, too, would have to climb the hill of Calvary. Ever since Shirō had been chosen as commander at Yushima, Jinbei had not spoken to him as a father to his son.

The memory of his grandmother's face on the night of his coming-of-age ceremony, when she had stroked his wrist and placed the sake cup in his hands, came drifting back on the waves.

Shirō wanted to ask his father, "How is Grandmother doing?" but his father was staring up at the sky.

It was impossible for Jinbei to truly know the suffering of his captive family without experiencing it himself. Time after time, he reproached himself for not having acted more quickly to bring them to his side. But there was nothing he could do now to relieve his feelings. As one of the leaders of the insurrection, he had to accept his situation as a trial sent by God. Moving a few steps to the side of the boat, Jinbei glanced at Denbei, standing in the sea breeze. Denbei's suffering was no less than his own.

Denbei had relied heavily on his eldest son Kozaemon, but now that he was captured, Denbei never spoke of his troubles, despite being in a situation that would have driven most people to insanity. He took the place of his son and once again served as village headman, and he continued to manage the *confuraria* flawlessly. Jinbei, as a samurai, felt tremendous respect for Denbei's firmness of character. It had not been a mistake to go to him first in planning the rebellion. He found that this elderly leader was far more capable than he had previously realized.

Shirō, Jinbei and all those on the boat gazed at the currents with determined expressions.

"Look—those ruins! That's Hara Castle!"

People clung to the side of the boat and gazed at the distant cliffs that rose above the coast. To those from Shimabara it was a familiar sight, yet no one on board was unmoved by the unmistakable revelation inscribed on the ruins of that castle.

When Shirō had announced his plan to occupy Hara Castle, the people from Arima had been greatly pleased. Even if only its stone walls were left now, the castle remained a special place for the samurai of the old Arima clan; a place marked by their unforgettable bond with the late Lord Arima Harunobu. From time to time, they recalled with pleasure the religious faith that had been shared among the lord and his vassals.

"I still dream of the days when I served at that castle."

"So do I."

"This morning I dreamed I was on guard outside his room and he came out with a big smile, holding a sweet bean bun in his hand."

Such conversations were often exchanged.

"Well, it's a good idea about Hara Castle," Matsushima Sadonokami said. "Since the stone walls of its foundation are still strong, if we can repair the board fences and the turrets and keeps, we'll have an almost impregnable fortress. On the back side there are steep cliffs, and on the front side there's a big nasty, mucky bog. Attacking that castle would be incredibly difficult."

The Arima samurai broke into animated talk, and their excitement spread to the others. Their despair seemed to vanish miraculously and once again spirits were high. *If it hadn't been for these remarks, most likely they would have sailed along in miserable spirits,* Jinbei realized.

He was astonished by his son's plan, coming as it did at this late hour. The booming roar of the waves resounded in the pit of his belly. They were passing the whirlpools of the Hayasaki Straits.

When the people in Kuchinotsu noticed a group of boats approaching on the sea, they ran down to the harbor. Among them were thc Kuchinotsu headman Hasuda Nisuke, and Matsukichi and Oume. When Shirō stepped ashore, people kneeled along both sides of the roadway. Some shouted in reverence, "Lord in Heaven!" Shirō, accompanied by his followers, walked toward the headquarters at the Hasuda family home.

When Shirō crossed the threshold and entered the house, Oume approached him slowly with her arms spread wide.

"While I'm still alive, I'm seeing you again. *Namu amida butsu.* Praise to the merciful Buddha."

She embraced him, clapping him repeatedly on the back with her stout hands. Their eyes met. The look in her eyes melted away all the strain that Shirō had been carrying in his heart.

Thank goodness she, at least, doesn't treat me as a god.

Enjoying a relief he hadn't felt for some time, Shirō stood still for a few moments.

Shirō stayed with the Hasuda family for some time. Before they could occupy Hara Castle, Jinbei and the other officers had to finish countless preparations, but this period gave Shirō a brief chance to do things like watch the leaves of the persimmon trees fall in the garden. Having lost the happy circle of his own family, this was to be his last taste of warm family life.

Ukon stopped by every day. One day, as he was standing in the storehouse thinking about past times, a shadow fell over the threshold. It was Shirō. Ever since Shirō had been appointed commander,

Ukon had been careful about how he spoke to him, but now, as he stood in the storehouse, memories of their past days together at the school came back.

Perhaps lost in the same thoughts, Shirō said with a serious look, "Elder brother, if we manage to take Hara Castle, let's start the school again."

This was the first time Shirō had called him "elder brother." Ukon was surprised. It was as if the mark of a flower petal had been impressed on his soul. He was struck with an awareness of how short is the time we are granted in this life.

"'Elder brother,' you called me?"

Ukon's voice quavered. And then, so did Shirō's.

"Yes. Especially at this time, allow me to call you 'elder brother.'"

Shirō was standing up straight as he faced Ukon, but then, as if swept up in a flurry of petals, suddenly he started to faint.

As his slender body began to fall backwards, Ukon quickly grabbed hold of him.

The collapse of their commander threw the headquarters into a great commotion. Immediately, they called for Gensatsu, the doctor from Ōyano. From the start, he had been a central figure in organizing the insurrection.

Ever since the meeting on Yushima Island, Shirō's days and nights must have been filled with extreme tension. But whatever pains he had suffered, he had never made others aware of his feelings. At his bedside, watching Shirō's pale face, Ukon was overwhelmed with concern. Yet his thoughts were mixed with the brighter feeling from just moments ago when he had caught Shirō in his arms.

Gensatsu rushed over immediately. When he finished examining Shirō, his worried expression lifted. He announced his diagnosis: "Extreme exhaustion."

"You're young, so as long as you take a good rest and get enough nutrition, you should be feeling well again soon. You need to take better care of yourself, since your body is not only your own now. If our commander falls ill, how will we be able to fight? It will take a while to move into the castle. This will be a time, granted by Deus-sama, for you to recuperate, so make sure you take it easy."

Gensatsu turned to Ukon and requested that the tea room, set apart from the main building, be used for Shirō's convalescence. In the main building, which served as the army's headquarters, voices carried too loudly, all the way to the back room. He also asked Omiyo and Oume to take special care in preparing Shirō's meals.

Ukon remembered how, among all the soldiers on the battlefield, Shirō had been such a light eater. Some people considered him a heavenly being who had forsaken eating, but Ukon understood Shirō's deep troubles. From now on, he would sit with him at meal times and make sure he ate enough.

A steady stream of people came and went from the Hasuda home to attend meetings, and there was scarcely a spare moment to catch a breath. At the same time, Oume and Matsukichi were carrying out preparations to occupy the castle. Any bulky household furniture and unnecessary items were to be left behind, while whatever could be used as provisions was packed in straw bags or barrels. This included hoes and other farming tools for growing vegetable inside the castle grounds.

Shirō recovered enough to go out into the garden. He had the acute sense that everyone in this old household was trying to live to the best of their ability, until the very end. He felt that this place was like a familiar home he had known since the distant past. As he lay on his back, gazing up at the roof, he found himself calling out, "Mother."

The day before the entire Hasuda household, including all the helpers, planned to move into the castle, Okayo came running into the house, alone. When she saw Daisuke, she sank to the floor in exhaustion and clung to him.

"I know I'm going against the wishes of you and your father, that I should behave myself and stay with my family in Uchino, but please, let me go with you. I heard from my brother that the Kutchinotsu forces are going to occupy the castle. I'm prepared for whatever may come. If you won't let me go with you, I'll die right here."

Her face was pale, yet she spoke with an eerie calmness. Daisuke was at a loss for words. *What has happened to the delicate, tender woman I knew?*

Nisuke, Omiyo, Oume and even Matsukichi came in and listened.

"It's good you're back. This is the way it should be."

With these words, Oume embraced Okayo and lifted her up. Okayo burst into tears and began speaking almost incoherently, like a child. That morning, still in the dark, she had slipped out of her house, leaving a note behind, and had run as far as the bay at Futae no Ura. With good luck, she had found a boat heading for Kuchinotsu. The night before, she had confided her plans to Suzu, who had promised to care for Ayame. As a parent, she may have been acting selfishly, but Ayame would be brought up safely in the home of her grandfather.

At first, Okayo's face had looked like a Noh mask, but when Daisuke saw it return to that of her young self, his heart filled with affection.

Nisuke sighed deeply. All his precautions had been in vain. Yet perhaps this, too, was the will of Heaven.

"It's good that you came back today. If you'd come tomorrow, no one would have been left in our house," he said.

Omiyo took Okayo's hands with joy and helped her step up into the house. Okayo couldn't hold back her tears. And then, when she smiled, it felt as if the brightness of flowers was shining in the house for the first time in ages.

They had made plans to hold a farewell party that night to say good-bye to the old house in which they had lived for so long. Takematsu brought crabs and turban shells to the kitchen, and the preparations for a fitting last feast were almost complete. Oume, Matsukichi and Kumagorō sat down to take a break and looked carefully around the room. Would they ever work in this kitchen again? There was no way to know what would happen after tomorrow.

At sundown, when Matsukichi was sweeping the front garden, he noticed an unfamiliar woman enter quietly through the gate. She was accompanied by an attendant carrying her luggage. Wondering who could be coming at a time like this, he stopped, broom in hand.

"I'd like to ask if this is the army headquarters. My name is Onami. I've come from Nagasaki, hoping to see Shirō-sama."

When Matsukichi relayed her message to those inside, Shirō and Ukon rushed out to meet her. Having already exchanged what they had assumed to be their final words of parting, it was almost beyond belief to now see their Nagasaki benefactress Okattsama. Ushered into the reception room, Onami—Okattsama, that is—bowed deeply, placing her fingers respectfully on the tatami mat.

"Congratulations on the rebellion."

Shirō found himself at a loss for words.

"After you left Nagasaki, I wrapped up my affairs there and had planned to go off somewhere on a trip. Then a rumor reached Nagasaki that the headquarters of an uprising of Christian forces had been set up here. I also heard that the leader was a young person named Masuda Shirō, who had come down from Heaven. So, right away, I understood. I already knew that I had no place to go in this world. I set my mind on asking the honor of joining your efforts, even at the tail end, but I didn't know where to look. I imagined that if I went to the school in Kuchinotsu and talked to people there, they could tell me where your headquarters were. Thank goodness, it seems I've found it."

Both Shirō and Ukon just stared at her, unable to speak. Although Okattsama's white hairs showed, she looked more graceful than ever.

She smiled at the two young men.

"I hope I won't be a hindrance here, but when I was at the harbor I heard that you're going to take over Hara Castle. When you get into the castle, you're going to need women's help. You'll need flags and clothes for fighting. I'm plenty handy with needles. And as for my skills in general—well, let's just say I'm not too bad at a lot of other things, either."

Okattsama laughed a bit mischievously.

"I'm not bad at throwing the *shuriken* star knives, for starters. I learned that from Yang, the Chinese sailor who taught Shirō magic."

Since this sounded plausible, they weren't quite sure if she had said it mainly in jest, or to offer a real possibility. Leaving the two men baffled, Okattsama beckoned her companion to open her luggage.

Immediately, an array of richly textured fabrics were set out in front of them: crimson embroidered cloth, luminescent white figured satin, damask woven with small rising waves in dark jade colors, and more. All were gorgeous materials. Picking them up one roll at a time and piling them on a Sōwazen lacquered stand that she also had brought, Okattsama announced reverently:

"I regard the attire of our leader as of utmost importance, so I brought some things I had stored away in the back of my shop when I closed my business. These are just a small token of celebration. Please accept them and use them."

As Omiyo listened, she gazed at the fabrics that had been laid out on the table.

Drawing a deep breath, she murmured, "My goodness, these are so elegant . . ."

With a sense of women's shared intimacy, Okattsama placed some lengths of cloth in Omiyo's hands.

"This is a famous Chinese textile. It's a figured satin from Rakushū. And this is a flower-patterned satin. It has quite a large pattern, so I think it should be suitable for making a *jinbaori* jacket and *hakama* pants to wear at the headquarters."

Omiyo blushed and was left speechless, so Okattsama said softly, "I'd like to ask for help from all of you in making clothing for Shirō and the others in the headquarters. I look forward to working with you."

That evening, Henmi Juan, along with Yazō and Ukon's mother and sister, joined the feast.

When Juan was introduced to Okattsama, he thanked her for the treasured gifts she had sent in the past, including the Christian books and the precious incense wood. As he gazed intently at her, he spoke with deep emotion.

"I must say, we have been joined tonight by a most esteemed ally. I think this is more encouraging, even, than the support of a brave general. Agreed, everyone?"

"Juan-sama, it looks like you're going to be enjoying yourself a lot more from now on in the castle," Yazō teased.

"Now don't start making fun of the old folks. But having this woman here is more important than having you as a guest at tea."

Laughter broke out all around.

Okayo, dressed in her best clothing, brought in a small *ozen* dinner table and placed it in front of Shirō. Omiyo had instructed her to put on makeup for the last time. She looked even more lovely than usual, and sighs went up all around the room. An innocent-looking young woman brought an *ozen* table to Okattsama.

Turning to Omiyo, Okattsama asked, "And whose daughter, if I may ask, is this young lady?"

"This is Ukon-sama's sister, Mizuna-sama."

"Well, Mizuna-sama looks like a very promising young woman."

"Yes, and what a trying time this is for us all."

Although the crimson lacquer had worn off in places, the bowls and *ozen* tables had come from Nagasaki years ago and were of the finest quality. Omiyo hoped they could take this lacquer ware with them when they moved to Hara Castle and use it morning and night.

She motioned to Mizuna and whispered as she passed her a sake bottle decorated with gold flakes, "First, why don't you pour a little sake for Shirō-sama."

Since the night of the big storm the previous summer when he had first spent the night with them, Shirō had stayed with the Ninagawa family any number of times. During that time, Mizuna had grown from the innocent and frank young girl he had met into more of an adult. He glanced at her a bit nervously as she kneeled in front of him, holding the bottle of sake. Dressed in her purple crepe-silk kimono, she looked like an entirely different person. While he was guessing that she must be about fourteen, she opened her rouged lips.

"May I fill your cup?"

Flustered as Shirō raised his cup, Mizuna poured his sake without expression, keeping her eyes cast downward. As soon as Shirō had emptied the cup of sake, Mizuna let out a stifled giggle, unable to suppress it. Shirō was happy to see her return to the way she had looked on the night of the storm, when she had cried out so wildly like a child.

The celebration was fitting for their last night in the house. Daisuke wasn't with them, since for the past days he had been making repairs at Hara Castle, but the rest of those present were all Hasuda family members or people with close connections to the family, and they shared deep feelings for one another. Noticing the hand drum that had been placed behind Juan, Nisuke made a request.

"That hand drum . . . Juan-sama, do you suppose we might get you to sing us some Noh verses?"

"Oh, you saw it, did you?"

Placing his sake cup on the table, Juan glanced around.

"Well, since the sake has put us all in good spirits, I suppose it's about time for some songs."

When Juan picked up the drum and started tuning it, everyone quieted down.

"I'm not sure if it's the most appropriate song for this evening, just when we're about to be separated from this esteemed house, but since it's the only one I know, I'd like to sing from *Matsukaze, Murasame*."

Sighs rose up all around the room.

Everyone knew this was Juan's favorite Noh play.

The story was about two sisters who were divers. Their names were Matsukaze and Murasame, meaning "wind in the pines" and "rain in the town." Yearning for two noblemen who had fled from the capital of Kyoto to Suma Bay, the sisters had died of broken hearts. On a moonlit night, their spirits returned to the beach to draw water, and there, with the moon reflecting on the water in their pails, they danced and sang as the past came back to them.

"Ukon-dono, would you dance for us? I've been teaching you since you were a kid, haven't I?"

Without hesitation, Ukon stood up.

"I'll dance the part of Matsukaze. Who'll do Murasame . . . ?"

Ukon looked at Shirō.

"I can do Murasame."

Nodding, Shirō stood up.

"I remember the verses. It may be rash of me, but I'll try."

Already, the two actors were holding white fans in their hands. Everyone watching drew their breath and fell silent as the sharp slapping sounds from the drum reverberated through the room. Juan's plaintive voice penetrated the evening air:

As they ladle water from the sea, look—the moon is shining in the bottom of their pails.

Ukon proceeded to the center of the room and began reciting

the lead actor's part:

The moon, too, is in this pail.

Then Shirō entered and sang:

How joyous, seeing the moon here, too.

Juan sang the chorus, his voice resounding deeply:

One moon and two shadows, carried upon the night chariot of the full tide, along the path of tides that know no sorrows. At last, the two women dance together gracefully. Two spirits that had been crazed with yearning, now beautifully sublime.

Day breaks, leaving behind neither dreams nor traces. Hearing the sound of a passing shower and looking about in the morning, only the sound of the wind in the pines remains.

The audience was speechless. Seated in the shadows of the partition screen, Oume wept and Takematsu's lips twisted. As the dance continued, Daisuke returned home and sat at the back of the room. Okayo sat beside him, wiping the tears from her eyelashes. On this last night, everyone was swept up in an intoxicated dream. Finally, they fell into sleep.

The following morning, they woke early and prepared for their departure.

According to Daisuke, who had returned from Hara Castle the night before covered in dust, the repairs were proceeding swiftly under the direction of Shirō's father Jinbei and the other samurai soldiers. They had finished reinforcing the main castle walls and were now waiting for Shirō to join them. Scouting boats had brought back news that a large number of war boats had gathered in the port at Takase in the Higo domain, with the flags of many daimyo waving above them; it seemed the generals had already arrived with forces sent by the *bakufu* to put down the rebellion. Shirō and his followers marched toward Hara Castle bracing themselves for battle, realizing that the events they had been expecting had finally arrived. It was the third day of the twelfth month.

Itakura Shigemasa, the *bakufu's* special envoy, had arrived at Takase on the first day of the twelfth month. He had met with the Bungo overseer and various daimyo from neighboring domains and they had drawn up plans. On the fifth day of the twelfth month, they moved into Shimabara Castle. There, for the first time, the daimyo of all the surrounding domains received permission to supply troops.

After their unsuccessful battle at Tomioka Castle, the Kōtsuura and Ōyano forces had rowed back to their island towns in Amakusa. As soon as their boats touched shore, they had rushed home, kicking up clouds of sand. On the boat, Tsunekichi had been thinking about how he had no family to return to. But when they landed and he saw all the others hurrying back to their homes, he, too, started to hurry, and before he knew it, he arrived at his ramshackle house in the bushes.

On the way to the battle at Tomioka Castle, Tsunekichi had seen farmers in other villages escaping from the frenzied rebel forces. As their houses burned, they had fled in confusion and tears. The small thatched straw houses had caught fire quickly, and the flames jumped to other houses until they were all consumed in fire. Once the fire reached the straw houses, nothing could be done to stop it. He could not forget the terror in the children's eyes.

Perhaps my house, too, will be burned by the Hosokawa or the Terasawa army. If I had a wife and child, what would I do? He had felt as if his dead wife were staring at him. Seized with a vision of a baby wrapped in flames—even though he no longer had a baby—he rushed into his small house. The house was filled with nothing but silence.

"Papa, mama, let's all go together now. Osaki, you carry the baby!"

Tsunekichi called out the name of his dead wife and grasped the memorial tablets of his parents and ancestors. After wondering for a while what to do, he spread out a thin futon and tried to wrap the tablets in it. He thought he should also take some pots, bowls and knives. The bottoms of the pots were black with soot. He couldn't wrap them without first scraping off the soot. Unsure what to do, he lost his temper.

"Damn—at a time like this, why aren't you here?"

Hunched beside the futon, he started to weep. Had he been talking to his wife who had died—or rather, who had been killed? Or to his dead mother? For a while, he was lost in thought. Then, suddenly, he realized, *I'm not leaving today. Our departure is still five or six days from now.*

On the boats as they headed home to Amakusa, the rebels had talked amongst themselves.

"We'll all be going Hara Castle together—our women and children and our old folks and everyone. If we left them behind, they'd all be killed. This way if we die, we'll die together."

"So it's time to move house. Bring your pots, pans and hoes, and grain and salt—and don't forget the stone hand mills—we're all moving out."

"What will you do about your house?"

"My house? I can't make up my mind if I'll burn it or not."

Hearing such talk, Tsunekichi had felt envious. He had been living alone since his wife died, so why was he suddenly feeling so lonely? If Shichibei's mother Osato were still alive, he would have rowed her boat. But she was no longer in this world. Loneliness sunk to the marrow of his bones.

Sitting on the floor of his house, he muttered, "I won't be coming back here. Better to burn it myself than have it burned by the Hosokawa army."

Speaking to the memorial tablets that he had laid on the cloth, he asked, "Mother, when I was little, what were our days and nights like? In this broken-down place . . . I must have had some good times, didn't I?"

Tsunekichi filled his remaining days on the island with things like wandering along the shore and stopping in at the Kōtsuura headman Umeo Shichibei's house.

Lately, the townspeople he met along the shore and on the mountain roads had become strangely kind, as if both they and he had taken on the spirit of plants. The movements of the women pulling up daikons to dry and bring to Hara Castle looked more like the gestures of dolls than of actual women at work.

Except for the leading families, most people had few household possessions to bother with. They had made up their minds that they were going to Hara Castle—their Spring Castle—to live, and would never return to their old homes. They were abandoning the land passed down to them by their ancestors. As they got ready to leave, they were filled with thoughts that were hard to put into words.

With hardly any preparations to take care of, Tsunekichi decided to check on his neighbors.

"Have you gotten your things together? If you need help, I can lend a hand."

"Thanks, but we don't have much left to do."

A neighbor who had always talked to him roughly in the past now spoke to him humbly:

"I think one of our ancestors may have brought this plum tree here. Every night the one who planted it speaks to me in my dreams. He says, 'It's going to blossom soon—won't you dig it up and take it with you?' What do you think I should do?"

"If you want to dig it up and take it, I'll help."

"Well, thanks, but do you think we could plant it at Hara Castle?"

The man's wife cut in and scolded, "How can you be talking about such trifles at a time like this? We have bigger things to worry about. What's so important about that plum tree? If you have so much spare time, I wish you'd go catch us an octopus and dry it. Tsune-yan, I have something I'd like you to do."

"What can I do for you?"

"He seems to have his mind set on planting that plum tree at Hara Castle and living a long and happy life there with it. You suppose you could run over to Shichibei-sama and ask him if we can take a plum tree with us on the boat?"

When Tsunekichi struggled to find an answer, the wife pressed the point again:

"I can't believe he's talking about something so annoying at a time like this. Do you think he's really planning to take that plum tree and leave people behind?"

"Well then, how about we dig up some narcissus to bring? They're the spirits of our ancestors," the husband said.

At this point, the neighbor's elderly mother came out and took the side of her son.

"That's right. Why don't we take some narcissus as a memory of our ancestors?"

Glancing quickly at Tsunekichi, the wife retorted, "What's this now, mother and son both talking about narcissus? Why are you two going to Hara Castle anyhow? Are you going there to plant flowers?"

Tsunekichi hung around a little longer, then left them, but a strange feeling lingered in him.

On the third day of the twelfth month, lines of boats could be seen from the hilltops of Kōtsuura, rowing from the bays along the Ōyano coast toward Hara Castle. They looked like flocks of birds flying away. On the fourth and fifth of the month, boats continued to cross over. A messenger boat came to warn them that the Hosokawa clan had noted this flurry of activity and was hastening to mobilize its forces.

On the sixth, a swift boat arrived, carrying a report from the Arima group:

"Someone has entered Shimabara Castle; possibly the commander in chief of the *bakufu* forces. And large boats, flying various flags, are coming in, one after another. They're likely the boats of daimyo from nearby provinces. You all had better move out as soon as possible. Shirō-sama has already arrived at Hara Castle. He got there on the third."

After relating this urgent news, the messenger quickly rowed back.

The reason the group from Kōtsuura was so late in departing was because they had taken extra time to gather everyone from the small surrounding villages and Shimotsuura and prepare their boats. But it had become clear to everyone that they shouldn't waste any more time.

"All right now, the time has come. We'll all sail out tomorrow night on the evening tide. No one must be late."

Shichibei's orders were passed from person to person, and Tsunekichi also ran from village to village spreading the message.

"Let's make sure we get every last family on board. We're leaving on the evening tide. They'll burn out anyone who's left behind—children and all."

What did the families talk about and what did they do? Even though many of the sounds of ordinary life had ceased, including even the crying of babies, no one spoke ill of it.

The parents who couldn't bear to take the lives of their young children piled their backs with things like half-foot sandals and bags of edible wild plants and dried seaweed, and family memorial tablets as protective talismans. Probably they wanted to show that their children would be useful. Children of twelve or thirteen years old were already quite grown up. On their backs they shouldered iron pans and rice cooking pots wrapped in straw mats, and in their hands they carried hoes. They realized that the hoes might also be used as weapons. Loaded down in front and back and holding their rag-tag baggage in their hands, the villagers gazed up at the star-filled sky. They stood for a moment in front of their houses, where they had left the lamps burning, and parents told even the youngest children to press their hands together in prayer. Finally, as if in a dream, they arrived at the beach.

As they walked through the darkness, they called out to each other, lest their families become separated, and made their way onto boats of all sizes. They rowed silently into the open sea. They gripped the gunnels of the boats and watched the peaks of the familiar mountains fade into the distance. The sea wind was cold and everyone huddled together in the center of the boats, trying to warm each other. The oars creaked and the fangs of the sea seemed to howl. How many scores of ships must there have been? On that night, more than two thousand seven hundred people from Kōtsuura crossed over the sea.

When morning broke, at just about the same time as the people on the boats were gazing up at the dawn-tinted, vine-and-shrub-covered cliffs around Hara Castle, Karatsu clan sentries and Hosoda clan soldiers were storming the now-deserted villages around Kōtsuura.

At the urging of an elderly woman who lived nearby, Tsunekichi had left his house standing because she had told him it was the place where his ancestors' spirits came to play. When the Hosokawa army searched the hills, they set fire to it, along with all the other remaining houses.

The people on the boats had woken early. It seemed that Tsunekichi's elderly neighbor, who was on the same boat as him, had woken particularly early. Since her body was pressed against his back, he could feel her heart beating softly.

"My goodness, we've made it," she muttered to no one in particular. "Those must be the cliffs! I know them! When the time comes, the cherries there will blossom. I've heard about the castle, the way it was in the old days—that it was so beautiful at sundown. And if you saw it from the sea with Mount Unzen in the background it was such a stunning sight.

"Ah—and I remember! When I was young, I rowed there with some girlfriends to see the cherry blossoms. Tsunekichi—you have to wake up now. Your mother was with me! We landed over there at Ōe Beach—right over there. We'd planned to go up and look around, but we were scared that the spirits of the old lords and ladies, who'd had their heads cut off, might have come back to see their beloved cherry blossoms. So we just dug a few clams at the beach and then rowed back home.

"Those lords and ladies were Christians too, and they were sent off to some far-away place where their heads were cut off. The ladies were dressed in fine clothing when it happened. We kept turning around as we rowed, half thinking we'd see them in the shadows of the trees, dressed just like they were when they died. I'll never forget it. I wonder if the cherries trees still remember those old days when they blossom.

"Your mother was still young then, Tsunekichi. She died when you were a baby so you don't remember her, but your mother was a petite woman. And you were so adorable. We were great friends. When you meet your mother in the world to come, please tell her that her next-door neighbor told you about her. Are you awake yet?

"I'm not sure what it means, but I heard that the cherry trees there blossomed last autumn. I feel like they were calling to us and now we've crossed over to their castle. Tsunekichi, don't you suppose your mother, too, might be on this boat?"

Tsunekichi felt the old woman's back growing warmer. She coughed. When he rubbed her back, he felt he was being blessed with an unexpected joy. The mother of the village headman, too, had been unexpectedly caring toward him. And now this woman, who had lived next door to him but with whom he had never been particularly close, was treating him so thoughtfully.

Your mother was a petite woman. And you were so adorable.

Almost in a daze, Tsunekichi reflected on her words. He had no memory of the face of his mother, who had died when he was a baby. To think that she had come to this very castle to view the cherry blossoms when she was young! He truly felt her presence on the boat. He wiped away his tears with his large palm and helped some children from his neighborhood disembark from the boat, carrying their ancestors' memorial tablets, straw sandals and other belongings on their backs.

The ruins of Hara Castle were covered with plume grass, bush clover, kudzu and colorful vines, and inside, more people than Tsunekichi had ever seen before were scurrying around. The new arrivals were quickly setting up stone cooking stoves to prepare their morning meals. It made an oddly animated sight.

Although all the castle's buildings had been dismantled, the stone walls and dry moats had remained sturdy. The new inhabitants felt overwhelmed by the dignity instilled in them by the old castle.

Above the stone walls, strong wooden fencing made from the planks of their boats had been erected, reinforced by thick earthen backing. The fence stretched on as far as two thousand yards. Behind the walls was a long dry moat. Likely, it had been constructed at great effort to allow the soldiers to move around safely within the castle. Shirō's headquarters had already been constructed within the main enclosure, near the cliffs at the far end of the castle. The farmers, however, had built small shacks inside the ruins of the second and third castle keeps, in areas allotted by town. They were simple dugouts covered with roofs, but very sturdy.

When the Kōtsuura group arrived, they were greeted with cheers of welcome and exchanged friendly greetings with those who were already living there. However, they didn't have much time to enjoy themselves, for as soon as they finished breakfast, they had to start their work.

First, they had to go to the beach where they had left their boats and disassemble them, then carry the boards back up to the castle. The groups that had already arrived had all done the same thing. With those boards, they had constructed the reinforced wall that the newcomers now saw in front of them. It was still incomplete in places, and there were other weaknesses in the castle's defenses. They wondered if the boards from their own boats would also be used for this fence. They also had to erect the shelters where they would sleep this very night. They needed boards from their boats for this as well. Everyone started to work feverishly.

"We've got a long stretch ahead of us. It'll be getting colder, and once they start attacking the castle, the arrows and bullets are going to fly. We'd better make our roofs as thick as we can."

They passed the day working and talking, and by nightfall, they had assembled rough housing. At the end of the day, Masuda Jinbei led several of the leaders on an inspection tour. When he told them to let him know if they needed anything, they felt reassured.

The people from the southern part of the Shimabara Peninsula and from Ōyano Island and Upper Amakusa Island held a meeting in Shirō's headquarters, where they decided on fighting units and duties. The newly-arrived groups from Kōtsuura were told to stay in the Matsuyama outer enclosure, located at the south end of the castle complex.

Some of the newcomers grumbled at being told this just when they had finished building their new shelters. But the military commissioner had asked them to move there without complaining, so the Kōtsuura group moved again to the outer enclosure.

Word went out that Shirō was planning to convene a large meeting in the early afternoon in the open space in front of his headquarters.

"Tsunekichi, are you going too?" Shichibei called to him.

Tsunekichi nodded.

Normally, Tusnekichi would have declined a suggestion to join such a meeting, but it had been ordered that as many people as possible should take part.

Thousands crowded into the open ground inside the main enclosure. Some of them even climbed the pines and cherry trees to see better. Since they had been working day after day, they were covered with dust and dirt. When they grinned, their eyes framed by unkempt hair, they looked like wild mountain bandits.

Next to Tsunekichi was a large man who stood some six feet tall. Tsunekichi remembered that when he was dismantling the boat he had come on, with every swing of his hammer this man had called out the words of the Buddhist chant *namu amida butsu*. Later, he learned that he had been a monk at an Ikkō sect temple in the mountains, some four miles from Kōtsuura. When he smiled, his tiger-like face gave a jolly impression, and Tsunekichi had taken a strong liking for him.

Kamizaki Daizen appeared at the top of the rugged stone walls that surrounded Shirō's headquarters.

"I want you each to take the message I'm about to give you back to everyone in your group. Today, we have over thirty thousand people inside this castle complex."

A stir rose up among the assembly and it took some time to subside. Everyone knew there were a lot of people in the castle, but it was astounding to think that such a large a number of farmers had abandoned their homes and fields to join the uprising.

"I feel so heartened by the strength of our faith, the grace of our Lord and the strength of our religion," Daizen continued.

He read out the plans for the organization and deployment of troops in the castle. He named the various leaders, starting with Masuda Shirō, the commander in chief, and continued on down through the councilors, the consulting members, the military commissioners, the flag bearers, the building and construction workers, the superintendents, the guards and the messengers, as well as the commanders of the main, second and third enclosure and of the Matsuyama outer enclosure and the leaders of the rifle-bearing artillery units. The list ran on to several dozen names.

"Well, everyone, for many days now you've labored hard to rebuild this castle. I thank you deeply for your efforts. But now the real battle is about to begin. The shogun has appointed General Itakura to lead the government troops and they've been ordered to hunt down and destroy all rebel forces. He's already arrived at Shimabara Castle, so we can expect that in a few days he and his troops will get here and start their attack on our castle. He's backed up by the renowned Lords Hosokawa, Nabeshima and Kuroda and their armies. Are you prepared for this? We're going to be completely surrounded, with not even an opening wide enough for an ant to crawl through, and the bullets are going to fall on us like hail."

"Get ready! Get ready!" someone bellowed.

Tsunekichi was startled. When he glanced around, he realized it was the Buddhist monk with the face of a smiling tiger.

Caught up in the spirit, a woman cried out tensely, "The women are part of this, too!"

Slowly, Daizen looked around to where her voice had come from and nodded.

"She sounds brave. Perhaps we'll be able to rely on you women more than on your husbands!"

Peals of laughter broke out.

"And so, everyone, with our spirits united, we're going to hold this castle. Our Lord Yesus-sama and Mother Maria-sama are our witnesses. And Santiago. Hurrah!"

Cries of "Santiago!" rose up all around. His body trembling, Tsunekichi raised his hands to the sky. He heard himself shouting wordlessly. Gradually, starting from the front, the voices settled down. When Tsunekichi looked up at the stone wall, he saw Shirō standing on top.

Dressed in a dazzling white kimono and an iridescent military surcoat embroidered with chrysanthemums on a hexagon-patterned material, with smart *hakama* trousers of the same material, Shirō was gazing up at the sky.

When the sunlight reflected off the cross on Shirō's chest into Tsunekichi's eyes, he staggered involuntarily, recalling the heavy weight of the wooden cross that had bitten so deeply into his shoulders when he had carried it in the procession of atonement. The monk standing beside him grabbed his arm, wondering what was wrong. Tsunekichi recovered somewhat, but was left with the feeling that a mark had been placed indelibly on his shoulders. It seemed he had been touched softly and firmly, as if by the hands of his late wife, or of his mother. He couldn't help wondering if they might even have been the hands of Maria-sama. He wanted to know whose hands they were, but as he was thinking about it, the feeling of the soft hands disappeared and he was left with a sense that something important was weighing down his shoulders and preventing him from moving. Even though the monk had been watching him carefully, he hadn't noticed this.

Shirō had just started to speak. With the intense light of the sky shining on his back, he looked like the incarnation of a white heron.

" . . . With our thanks to infinite mercy, from today on, in this castle we are literally committing ourselves to living together. Our fate has become one, and it will remain one in the hereafter. Let us decorate our bedsides with the broken wild chrysanthemums that are still blooming in the fields. Just as a divine light dwells in these flowers, the grace of God shines on each of us. And from this evening on, in this castle that we have rebuilt, the thundering of the hooves of the horses of God will resound. Santiago, the Spanish saint of war, will come to us at night on his divine horse to give courage to us, and to our esteemed relatives from Shimabara and Amakusa who have overcome endless hardships and already achieved martyrdom.

"Our lord alone teaches us that we should love others as we love ourselves. From this night onward, let us pray for the beautiful dreams of all, from the elderly who have just a short time remaining on this Earth to the youngest among us."

Shirō paused for a moment, then continued.

"Our Lord is watching over us now, overflowing with joy. The teachings of our Lord have become visible, right before our eyes. We are no longer individuals, but brothers and sisters, joined in waging God's holy battle. God's country lies before us. We must summon all our strength and move forward."

Holding his rosary beads, Shirō began to recite an *oratio*.

As the light started to change the colors of the mist, the congregation looked up to the sky. All knelt down and brought their dirt-covered hands together in prayer. As they recited the *oratio,* their voices rose into the sky, layered upon each other. Their prayers spread from the courtyard to the neighboring headquarters, and then to other headquarters beyond, until finally the entire castle, towering above the coast, was enshrouded in prayer.

On his way back to the Matsuyama outer enclosure, Tsunekichi said to the monk, "I'm Tsunekichi. I've been working for the headman of Kōtsuura village as a messenger, but Reverend, might I ask your name?"

"Me? I'm Sainen."

"You're a Buddhist monk—but you're with us Christians?"

Sainen looked down at Tsunekichi with a puzzled face.

"I haven't changed my religion, you know. You can call me a monk, but before that I was a farmer, and my farmer's blood has been stirred and it brought me here."

"As for me, my parents were Christians, and I'm also a Christian, but in name only. I don't understand all of it. But when I heard Shirō-sama speak just now it sent shivers down my back. *Paraizo* isn't in the world beyond. It's in this world. For the first time, I felt that in my heart. What did you think about his sermon, Reverend?"

Tsunekichi realized that he was feeling freer and speaking more smoothly than usual.

"Well, in my religion we talk about the Western Pure Land of Amida . . . but I'll pray to Maria-sama and chant *namu amida butsu* too. Seems to me there's no big difference between those two things. I'm the son of Hiroshima farmers who went broke, and I was taken in by a temple when I had no place to go. Then I wandered south and ended up in Amakusa, here in Kyushu. But I don't have much taste for giving sermons. The people in Kōtsuura were good and friendly and somehow, I spent four or five years there. The townspeople treated me kindly and started calling me 'Reverend,' and I wanted to stay with them. And then Shirō-sama came along. He was such an impressive, good-looking kid. I had to follow him—like Benkei of old."

When Tsunekichi looked up at him in surprise, Sainen smiled, as if enjoying a joke.

Below the castle, from his boat on the shore of Ōe Beach, Yazō listened to the *oratio* floating in the evening sky. *How many thousands or tens of thousands of voices could there be?* Never before had he heard so many human voices. It seemed as if this rainbow of voices was sinking into the quiet ripples of the sea and being carried toward Amakusa.

The voices were not shouting and clamoring. They were very soft. They could not but serve as prayers of purification and self-renunciation; prayers of supplication to Heaven; prayers rising from a people born of this earth. Yazō and his crew members dropped to their knees. The sounds of the *oratio* resounded from high above the cliffs and echoed through the fortress until their lingering tones faded into the waves of the sea.

Yazō gazed across the undulating waves. He saw no sign of any other boats. Except for his one fast boat that was being used for reconnaissance, all the others had been dismantled, their wood turned into the walls of the castle.

There had been some discussion at the headquarters about whether or not to save this last fast boat with its thirty oars. Some had been reluctant to take it apart, given how valuable it was for reconnaissance and transporting people. There was no telling how things would unfold, so most people had felt they should save this one last boat.

"This boat has put in a lot of work for us, and now I guess we can let her sleep on this beach, loaded with our unfinished dreams."

Yazō remembered these words that Juan had spoken with a smile as the meeting came to a close.

"All right then, shall we pull her up onto land before it gets dark?" Yazō said, looking up at the castle walls as the last strains of the *oratio* rose into the sky.

Gazing out over the sea, Yazō stroked the boat's mast and gunnels, and then made the formal sign of the cross, which he rarely did. His crew members joined him in the gesture.

Starting in his youth, Yazō had sailed on foreign ships and traveled to far-off places like Macao and Formosa, and of course to all the ports of Western Kyushu, and he had gotten into many dangerous scrapes. He had little desire for riches and was well trusted, and he enjoyed working to gain people's trust. He had been helped greatly by his friendship with the Hasuda and Ninagawa families, and by Juan-sama; but he had worked especially closely with Onami. At the time of the great martyrdom at Genwa, he had gone with her to the execution grounds to see her "dear ones" through to their last moments. He was not a particularly devout follower of his family's religious tenets, however, and he had often told Juan that he considered himself a Christian in name only. He was more interested in the mundane lives of ordinary people.

Yazō looked up at the scarlet flag above his boat, waving

brightly in the slanted rays of the sun. The flag was trimmed with a Chinese-style gold fringe and emblazoned with white characters for the sun and moon. With this flag, Yazō's boat could be recognized from far away.

But how could I ever have imagined that Onami-sama would come to this castle?

He took down the crimson flag. When he was finished, darkness had settled on the land.

Yazō stared at his boat and sighed.

"You stay here and dream for a while. As for me, I have much to do."

Early the next morning, Sasuke went out from the third enclosure and stopped in at the Kuchinotsu village headquarters. After their retreat from Tomioka castle, most of the men from Futae had returned home and hadn't gone on to Hara Castle. But a few of them had ventured to join those inside the castle. Satsuke and some of the other young people from Uchino were now living with them, out along the edge of the third enclosure.

From the time Sasuke arrived at the castle, he had been busy every day and hadn't been able to visit Daisuke. At the big open meeting at the main enclosure the day before, it had been too hard to find Daisuke among the crowd of people. The Kuchinotsu headquarters were said to be located "at the far end of the second enclosure." At last, Sasuke found Daisuke's hut.

"Sasuke-don, you found me! Today, finally, I have some free time and I was just about to take a look around the castle with Kumagorō. I'll bet you haven't seen it all yet, either. It's really a huge castle."

First the three men explored the second enclosure. It was built on land a level higher than the third enclosure, and on its spacious grounds were countless little huts. The smoke from breakfast fires still hung in the air. In the back, near the cliffs by the sea, was a large lotus pond with several hundred ducks on it.

They climbed to the lookout of the main enclosure. At its entrance they were questioned by guards, but when Daisuke told them he was the son of the headman of Kuchinotsu, they quickly let them pass.

Looking out from the top of the central fortress, they could view the entire castle complex. The third, second and main enclosures were connected to one another, curving along the coast from north to south. South of the main enclosure was the long, narrow Matsuyama outer enclosure. Below the cliffs under the main enclosure were the Ōe inlet and the rear gate of the castle. The main gate was in the third enclosure. In the back of the castle compound were sheer cliffs that plunged into the sea, and in front were marshlands and the salt flats of the inlet that flowed into a small bay. It would be no easy feat for an enemy to scale the walls and enter the castle.

"This sure is quite a structure. Shirō-sama has planned well," Daisuke said with a sigh.

"So, this is our castle," Sasuke said, then fell silent, perhaps feeling overwhelmed.

Kumagorō clenched his hands and raised and lowered his shoulders.

"We've never had much to do with castles. I just thought of them as places where we paid the land taxes."

Not having had time recently even to shave, Daisuke had grown a beard. Stroking his cheeks, he looked toward the main road.

"With that beard of yours waving in the wind, you look like a great general."

"Oh, come on, stop joking. If I'm a general, then I'm a beggar-general. But being here in this castle with my whole family makes me so happy. And Kumagorō is with us, too. It's the same for every family. What happiness, for parents and children, brothers and sisters to all be together."

Suddenly, Daisuke fell silent. He had remembered that Sasuke's parents and wife and children were in Uchino. Sasuke, however, looked up and said proudly, "My brother, I, too, am happy. Only five or six people came from my village, but in this place, there's no difference between my village and the others. With all of us piling up sandbags together, our spirits have become one. This is the first time I've ever felt this way."

Daisuke peered into Sasuke's face. Whether it was owing to his good upbringing or something else, he seemed to feel no ill will whatsoever. Being addressed as "brother," Daisuke felt a wave of affection, mixed with a twinge of pain, for this straight-forward young man.

Just then, Kumagorō shouted wildly, "They're coming! They're coming! Over there—they're coming!"

In the distance, in the direction Kumagorō was pointing to, dust was rising from the road. In wave after wave, a great army of thousands, or tens of thousands, was advancing like an enormous swarm that far outnumbered the forces in the castle. The three men ran off to the stockade on the north side of the main enclosure. In an instant, it was crowded with people. Those who were running to the main headquarters to bring the news met others who were rushing back to their own quarters, and the entire place was filled with a tremendous clamor.

Kumagorō was trembling. From the depths of his heart, he shouted:

"You fools, just wait and see! Father, Mother, Sankichi—we'll take revenge on our enemies!"

Itakura Shigemasa, the shogun's chief envoy, had left Edo on the ninth day of the eleventh month and arrived in Takase in the Higo domain on the first day of the twelfth month. Shigemasa was the third son of Itakura Katsushige and had shown his ability as the shogun's military governor in Kyoto. When the daimyo were transferred in the ninth year of the Kanei era (1632), he had been sent to Kyushu as the shogun's envoy, so he was already well-acquainted with the situation in the area. He was fifty-one years old.

When Shigemasa entered Shimabara Castle on the fifth day of the twelfth month, he was following orders from the *bakufu* to organize the shogun's troops from Hizen, Higo and Chikugo into a large punitive army. Under him, he had ten thousand troops of the Nabeshima clan from Saga and eight thousand troops of the Arima clan from Kurume, along with others from the Tachibana clan in Yanagawa and the Matsukura clan forces. After setting up encampments in front of Hara Castle, they launched an offensive on the eighth day of the twelfth month.

Since the outbreak of the rebellion, all the daimyo in Kyushu had vied to prove their loyalty to the government and express their eagerness to fight, but among them, the Nabeshima and Hosokawa daimyo had been particularly aggressive. In the past, at the Battle of Sekigahara, the Nabeshima army had suffered disgrace owing to its having taken the side of the western army, so now it had a particularly strong motivation to restore its honor. The Nabeshima Lord Katsushige had even boasted to the *bakufu* that he wanted to destroy the entire rebel army with his own forces alone.

In the past, the Hosokawas had held strong ties with the Christians. Hosokawa Tadaoki, the former lord, had not actually converted to Christianity, but he had been close friends with Takayama Ukon, and through that connection his wife Gracia had become an ardent believer. Even after his wife died, he had continued to show his liking for the Christians. The Jesuit priests had placed their highest trust in him. Even after the suppression of Christianity began, he had helped to protect the missionaries in the Kokura fief.

However, precisely because of this past history, Hosokawa Tadaoki and his son Tadatoshi had been forced to show even stronger zeal than others in suppressing the Christians. The southern half of the Higo domain had formerly been part of the domain of Konishi Yukinaga, and although Christianity had been subdued, at least on the surface, there were still quite a few people in the area who steadfastly maintained the Christian traditions. The daimyo could not overlook the possibility that the Christian rebellion that had broken out on the Amakusa Islands might affect his own domain, just a short hop across the Shiranui Sea. The Hosokawa clan spared no effort in patrolling and preparing the coastline for war, gathering information, and other painstaking operations.

Since the outbreak of the rebellion, a stream of refugees had been crossing over the Shiranui Sea from the Amakusa Islands to the shore of the Hosokawa domain in Higo. By the twentieth day of the eleventh month, two hundred thirty people had fled to Ashikita County, another two hundred had gone to Yashiro, and seventy had fled to Uto County. None of these refugees had supported the Christian rebellion, and they had felt in danger. The Hosokawas questioned them relentlessly about affairs in the area.

On the seventh day of the twelfth month, following orders from chief envoy Itakura Shigemasa, the Hosokawa clan brought its large army of 16,000 over to attack Amakusa. They were prepared to fight, but when they discovered that the Christians of Ōyano and Upper Amakusa had already left for Hara Castle, all they could do was set fire to the deserted houses, fields and hills and pull back to the port of Kawajiri in Higo.

The besieging army began its attack on the castle on the tenth of the month, but the rebel defenses proved formidable and the clan soldiers were unable to readily force their way in. Meanwhile, the *bakufu* government had received the shocking news that the rebel army was far larger than it had imagined. The *bakufu* leaders decided to dispatch senior statesman Matsudaira Nobutsuna. He left Edo on the third day of the twelfth month.

CHAPTER TEN

IN FLAMES

The Kuchinotsu troops led by Ninagawa Sakyō were stationed in the second enclosure, a critical location on the front lines of the fighting. Yazō and his boat crew had also joined their ranks.

The next morning, Yazō climbed the castle walls to assess the state of the enemy forces. Daisuke joined him.

"I thought they had quite a gang out there, but it turns out even the Arima and Nabeshima fighters are nothing special."

Daisuke was talking about the previous day's attack. After learning the basics of using a rifle at Tomioka Castle, he had become an able marksman. Just yesterday he had shot down an attacking Arima general on horseback.

"Maybe not, but they're just getting started. Judging from the flags out there, the Hosokawa troops haven't arrived yet. The real battle is still to come. As for me, I'm like a fish out of water up here on land, and it's getting to me. I'm no good cooped up like this. The open sea is where I belong. What do you think, Daisuke?"

With Yazō bantering away, his voice and eyes so spirited despite being constrained within the castle, Daisuke felt at ease.

"Across the seas you'll find all sorts of countries. The waves are like mountains, but when you get past them you feel like a real man. Out there, over the seas, there's all kinds of people. When you bargain and trade with them you feel a bit like a pirate. What do you say—when the fighting's over, how about you come on board my *Higetsu Maru*?"

Daisuke glanced quickly at Yazō. Did he really think they would be able to get out of this castle alive?

"Sounds good to me. If you'll take me on the *Higetsu Maru*, I'll work hard to become a great pirate."

Laughing, Daisuke felt as if, somehow, bright rays of sunlight were shining on the castle.

The *Higetsu Maru* had carried some remarkable goods. The rebels had already brought over everything remaining in their storehouses in Kuchinotsu and Nagasaki, including the magnificent contributions from Okattsama—that is, Onami-sama. When they were brought to Shirō's headquarters, everyone had gasped in amazement. Such goods carried a whiff of the distant lands of China and Europe. People had heard that far across the seas to the south of Amakusa was the Portuguese port of Macau. They wondered if her things had come from there. When Daisuke thought about their situation inside the castle compared to the wider world beyond, he felt a little dizzy.

"Yazō, tell me more about what's out there beyond the seas."

"Well, I'd like to, but I don't know if we have time for a chat now. It all depends on our enemies, I guess," Yazō said, gazing out at the enemy encampment, where activities seemed to have lulled.

Such an immense knowledge of those far-off lands and people is stored up in this man. If he should die, all those memories will go with him. That would be a sadder loss than losing any sort of riches.

Yazō glanced at Daisuke.

"Hey, with that beard of yours, you're looking a lot more manly these days. I hear Okayo-dono has fallen in love with you all over again!"

Embarrassed, Daisuke raised a hand to his face.

The previous night, when Okayo asked him to shave, he had surprised her by replying that he didn't plan to go back to being clean-shaven.

Shirō's headquarters also served as the chapel. Now furnished with the gifts from Onami—mother-of-pearl inlaid chairs, a Chinese desk, large brass candlestands—it had taken on an imposing appearance. The inner quarters were decorated with sumptuous crimson damask silk.

Shirō's assistants were young men, about fifteen to twenty years old, who had been chosen from among the most loyal supporters of the rebellion. His headquarters were at the very back of the castle, just above the cliffs. Thanks to this location, those inside could only faintly hear the battle cries and gunfire, and remained somewhat removed from the general air of tension. On days when the castle wasn't under attack, some of the young assistants lounged in the old-fashioned ebony chairs and chased each other around the tables for amusement.

Ukon watched them for a while with a bemused smile, but finally said, "All right now, enough horsing around. Don't you hear the gunshots over in the second enclosure?"

As they rushed out to look, he shouted, "Wait—don't go running off now. I have something to talk to you about, so pull your chairs together and take a seat."

Ukon remained standing, straightening his posture.

"I suppose you'd like to run out and see what's happening now, but your job is to look after Shirō-sama. Despite your youth, you've been chosen as his assistants, so you must stay calm no matter what happens. And I'm not just saying you have to be on your best behavior. Soon the devouring flames of the end of the world will reach us, and even then we must preserve these headquarters as a place of tranquility. To do that we have to keep our spirits strong and the eyes and ears of our hearts open.

"What do you make of this headquarters? Why do you think we've shut ourselves up in this castle? In protecting the house of the Lord and those within this castle, we're casting off our individual selves and becoming one with the glory of God's mystery. In the long history of humans, there have been times when exceptional events occurred; events deeply inscribed with the mark of God. I ask you to think of the battle we're waging inside this castle as a part of this glorious history that will be passed on to the world to come. Along with Shirō-sama, you are carrying this glory.

"Our days in this castle mark a time shining with light and immortality, such as we will never again experience. Can't you hear the ticking of the flower clock that measures this time in our lives? So, gather yourselves together, make of yourselves a single arrow, and strive until you become as beams of light. This arrow of spirit will not fail to reach the world of the hereafter, where you will be reborn in eternal life."

Shirō and Juan were standing behind Ukon, nodding solemnly.

In a room facing a wide porch, Onami was busy sewing, helped by Omiyo and her assistants. She asked two of the women to take an end of a large piece of white silk cloth, and then she stood up.

"We've finished the banner," she said.

Everyone sighed in admiration. In the center of the banner was a sacred chalice, flanked by two worshipping angels. Above it were Portuguese words that Juan read out.

"*Lovvado seia o sãctissimo sacramento.*"

"What does that mean?" someone asked.

"It means 'Praised be the most holy sacrament.'"

The design had been painted by Yamada Yomosaku. He had been given a room near the headquarters to devote himself to painting religious pictures. His finished works were displayed in the headquarters.

Onami thought back to the day she gave Ukon the valuable Christian books. What strange times had passed since then. Her ties with Shirō had also been her ties with Ukon. How mysterious that, as a result of these well-nurtured ties, just now she had heard the normally-quiet Ukon speaking so passionately in the fortress of this castle.

From the first time she met Shirō she had felt a special affection for him, but she had never imagined they would end up together in a castle fortress like this. She recalled for a moment her time as a prostitute. Those days—including when her Christian parents had been forced to sell her, their own daughter—seemed to belong to the world of the distant past.

Looking outside, she could see the boat-plank fencing stretching into the distance, enclosing the little dugout huts. A mild winter sun was shining on them. To Onami, the entire castle complex seemed like a living being breathing in and out a faint light from the earth at its center. And she herself was like a clump of moss taking in this faint light from her warm, sunny spot on a hill.

Everything was coming to an end, and although she had meant to set out on one final unmoored voyage, she had somehow been called to this place of death, as if she was in the most beautiful, exquisite dream. As sundown steeped the castle in a deep crimson light, a vision appeared before her. A curtain the color of flickering flames covered the hills and then rose up into the sky. *How beau-*

tiful—the world is ending, she whispered to herself as she gazed up at the sky.

Snapping out of her reverie, Onami realized that her hands were cold. The three women nodded. They held up the newly made banner for the headquarters, slid a pole through its sleeve, and spread it out on the Chinese-style table.

"With this flag, the spirit will be with us. This sacred flag, with its special design, is exactly right for our cause."

The young men raised it high on the stone wall of the headquarters.

The rebel forces struggled on, surviving for another month inside the castle. The nights they passed inside their small huts were bitterly cold. People slept on straw-strewn dirt floors, covered only with thin cotton blankets, their bodies huddled together for warmth.

A second attack was made on the castle. The rebel forces fought off the attackers by firing rifles and throwing rocks so the enemy couldn't scale the castle walls. Everyone was amazed at how, in this time of need, they seemed to have mustered a strength far beyond that which they normally possessed. Especially when they faced the Matsukura forces, their strength seemed to be multiplied several-fold. When the enemy retreated, Shirō's headquarters overflowed with worshipers.

On the first day of the first month of the fifteenth year of the Kanei era (1638), Itakura Shigemasa had taken sole command of the united attacking armies. However, the *bakufu* leaders had previously received reports warning them that the rebellion was not likely to be easily crushed, and had already appointed Matsudaira Nobutsuna as the shogun's deputy. Nobutsuna, who had much experience in war, had left Edo on the third day of the twelfth month. It was said that Itakura Shigemasa felt disgraced by this and may even have rushed to an early death because of it, although this remained unclear. In any case, on the day of the second attack, the front-line Arima army retreated after suffering a clear defeat and the Matsukura forces, too, fearing the rebel army inside the castle, failed to advance. And so Itakura Shigemasa charged through the front lines on his horse and was struck in the heart by a bullet and killed.

Matsudaira Nobutsuna arrived at Hara Castle on the fourth

day of the first month. On the following day, the twenty-three thousand men of the Hosokawa army were added to the *bakufu*'s attacking forces. Along with the thirty-five thousand Nabeshima forces and the eighteen thousand Kuroda forces, the total number of men participating in the siege now amounted to over one hundred twenty thousand. Nobutsuna's basic strategy was to starve the rebels out. He anticipated that the food and other provisions in the castle wouldn't hold out for long, and therefore avoided making unnecessary attacks. He drew a tight cordon around the castle, built artificial hills, erected observation towers and established the foothold for an eventual decisive attack.

Nobutsuna again shot an arrow into the castle, with a message calling for the rebels' surrender:

What ill will or grudge led you to start this uprising and confine yourselves in this old castle? If you have some complaint against the Matsukura administration, we will do all we can to meet your requests. Leave the castle soon, return to your homes, and resume farming. If you do this, we will provide you with two thousand koku *of rice and grant you an exemption from this year's land taxes, as emergency measures. Furthermore, from now on, we will reduce the land tax to thirty percent and exempt you from other taxes, which will make your lives easier.*

When the message was unrolled and read at Shirō's headquarters, everyone laughed derisively. It was clear to them that this "invitation" was no more than a ruse—one they did not intend to accept meekly. What was its aim? To seed confusion and discord in the castle?

"We'll reply by feigning ignorance."

As for our occupation of this castle, we have no intention of establishing our own country or of disobeying the daimyo. We have no ill will toward the country or our neighbors. If you do not object to our faith, we have nothing more to say. Let us be. Our concerns are only about our religion, and about making a strong new start.

Respectfully

For some time, an exchange of arrow messages continued.

This battle of words was not limited to official exchanges between the *bakufu* and rebel forces. From time to time, for example, the painter Yamada Yomosaku exchanged messages with the forces of the Matsukura and of the former Shimabara Lord Arima Naojun, who had renounced his Christian faith.

Yomosaku had painted folding screens on commission for the Matuskura lords and their chief retainers, and he hadn't intended to join the uprising. The Christians in his town had threatened to burn his property if he didn't support them and had taken his wife and children hostage, so his only choice had been to join them in the castle. In the arrow messages, the former Lord Arima Naojun tried many times to change Yomosaku's mind. In the end, Yomosaku decided on betrayal.

Among the arrow messages from the rebels, some appeared to be forgeries. One notable example bearing the signature of Amakusa Shirō read, "*In order for us to arrive smoothly in the Paradise to come we must trample on the Buddhist books of Enma the King of Hell, and dance our way through the bloodbath of Asura. Such actions will, no doubt, be necessary.*" But even though the Christians' beliefs were deeply intertwined with local customs and Buddhist traditions, it was hard to imagine that Shirō would have used such inherently Buddhist phrasing as the "King of Hell" and the "Paradise to come." In contrast, a message he sent to Hosokawa Nakanori and his chief counselors on the nineteenth day of the first month contained few such excessive flourishes and more directly conveyed the rebels' claims.

The reply from the government side read, "*A message containing requests from those inside the castle has come to the attention of the shogun and there are some questions regarding its veracity. As for now, rest assured.*" This message merely appeared to state that the government side had received the previous message and that it had been passed on to the shogun. In other words, little scraps of truth and falsehoods were being exchanged between the two sides.

When the government accused the rebels of "*unthinkable acts against the country*" and "*causing the deaths of countless people,*" the rebels replied that, "*We did not initiate these aggressive acts. We were merely responding to the death and destruction you have caused in Amakusa and Shimabara and trying to prevent further calamity. If you look at the situation from the very beginning, all is clear. The crucial point is that we have been set ablaze by God's mysterious will. It may be difficult for you to understand this, as it relates to the essence of our religious belief.*"

When Lord Matsukura Katsuie inquired about an "*ill will or grudge*," the rebels had replied, "*We have none. As long as you don't interfere with our religion, we have no complaints.*" Their response to a rumor about having ordered an exile-execution of Katsuie was, "*This is so absurd we can't help laughing.*"

In regard to questions about Shirō, the reply began, "*I will try to answer.*" The writer introduced himself and then continued, "*I must say that he is an angel. He is most graciously born and wise, such as ordinary minds can never imagine.*"

However, the sections of the rebels' message that attracted the most attention were those that distinguished between "*matters of this world*" and "*matters that are important for the world to come.*" The words "*matters that are important for the world to come*" were also used in Buddhist scriptures, but of course for the Christians they referred to their hope for salvation in the next world. The rebels had written that, as for "*matters of this world*," they had no intention of going against the government. On the contrary, they claimed that if the government were to find any sign of treason among the believers, it would be their duty as Christians to lay down their lives. This was no falsehood. But as for "*matters that are important for the world to come*," they had resolved that, following the angel's holy orders, they would not retreat even one step.

This was how they interpreted the Bible's teaching to "Render to the Emperor the things that are the Emperor's, and to God the things that are God's." Their claim to have no intention of defying the government should not be understood as a sign of ideological limitation. Rather, they were declaring that, even if the orders came from the shogun himself, they had no intention of obeying when "matters important for the world to come" were involved. Such matters were of a different dimension.

What stood out above all else in the arrow messages was the

rebels' total commitment to their cause. To the sweet-sounding suggestion that they might return home with their families if only they surrendered, they replied, "*It is our desire to dwell in the treasured land of the great infinite, and so we have no wish to inhabit this land of pain and suffering.*" In conclusion, they wrote, "*In accordance with the above-stated message, any further efforts and offers will be futile. We are resolved to send no more, and it will be pointless for others to send us any further such communications.*" It was a strikingly bold reply.

For some time, days passed without any fighting. Those inside the castle found it curious to watch the attacking forces busy at work constructing man-made hills. With tremendous energy, they transported bundles of bamboo and erected bridges over the marshes and tide pools that surrounded much of the castle, and set up bases for staging an attack. Day by day, their man-made hills grew higher. Then, on the hilltops, they erected observation towers. Huts went up in places where just the previous day there had only been fields. Roadways were built. Small stores were even set up to sell things to the soldiers.

"Now that's something you won't see more than once in a lifetime—or once in several ages!" people said to each other.

"I wish I could leave this story behind for future generations."

People fell silent. Everyone was thinking of how the scene might look in their final days.

"So, everyone in those armies came here on orders from the shogun?"

"Of course they did. Otherwise, do you think they'd have rushed here from all over the country just to pickle themselves in that bog?"

It was news to many in the rebel forces that the shogun's name was Iemitsu and that, of late, he had become very irritable and somewhat ill. Until recently, they had been aware only that, higher up beyond the feudal administrations of clans such as the Matsukuras and the Terasawas, there existed a *bakufu* national government. But this had seemed distant and of little concern to them. The discovery that the *bakufu* was a force that could appear so suddenly, right before their eyes, triggered deep reactions. The farmers inside the castle were ready to announce themselves proudly in defiance of this shogun.

There were nights when the main enclosure by the edge of the sea was buffeted by bitter winds and snow. There were also days when the sea was bright and calm. Inside the abandoned castle, the plum trees that remained from older times opened their fragrant blossoms and the buds of the peach trees were swelling. It was under a particularly large old cherry tree that the Hasuda family had managed to set up their hut.

"Now that we've abandoned our old home, we're going to be granted the greatest show of cherry blossoms ever, right here," Nisuke said.

Omiyo broke into a warm smile and looked to Oume for agreement.

"That's right. Flowers don't belong to any one person. That's something I've come to understand at my age."

Oume glanced at Omiyo, her constant partner in conversation. Oume was busy cutting up and sorting *arame* roots and dried hijiki for the evening meal.

The attacking armies found it much more difficult to capture this fortress than they had imagined. The clan armies were discovering that, no matter what schemes they came up with or how many men they deployed, they could achieve nothing without a solid foundation from which to launch their attacks. In front of the castle lay a morass of soggy fields, marshes and tidal flats that made it extremely difficult to scale the castle walls. On the back side of the castle was the ocean, and any attacking boats confronted sheer cliffs along the shore. After suffering an unexpected defeat in their first attack on the twentieth day of the twelfth month, they had put all their efforts into laying the foundations for a proper attack. In this way, their plan for taking the old castle became what might be regarded as a great engineering and public works project.

The Hosokawa clan forces were well prepared for the toughness of the rebel forces, having arrived late in Shimabara after carrying out their extensive search of the areas around Ōyano and Kōtsuura. Following their lord's orders, they had brought with them a number of large cannons from Kumamoto Castle. To construct the artificial hills, they had also acquired some 80,000 empty sacks, 2,000 bundles of rope, 10,000 bamboo poles and 5,000 trees from the surrounding areas and loaded them onto boats. They had to build housing for the leaders, and to do that, records show that they brought in 312 tatami mats, 100 *usuberi* cloth-bordered rush mats, 370 straw mats, 110 rush mats for enclosing the premises, numerous folding screens, *kotatsu* heaters, futon bedding, fire shovels, wash basins, lamp stands, candles, brooms, dustpans, letter cases, oiled paper, mortars and pestles, charcoal stoves, 5 iron fire stands, 5,000 pairs of cedar chopsticks, 10 large sacks of rice, 2,000 *mochi* rice cakes, 10 large sacks of soybeans, 5 tubs of miso paste, boxes of incense, 5 casks of sake, 1 cask of soy sauce, casks of vinegar and oil, 5 large sacks of salt, 100 slabs of dried duck and bonito, as well as considerable supplies of yellowtail, daikon, burdock, charcoal, firewood, sugar and straw. Using 300 wooden buckets and 270 horse buckets, they continually brought in new stocks of rice and soybeans. The records also include the numbers of laborers and porters. Considering that these figures relate only to the army's leaders, one can imagine just how immense the whole operation was.

When the people inside the castle had spare time, they relaxed by bantering and joking about the enemy, as well as singing and dancing. During the reinforcement of the fortress, the workers had left some observation holes in the earthen banks, and people often gathered behind them to watch the enemy. They often saw the laborers hard at work transporting bundles of bamboo poles, filling sandbags, constructing bridges, and filling in the marshes.

"Look—those guys sure are busy. It's damn hard to be in a battle when you have to start out by building roads."

The rebels enjoyed this kind of banter and were happy to talk to anyone at hand.

"Don't be too impressed by that. When we ran off to war ourselves, we had to start by digging holes."

"Maybe so, but whatever they're up to now looks pretty impressive. It's like they've come for a festival."

"A festival? Well, you may say that now, but wait till the battle starts."

They all felt good just seeing each other's faces. The peaceful days continued for a while, but on the first day of the new year a surprise, all-out attack was launched on the castle.

In his records, Ishimaru Shichibei of the Okayama clan called the rebels' fighting "very strange":

> *As for the meeting held at dawn, some of the groups had arrived at two in the morning and others at dawn. We all attacked at once, but we failed. When we approached the walls, they dropped stones and scattered sand and ashes. When we grabbed onto the walls with our hands, they cut them off with their long swords. It was very strange. If things go on this way, it looks like we'll have to kill all the rebels.*

Four days later, Suzuki Saburō Kurō Shigenari, who later was appointed governor of the Amakusa region, joined Matsudaira Nobutsuna's forces. He was very interested in what he heard about this attack.

He had also been employed as a commissioner of levees and embankments, so he was well-informed about construction and river engineering. In a report he sent to the Osaka administration, he recorded his perceptive observations about the formidable castle fortress:

- *The old castle that the rebels have occupied has very solid walls and an inner fortress, both of which are generally in good condition.*
- *The walls are about fifteen feet high. Around them, they have erected bamboo fencing, and inside they have constructed a strong earthen embankment about five feet wide, which, it seems, also serves as a roadway for their troops. The walls aren't covered, so our spies have been able to sneak up at night and see how their arrows and other things are being constructed. They seem to be very strong.*
- *In their headquarters inside the main enclosure they have left the old stone walls as they were. Inside, they made a chapel for religious services. The rest of the buildings look like small portable huts.*
- *Amakusa Shirō is fifteen or sixteen years old. The people in the castle worship him. He seems to be a descendant of a*

higher-class family. People beneath him are not allowed to look up at him. A defeated warrior said this. Yesterday, one of their people who was out gathering firewood was captured by Etchū-dono (Hosokwa Tadatoshi).

- *Inside the walls, which are about seven feet wide at the base, they live in small huts. In them, they dig holes, where they store bamboo shields. They treat their rifles with great care. That's how they get along. They haven't become weaker.*
- *Usually, they don't fire their guns from the castle. It seems their leaders are being very careful about using their gun powder.*

Inside the old castle, with only its stone walls and trees remaining, the rebels had built a roadway along the dry moat, with a high embankment around it facing the outside. When this work was complete, the people living inside the castle felt a love for one another such as they had never known before. They also felt a sense of liberation, as if they were inhabiting a new world.

Tsunekichi, who often visited the chapel in the headquarters, became friends with Takematsu, who worked there as a cook. One rainy night when the enemy's rifles were quiet, Tsunekichi went out with Sainen to Takematsu's hut. From there they went to visit the Hasudas in the second enclosure to talk about celebrations for a belated Christmas, which they had missed due to the commotion of moving into the castle. When the three of them arrived, they were warmly welcomed by the Hasuda family. Tsunekichi felt as if he were among old friends. Yozaemon's son Chōichi was also there. Chōichi had been known as quite a talker in the past, but ever since his beloved wife was killed, he had become a quiet man. That evening he seemed more relaxed than usual, and from time to time, a thoughtful smile showed on his face, and he even joined in the talk.

With deep emotion, Tsunekichi asked, "Well, Sainen, with all of us here together and all these new houses, what do you think we should call this place? A town?"

"I suppose you could call it a town, or a village, but to me it seems more like the start of a new world."

Everyone seemed to agree with the Ikkō monk's reply. He had said as much in public before.

"I haven't changed religions, have I? I came here to repay my gratitude to the farmers who fed me."

During the second attack on the castle, everyone was astonished to see Sainen wield his so-called "battle-axe sword," cutting down enemies who attempted to scale the castle walls one after another. He became known as the "Benkei of the present-day."

"A 'new world,' you say? It sounds like our monk has studied a lot," Takematsu teased.

"What's this talk about study? Aren't we all just getting caught up in a drunken dream?" Sainen answered, feigning innocence.

Tsunekichi and Kumagorō replied that they agreed completely. And although they had said this very seriously, Chōichi cracked a smile. Nisuke, who seemed more at peace than usual, turned slowly to look at them.

"Well, that's good. Just yesterday, after his prayers, Shirō-sama was talking about the celebrations for *Natara*—the Nativity and Christmas season."

"I heard him too. The women and children will be happy about that," Sainen replied, but thinking he couldn't say much more on the topic, he looked at Tsunekichi encouragingly.

"Right. Yesterday we talked about it with Shichibei-sama and Kanzaki Daizen-sama."

Oume, who was busily weaving straw sandals, looked up. Thanks to the fact that they weren't serving alcohol this evening, she was making good progress.

"I heard it too. He talked about the sacred procession they used to hold in Nagasaki back in my parents' time.

"Yes—the Nagasaki procession. My parents were in Nagasaki when they were young."

To everyone's surprise, Chōichi was talking.

"My father told me he saw the baby Chirisuto-sama in the procession, riding on a pedestal covered in purple velvet."

Everyone stared at Chōichi. They all knew that his baby had died together with his young wife in the water dungeon.

"A sacred procession, was it? Just the thought of it is beautiful. We'll have a wonderful Christmas Eve."

"What do you think, my dear? Shall we lead a procession

through our part of the castle, with candles and lanterns too?" Omiyo said, as if she could no longer keep the idea to herself.

"A candlelight procession along the road above the moat—what a sight that will be! And when it's finished, I'll bet people will bring sake and make offerings," Takematsu said, trailing off at the end so that no one answered.

"On the night of Chirisuto sama's birth," Oume whispered. "Takematsu-don, if you can rouse the budding plums, you'll get drunk for sure."

Takematsu's eyes lit up like a child's. He placed his hands on his knees and, for a while, rested his chin on them.

At the end of the first month of the year, after having been in the castle for almost two months, Shirō had announced plans for the Christmas celebration.

"Since we've been so busy settling in the castle, we weren't able to observe the birth of our Lord at the regular time, so let's celebrate it three days from now. This celebration will be a little different from other years. We've joined our hearts, and together we've rebuilt this castle, and twice we've fought off attacks from an enemy with ten or twenty times the men we have. The glory of these feats will remain in the world to come.

"We have forsaken this world, so let us fast and take only purified food and drink and live solemnly in our limited remaining days on this earth, since at long last the dawn of our rebirth has arrived. The pathway we have built ourselves has led us here, and to the evening of the Nativity. On the day of Chirisuto-sama's birth, especially, we will be ready to present ourselves, body and soul, to our Lord.

"From each of our villages, let us bring the candles we've set aside, and with our children singing hymns and dancing, let us go forward in glory and utmost sincerity."

Shirō's suggestions were met with tremendous joy.

The people had transformed their sadness from not planting crops for the next year and abandoning their homes and towns into the energy to build the fortress that would protect them. Men, women, and children had all worked. With their own hands, they had dug the earth and built the rugged embankment that circled the castle, and they had reinforced it with planks from their boats. Now the surrounding enemy was firing bullets at them from below, but the bullets just sank into the thick embankment and never reached the roadway that encircled the moat inside. They lived in makeshift huts, but inside their dug-outs they were safe. Even when the earthen embankments were damaged by cannon fire, they were able to repair them quickly.

They had built the fortress with their own sweat. People from the different towns who met each other there for the first time soon formed bonds and lived as members of one community, so that no one would have imagined that a short time ago they were strangers. When Shirō called them brothers and sisters, they trembled. The roadway they had built around the castle compound became a playground for the children.

"Surrounded by enemy forces that outnumber us by ten or twenty times, this holy celebration of the Nativity will be most glorious. May Heaven be our witness! Let us pray as never before."

After these concluding remarks from Juan, people from all the villages chatted cheerfully about how they would soon begin a Christmas celebration the likes of which they would never experience again in this world.

The idea of holding a great celebration surrounded by enemy forces strengthened their morale more than they had imagined. Simple litanies were chosen, and people promised each other that this time, they would really learn the words they only vaguely knew before.

"We should take our inspiration from that last celebration in Nagasaki twenty years ago. We need the best ideas of every town and village."

Impassioned words filled the air as people went about planning the event.

"Do you think we'll make it before the next attack comes? We have to keep our spirits high."

"Holding our celebration in the headquarters of God's battle is a joy we won't have again."

The day arrived. When darkness fell over the entryways of the houses, people raised their lanterns together. If observers could have looked down on Hara Castle that night from up in the sky, they would have seen faintly-lit scenes of women holding up their kimono sleeves to protect the flames of their lanterns as they watched the children's holy procession pass by the countless huts alongside the embankment road, and of the festive lanterns shaped like cocoons, hung on poles at entryways here and there, flickering in the air of the ancient castle.

Shirō's chapel, surrounded as it was by stone walls, couldn't accommodate all who had joined in the procession. As people chanting litanies came from every corner of the castle complex and gathered outside the walls, children dressed in white vestments came out and sang hymns. The baby who had been chosen as the infant Chirisuto was sleeping soundly, wrapped in soft silk brocade in a straw manger under a sign that read "Tree of Life." The scene brought peace to all who saw it. The flow of celebrants continued through half the night.

After the procession ended, the *confuraria* of Arima samurai—unable to hold back their excitement—sang the ancient song "Saibara" to entertain the party. The people nearby began dancing to the song.

Oh holiness—the holiness of today. From ancient days, Hallelujah!
Since ancient times it has been like this—the holiness of today!
Even had we been there—the holiness of today!

Since everyone enjoyed the celebration that night so much, they began holding events with singing and dancing whenever they could. The attacking armies watched the festivities. The Hosokawa camp had set up a tall ship's mast on the top of one of its man-made hills and attached a box to it, from which observers could view the goings-on inside the castle.

In a letter from Hosokawa Nakanori to his father Tadaoki, he warned that the castle was strong and that it would be difficult to attack, and that it was surrounded by a moat and any number of traps and pitfalls. He wrote, *If we make a reckless attack, we will suffer heavy casualties, so for now we're concentrating on building observation towers to keep a close watch on them.*

He added, *The people inside the castle appear to be hanging out big lanterns and flying kites for the amusement of their children.*

With the help of the Nagasaki magistrate Tsunetsugu Heizō, the *bakufu* arranged with Nicolaes Couckebacker, the chief of the Dutch trading post in Hirado, to borrow some large cannons, gunpowder and other munitions. For the *bakufu*, such dealings represented not only a request to use Dutch weapons and ammunition in a time of revolt, but also the granting of permission for increased foreign trade. Foreign ships were permitted to dock and conduct trading activities in Hirado, near Nagasaki. Using the rebellion as a pretext, the merchants could gather detailed information about the state of the war, the numbers and movements of troops, the progress of the fighting and so on, enhancing their opportunities to develop trade relations. The Dutch entertained the high-ranking officials, treating them to dinner parties and gifts, and with a business-minded spirit, kept their eyes on what was happening in the war.

On the twelfth day of the first month, an arrow message signed by the shogun's envoy arrived urging the rebel forces to surrender. On the same day, a Dutch ship sailed from the harbor in Hirado and dropped anchor offshore from Hara Castle. Immediately, the Couckebacker group landed and proceeded to visit the headquarters of the shogun's envoy Nobutsuna. Using maps and drawings of the castle, they decided on the objectives of an attack.

Suzuki Saburō Kurō Shigenari, the artillery commissioner who had come with the cannons from Osaka, asked, "Couldn't we use our artillery to set fire to their straw houses?"

The representatives from the Dutch delegation replied that they doubted such a plan would work. "Destroying houses made of straw and matting will be difficult. Any bullets or cannon balls that managed to hit them will just make holes. It would be easier to demolish them if they were made of stone or wood."

The thirteenth brought fine weather. According to the notes in Coukebacker's diary, although the attacking forces had been advised not to waste cannon balls, on the next day they fired fourteen test shots from the deck of the ship. On the following day, they fired twenty-seven shots. From then on, cannon attacks continued and the castle suffered some damage. However, as Coukebacker observed from his boat, the rebels were able to repair the holes in the walls quickly, sometimes as fast as overnight.

Since Takematsu was single, he had been assigned to work as a cook in the headquarters. Working so close to Ukon was the fulfillment of his long-held wish. Still able to put his strong diver's arms to good use, he kept his harpoon and halberd sharpened and close at hand. Privately, he was convinced that his trusty old weapons would be far more effective in time of need than any fancy spears.

Perhaps because he was so slender and delicate, the women cooks often chatted with him. Sometimes, at his invitation or theirs, they would go down to the beach together to gather conches and seaweed.

One day they went out as usual from the second enclosure. But when they got to the outer enclosure and saw the enemy laborers working in the marshes, they noticed that the workers were unusually close.

"They're awfully close to the bridge. That bridge looks real strong. The construction boss over there did a good job," Takematsu said.

"And look at that!" one of the women yelled, leaning over the fence and pointing. "That lookout tower—I think it's gotten taller since last time we saw it."

"Maybe there'll be another attack on the castle soon," Takematsu answered.

Perhaps this made the women anxious, because they started jeering at the workers.

"Hey, you there, where'd you come from? When you get back home, you're gonna be farmers again, just like us," one of them said in a loud, strong voice.

The other women began to laugh. The men stood up and looked around with puzzled faces, as if asking, *What was that we just heard?* The women laughed even harder.

"Hey, instead of getting hit by bullets and stones, you'd be better off hightailing it back home. I bet you have wives and children, too."

"Don't you want to get it on with your wives?"

"If you don't hurry back, someone's gonna get your women."

"Around here, our rain of stones is about all the jollies you can look forward to."

The women continued their heckling in the lyrical intonation of the Amakusa dialect.

Hearing their bawdy catcalls, Takematsu looked up at the sky and laughed. The workers tried to hide behind their bamboo shields, but they couldn't move their legs freely in the muck of the marsh. They realized that if a battle should break out, these same women might knock them down with stones.

Suzuki Shigenari watched from the top of an observation hill near the castle. *What sort of women are they?* he wondered, smiling ruefully. He hadn't witnessed any major battles since his arrival, but he had heard that during the fighting on New Year's Day, the women in the castle had tied their hair back, put on headbands marked with the cross, and pelted the enemy with a steady rain of rocks and stones. Apparently this had unnerved the attackers so much, they had been unable to continue fighting.

When Shigenari saw the closely packed rows of houses inside the castle, it brought back vivid memories of an unforgettable incident from his past. In his previous post in Osaka, he had served both as the regional magistrate of Settsu and the commissioner of rivers in Kōchi. His elder brother Suzuki Shōsan had paid him a visit during a preaching tour, dressed in his Buddhist monk's robes. Shigenari had recently discovered that there were many unregistered fields under his jurisdiction that farmers were cultivating, and this become a big problem. Shigenari had sympathized with the farmers, who just wanted to feed themselves by using a little of that neglected land, and he knew that he could help them simply by overlooking the unregistered fields. But eventually someone leaked the information and it became impossible to hide his discovery, so he brought it up with the Fushimi magistrate Kobori Enshū. Enshū was known as an accomplished devotee in the arts of tea ceremony and landscape gardening. Shigenari had intended to ask him for a reduction in the penalties for the farmers, but strict orders were instead issued to punish the offenders by death—both men and women. Shigenari became discouraged and, when his revered brother visited him, he told him of his plight, practically clinging to him as he asked for help. Shōsan had counseled him severely:

"Sanyō (ruler of the Mikawa region, later given the name Tokugawa Ieyasu) would never punish a woman for this sort of thing. If you don't fix this problem now, it will be an act of disloyalty and a sin against the gods and the Buddha. You must plead their case, even if you end up paying with your life."

By "disloyalty," he meant not so much the people's betrayal of their lord as the lord's betrayal of the people. Moved by his brother's words, Shigenari pleaded the farmers' case repeatedly, and in the end the women prisoners were spared on the very eve of their execution. Shōsan had chanted sutras and they had hoped to save the male prisoners as well, but they had not succeeded. In Shigenari's mind, a vision of those farmers was layered over the sight of the women from Amakusa in front of him now. A faint flash of lightning lit up the image. Farmers' revolts were certainly terrible affairs. But even so, entire families and villages had shut themselves up in this freezing castle, practically throwing away their lives. What could have driven them to this?

Shigenari wished he could have seen the lives of these women through their own eyes. His elder brother Shōsan had chosen not to take up a samurai's career at the Osaka headquarters, instead becoming a Zen monk and writing many works. He had an imposing stance and an intrepid spirit. He maintained that when sitting zazen, one should always do it with the daring spirit of the two guardian Deva kings, and when saying prayers to Amitabha, one should fix one's gaze firmly, as if in a duel. If Shōsan could see the nerves of steel these farmers had, what would he think?

Shigenari had been dispatched by the *bakufu* as the commissioner in charge of artillery and, under orders from Matsudaira Nobutsuna, he had procured cannons and gunpowder for their forces. Those cannons would likely be spouting fire from atop the man-made hills before long. A vision passed before his eyes of the destruction that would come to the farmers' homes in the second enclosure when they were blown apart. It was not a pleasant one.

At the time, he could not have foreseen that he would one day be appointed governor of Amakusa, and that for some twelve years he would devote his life to helping the scattering of people who remained after the rebellion. Much less could he have imagined that, after the failure of his many requests to the government to halve the farmers' excessive land taxes of 42,000 *koku*, he would end his life by committing *seppuku*.

During a pause in the battle of arrow messages, Matsudaira Nobutsuna summoned to Shimabara Castle Shirō's mother Oine; his sister Regina and her son Kohei and daughter Man; and Watanabe Kozaemon, all of whom were being held prisoner by the Hosokawa clan.

Since her capture, Oine had been using her Christian name, Marta.

"Marta, come here."

When summoned in this way by the Hosokawa officials, she couldn't help but hold her two grandchildren tightly, expecting that the men might soon cut off her head. Her interrogation and prison treatment had not been as harsh as she had feared, and she had learned from the officials that Shirō was now commander of the rebellion at Hara Castle.

But the officials sneered and taunted her. "Your son's been deceived," they would say. "A sixteen-year-old commanding general? Come on now—he's being used as a puppet."

Each time, she replied from the depth of her heart, "No—my son is God's angel."

Naturally, she cowered when called before Matsudaira Izumamoru (Nobutsuna). He ordered her to write a letter to Jinbei and Shirō, who were inside Hara Castle. She was somewhat relieved that Nobutsuna had spoken to her gently. He had suggested that she and her family might be released and sent to the castle in exchange for some Buddhists who had been forced by the Christians to stay in the castle. Oine dearly wanted to believe his words.

In her letter she added, without much thought, *I am sad that we have been forgotten here.* Tears blurred the words on the paper as she wrote that since Shirō was now the leader, it would be difficult to meet with him, but she would be happy even to see his face through a chink in the castle wall.

The letter was delivered by her eight-year-old grandson Kohei. He was the son of Shirō's older sister Regina and Watanabe Kozaemon's younger brother Satarō. Not sure of what his role would be, Kohei was simply happy that he was going to be taken to the castle to meet Shirō in the company of his father and both of his grandfathers, Jinbei and Denbei. Kohei went to the castle escorted in front and behind by samurai.

With both sides observing a ceasefire, the group arrived at the beach and were met by representatives from the castle. They were relatives whom Kohei knew well.

"Kohei, how wonderful to see you. You remember your Uncle Nakamura, don't you?"

Calling out as they approached, the relatives politely conveyed greetings from Shirō and Jinbei to the samurai. Then they embraced Kohei and disappeared with him into the castle.

When a signal was given that evening was approaching, Kohei was sent back out from the castle. He was holding a large paper sack in front of his chest. In it were persimmons, tangerines, sugar, oranges, sweet bean buns, potatoes and other presents.

In prison, Oine opened the sack. As she imagined who might have put the presents into it, and with what gestures, tears welled in her eyes. She set them in a row, one by one, imagining how immensely precious these gifts must have been to the nearly starving people inside the castle. And still, they had sent them with Kohei. As she thought about this, she read the stirring letter.

"Are all of these things from your father?" she asked Kohei.

"Not only from Father, but from Grandpa Denbei and Shirō, too. And the persimmons are from one of the old women."

Oine imagined many faces. *Who might that have been? It must have been someone who knows Kohei well.*

"Look, a girl gave me this tangerine."

The boy said she had come running up and pressed it into his hand as he was leaving. He looked up happily as he held it.

"How was Grandpa Jinbei?"

"When he held me, his beard felt rough. It kind of hurt!"

"And how was Uncle Shirō-sama?"

"He told me, 'We'll meet Mother and Sister soon, so be patient.' He smelled like nice incense."

He had meant that soon they would all die, himself included.

Kohei had brought back a reply signed by his father Satarō and his grandfather Denbei. The message was too short for Oine to guess their deeper feelings. Not having received any reply from Jinbei and Shirō, she felt disappointed.

A few days later, Kohei was sent back to the castle, this time accompanied by his younger sister Man. With them, they carried a letter from Oine and Kozaemon that expressed their hope to get away from the non-Christian pagans quickly and be taken into the castle.

Oine added:

Think wisely, once again. Please take us into your place . . . Please do not refuse us.

A reply arrived from Satarō:

The cherry blossoms on the castle hill are a spring storm rushing towards Paraizo. *I am writing this letter using my tears as the water to grind spirit into black ink . . . I will see you in* Paraizo.

In the setting sun, the young brother and sister held hands as they took this final letter from the castle, receding from the darkening shores of this life. Two or three hundred people from the castle had gathered. As they saw the children off, they held the sleeves of their kimonos up to their eyes. It was said that Man was holding a gold ring and a ball of soapberries she had received from Shirō.

Although the spirit of solidarity deepened among most of the people inside the castle, a few deserters started to appear.

The cold of midwinter set in, and the thirty-some thousand people locked inside the castle on the narrow plateau needed to warm themselves and cook their meals. First, they began to run short of firewood and charcoal. Their supplies, of course, had almost been used up. To obtain fuel, little by little they began removing the wooden planks from the fence that separated them from the enemy and cut trees and roots from inside the castle to burn. In every hut, they searched for hidden supplies of grain and other items to share.

Hearing the sighs of the women holding infants and seeing their faces, Sainen the monk from Kōtsuura thought, *I'd like to help them out of here. But they would end up getting caught. We have no way to ensure we'll stay alive. After they cut off our heads, they'll split open our bellies and see what's left in our wasted guts—the dregs of sesame seeds and soy beans and seaweed from the shore, no better than bird feed. Any way you look at it, it's miserable.*

The people in the castle likened their privation to the coming celebration of Lent. This would be their last chance to think about the sufferings of Christ. On the first day of the second month, a statement signed by "Masuda Shirō Francisco" was issued, urging everyone to abstain sincerely from eating meat and fish, and to practice fasting and deep prayer:

> *For all of us sheltered here inside this castle, not even our salvation is decided, owing to our sins in this life. We have been granted this time with immeasurable kindness and we have become friends until the life hereafter. This is a most precious blessing.*
>
> *Furthermore, let us not neglect our* oratios *and our daily prayers of gratitude. It is most important that we do this.*

The statement noted that since there were many people who could not recite the *oratios* properly, care should be given to helping these people. They should be instructed with love and in simple terms so that, "*one by one, everyone may come to an understanding.*"

Taking this as a personal call to action, Sainen opened the Christian book of scriptures for the first time.

Even I can read this out loud to the farmers. It's easy to recognize forsaken people, people who want to run away. If they're caught while their souls are wavering and their empty bellies are ripped open, that won't help them much in the afterlife. I'll bet the Christian Hell is even worse than the Buddhist one. If they're going to die anyway, I might as well say some last words to them to help their souls, and then I wouldn't mind dying right alongside them.

He chose a few easy-to-understand passages from the rather lengthy scriptures and went around to the huts, doing exactly what he had never wanted to back at his temple, which is to say, reading to the people from the long, fluttering scroll and explaining the words to them.

"I've been a follower of Shinran-sama, but this scripture is just like what the Buddha teaches, so it's easy to understand," he told them.

"It tells us the present world is only temporary. And our lives in this castle may be even shorter still. During this time, we have to faithfully say our prayers, day and night, to show our thanks for each day and to apologize for what we did in the past.

"Is everyone okay now? You follow me? The Buddhist teachings say the same thing; the present world is just a transitory thing. In other words, we're only here on Earth in passing. Soon our temporary lives shut up here in this castle will come to an end, and we'll be released from all our suffering. Shirō-sama has told us that this is a matter of great joy. So that we may put this present world behind us and be granted a good rebirth, let us remember even our darkest moments and be penitent. In our remaining days, let us give thanks and say the *oratios*.

"Personally, I think saying *namu amida* to the Buddha is also good. If I can forget myself and say it with all my heart, I'll be granted life hereafter by saying the Original Vow of Amida Buddha.

"You get what I'm saying? Our time in this world is running out. I'm in this with all of you. Somehow, our fates have come together in life and death. It's difficult to say goodbye, but our time is running out. Even in the short time that's left, try to inspire yourselves and others for good and free yourselves from the hardships of this world. People who see the light of religion can help those who are in the dark.

"Especially in this time of year called Lent, the sufferings of Chirisuto-sama become apparent again on Earth. We've entered the period when we carry the weight of this suffering as we abstain from eating meat and fish and we fast and strengthen our prayers as never before. Let's pray for the purity of everyone's *anima*, join hands, and receive the light of the life to come. Shirō-sama has said that all who have come here to serve inside this castle will remain as friends in the life hereafter."

Although Sainen's preaching may have seemed slightly odd to those gathered around him, they welcomed his passion. The most comforting thing of all was that this rough-speaking monk had the spirit to assure them that even if they went to Hell, he'd go right along with them. Yazō and Nisuke thought he was an outstanding monk. Some people even said that Shirō-sama had possessed him.

A rule was made that no one was to go outside the castle to draw water unless they received permission, since many people had been captured in this way.

In the Hasuda family's hut, Oume was turning a stone mortar. Because of the cold, she was seated on a pile of straw. She hadn't been doing it every day of late, since there wasn't much to grind.

At first, when the rebels had just entered the castle, portions of unhulled brown rice had been distributed to everyone, but by the middle of the first month this had stopped, and now they were being told to scrape by on the supplies they had brought themselves. Tiny amounts of sesame seeds, soybeans, and adzuki beans were handed out, but it hardly amounted to anything, so everyone started digging bracken and kudzu roots and collecting shellfish and seaweed from the shore. The Hasuda family had managed to get by thanks to Oume's resourcefulness, but some families from Kuchinotsu were in dire circumstances.

Oume was grinding fava beans. The fasting for Lent would begin the next morning, so on this night they were preparing a porridge of the precious beans to celebrate. Beside her, Omiyo spoke in a restrained voice.

"I imagine that those from far-off villages haven't brought much to eat, so they must be having a hard time."

She felt somewhat ashamed that only those in her hut would be eating fava beans. Oume often complained that their store of grain would soon be empty thanks to her habitual generosity to neighbors.

"The other day I gave them half of what we had left, and now we only have a little left," Omiyo said.

"Well, somehow we have to find a way to share and also get by ourselves. Let's take a little to the people in the hut with the old folks," Oume said, looking down at the mortar. "If we have nothing to eat, we'll simply die together. As Shirō-sama has said, this is an important time when we are being tested, to see if we'll remain friends in the next life or not."

Nisuke was sleeping in the back room. His knee had been injured in the cannon attacks from the Dutch ship that had started about ten days ago. Daisuke, Matsukichi, Kumagorō and others had been rushing around, trying to keep up with repairing walls and embankments damaged by the cannons.

The rebels sent an arrow with the taunting message:

We are only farmers, yet the government had to order daimyo from all over Kyushu to come fight us. And even that wasn't enough, so they had to ask for help from foreign ships. What a disgrace to this country and a stain on the honor of your samurai! Japan must be the laughing-stock of other countries.

On a night when the sea was so tossed by storms that the Dutch boat had to suspend its cannon bombardment, Daisuke stopped in to join the service at the chapel in the headquarters.

Casualties from the salvos from the Dutch boat had been quite high. Even Umeo Shichibei from Kōtsuura, who had once been so full of energy he claimed he would live two lifetimes, was among the victims.

Every evening in the chapel, solemn and beautiful with its hanging lanterns, Shirō held services for those who had died in battle. It was hard to imagine that the children dressed in white Western vestments and singing hymns were in the same castle where bullets had flown in the daytime.

When Daisuke returned to the hut, Nisuke asked, with eyes closed:

"Have the lanterns been lit at our house?"

"Yes, they have."

"They're the ones that were specially ordered when we got married," Omiyo said. She had not been back to the headquarters since she helped sew the flag.

"And I put them up before I brought you home."

In the areas around Nagasaki and Shimabara, whenever an important event took place, people hung lanterns from the eaves of buildings. The Christians also put them up on their celebration days.

"They've hung the lanterns we ordered for Okayo's wedding outside the headquarters," Daisuke said, remembering when Okayo came by boat for their marriage.

"How wonderful—mine are there too!"

Ever since Okayo returned from her hometown, she had been calm and always smiling. Even when the cannons began to thunder, she just ducked her head and said with a smile, "Ah—that's a surprise."

"I've never had so much free time in my life, so I've been thinking a lot lately," Nisuke said. "I feel like I'm turning into some kind of insect, sleeping down here in this cellar of a hut all the time."

"To tell the truth, that's how I feel too," Oume answered as she shelled beans. "I must have been an insect or a fish in a former life."

"Yes, that's it! And when we were insects, do you suppose we worshiped the light?"

"Well, insects love light . . . And they say that farmers are like insects. But there are all sorts of insects living above ground and below ground. They're so lovely. And there are pious insects too. I'm sure of it."

"Hmm. Well, since you've worked so much with your hands in the earth, you know a lot more than I do about things that live in the ground."

"I don't know all that much, but it strikes me that insects know the difference between day and night."

"And the insects bring messages, too," Okayo added. "When I went back to Uchino, there were so many crickets singing by my bedside. It made me so sad and I thought they were messengers from Daisuke, so in the end I made my way back here."

Okayo turned to Oume for confirmation.

"Certainly, they must have been messengers from Daisuke-sama. And not only the insects; the winds and the birds are messengers, too, but you can't hear them unless you have ears for them."

Omiyo wiped her tears with her kimono.

"And you know how the dogs and cats, and the birds and frogs close their eyes when they sleep? I can't help but loving them. This morning I sent a message over to Uchino with a crow."

Okayo found it hard to go on. *She's thinking of how she wants to be with Ayame*, Omiyo thought. But she knew if she tried to speak she would fall apart, so she kept on silently warming some ointment to rub on Nisuke's knees.

"I send messages too," Nisuke added. "This morning in my dream, I asked a mole to send one."

"A mole, did you say?" Omiyo asked. Some of her tension

seemed to leave her at the thought.

"At times like this even a mole in a dream is better than nothing."

"Speaking of dreams, when the frogs and the *okera* bugs are sleeping in the winter fields, you can put them in your hand and they'll just rest their jaws on your palm and go on sleeping."

Oume squinted her eyes like a sleeping frog or *okera* bug.

"My parents taught me about these things. So when someone calls you an insect because you're a farmer, don't be sad. Birds and animals and insects are all messengers of the Buddha. We're working, and they're working, too. Maybe we do it to have food, but I think there's more to it. It seems to me they all have their parts to play, and so do we.

"At the beginning of summer, the fireflies light up, and in the fall the insects sing. Their lives may be short, but they still join their hands in prayer and sing for Hotoke-sama, the Buddha who gave them life, to let him know they're alive.

Hazy moon, quaking with longing,
Three thousand worlds of falling petals

"I've never given birth to a child, but helping with Daisuke-sama's birth and raising him has been my treasure as I pass through this world to the next. When he used to cry at night, it was heart-breaking. When he was a baby, his wails made me wonder, *Daisuke-sama, what are you thinking about when you cry like that?* I could understand the shock he must have felt to leave his mother's womb, but when I heard him cry like that, it seemed like sorrow from a previous life. He cried like he would be alone in the world from that moment on. It was such a sad thing."

Clasping both of his knees and nodding slightly, Daisuke gazed at Oume's face.

"The cries of a baby who can't yet recognize the faces of its own parents are so sad. From then on, we humans in this world are alone—right, Danna-sama?"

"Listening to you, I had the same thought," Nisuke said, hoping to encourage her to keep talking.

"Babies reach out to the far-off light without knowing why

themselves, and that's how they grow up."

"I suppose you're right," Nisuke replied vaguely.

"I finally found it."

"Found what?"

"This family."

With extreme reverence, Oume bowed her head.

"I, too, was a lone child on this earth. When you took me in, I learned the meaning of affection and ties among people. For me, *Paraizo* has been the household in Kuchinotsu."

"I don't know what to say . . ."

Nisuke stammered and silence filled the space.

Wind and rain began to blow and the trees tossed and moaned in the gusts from the sea. Omiyo placed a thick paper screen around the dish where a wick was burning, to protect it from the drafts.

As the quavering lamplight stilled, Nisuke could see Oume's face clearly from his bed. It was, to him, a good face. It was well-tanned and deeply wrinkled from exposure to the sun, but her eyebrows had a relaxed look that reminded him of a wooden carving of Kannon-sama. Never having looked directly at the face of a Kannon Bodhisattva, Nisuke was surprised at himself for seeing Kannon-sama's face in hers.

On the night Nisuke first talked to her about the rebellion, Oume had told him why she had never been baptized. When she was a small child, her father had worried about her frailty and had carved a small statue of Kannon using her as a model to pray for the health of his beloved child, presenting it as an offering to the Kannon of Iwato. Later, he had wept when he learned it had been destroyed and used as kindling, along with all the other Buddhist sculptures, on order of the padres. Nisuke hadn't forgotten Oume's words that night:

"If Maria-sama and Kannon-sama could meet, I'm sure they would get along so well and be even kinder."

Now, as Nisuke listened to her talking much more than usual, he felt as if a cover had been lifted from her heart.

"Kannon-sama, too, is very beautiful," he sighed.

Everyone was surprised to hear him unexpectedly praising the Kannon-sama so revered by Buddhists. But soon they understood.

Nisuke thought it would be inexcusable if he didn't pay proper respect to Oume's precious Kannon-sama.

"Oume, for so long you've kept the memory of that destroyed Kannon-sama safe in your heart. When I think of how much you've done for our Deus-sama, I realize I've only thought of my own religion and I have forgotten to be humble. I feel ashamed. Now I can see that you are the embodiment of Kannon-sama. Listen, everyone, Oume may be the real lantern that lights our house. We are the little insects who are flying around her light. It's like a dream, isn't it?"

Oume became flustered and backed away.

Daisuke slid on his knees toward her and clasped her hand.

"Since I have no way of knowing what will happen tomorrow, I want to say this to you now. Oume, thank you for raising me. Even the memory of how I swung that snake around and around and you scolded me and tied me to the persimmon tree is dear to me."

"Oume-yan, thank you for bringing up Daisuke-dono," Okayo said.

It seemed to Oume that there was no place to hide.

"Oume-yan, you were talking about *okera* bugs," Okayo went on, noticing Oume's discomfort and changing the subject. "Well, in my town, I used to see the little shrimp clinging to the grasses along the banks of the river inlet, sleeping there. When the sun came up, the river took on the colors of the sky and the shrimp started to move slowly and touch their neighboring shrimp with their long claws as they exchanged greetings. And the little *shijimi* clams, too, they'd open their two eyes so brightly on the river bed. Sometime soon, Ayame will play with them—isn't that right, Mother?"

"Yes, she will. She will!" Omiyo replied.

Omiyo felt a deep sadness for Okayo. *Even though she chose to leave home to die with her husband, she must be feeling so much for Ayame. And with both Okayo and her brother here in the castle, it must be so hard for her family, too. If she and Sasuke die, I hope they become fireflies or autumn insects and go back to apologize. Otherwise, it will be all too sad.*

Nisuke continued thinking about his conversation with Oume. She had talked of how all things in this world, from the tiniest specks to those too large even to measure, have equal value and must be accorded respect. Here was a farmer, a woman of quiet dignity who had deepened her heart with the humility that Chirisuto-sama teaches. As they waited for their lives to end, their home was being visited by an unexpected beatitude. How could this be anything other than a time given to them by God? Lying on his back, Nisuke made the sign of the cross.

Takematsu, Sasuke and Chōichi rushed into the hut, rain splashing in with them. Sasuke held a branch of peach blossoms.

"We wanted to see how Nisuke-sama's getting along. With this rain, there's a break in the fighting."

"You've come at a good time. I was hoping to see you tonight. Don't you think it looks like things are finally coming to a head?"

"It sure seems that way. That's why we came over to see you."

"We've been telling old stories. Omiyo, with all these folks here now, how about breaking out the special Ryukyu sake from Yazō-dono that we've been saving?"

"Yes, let's bring it out. What do you say, Oume?"

Takematsu's nose twitched. He could hardly ignore the mention of Ryukyu sake. He hadn't had a chance to drink sake at leisure since coming to the castle.

"Maybe we should fill you in on our conversation."

"We've been having such a good talk."

Judging from the expressions of the Hasuda family, Takematsu could imagine the sort of discussion that had been going on. A strong, indescribable fragrance wafted up from the small brown pot that Omiyo brought in.

"Well, there's not much really, but let's drink it, one cup each. We don't have any side dishes to go with it."

"Well, actually, I brought some. I have some sea lettuce and some limpets. With the Hosokawa boats out there patrolling, this was all I could get."

The limpets were small sea snails that clung to the rocks near the shoreline. Oume peeked into the basket he was holding out to her. She picked out the sea lettuce and savored its fragrance. It had the fresh green color of spring.

"Ah, such a good smell. It's the first of the season. Already, it's the time of the Girls' Festival Tide."

With somewhat sad expressions, the women watched Oume's fingers.

"You're right, the Girls' Festival Tide."

Every year, local people waited eagerly for the time when the big spring tides came in, around the third day of the third month. On this day, the ebb tide receded all the way back to the offing, and everyone would go down and look, drawn by the abundance of life in the sea. That big tide was now starting to rise along the shoreline.

"Today's the twenty-sixth day of the second month," Nisuke said. After pouring some fresh hot sea lettuce soup into the reddish-brown earthenware bowls, Daisuke propped Nisuke into a sitting position.

Okayo passed out cups and filled them with sake. When she had finished serving Matsukichi and Kumagorō at the back of the room, she picked off some petals from the peach branch that Sasuke had brought and placed one petal in each of the sake cups.

"This is Ayame's first Girl's Festival."

After bowing deeply, they drank their sake in silence.

"Early this morning, a white bird was flying toward Uchino and I sent off a lot of messages with it," Sasuke said brightly.

Quite likely he had wanted to say that he had sent a message to Ayame, too. The drinking party grew quiet.

"I wonder, do you think there's sake in *Paraizo* too?"

Everyone smiled at Takematsu's humor. As Oume looked at Chōichi's face, she realized what a good-looking young man he was. She recalled the time she had eaten pieces of pomelo that his wife Okimi had given her.

Past noon on the next day, Takematsu went out with his halberd to the beach below the cliffs by the second enclosure. There he saw three or four thousand people. With their food supplies so low, they were scouring the shoreline for clams and seaweed. To Takematsu, it looked like a swarm of fiddler crabs had come out from their holes.

Then, although there was no wind, the reeds and bamboo along the shoreline started to tremble. From their midst, the flags of the Hosokawa troops appeared in the direction of the main gate. Takematsu ran back to the corner of the cliff. An unending stream of warriors suited in armor and carrying banners and spears was flooding the beach below the main gate. Takematsu raced up the hill on his usual pathway and yelled with all his might, "Ukon-sama!"

On the twenty-seventh day of the second month, the *bakufu* forces ended their siege and began an all-out attack. Mizuno Katsunari, the seasoned warrior and lord of Fukuyama Castle, had arrived with his army on the twenty-third, on orders from the shogun. His arrival gave Nobutsuna confidence to launch the attack.

In any case, Nobutsuna's decision to begin the attack was likely based mainly on his estimation that the supplies of food and ammunition inside the castle had mostly run out. In recent days, there had been a steady flow of escapees from the castle and they had testified to the dire situation within.

Moreover, on the night of the twenty-first, the rebel forces had launched an attack on the camps of the Kuroda, Terasawa and Nabeshima clans and their three thousand elite soldiers who had been sent in from Oeguchi. This had thrown the government forces into utter confusion and they had just barely managed to drive the attackers back. The rebels had killed nearly three hundred government soldiers, but nearly one hundred of their own men had also died and close to three hundred had been injured. On their way back to the castle they had seized as much ammunition as they could. They had also eaten and drunk goods from the small shops. It was clear that their main objective had been to collect food and ammunition. Upon examining the slashed-open stomachs of rebels' dead bodies, it was evident that they had been eating almost nothing other than beans and seaweed.

Also, the lengthy siege had led to a somewhat relaxed attitude among the government soldiers. They vividly recalled the fierce fighting of their earlier attack, in which General Itakura was killed, and a vague distaste for "seizing the castle" was widespread. The Matsukura forces in particular had gained a reputation for fearing active battle. Lord Matsukura Katsuie appeared ashamed at having caused this big rebellion; one of the Hosokawa samurai sent a message to his chief counselor stating, "Matsukura-sama has become rather pathetic. He walks around all bent over and shrunken." With their lord so weakened, the Matsukura samurai could hardly have been expected to maintain their zeal.

The dull routine of waiting for the peasants inside the castle to starve had become an affront to the samurais' dignity. Clearly, Nobutsuna had been looking for a chance to storm the castle in a decisive final attack. And then the chance came. An all-out attack had been planned for the twenty-eighth, but at about one o'clock in the morning of the twenty-seventh, the Nabeshima forces, unable to restrain their yearning for action and honor, assembled outside the second enclosure. Nobutsuna immediately made the decision to mobilize the armies of all the clans.

By the time Takematsu reached the top of the cliff, the leaders in the headquarters already knew that the Nabeshima forces had breached the second enclosure. But they didn't immediately realize that this was the prelude to an all-out attack. Masuda Jinbei, Kanzaki Daizen, Chizuka Matsuemon and other leaders rushed to the cliff edge overlooking the second enclosure. There, outside the walls of the third enclosure, they could see the armies of the Hosokawa and Tachibana clans. Outside the walls of the second enclosure were the armies of the Matsukura, Arima and Nabeshima clans. Outside the main enclosure were the Terasawa forces. And in front of the Amakusa enclosure were the Kuroda forces. They all were advancing at once.

"For the past two or three days, kites have been flying around the Arima hillsides. This must be what they were trying to signal us about," Jinbei moaned.

Some of the Christians outside the castle had been scouting for information and had sent up the kites to warn their allies inside.

"What do you think we should do with Yomosaku?" Matsuemon asked.

"Shirō said to leave him be."

"All right," Matsuemon replied simply.

There was little point in executing Yamada Yomosaku at this late hour.

In the flurry of arrow messages, Yomosaku had sent a secret message to the former Lord Arima Naojun saying, "With my eight hundred men, I can get Shirō out of the castle and make them surrender." An arrow message from the Arima group had disclosed Yomosaku's plot, and now he was being held, tied up in a corner of the main enclosure.

"This must be like what Chirisuto-sama faced as his hour of death approached. There are many sides to the human spirit. We know the example of Judas, so if he wants to sneak off, let him go."

Those had been Shirō's words. If they let him go and he was rescued by the Arima forces, then the story of their time in the castle would be told from his viewpoint. *But so what? Go ahead and say whatever you want, Yomosaku*, Jinbei muttered to himself unexpectedly.

The attackers sounded their trumpet shells continuously, while inside the castle warning drums boomed a wild reply. Here and there, sword fights broke out amidst the sound of rushing footsteps, heavy breathing, gasping voices, gunshots and cannon explosions. Living bodies fought for their life like molten stones tumbling out from the earth and striking each other.

"At last, they've come."

"It's been a long wait."

Kanzaki Daizen appeared quietly at Jinbei's side.

"I didn't enjoy being starved, but finally they've come. There won't be any easy way home."

Jinbei surveyed the area. Takematsu was standing next to the headquarters with his halberd in hand and his eyes fixed. Without anyone noticing, he had changed into the white robe that Onami-sama had sewn for him.

"Takematsu—you take the women and children to the dry moat. And be quick about it."

Raising his halberd and nodding, Takematsu dashed off.

The second enclosure was swarming with enemy troops who were setting fire to the thatched-roof houses, and the fires were spreading quickly. Since the little huts had been dug partly into the ground, their eaves were low, which made it easier for the invaders to ignite them with their torches. The attackers appeared to be following a set plan to burn all the dwellings as soon as they broke into the castle.

Jinbei's heart filled with a sorrow beyond words. For almost three months, families had lived together in those little huts, through all their hardships. He thought of his own family members who had been captured early on by the Hosokawas, and especially of his two young grandchildren who had been sent to the castle as messengers.

Although he had plotted the rebellion himself, he had not brought it this far on his own. All of these people who had given up their homes and land to live in this abandoned castle like moles in the ground and dreamed of building a kingdom of God—they had stretched themselves to their limits. During this time, one by one, they had overcome the bounds of endurance. And now the day for casting off their mortal selves and ascending to Heaven had arrived.

I put my heart and soul into this rebellion. But in the end, was it only a shallow fantasy? Soon, some thirty thousand lives will be extinguished from this earth. Was it I who brought on this tragedy? No, even this thought may be too arrogant. I realize my own insignificance. I don't know what our Lord's plan is, but His will has brought us here. Deus-sama is carrying out great work. My comrades have endured until this day, and now we must carry out our final obligations.

Fierce fighting was going on inside the second and third enclosure, where the attackers had broken through. He could see that the elderly and children had banded together and were moving into the main enclosure, driven by the raging fires. Even with the terrifying battle cries and gunshots piercing their ears, they moved along calmly, as if to say there was nothing in this world to get flustered about. Jinbei watched them for a while, then turned toward the main enclosure. Already, Kanzaki Daizen was leading the last of the reserve troops into the second enclosure.

Suzuki Saburō Kurō Shigenari saw off Hosokawa Tadayoshi after their meeting at Matsudaira Nobutsuna's headquarters to plan the attack on the castle. On his way back, he wanted to get a good look at the camps. Fierce fighting had already broken out in the second enclosure, which the Nabeshima forces were attacking amidst the sharp cries of rifle fire. The all-out attack had been scheduled for the next day. So what was happening now? He could hear angry screams and shouts. Shigenari quickly climbed the nearest lookout hill.

As he had guessed, the Nabeshima troops had scaled the stone castle walls, and some were already inside.

"The Nabeshima stole a march on us!" he shouted impulsively. He could see messengers dashing out of the allied clans' headquarters. Orders to attack must already have been sent to the camps of all the clans. Shigenari ran from the lookout hill to his own camp, which was equipped with large cannons. When he arrived, he learned that orders had just been given to start the general attack. Since his camp was on high ground, he had a good view of the assault. On the left, in the Hosokawa camp, flags with the clan's nine-circle crest were waving restlessly, and already advance soldiers were fighting their way past the outermost walls of the third enclosure.

Shigenari was in charge of distributing all the artillery and ammunition procured by the *bakufu,* and he had carefully studied how to use these armaments most effectively, according to the structure of the castle. However, when the battle began before his eyes, he was bewildered by the emotions that rose up in his heart.

War is a cruel, merciless affair, and the military leaders had already decided to slaughter everyone inside the castle—the women, children and elderly included. Now the massacre had begun. Images of the countless victims who would be piled one upon another lodged in the back of his mind and there was no way he could shake them out.

Still, the rebels resisted fiercely. When a wall was damaged by the cannon bombardment and he peered through an opening in it, he saw a hut going up in flames and its inhabitants fleeing, carrying one of the wounded. It appeared to be a man whose knee was injured. The man seemed to be motioning to the others to leave him there and escape. Two people, apparently the man's wife and son, carried him to the base of a large old cherry tree. Then the big young son rushed back to the castle wall and began throwing rocks down on the Nabeshima troops. Young women and men ran to assist. They threw down lumber. They threw down burning straw mats. More and more Nabeshima soldiers were scaling the walls. The women, gathered together along the top of the castle walls, started throwing down pots and pans, and even hoes. Some threw down ashes and mud from their colanders. Shigenari sighed deeply.

Then he saw a most unbelievable sight. An elderly woman was

lugging a stone grinding mill to the edge of the parapet. Planting her legs firmly, she lifted it up, her body shaking, and with a mighty heave and a shout, hurled it outward. Several Nabeshima warriors who were scaling the wall went tumbling down. The woman's white hair was blown straight up by the wind gusting along the walls. She stood there for a moment, seemingly dazed, and then a red spot appeared on the breast of her white clothing. She staggered, fell, and didn't rise again.

That woman was Oume. Shouting, "*Yoisho! Yoisho!* Here it goes!" she had hurled the stone grinding mill that she had carried from her burning hut. As she did, she had caught a glimpse of Nisuke and Omiyo beneath the cherry tree.

"Forgive me for going first," she had called out.

As if in a dream, Omiyo had watched Oume haul the stone grinding mill to the edge of the parapet.

As she lifted the grinding mill, Oume had chanted "*Maria-Kannon-sama.*"

When Omiyo saw Oume collapse, she ran to her. Around Oume's breast, a red flower was blossoming. As Omiyo raised her body and cradled her, Oume closed her eyes and an indescribably tender smile settled on her lips.

Omiyo set her clear, pale eyes on Okayo, next to her.

"It is as we planned. And so now, my dear, let us not delay."

Omiyo returned to the cherry tree and remained close by the side of her husband, who couldn't stand. Nisuke drew his short sword.

"My dear."

Gazing for a moment on the face of his wife, whose hands were folded in prayer, he said, "All right, now." He plunged the sword into her chest and as she fell onto his knees, he slashed his own throat.

Kumagorō, after having thrown down his store of rocks and stones, rushed past. He clasped the still-warm bodies of the couple. His body trembling, he broke into tears. "They were my parents. And now they're gone—before I could return their kindness," he cried.

Kumagorō picked up Nisuke's long sword, which lay beside him, and unsheathed it. He staggered forward, stood firmly with his soot-covered face looking up at the sky, and cried out:

"Sankichi—I did it!"

Just as Kumagorō was calling to Sankichi as if he were actually standing in front of him, a soldier who had come up the roadway along the moat pierced his side with a spear.

At almost the same moment, Daisuke felled the soldier with his last bullet. It seemed the entire battlefield had become a mountain of corpses and a sea of blood and gore. Daisuke hadn't yet realized that both his parents were dead. Although he had tried to save Kumagorō, he had been an instant too late. When Daisuke looked beyond Kumagorō's fallen body, he saw Okayo kneeling beneath the cherry tree, beckoning to him with both hands waving, as if dancing.

Daisuke ran, feeling his legs had been injured. At that moment, he caught sight of the first of the cherry blossoms opening above Okayo's head. He also saw the bodies of his parents.

Back when they built their hut, Okayo and his parents had taken great joy in the fact that the great old cherry tree stood right beside it.

From time to time, Nisuke had muttered, "What fate was it, I wonder, that brought us together with this cherry tree?" After they had abandoned their big home and come to live a life without gardens and trees, the old tree had brought great comfort to Nisuke, who had loved trees so much.

Any number of times, Okayo had asked her husband, "We'll be here until the cherries bloom, won't we, my dear?"

"If we die, I hope it's beneath the cherry blossoms," she had said with a smile.

As flames raged behind them, the cherry branches with their swelling buds trembled. The bodies of Daisuke's parents lay beneath them.

"Mother told us not to be late."

Holding Okayo, who was clinging to him, Daisuke stared at their hut as it went up in flames. Okayo understood his thoughts instantly.

"My dear, your mother said to use this."

Slowly, Okayo loosened the tasseled chord around the sword that Omiyo had given her. Already, Daisuke was no longer thinking about how their religion forbade the taking of one's own life. He simply didn't want Okayo to be killed by the enemy's hands.

"Okayo, look, the cherries are coming into full bloom."

Holding his wife at his breast with one hand, Daisuke pointed above his head.

"Ah, the cherry blossoms."

In place of the cherry blossoms, flames and sparks were swirling high.

"I am happy."

As he said this, Daisuke cut her throat and then his own. The couple fell on top of the bodies of his parents.

Someone stumbled towards them. It was Sasuke. His disheveled hair was hanging loose and his white clothing was smeared with blood and grime.

"Daisuke-dono! Okayo!"

He staggered to the old cherry tree. There, in a pool of blood, he saw the bodies of the Hasuda family. In despair, he sunk to his knees.

"Ahh, I'm too late! We promised to die together. My brother! Okayo!"

Sasuke drew the two bodies to his chest and held them. A Hosokawa soldier ran up behind him and perfunctorily swung his sword.

As Takematsu rushed around directing the elderly and children, he, too, saw the Hosokawa forces break through the second enclosure and advance on the main enclosure. He dashed up to the headquarters.

Smoke had started pouring from the Matsuyama enclosure, where the Kuroda forces were attacking. Although desperate fights that seemed to twist the heavens and earth were breaking out in every direction, within the stone walls of Shirō's headquarters votive lamps were burning and prayers were being chanted in low voices, like in a separate tranquil world. Takematsu felt as if he had arrived at the bottom of the ocean.

Takematsu had always felt Shirō's presence was like a flame casting light into the water, but Ukon-sama, so completely devoted to Shirō-sama, was also different from other people.

Come to think of it, that might be true about me, too, he reflected. *I don't get along so well with people. Usually, I'm either out at sea or drinking. I've never had much to do with other people. Was it that way for Chirisuto-sama, too? Maybe it's a sin to compare myself to him, but with his ascetic training in the wilderness and his offering himself on the cross, perhaps he, too, felt in some way uncomfortable around people. But then, he didn't act the same as ordinary people like me. The best I could do was get close to Maria-sama when I was drunk. Drinking was my doctrine and my creed. If I were to confide these things to Ukon-sama, I suppose he'd just smile.*

Takematsu looked up at the lighted lanterns. A deep fragrance hung in the air. Most likely it came from the incense that Onami-sama brought with her. The chapel was crowded with people. Seated upright in the front row were Ukon and his pageboys. The bands of pure white cloth tied tightly around their heads must have been prepared especially for this day. In the back, he could make out the figures of Shirō and Juan. He also recognized Onami-sama's face. Everyone, including the women, held a sword in one hand. The sounds of an *oratio* filled the room. Takematsu noticed the clear, fresh light shining from Shirō's pale face. He supposed that he had been fasting. The thought pierced his heart.

The congregation could hear the attacking soldiers' feet striking the ground outside the stone walls surrounding the headquarters, mingled with the sounds of frantic breathing. It seemed that the fighting had reached them. Juan and Yazō stood. They cast a calm, decisive look at Onami-sama and then stepped out. When the enemy had entered the second enclosure, the leaders had gone out to strengthen the main enclosure's defenses. Now it appeared those defenses were collapsing.

After nodding at Juan and Yazō's receding forms, Shirō surveyed the chapel again. Among those gathered were the pageboys, the elderly, a hearing-impaired former student of the *seminario*, the young female attendants including Mizuna, dressed in their embroidered kimonos, Onami, Ninagawa Sakyō, the wives of Matsushima Sadonokami and others, and about a dozen samurai guards. Shirō, however, could not really see them. His eyes, clear like the winter sky, acknowledged Ukon for a moment and then took on a look of deep loneliness. Now he was obliged to carry out his final duties. He managed to speak in fits and starts.

"Virgin Maria and all the angels, from this castle we raise to you our humble praise. Now, today, with your grace, we are about to set off together for His land."

His voice grew hoarse.

"Out of our love for our families . . . and for all of our children, who we have brought to this castle . . . with your profound grace may we be granted rebirth."

Having finished his recitation, Shirō paced slowly toward Ukon, moving like a bird that had lost its sight.

When they heard Shirō's words "with your profound grace may we be granted rebirth," the women embraced those who were beside them.

The smell of the smoke blowing into the chapel began to mix with the incense. Ukon grasped Shirō and helped him to sit down, then stood and opened the shutters. The smell of smoke and blood poured in. Outside, it was already growing dark. The force of the flames in the outer two keeps seemed to be waning, but from time to time, embers and sparks continued to spout high into the sky.

Shirō asked, "How close have the fires come?"

Ukon was surprised. *Is Shirō unable to see? Has his frequent fasting caused him to lose his eyesight?*

"The flames in the second and third enclosure are dying down, but the main enclosure and outer enclosure have caught fire."

A faint smile spread across Shirō's lips. Falteringly, he stood up.

"There's no need for our defensive forces any more. Run out to the defense gates."

A number of people rushed out into the embers and sparks but quickly ran into Hosokawa forces. Sword fights broke out. The winds from the battlefield swept into the chapel. Shirō spoke as if his words were slipping out from the depths of his soul:

"Brother, at last the end has come."

Ukon held out his trembling arm.

For what purpose were some thirty thousand people now to be sacrificed? No doubt Shirō, too, had wondered the same thing any number of times. Now Shirō, himself, was to climb to the place of sacrifice. Ukon held his withered wrist and said, "Now, dear Lord, the time has come."

Shirō nodded, and for a brief moment passed his finger over

Ukon's eyelids.

Takematsu grasped his sword. He rushed out into the battle that was raging in front of the chapel. The brief moment of happiness he had enjoyed at Nisuke's hut the previous night flashed in the back of his mind. What had happened to the people in that family? Before he could even reflect on how good it was that he had gone there, his halberd cut through a chink in the armor of an oncoming soldier.

This was different from when Takematsu was at sea. He didn't have the feeling of having killed anything. It was a strange feeling, different from that of catching an octopus or a fish and it confused him. But his opponent let out an eerie cry and then fell back, face upward.

Ukon, too, rushed out of the chapel with his sword in hand. Vowing that, as long as he was alive, he wouldn't allow a single attacker to enter Shirō's chapel, he struck at the hands of a soldier charging forward with a spear, and then, sinking to one knee, cut him down with a sweeping side blow. He watched the attacker fall with his leggings slashed open, then glanced up at the sky. His eyes met those of Takematsu. Ukon could sense his knit brow relax into gentleness, like ripples on the sea.

Seeing Ukon's youthful gallantry brought Takematsu immense pleasure. He thought that if he could be reborn, he would like to be a person like Ukon-sama. Just then, he felt a shock at the base of his neck.

"Bastard!"

Moaning, he wheeled around and jumped on the attacking foot soldier. Ukon ran to him and pierced the assailant's side with his long sword.

Takematsu continued grappling with the soldier until Ukon pulled him loose. Takematsu was still breathing. Ukon cradled Takematsu's neck in his arms.

"Well, well," he whispered contentedly. And then, calmly, he passed away.

Cut off by the intense fires, the approaching attackers had to halt their advance. If they broke into the headquarters, would they be killed? Should they retreat? For a moment, quiet returned to the courtyard outside the headquarters.

Noticing the silence, Shirō walked toward the door but bumped into the Chinese table. Jinbei caught him in his arms.

"Can't you see?" he asked, speaking in a fatherly way for the first time in many days.

Supported by Jinbei, Shirō made his way to the chapel door. The stench of blood was overwhelming. As he was about to make the sign of the cross, a bullet pierced his shoulder. Onami rushed to him and tended his wound, her face pale. Ukon noticed a quiet relief spread over Shirō's face as he lay in the arms of the woman he had so revered. It seemed he had fainted. Ukon watched them from below the stone steps of the chapel—the Virgin and Child, hovering above the burned-out ruins of Spring Castle.

As the castle sank into darkness, the light of the flames shone on the countless women who were taking their lives by walking into the burning buildings. It was a scene to silence the heavens and earth. Hosokawa Nakanori, who witnessed it, wrote in a letter to his father Tadaoki:

> *In the main enclosure, dead bodies were piled seven and eight upon each other. Many people had pushed their way to the burning fort, entered it, and died. I hardly saw anyone escape. How strange this was to a Buddhist. They entered the second enclosure more than the third, walking not a bit faster than usual. It was the way of dying of strong men and women.*
>
> *Many of us saw the bodies of the Christians who had taken their own lives, in their charred kimonos. Many had pushed their children beneath them, placed themselves over them, and then died. These were praiseworthy deaths of common people. It cannot be expressed in words.*

Suzuki Saburō Kurō Shigenari wanted to observe the situation in the main enclosure, the last to go up in flames. In a stiff, unnatural voice he called out, "Captain of Firearms—let me through!" and made his way through the crowd of soldiers so he could watch at a slight distance from Nakanori and his men. The samurai were watching speechless as the women entered the flames.

Caught in the flames, the women's long hair stood up straight and the silken sleeves of their kimonos were lofted in the air, dancing about like the scarves of heavenly maidens. Involuntarily, Shigenari closed his eyes. It was a sight beyond belief. Shock overtook him and he could not rid himself of it.

The *bakufu* armies took full control of the castle at around noon the following day, the twenty-eighth, having finally crushed the revolt. On the *bakufu* side, some one thousand one hundred lives had been lost and some eight thousand had been wounded. It was the Hosokawa clan's field commander Jin Sukezaemon who took Shirō's head. His mother Marta was forced to identify the decapitated head.

"What trials he must have gone through," she moaned. She lamented the cruelty of the letters she had written to him without knowing his true suffering.

The sun was warm and the peach blossoms had already begun to fall.

Suzuki Saburō Kurō Shigenari crossed the Hayasaki Straits and landed in Amakusa at the bay of Futae.

He had been passing the whirlpools of those straits often recently, having been charged with the task of rebuilding the devastated lands of Shimabara and Amakusa.

At low tide, the shoreline was colored with a rich carpet of seaweed. Wrapped in the smells of the shore, he wondered if spring began at the bottom of the sea. He felt a shiver of pain in his chest. The year before, at just about this same time, he had gazed down from the cliffs of Hara Castle and seen the Amakusa Islands in the distant haze. Why had the believers gone all the way to that castle simply to die? On that day, just a hundred yards or so from where he had been standing, the last survivors were being beheaded. It had seemed as if a curtain of bloody smoke was hanging from the skies. Such a tremendous number of people had been slain. The executioners had grown exhausted, only half conscious as they struck on with their swords. Not even the last women and children were spared. Two girls remained at the end. They looked at a glance like sisters, about seven and three years of age. They held hands and the younger one looked up at her older sister and said in the local dialect, "Let's be off now, quickly."

Where had they expected to go to as they knelt with their knees pressed together in front of the executioner, almost joyfully?

The deserted villages were enveloped in tall grass and weeds, and here and there peaches and apricots bloomed innocently.

Sensing someone near him, Shigenari snapped out of his reminiscence. A very young girl was standing in the sand a few yards in front of him. She placed a round seashell she had just picked up into her palm and toddled toward him, as if expecting to be praised. A short distance behind her, a girl not more than ten years old was squatting with a basket of shells in her hand. Seeing the movement of the little girl, she stood up. Then, noticing the presence of this unknown soldier, she anxiously tugged at the little girl's hand. The seashell fell and the little girl stamped her feet and started crying. Instinctively, Shigenari walked over, picked up the shell, brushed off the sand, and placed it in the hand of the girl, who could have been his grandchild.

Her tearful face changed into a smile, like a peach blossom opening. She held the shell out to him and broke into laughter.

The older girl looked him over carefully and then bowed in a graceful manner, such as could hardly be seen even in Kyoto or Edo. He had no choice but to accept the unexpected gift. As if asking to be picked up, the little girl raised her sand-covered hands and touched his *hakama* trousers.

"Aya-sama, you mustn't do that," the older girl scolded softly.

The two girls were Ayame, the granddaughter of Nisuke, the village headman of Kuchinotsu, and Suzu, her caretaker.

The following year, Suzuki Shigenari was officially appointed magistrate of the Amakusa Islands. He held memorial services for the dead, instituted a benevolent administration, and made repeated, though ultimately futile, appeals for the reduction by half of the land tax. Still not imagining that he would end his life by committing *seppuku*, he enjoyed some good years bathed in the bright light of the sea.

The people who worked for him recalled that he kept a single round seashell on his desk until the end of his life, and that, from time to time, he would clasp it in his hands.

Michiko Ishimure

Michiko Ishimure (1927-2018) is regarded as one of Japan's most important modern writers. She published over 50 works ranging from novels, non-fiction, Noh drama and poetry to essays, memoirs and children's stories. She received numerous international and Japanese literary awards including the Ramon Magsaysay Award from the Philippines (1973) and the Asahi Prize for literature in Japan (2001). Her best-known work, *Paradise in the Sea of Sorrow: Our Minamata Disease* (1969), went through over 30 printings in Japan and has been translated into English and several other languages. This work, along with several other books focusing on the Minamata Disease incident, led to her being known as the "mother of the Japanese environmental movement" and the "Rachel Carson of Japan."

Bruce Allen

Bruce Allen is retired professor of translation and global environmental literature at Seisen University in Tokyo. His translations include *Japanese Tales of Fantasy and Folklore*, Michiko Ishimure's novel *Lake of Heaven* and *Toward the Paradise of Flowers*, a documentary film on Ishimure. He is editor of *Ishimure Michiko's Writing in Ecocritical Perspective: Between Sea and Sky*. His translation of several chapters of *Spring Castle* received honorable mention from the Kyoko Iriye Selden Memorial Translation Prize of Cornell University.

"Books to Span the East and West"

Tuttle Publishing was founded in 1832 in the small New England town of Rutland, Vermont [USA]. Our core values remain as strong today as they were then—to publish best-in-class books which bring people together one page at a time. In 1948, we established a publishing outpost in Japan—and Tuttle is now a leader in publishing English-language books about the arts, languages and cultures of Asia. The world has become a much smaller place today and Asia's economic and cultural influence has grown. Yet the need for meaningful dialogue and information about this diverse region has never been greater. Over the past seven decades, Tuttle has published thousands of books on subjects ranging from martial arts and paper crafts to language learning and literature—and our talented authors, illustrators, designers and photographers have won many prestigious awards. We welcome you to explore the wealth of information available on Asia at **www.tuttlepublishing.com**.

Published by Tuttle Publishing, an imprint of Periplus Editions (HK) Ltd.

www.tuttlepublishing.com

Library of Congress Control Number: 2025937361

ISBN 978-4-8053-1965-9

28 27 26 25 5 4 3 2 1 2506TP
Printed in Singapore

Distributed by:
North America, Latin America & Europe
Tuttle Publishing
364 Innovation Drive
North Clarendon, VT 05759-9436 U.S.A.
Tel: 1 (802) 773-8930
Fax: 1 (802) 773-6993
info@tuttlepublishing.com
www.tuttlepublishing.com

Japan
Tuttle Publishing
Yaekari Building, 3rd Floor, 5-4-12 Osaki
Shinagawa-ku, Tokyo 141-0032
Tel: (81) 3 5437-0171
Fax: (81) 3 5437-0755
sales@tuttle.co.jp
www.tuttle.co.jp

Asia Pacific
Berkeley Books Pte. Ltd.
3 Kallang Sector #04-01, Singapore 349278
Tel: (65) 6741-2178
Fax: (65) 6741-2179
inquiries@periplus.com.sg
www.periplus.com

GPSR representative
Matt Parsons matt.parsons@upi2mbooks.hr
UPI-2M PLUS d.o.o., Medulićeva 20,
10000 Zagreb, Croatia